BLACK MARKET
TRUTH

ANCIENT GREECE, 4th Century BCE

ILLYRIA

ADRIATIC SEA

EPIDAMNUS

APOLLONIA

MACEDONIA

EION

THERMA

PELLA

STAGEIRA

XE

METHONI

OLYNTHUS

AEGAE

PYDNA

POTIDAEA

EPIRUS

THESSALY

KASTHANAIA

DODONA

LARISSA

PHERAE

SKIAT

PHARSALUS

KORKYRA

EUBOEA

KASSOPE

AMBRACIA

ACARNANIA

CH

ANACTORIUM

AETOLIA

PHOCIS

DELPHI

BOEOTIA

TH

LEUCAS

NAUPACTUS

MEGARA

CEPHALLENIA

CALYDON

ACHAEA

CORINT

PATRAS

ELIS

PHLIUS

ARGOLI

ELIS

ARGOS

ARCADIA

OLYMPIA

TEGEA

ZAKYNTHOS

MESSENIA

SPARTA

MESSENE

LACONIA

METHONI

EUROPE

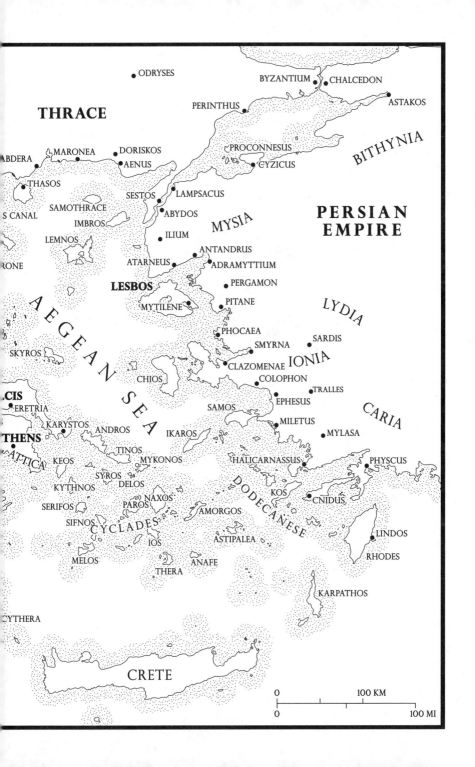

αηρ ~ Air
πυρ ~ Fire
υδωρ ~ Water
γη ~ Earth

THE ARISTOTLE QUEST

BLACK MARKET
TRUTH

A DANA McCARTER TRILOGY
BOOK ONE

Sharon Kaye

PARMENIDES
FICTION

Las Vegas | Zurich | Athens

PARMENIDES FICTION™
Las Vegas | Zurich | Athens

Published 2008
Printed in the United States of America

ISBN hard cover: 978-1-930972-30-8
ISBN soft cover: 978-1-930972-31-5

Library of Congress Cataloging-in-Publication Data
Kaye, Sharon M.
  The Aristotle quest : a Dana McCarter trilogy. Book I, Black market truth / Sharon Kaye.
      p. cm.
  ISBN 978-1-930972-30-8 (hard cover : alk. paper) — ISBN 978-1-930972-31-5 (pbk. : alk. paper)
  1. Classical antiquities thefts—Fiction. 2. Aristotle—Manuscripts—Fiction.
  3. Women scholars—Fiction. 4. Police—Italy—Rome—Fiction. 5. Religious adherents—Fiction. I. Title.
  PS3611.A918A89 2008
  813'.6—dc22

2008035273

Typeset in Perpetua and Din by 1106 Design
Printed by McNaughton & Gunn in the United States of America
Cartography [Map of Ancient Greece in 4th century BCE]: Mike Powers, Maps.com

FSC
Mixed Sources
Product group from well-managed forests, controlled sources and recycled wood or fiber
Cert no. SW-COC-002283
www.fsc.org
© 1996 Forest Stewardship Council

Parmenides Fiction™ chose to print this title on materials with postconsumer recycled content or Forest Stewardship Council (FSC) certified. FSC materials are independently certified to assure consumers that they come from forests that are managed to meet the social, economic and ecological needs of present and future generations.

1-888-PARMENIDES
www.parmenidesfiction.com

For Tris and Audrey

Preface and Acknowledgements

I had my first grown-up encounter with Aristotle as a brand-new graduate student at the University of Toronto in 1992. I was there to pursue a PhD in philosophy, but I hadn't yet determined my area of specialization.

I started hanging around with students working in the classics, fascinated by the way they would spend hours and hours learning dead languages and discussing ancient history as though it were the evening news.

One day, an announcement that the great Joseph Owens was to give a seminar on Aristotle generated considerable excitement among these scholarly creatures. Father Owens, in his early eighties at that time, was a world-renowned Aristotle scholar (he is now deceased). His talk was to be given in the famous seminar room at the Pontifical Institute of Mediaeval Studies, which had hosted many other great classicists, beginning with the legendary Étienne Gilson in 1929.

Wanting to know what all the fuss was about, I decided to attend. On the appointed day, I parked my bicycle outside the Pontifical Institute and scurried inside just minutes before the seminar was to begin. Out of breath and disoriented, I scanned the room. It was smaller than I expected, dominated by a majestic old oak table. The table was surrounded by chairs and there were benches all along the walls. The room was already packed with expectant listeners speaking in hushed tones. There was just one seat left at the oak table, so I sat down.

The room fell completely silent. Digging through my satchel for a notebook and pen, I assumed the famous speaker must have arrived. I looked up. He hadn't. Was I imagining it, or was everyone looking at *me?*

Finally, mercifully, the man sitting to my left leaned over and whispered in my ear: "You're sitting in Father Owens' chair!" Blushing furiously, I popped up and squeezed onto a bench along the wall just as Father Owens strode into the room and came to roost upon his (my?) seat. I always wondered whether he noticed that it was already a little bit warm.

Father Owens' seminar focused on how Aristotle paved the way for Christianity. Call it sour grapes for having been ejected from my place at the table, but from the very beginning, I found the whole idea extremely suspicious. On that day, I vowed to find out who Aristotle really was. As time went on, the more I learned, the more I realized that nobody, not even the great Joseph Owens, really knew the answer.

Throughout my time at graduate school, I was told I had far too much imagination to be a historian. Maybe it's just as well, therefore, that I have never been able to write a scholarly monograph about Aristotle. A novel—or two or three—will have to do.

The Dana McCarter series is based on the scant information we possess regarding Aristotle's life and times. I wrote an essay called "Fact and Fiction in *Black Market Truth*" explaining the historical elements of the novel. It is printed in the Afterword at the back of this book. Spoiler alert: you wouldn't want to read it first!

I would like to thank John Carroll University for supporting my research and for providing a wonderful community in which to teach, learn, and grow. I would also like to thank Eliza Tutellier, my editor at Parmenides, for taking a chance on me and providing such sound guidance throughout the process. Finally, I would like to thank Dr. Robert Martin for teaching me how to write about philosophy.

"Happiness depends upon ourselves."

—Aristotle

Chapter One

 Domenico Conti liked dead bodies, provided they were still warm.

Most people, making no fine distinctions, think a dead body is a dead body. Having worked homicide for twenty years, however, Conti knew there was a difference between warm and cold.

The colder the body, the colder the trail to the killer. The colder the body, the worse it looked, and the worse it smelled—unless of course it was *freezing* cold, which entailed a whole different set of problems.

Conti was aware of numerous reasons why one might prefer the rare warm body. But he was not aware of his own real reason.

The truth was that, although he was not conscious of it, he not only preferred warm bodies, he also preferred bodies that had been killed over those that had died of natural causes.

The body lying at his feet now was both killed and warm—probably dead no more than three hours. It belonged to a guard at St. Paul's Basilica, just outside the walls of Rome.

The Basilica of St. Paul Outside the Walls was the largest church in Rome after St. Peter's. In December of 2006, after four years of excavation, archeologists unearthed the sarcophagus of St. Paul, which was buried under marble slabs beneath the altar. Although the Pope authorized public viewing of the sarcophagus, he declined to authorize its opening.

Now, someone had broken into the basilica in the night, leaving the sarcophagus empty and its guard dead. The crime had been called in by the archpriest an hour ago.

It was just past seven on a Saturday morning in mid February. The crime scene was already abuzz with various professionals. Conti needed to work fast.

He knelt close to the body, careful not to touch it. A young man. Maybe twenty-five. Throat cut. He leaned in and inhaled deeply through his nose. No unusual odors.

Just fresh death. Fresh kill, that is. What is it about fresh kill . . . ?

"Scusilo, Ispettore Conti!" It was the voice of Conti's assistant, behind him.

"Un momento," Conti barked. He leaned in again and breathed, taking in the heat still radiating from the man. He closed his eyes. After another deep breath, he looked down the length of the body. That's when he saw it: a small smudge of blood on the guard's elbow. Based on the pattern of spatter from his neck wound, this blood could not belong to the guard.

Conti sat back on his heels and called a technician over, instructing him in rapid Italian to take a sample of the smudge for comparison against a sample from the victim, and then, presuming that they did not match, to run the smudge sample through the criminal DNA database.

"Excuse me, Inspector," the assistant repeated.

"What is it?" Conti asked, without taking his gaze from the body.

"Someone to see you, sir."

"Thank you," Conti said absently, finally turning to look.

A silver-haired man in a long black robe and red skullcap was kneeling in front of the rubble that was St. Paul's Tomb. Conti recognized him immediately: Cardinal Giuseppe Torelli, the most visible member of the papal curia. Cardinal Torelli had been in the news recently, promoting his new book about inner-city poverty. The proceeds were being donated to youth recreation facilities all around Rome, including one in the neighborhood where Conti lived.

Conti snapped to a standing position and straightened his trousers.

The cardinal was praying aloud in Latin, his voice cracking in lament. He turned and rose when he heard Conti approach.

"Your Eminence," Conti said.

"Ah, Inspector," the cardinal replied, reaching out his hands for a double-handed grasp. "It is unspeakable, this crime. You must forgive my dishevelment. I came as soon as the archpriest called."

"It is a great honor to meet you," Conti said. "I only wish it were under better circumstances."

They surveyed the damage together: thick stone sarcophagus and protective barriers blown to pieces with precision explosives. The crumbled blast area made a stark contrast with the opulent interior of the church, an enormous space flanked by marble columns and topped high above by a gold-encrusted ceiling.

After a long, deep sigh, Cardinal Torelli turned back to Conti. "Inspector, this place—it is very sacred and especially dear to the heart of the Most Holy Father. Every year, the sarcophagus is visited by millions of pilgrims who need to feel the power of St. Paul's healing spirit. This desecration, it is unbearable."

Cardinal Torelli looked imploringly at Conti. His face was deeply lined with all the troubles of humanity. He stalled, his lips parted, as if there were no words for what he needed to say.

Conti wished he could supply them. Instead, he creased his brow solemnly.

At last, the Cardinal shook himself and continued slowly, "For your investigation, I came to offer my help. You will, no doubt, be focusing your attention on apprehending the murderer—as well you should. The Holy See is also especially concerned, however, that you make your most wholehearted effort to recover the contents of the sarcophagus."

Conti looked at the cardinal inquiringly. Would "the contents" be bones? A shroud? Dust? What would be left of a body entombed for nearly two thousand years? He didn't know how to express his questions respectfully.

"You will not be looking for the remains of the blessed St. Paul, Inspector," the cardinal added, as if reading Conti's thoughts. He smiled ever so slightly.

Conti cocked his head, even more puzzled.

"Inspector Conti," the cardinal said, "please be aware that I tell you the following in the strictest confidence."

"Of course, Your Eminence." Conti waited, watching the cardinal formulate his story.

"In the year of our Lord three hundred and ninety," the cardinal explained, "Emperor Theodosius built this basilica with a proper sarcophagus for the blessed St. Paul. The intention was to transfer his remains from their original resting place."

He paused and cast his eyes upward, reminding Conti of the way his grandfather looked when he talked about the old days.

"But it was not to be," the cardinal continued. "In the Vatican's most restricted library, there is a document issued by Emperor Theodosius. It states that St. Paul's body could not be recovered for interment, and that his library was interred instead."

The cardinal peered at Conti to see how he was taking the news. Conti nodded soberly.

Neither spoke for some time. Finally, Conti cleared his throat. "So, I'm looking for books?" he ventured.

The cardinal nodded emphatically. "It will be scrolls. Five of them, most likely," he said. "But that is not all."

Conti stood as still as a statue.

"There is further information in the document that we feel may be of the utmost importance for solving this crime." The cardinal's voice diminished as he spoke so that he ended in a whisper. Conti leaned in, willing the cardinal to tell him more.

But the cardinal backed away and turned the volume up again. "Inspector, you can appreciate the delicate nature of this operation. These scrolls were buried for a reason. It would be unsuitable for them to become the object of public curiosity."

"I understand, Your Eminence," Conti assured him.

"I knew you would," the cardinal said, crinkling his eyes. "And so, Inspector, due to our special concern, we would like you to report your progress to us. To me, that is."

Conti blinked. The cardinal noticed.

"I may be able to assist you," the cardinal explained.

Again, Conti nodded soberly. The two men surveyed the damage before them once more. Then Conti cleared his throat and spoke. "Your Eminence, I can assure you that I will conduct this investigation swiftly, effectively, and with the utmost discretion. Can you tell me what the document says about the scrolls?"

"Indeed, Inspector, that is the question," the cardinal mused. "Can I?"

Conti felt the weight of the Church, the magnitude of his own faith, settling squarely on his shoulders. "You can," he averred.

The cardinal put his hand on Conti's shoulder, as if aware of the weight there. "The document states," he whispered, "that the scrolls were buried 'that the cult of Dionysus be forever laid to rest.'"

Chapter Two

High over the Middle East, a Boeing business jet hurtled toward Muscat, the capital of Oman. Upon one of its sky-blue leather couches sat Achille Benevento, a small, dark man with pock-marked cheeks. He held on his lap a black duffel bag containing a tarnished silver box. Inside the box were five scrolls.

Benevento was alone in the cabin. Apart from the crew, he had the entire plane to himself. It was sumptuously decorated in the whimsical colors favored throughout the Middle East—fuchsia curtains, jade-and-white checkered tiles, gold trim. Festive Arabic music pulsed through unseen speakers. But Benevento was not feeling festive. He sat stiffly, talking to himself from time to time.

To look at him, you would never suspect he was one of the most talented thieves the Italian mafia had ever known.

A lithe stewardess emerged from somewhere behind him to check his untouched water glass and to ask if anything else would please him at this time. Benevento brusquely waved her away.

He knew he should eat, but his stomach was churning with acid. What a shame he couldn't enjoy such an extraordinary flight. How much had this jet cost? How much had his host paid to have him whisked through the airport so quickly and discreetly? He was sure even the mafiosi would be impressed.

Benevento unwrapped the bloodied handkerchief from his right hand and palpated the wound to be sure it was done bleeding.

The pain fed his anger. *There is no way around it: I will have to retire. And the Omani will have to pay for it.*

As the plane descended toward Muscat's airport, Benevento was momentarily distracted from his internal tirade by the spectacular view from his window. A long stretch of desert finally gave way to burly mountains that sloped straight down into the sparkling sea. Old stone forts stood guard at regular intervals along the coast. The city of Muscat was a tumble of ivory buildings amidst lush vegetation. Benevento gazed at the traffic in its busy harbor, wishing he were arriving for a holiday.

On landing, Benevento was escorted through the airport to a black Mercedes sedan. The morning was blindingly bright, especially to a man accustomed to sleeping by day and working by night. As they drove to the Sultan's palace, Benevento studied the streets.

The people of Muscat went about their business without a glance at the Mercedes. They were dressed in traditional Arabic garb. Men wore full-length gowns without collars—most often white, though sometimes sky blue or lavender—along with turbans or short cylindrical hats. Women wore black or richly patterned dresses over slacks. Their headdresses sometimes included face covering.

At a traffic light, Benevento watched a boy on a bicycle. He careened to a wobbly halt to wait for the light. There was a bulging sack strapped to the rack over his back wheel. It was clumsily tied, hanging heavily over each side. When the boy bent to adjust his sandal, the sack slid and pulled the bike over. He climbed off and attempted to readjust it.

The sack was grey with rusty streaks. It looked to Benevento just like a dead pig.

When he was a child, Benevento had seen plenty of people bringing fresh meat to market on bicycles. He had carried fish that way himself.

This boy's sack was not, of course, a dead pig. *Not in Oman. There would be no pigs anywhere at all in Oman,* Benevento reflected.

When the light changed, the boy climbed hastily back on his bike, and the Mercedes moved on.

That's me, Benevento thought morosely. *Off to market with a dead pig.*

Before agreeing to do business with the Omani, Benevento had done some homework. Oman was an old-fashioned Muslim monarchy ruled by a sultan named Qaboos ibn Said. Qaboos seized power from his own father in 1970, proceeding to reign in peace and prosperity for nearly forty years. He was a flamboyant bachelor, more interested in fashion and music than in politics. Perhaps this was the secret of his success. At any rate, Qaboos was almost never in attendance at his Muscat palace and would certainly not be at the meeting today. Benevento had been contacted by a minister in the sultan's appointed cabinet, who made it clear that their arrangement was off the record.

I will have to be very careful with these people, Benevento reflected, *despite my own Middle Eastern roots.*

Benevento came from a family of Arab fisherman who migrated from Tunisia to southwestern Sicily. His mother became pregnant with him at the tender age of eighteen. She was permitted to have her baby and raise him only because she claimed to have been raped by a stranger. She confided to Benevento alone that his father was an Italian merchant whom she had loved with all her heart. Looking unmistakably like a mixed breed, Benevento was never accepted in the fishing village. To make things easier on both himself and his mother, he left Sicily for Rome as soon he was old enough to take care of himself. There he found he had a special knack for the life of crime. He adopted his father's name in an effort to fit in among his Italian "business associates." The older mafiosi called him "Mufti" behind his back and despised him for his mixed heritage; the younger ones, however, respected his work too much to hold it against him.

That Benevento was a Muslim was a major factor in landing him such an important job with the Omani. But it would not give him any further advantages. The Omani were Ibadi Muslims, believing that only other Ibadi Muslims were deserving of *wilaya*, the friendship shared among believers. Non-Ibadi Muslims were regarded with an attitude of detachment consistent with business relations.

Benevento set his jaw. *I will finish my business and be on my way as swiftly as possible.*

Soon they arrived at the sultan's palace. It was a surprisingly modest building, with a flat, square roof balanced on trumpet-shaped columns of sky blue and gold. A red flag stood atop the roof, snapping smartly in the breeze.

Upon entering the foyer of the palace, Benevento was met by a mustached receptionist who led him up a curving staircase to a white-washed conference room with open windows overlooking the sea.

Benevento tried to relax. He poured himself a glass of water at the sideboard. Before he could sit down, three men wearing elaborate turbans and cloaks edged with silver and gold embroidery entered the room. From their belts hung khanjars, the traditional curved daggers of Oman.

The tallest of the men stepped forward and proffered his hand. "Assalamu Alaikum," he rumbled in Arabic. He continued in English, "Thank you for coming, Mr. Benevento. I am Maged Salah. We spoke on the telephone."

Benevento reached out his hand to shake but said nothing, not remembering the correct reply to the greeting in English or in Arabic.

Salah turned to introduce his companions. "This is Mr. Mohammed Al Asmy," he said, indicating a man with a full white beard who carried a metal briefcase. "He is a senior minister in the cabinet."

Benevento shook Al Asmy's hand, adopting the soft-touch Arabic grasp he received from Salah.

"And this is Dr. Basim Al-Dahadha," Salah said, indicating a plump, bespectacled man. "He is a professor of ancient Persian history at Sultan Qaboos University."

Benevento and Dr. Al-Dahadha shook hands.

"I hope you do not mind if we conduct our business in English, Mr. Benevento," Salah said, "as not all of us know Italian."

Benevento reluctantly grunted his assent. "I can do it some," he said.

"The assistant we sent to collect you has informed us that your efforts were successful, praise be to Allah."

"Yes, I have the box," Benevento said, proudly patting the black duffel on the table.

Salah smiled. "Excellent. Congratulations. A most impressive accomplishment! We have brought Dr. Al-Dahadha to examine its contents, if you don't mind."

Benevento tensed. "What about the money?" he asked.

Salah bristled almost imperceptibly at his guest's boorishness. "Mr. Al Asmy has a portion of your payment in his case, sir." He tipped his head, indicating that Al Asmy should put the case on the table. "The rest will be deposited into your account on our command. A total of five million, just as we agreed." Salah opened the case, presenting its contents with a flourish, and then moved toward the duffel bag.

Benevento didn't budge. "Five million is not enough," he blurted. "There was a, how you say . . . guard. I have to kill him."

Salah stopped in his tracks. His smile faded.

"I want ten," Benevento concluded.

Salah smiled again, this time less mirthfully. "Mr. Benevento, please understand. The amount is not negotiable. There are certain risks in your profession. We cannot possibly—"

"But you were supposed to take care of all the guards," Benevento hissed in Italian. "That was the deal. You didn't do your part."

Alarmed by Benevento's unexpected hostility, the portly Dr. Al-Dahadha glanced nervously at the door. The bearded Al Asmy glowered.

Salah, however, received Benevento's words with apparent equanimity. "Mr. Benevento, to save us endless discussion of the original agreement, allow me to tell you plainly up front: we do not have any more than five million to give you. It was extremely difficult for us to raise even this amount." He paused for a moment, thinking fast. "We know that, once our plan is complete, and the sultan sees its magnificent results, he will be very grateful. Perhaps he will reward you further then."

Benevento breathed deeply, restraining himself and changing tactics. "My hand," he said in English, displaying the wound for his Omani hosts to see. "I cut my hand . . . and I am bleeding there . . . in the church. The polizia, they know my blood." He looked at Salah imploringly. Then he added in Italian, "I have to leave Italy. I have to disappear."

Salah frowned at Benevento's hand. He looked at his companions and then, slowly, back at Benevento. "I see," he said. "Please. Let us sit down." He went to the door and called to someone.

As each man took a seat around the table, the receptionist came in with a tray of coffee, dates, and pistachio nuts. After everyone was served, Salah gave further instructions in Arabic to the receptionist. Then he asked Benevento some polite questions in Italian about his flight. Benevento responded curtly, barely disguising his impatience. Soon the receptionist returned with some disinfectant and a bandage for Benevento's hand. Benevento tried to wave him off, but finally conceded to being doctored.

Once the receptionist had left, closing the door behind him, Salah began again in English. "I deeply regret your misfortune, Mr. Benevento," he said. "As a fellow Muslim, however, I ask you to bear in mind the ultimate purpose of this venture."

Benevento shifted uncomfortably.

"Please, sir," Salah insisted. "Allow us to explain."

Benevento nodded grimly.

"Dr. Al-Dahadha," Salah said, touching the professor's shoulder, "Please tell our guest about the gift that Allah recently bestowed upon you."

Dr. Al-Dahadha took a sip of coffee and wiped his lips with a napkin. "Approximately six months ago," he reported in a soft, almost feminine voice, "I arranged for our university library to purchase a very rare Persian manuscript dating to the fourth century CE. This manuscript revealed the existence of five scrolls in a silver box, entombed in the sarcophagus of the Christian St. Paul in Rome."

Dr. Al-Dahadha paused, noticing that Benevento was having trouble following his English.

"Yes, my friend," Salah prompted, "and tell him what the manuscript attests."

"The manuscript attests," Dr. Al-Dahadha continued in a louder voice with exaggerated enunciation, "that the scrolls in the silver box, the scrolls you brought us right here—" he broke off and cast a hand toward the duffel bag, checking to see that Benevento understood, "—prove that Christianity is a fraud."

Salah looked at Benevento triumphantly, murmuring, "Praise be to Allah."

Benevento was not sure what to make of this revelation, nor did he understand what bearing it had on his problem.

Observing that Benevento displayed less than the desired response, Salah tried again. "Mr. Benevento, we believe that these scrolls have the potential to destroy the foundation of Christianity once and for all."

Benevento roused himself as best he could. "That's good, real good, Mr. Salah," he said. "But how does it help me?"

Salah was visibly disappointed. "Mr. Benevento, do you not see? We have not undertaken this venture for profit or for prestige. We have undertaken it as an obligation of Islam. Exposing the false claims of the Christian faith is the rational way to wage *jihad*." Salah raised his right hand, joined his thumb to the tips of his fingers and hammered the air as he spoke. "Once the Christians hear the truth and see the proof they will no longer persist in their error. The religious war can finally cease. Allah will be victorious once and for all!" With this last pronouncement, Salah raised both hands in an expansive gesture. There followed a resounding silence.

"I don't believe this," Benevento finally erupted in Italian. "Are you asking me to take a hit for Islam?"

"We are asking you, sir," Salah explained patiently, "to accept our five million for the scrolls in your line of duty as a Muslim."

"No deal," Benevento declared. "You say you are constrained by your financial circumstances. But so am I. In a matter of days, I need to create a new identity for myself and start a whole new life outside of Italy. Five million is not enough to see me through. I want ten and I want it now."

The Omani were astonished at their guest's religious indifference. Dr. Al-Dahadha coughed into his napkin. Al Asmy and Salah eyed each other. An unseen signal passed between them.

Finally, Salah spoke. "Mr. Benevento, forgive us, but your unanticipated demand makes it necessary for us to consult with one another in private. Please, help yourself to some more refreshments. We will return shortly."

"I don't have time for games, Salah," Benevento growled, rising from his chair. "I'm warning you—" He broke off, debating what sort of threat to hurl. It didn't matter. The three Omani did not so much as pause to listen. They got up and left, taking the briefcase with them.

Benevento collapsed back onto his chair. Then he grabbed the bowl of pistachio nuts and began shoveling them into his mouth.

The three Omani marched downstairs without a word, entered an office, and shut the door.

Salah hit his fist into the open palm of his hand. "We have no choice but to kill him," he raged.

"No, Maged," Al Asmy protested. "It is not *halal*. This man is a Muslim."

Salah scoffed. "Is he? What kind of Muslim shrinks from the *jihad*? He certainly is not Ibadi. He is *Kafir,* that's what he is."

"Maged," the older man persisted. "We must find another way."

Salah snapped his head back and clicked his tongue. Then he crossed his arms and strode to the window to look out at the garden.

Al Asmy turned to Dr. Al-Dahadha. "Basim, does the Persian manuscript refer to all five of the scrolls as proof of the fraudulence of the Christian faith?"

Dr. Al-Dahadha thought for a moment, scratching the hairy back of his neck. "Well, yes. They were all kept together for a reason. However, it refers to one, or perhaps two, more than the others."

"Well then, gentlemen," Al Asmy announced, "here is our solution: we buy two scrolls for five million, and Benevento can sell the others elsewhere to make up the difference."

Salah turned from the window, his long fingers splayed in protest.

There ensued an intense argument between Salah and Al Asmy. Dr. Al-Dahadha watched with grudging interest, like a man dragged to a tennis match against his will.

In the end, the senior minister prevailed.

Salah folded his hands in front of him resignedly. "Mohammed, I thank Allah for your wisdom. We will do as you say. And we *will* make it work. In a matter of time, the sultan will know that five million dollars have disappeared from the treasury. He will find out we fabricated the conference in Italy in order to gain use of the jet and the special agents—who apparently failed to accomplish their mission at the church." Salah paused, shaking his head wearily. "In a matter of time, all of this will be found out and traced to us."

Dr. Al-Dahadha frowned at this, not liking the way Salah's use of the term "us" seemed to include him.

"Mohammed," Salah continued, "*you* can retire at any time with an illustrious career behind you. But *I,* at the opposite end, am gambling my entire future on these scrolls."

Al Asmy nodded reassuringly. "If our plan is successful, we will be heroes of the Muslim world."

Salah smiled, color returning to his cheeks. He did not tell his colleagues that he hoped—more than hoped, he *knew!*—that the aging and childless sultan would be so impressed with the initiative that he would name Salah his successor.

"The mission cannot fail!" Salah proclaimed, reaching to touch the shoulder of Dr. Al-Dahadha, who nodded vigorously a beat later.

When the three Omani returned to the conference room, they found Benevento pacing by the window. Nearly an hour had passed, and he was beside himself with muted fury.

"Mr. Benevento," Salah opened with a smile. "We have arrived at a solution that I trust you will find more than generous. As I have already informed you, we are strictly limited to five million dollars. But we are willing to give you this amount for just two of your scrolls. You can sell the others elsewhere."

Giving up on English, Benevento fired back in Italian. "Unacceptable! I have no place to sell scrolls and no time to waste. What good is five million dollars to a man in prison? I tell you, if you do not give me ten million for all five immediately, I will turn myself in and implicate *you* for a reduced sentence!"

On the word "you" Benevento pointed forcefully at them. They reacted as though they had been slapped, raising their hands, backing away, and complaining angrily in Arabic. Dr. Al-Dahadha headed toward the door. Salah recovered first.

"Please, Basim, come back. Everyone, let us calm ourselves. Mr. Benevento does not know that in our country, we point the finger only at animals."

Benevento stood with his hands on his hips, glad he had insulted them.

Al Asmy spoke to Dr. Al-Dahadha in Arabic. "Basim, where did you buy your original Persian manuscript?"

Basim shrugged. "From an Internet dealer."

"Would this dealer be able to sell three of these scrolls?" Al Asmy asked.

"Perhaps," Dr. Al-Dahadha replied.

Salah was listening carefully to their exchange. He nodded.

"Mr. Benevento," he announced in English, opening his hands in front of him. "We know a dealer who will sell the remaining three scrolls. This can be handled quickly and conveniently. Considering the value of the scrolls, you will likely come out with a net gain of more than ten million."

This gave Benevento pause. "Considering the value of the scrolls," he countered, "I require five million for just one along with your help selling the remaining four."

Salah crumpled as if in great physical pain. He swallowed hard and looked to Dr. Al-Dahadha. Dr. Al-Dahadha fidgeted and averted his eyes, but Al Asmy looked unwaveringly at Salah and nodded emphatically.

"Mr. Benevento," Salah croaked. "We find your terms very burdensome. Nevertheless, we are prepared to accommodate you—such is our determination to serve Allah faithfully. Dr. Al-Dahadha will select the scroll we want and give you the contact information for the dealer."

Hearing his cue at last, Dr. Al-Dahadha hustled over to the black duffel bag on the table, pulling on a pair of clear plastic gloves. He bent like a surgeon over the bag and began extracting its contents.

Benevento steadied himself against the sideboard. He tried to ignore the voice in his head telling him he had just cut the worst deal of his entire career.

The worst deal is always the last deal.

But the truth was, he had no choice. He knew it. They knew it. And it was all over. It was over the moment he had agreed to do this insane job.

I should have stuck with jewels and drugs. I'm good at those. There's nobody better. Who'd have thought ancient artifacts would be such a curse?

Benevento's future was dim. The only thing he could hope to save now was his dignity.

"If these scrolls are what you say they are," he muttered, "then they're worth at least a hundred million each."

Salah snapped his head backward, clicking his tongue as before. "Enough, Mr. Benevento!" he rasped. "You are lucky just to be leaving alive."

Chapter Three

 The day it happened, Dana hadn't even finished unpacking
the boxes in her new office.

She knew that leaving Columbia University, where she had taught
for thirteen years, would be a risk. She was camouflaged there. She had
become famous for her work on ancient Greek manuscripts so slowly
that no one had taken much notice. She was just another professor
of some obscure subject that only Europeans really cared about. But
becoming the first director of New York University's newly established
Advanced Institute for the Study of Antiquity had suddenly thrust her
into the spotlight.

It's because of the money, she reflected. *The spotlight always follows
the money.*

One year ago, it was announced that the Institute would be established as a discrete entity within NYU, with its own board of trustees
and its own endowment. An anonymous benefactor had left untold
millions for the endowment, far surpassing sums ordinarily reserved
for the glitziest high-tech fields. The benefactor had issued a single
statement with the bequest:

Human beings have begun the twenty-first century in a state of
crisis. Rapid, uncontrolled change has eroded our sense of direc-

tion. Lost on a dark path, we cannot risk going any further until we know where we have been.

This Institute will be a beacon of hope that shines a bright light from the past to the future. Penetrating the origin of Western civilization, it will reveal the truth about who we are. The time has come for us to face the secrets that lie buried in our history.

The Institute had come to life with extraordinary energy. First, prime office space was acquired on 84th Street, across from the Metropolitan Museum of Art. Then, the hiring began: two office managers, three librarians, five tenured professors, and a director of international stature. Next, the Institute would admit ten exceptional PhD students who would also serve as research assistants.

It wasn't so much the money that had attracted Dana but the concept—that the key to the future lay in the secrets of the past. She knew that was true. If it was true for individual human beings, why wouldn't it be true for civilization itself? Furthermore, she knew her work would skyrocket in a specialist environment, free from the bureaucratic constraints of a traditional university department.

She had not, however, counted on all of the attention. Since awarding her the directorship four months ago, NYU had paraded her around in a series of invited lectures and interviews showcasing her vision for the Institute. Although Dana was pleased to see burgeoning interest in such a neglected field, she was asked so many questions—questions that often crossed over into her personal life—that she felt exposed.

And so, when it happened, that Wednesday morning in late February, she naturally assumed the Institute spotlight was to blame.

She was standing at the east window of her office, trying to decide whether to order blinds or curtains. Someone knocked on her door.

"Come on in!" Dana called, expecting one of the two office managers, Eva or Ann.

"Dr. McCarter?" It was a man's voice. Dana turned.

"Yes," she said warily. The man did not look like someone she wanted to talk to. He was short and fat, with a balding head of prickly brown hair. Smiling broadly enough to show a gap between his front teeth, he had the ruthlessly confident air of a reporter. *Newspaper rather than television,* Dana surmised.

She crossed over to him, less to shake his hand than to block any further intrusion of her sanctum.

"Hello," he said, slightly out of breath and with an indeterminate accent. "My name is Turk Selenka. I'm an independent collector of ancient manuscripts, and I was wondering if you would be willing to give me your expert opinion on one of my recent acquisitions." He held up his briefcase, indicating that said acquisition was inside.

Dana was annoyed—more annoyed, in fact, than she would have been if the man had been a reporter.

"I'm sorry," she replied with impeccable politeness. "I'm afraid I don't do appraisals."

"Really?" he said, undaunted. "This is a very important manuscript. I would think it would be like candy for you. Come on—just one little look?"

Dana laughed awkwardly. "I'm sorry. I can't help you."

She started to turn away, hoping he would too. He didn't.

"I'm surprised they let you in, actually," she said, turning back and glancing down the hall to see if anyone was there to help her remove him. "The Institute isn't open yet. But even if we were, we wouldn't be doing that kind of work."

"You mean this isn't *Antiques Roadshow?*"

Dana planted her hands on her hips.

"I'm just kidding," he chuckled. "You are a tough nut to crack, all right." He looked at her searchingly. "But I'm afraid I can't leave until you tell me about this scroll."

"Excuse me, what was your name again?" Dana asked, adrenaline pumping now.

"Turk Selenka, at your service," he answered, smoothly producing a business card from his breast pocket.

She waved it away. "Mr. Selenka—

"Call me Turk."

"Mr. Selenka, please," Dana persisted. "I'm asking you to leave."

At first, he looked hurt. Then he straightened his shoulders and looked her in the eye. "No, Dr. McCarter," he countered, matching her tone, "you wouldn't want to do that. Because if I leave here without the information I need about this scroll, I'm going to have to tell someone about your little habit."

Dana froze for an instant. Then she looked at him with incredulity. "I don't know what you're talking about."

Selenka raised his eyebrows in mock surprise. "Oh, but I think you do." He moved to her desk and cleared a space for his briefcase.

"This is outrageous," Dana muttered, heading for the door.

"I wouldn't do that, Dr. McCarter," Selenka warned.

Dana slowed and stopped just beyond the threshold. A young woman's voice from down the hall called, "Did you want me, Dana?" It was Ann.

Dana looked back toward the man in her office and then down the hall toward Ann. She smiled wanly. "No, that's okay. I thought I did. But never mind. Thanks."

She moved slowly back into her office and closed the door behind her. Selenka was pulling up a chair alongside her desk. He opened the briefcase.

Shaking now, Dana watched him from the door until he turned toward her. "What do you want with me?" she finally asked.

"I told you," he said calmly, almost apologetically. "I just want you to tell me about this scroll."

"And I told you I don't do that," she spat.

"Ah yes," he recalled. "And then I referred to your little habit, and you suddenly seemed agreeable—do we really need to go through all of this again?"

Dana glared at him.

"Oh, I see!" he exclaimed. "You have more than one little habit and you need me to clarify which one I'm referring to. Forgive me! I am so naïve." He was enjoying himself, clearly hoping she would warm to him.

She didn't.

He was disappointed. "Look—Dan—Dr. McCarter," he started. "I'm talking about the manuscripts, okay? The illegal ones. The ones you procured without documentation from certain, well, let's just say the word 'black market' wouldn't be entirely out of—"

"That is a ridiculous, empty accusation," Dana objected, a little too quickly.

"You want me to be more specific?" he plowed on. "Okay, no problem. The Aristotle letter alone is enough to land you in serious trouble. Purchased approximately one month ago, from an Internet dealer called the 'Palatine Library.'"

He checked her face to see how he was doing. She was close to breaking.

"I swear to you," he sympathized, "I didn't want it to come to this. I will go away and leave you alone if you will just help me with this scroll."

He reached into his briefcase and pulled out a clear plastic bag containing a tan cylinder about ten inches long and four inches wide.

Dana's mind was racing. *Who is this man? How does he know about the Aristotle letter and the Palatine Library?*

This was the moment she'd been dreading for nearly ten years now, from the day she'd bought her first black market manuscript. At one level, she knew it was inevitable; at another level, she had somehow believed she could avoid it.

Did I really think I could avoid it, or was it just that I couldn't stop?

It's not as though she had gotten involved in the black market on purpose. She didn't even really know the first purchase was illegal. In her line of work, it was natural to encounter individuals with things—very interesting things—for sale.

When someone tells you that something you would absolutely love to have as your very own is for sale, you don't ask where it came from. You don't demand to see the paperwork. You simply regard it as your right to free trade.

The manuscript was illegal because it lacked provenance—documentation of history of ownership. International agencies had begun imposing artifact provenance regulations in the 1990s. Their goal was to curtail rampant tomb raiding, which was occurring primarily in South America and Persia. Both of these areas, however, fell far outside Dana's purview. She was only interested in ancient Greece, and only for the sake of her research.

Everyone celebrated Dana's groundbreaking work, not realizing it was achieved by stepping outside official channels. She pitied her colleagues, who toiled away over the same old manuscripts as though reading them yet again would suddenly shed new light.

In order to make real progress, you have to go beyond the stockpile.

There were dozens of collectors out there who had no idea what they were sitting on. And they didn't dare find out because, more often than not, finding out meant being told you were not the rightful owner. This was why so many invaluable ancient manuscripts were squirreled away in safes full of forgotten family heirlooms or—worse yet—uselessly displayed as mansion kitsch.

At first, Dana thought of herself as a kind of Robin Hood scholar, working for the greater good. But things slowly got seedier. She started buying things she didn't really need, telling herself she could trade them for the things she did need. At first she cringed at every transaction; then, little by little, she began to enjoy the rush. She vowed she would quit last year when a dealer she knew was arrested and imprisoned. She was clean for months after that. Then along came the Aristotle letter.

Dana was angry. She was actually angry at herself for letting it come to this, but she thought she was angry at the obnoxious son of a bitch sitting in front of her.

"How dare you!" she seethed.

"Why won't you just look at my goddamn scroll?" he erupted. "Jesus Christ, woman! I'm not a monster. I just want some cooperation here. I don't have time to pussyfoot around."

"If you're not a monster," she shot back, "then tell me where you got it and what you need the information for."

He shook his head resolutely.

Dana knew perfectly well that he bought the scroll on the black market and needed information in order to fake convincing provenance papers. He was probably going to try to sell it at Sotheby's or some semilegitimate venue.

Dana considered her options. If she called the police, Selenka would dash for the door and then call the police himself with an anonymous tip about her. Prior to her appointment as director of the Institute, that wouldn't have been much to worry about, especially if there was no hard evidence. But now, while she stood in the spotlight, a tip like that would ignite a scandal that would ruin her career.

Dana tried to calm herself, knowing that everything hinged on her ability to regain control of the situation. "Look, Turk, or whatever your name really is . . ."

He smiled disarmingly at her.

"I don't want any trouble, okay?" She inched toward him. "I thought you were trying to involve me in something illegal. And I would never consent to that. If you can assure me that you came by this scroll legally—"

He winked. "Consider yourself assured."

"Well, all right then." She pasted on a professional smile. "Let's have a look."

Dana cleared off her desk and wiped down its glass top with window cleaner. While it dried, she pulled a pair of latex gloves and a magnifying glass out of the top desk drawer. Then she carefully unwrapped the scroll.

"I can't believe you're carrying this around in a plastic bag like a sub sandwich or something," Dana scolded.

Selenka snorted and shrugged.

Dana was not expecting much. In all likelihood, it was a bible scroll. During the Middle Ages, hundreds of myopic monks had copied the same old religious stories for hundreds of years, and hundreds of copies had survived. Dana found bible manuscripts so boring that she had allocated no funding for them in the Institute library budget.

When she unrolled the scroll on the desk in front of her, however, she saw immediately that it was unique.

"What?" Selenka asked, observing her reaction.

"Where did you get this?" she demanded.

"I'm the one asking the questions, remember?" he snapped. "Tell me what you see. Tell me everything."

"Right. Okay," she conceded. "Well, first of all, it's parchment, not papyrus. Papyrus is made from reeds, so it has a rough texture. Parchment is made from scraped animal skin, so it's smooth like this." She handed him her magnifying glass. "See?"

"Okay, so it's parchment," he concurred. "What does that tell you?"

"Well, papyrus was preferred for all formal writing in the ancient world," Dana lectured, in her element now. "The ancients used parchment only for informal purposes, like notes. It was only after the papyrus supply ran out that parchment became the norm."

"When was that?"

"Around the fourth century CE."

"So this scroll would date to sometime after that."

"Well, no," Dana corrected, "because then it would be in book form rather than scroll form. Once parchment became the norm, they started folding it into books rather than rolling it into scrolls. If I had to guess, I would say this scroll was made before the transition to parchment books—someone's personal copy of a formal papyrus scroll."

"I see," Selenka said. "What is it a copy of?"

"Let's find out," Dana murmured, more to herself than to him, as she picked up her magnifying glass. The long, crinkled page lay horizontally before her. Ten neat columns lined up from left to right, each consisting of rows of letters without spaces.

Selenka stood to peer over her shoulder. "Is it some kind of code?" he asked.

"No," Dana sighed, wishing he would shut up so she could concentrate. "In ancient times, it was standard to run the words together to save space. Writing materials were very expensive."

Selenka nodded and was quiet, but only for a moment. "What does it say?" he prodded.

Dana started to reply, but the words caught in her throat.

"What?" Selenka demanded.

She ignored him, squinting at the text.

He leaned in, scanning the exotic lines. "What did you just see?" he asked.

Dana could feel his breath on her neck. It smelled sour.

"You know what?" she announced, rising abruptly to her feet. "This isn't going to work with you hovering over me. You're going to have to give me some time."

"Okay," he said, taken aback. "You're right. I'm sorry." He glanced around the room. His eyes landed on a short, green couch amidst a conversational grouping of furniture. "I'm just going to go sit over there. You take your time."

And so she did.

Chapter Four

It was four o'clock in the afternoon before Dana finally came up for air. Her back was stiff and she was starving. Selenka was snoring unbecomingly on her sofa. She snapped off her gloves and trotted down the hall to the bathroom. On returning, she went to her kitchenette, put a pot of coffee on, and selected a box of peanut butter granola bars from the cupboard. Then she sank into the rocker across from Selenka. As she rocked, munching a granola bar, she considered what to tell him. Her only objective now was to convince this impertinent little man to sell her his scroll.

"Finished?" he slurred, popping one eye open.

Dana gave a start. "For now," she answered.

Selenka sat up and stretched. She offered him a granola bar and went back to the kitchenette for two cups of coffee.

Selenka accepted her refreshments gratefully. "So, what's the verdict?" he asked.

"Well, proper study will take months," Dana replied. "As it happens, this scroll is just the kind of thing we're looking to purchase for our library here at the Institute. We have a substantial acquisitions budget and can offer you a generous price."

Selenka blinked at her. "I'm sorry, Dr. McCarter—"

"Call me Dana."

He smiled groggily. "Dana. I'm sorry, but it's not for sale."

She pretended not to hear him. "You know, it's very common for there to be problems with provenance papers. I know a man who has done some documentation for Sotheby's. He's a miracle worker. I bet he could help you gather the documents you need." She checked to see if he looked like he was ready to negotiate. He didn't.

He was watching her steadily. Her lustrous dark brown hair was pulled up in a loose twist. Her small frame was tucked effortlessly into a dark blue skirt and white blouse. She spoke with an alto voice and sometimes punctuated her sentences with a crooked little smile. Her earrings didn't match: one was a tiny diamond star, the other a tiny diamond moon. He wondered if she knew. After she stopped speaking, it took him a moment to realize it was his turn.

"Dana," he sighed. "It's not for sale. I'm only here to find out what it is. Can you tell me what it is?"

She took a sip of coffee and brushed a crumb from the arm of her chair.

"Yes," she finally admitted.

There is no point in lying. I can tell him what it is without telling him that he is sitting on the most important manuscript find of the century. I can use his ignorance to my advantage.

He looked at her expectantly.

"Well, I'm pretty sure it's a dialogue by an ancient Greek author named Aristotle," she reported flatly.

"You mean Aristotle, the philosopher?" he asked.

"Yes," she conceded, disappointed he knew that much.

He ran a hand over his shiny head and sat back against the sofa. "That makes it really important then."

She shrugged. "Every ancient manuscript is important, Turk. It's just that the Institute takes a special interest in fourth-century Greece.

This manuscript is a piece of the puzzle we're working on. That's why we need it for our library."

"What do you mean, puzzle? What puzzle?" he asked.

"Not a puzzle, really," she amended, as carelessly as she could manage. "It's just that there are some things about Aristotle that we don't understand."

"Like what?" he demanded.

Dana waved her hand dismissively. "During his life, Aristotle published twenty-one dialogues. While fragments from the first half of them have been found, the others have vanished without a trace, except for the titles. The complete works attributed to Aristotle today were precariously compiled from a set of lecture notes in the library of the Lyceum where Aristotle taught. They were never intended for publication. Is Aristotle even the author of those lectures? Why did *they* survive while his dialogues didn't? These are the questions we are trying to answer."

Selenka nodded slowly. "So it looks like one of those dialogues survived after all. Which one is it?"

"It's the *Eroticus,* which turns out to be a dialogue about love between two characters called Herpyllis and the Stranger."

"Herpyllis? Oh my God, I hope he used a condom!" Selenka guffawed. "Ew! Can you imagine—'I'd like you to meet my girlfriend. We call her "Herp." Just don't get too close!' Oh, my God!" He slapped his knee and shook with laughter.

Dana cringed. "Turk, Herpyllis was a perfectly ordinary name in ancient Greece. It was the name of Aristotle's second wife."

"Really?" he marveled, wiping moisture from the corner of his eye. "So Aristotle made his wife a character in one of his dialogues?"

"That's not unusual either," Dana assured him. "Plato, in his dialogues, made characters of his mentor Socrates, his brother Glaucon, and other real people."

"Okay," he said. "Okay, I'm with you. So, what does Aristotle say about that crazy little thing called love?"

"Well, I can't give you a detailed exposition after just a few hours," she protested. "Basically, they discuss two different theories about what true love is, and then, at the end, the character Herpyllis presents her view. And we gather that this would be the author's view—namely, Aristotle's."

"And what was Aristotle's view?" he asked.

"Well," Dana answered, "in modern terms we would say that, through Herpyllis, he attacks transcendent realism as well as immanent realism in favor of nominalism."

"Yikes!" Selenka squealed. "You're going to have to put that in English. In fact, never mind. Just tell me how the dialogue helps you solve your puzzle."

Dana took a sip of coffee, stalling. Would telling him help her win him over, or would it make him tighten his grip on the scroll? She wasn't sure. Then she thought about her students—how their eyes glazed over whenever she tried to explain the nature of her research. Even her colleagues had trouble understanding her excitement. Surely she could bore Selenka into submission.

"Well," she explained, "in the published lecture notes that we today know as 'Aristotle's complete works,' all three of the views I just mentioned are present. This has led to a great deal of controversy among scholars concerning which was Aristotle's true view. This scroll, if it is authentic, clearly indicates that Aristotle's true view was nominalism."

Selenka waited for more. Dana shrugged, indicating she was finished.

"That's it?" Selenka finally remarked. "That's the big puzzle this billion-dollar Institute is working on?"

"Pretty dull, huh?" she agreed. "Which is why you should sell me the scroll and let us boring people do our boring work. I think my Sotheby's man is our best——"

"Dana, I told you," he interjected, leaning forward and speaking slowly and loudly as if she were retarded. "It. Is. Not. For. Sale."

She sighed.

He smiled apologetically and looked her over again. *Of course she knows her earrings don't match. Dana is clearly as sharp as they come. She's not going to make a mistake like that. Probably the pendant on her necklace has both a moon and a star on it. It probably came with the earrings. . . .*

Dana wore the top button of her blouse open, but the pendant of her necklace hung just too low to see. Turk craned his neck a little.

Dana noticed. She cleared her throat. "Can I get you more coffee?" she offered.

But Turk was entranced. "What's a beautiful girl like you doing mousing around with such dusty old stuff as this anyway?" he asked.

Uh oh, Dana thought, knowing exactly where the conversation was headed. *I would do a lot for this scroll, but not that. Not with him, anyway.* She could feel herself beginning to perspire. Not that she was afraid of him. She just didn't want things to turn unpleasant again.

"Turk," she asserted forcefully, in an effort to break the spell. "You have to understand that no individual piece of the puzzle is going to be impressive by itself. You have to keep your eye on the big picture. That's what this Institute is about. We're piecing things together with the conviction that an accurate picture of the past will give us profound insight into who we are today and where we're going."

"Hmm."

Dana sized up her quarry. Could she sell him on the Institute's vision? She got an idea.

"Let me ask you a question," she proposed.

"Sure," Selenka granted gamely.

"What thing in life do you fear most?" Dana asked. "You know, like snakes, or heights, or drowning."

"Knives."

"Really?"

"Yeah. I have nightmares about being stabbed." He pantomimed being stabbed, howling grotesquely. "I think a stab wound would be the worst possible way to die."

"Okay," Dana said. "What would you think if I told you that your fear and your nightmares are due to a childhood experience—a bad experience with knives."

"I guess it's possible," Selenka admitted. "But I don't remember anything like that."

"Of course not," Dana returned. "You've repressed it. Now, most fears are harmless, and everyone has some. But people with debilitating fears who seek professional help often learn they can overcome their condition by confronting certain childhood experiences."

Selenka picked a piece of granola bar out of a lower left molar with his pinky finger. "That's not very surprising, I guess."

"No, but what people don't realize is that our civilization as a whole is the same way. Cultural dysfunctions can be traced back to historical secrets. We have to learn the truth about the past in order to heal and move forward in a healthy way."

"It's like mass therapy," he chimed in, not a little sarcastically.

"Call it what you like," she said, folding her arms on her chest. "That's what this Institute is about. And if it works, it will be worth any amount of money."

"The operative word being 'if.'"

Dana rolled her eyes in what she hoped was a jocular manner. "Look, you don't have to share the Institute's vision. What I'm telling you is that the Institute is going to value your manuscript more than anyone else ever will. It's an informal copy of an obscure Aristotle dialogue that none of the other collectors know or care about."

"Oh, come on," he objected, "collectors love obscure things."

Dana smiled to herself, ready at last to drop her bomb. "Well, they might love it if it were a clean copy."

"What do you mean?"

"I mean the Aristotle dialogue isn't the only thing on the scroll. Whoever copied it also copied a passage of First Corinthians at the end."

"First Corinthians?"

"Yes. You know, the bible verse they always read at weddings: 'Love is patient, Love is kind . . . '"

"Not really."

"Well, anyway, it's tacked on at the end of the dialogue."

"Why?"

"Who knows? You have to remember, your scroll is just some-body's notebook. Its owner was probably at a library copying what-ever he liked. He evidently liked a little bit of Aristotle and a little bit of St. Paul."

"St. Paul?"

"Yes. St. Paul—the disciple of Jesus. He wrote First Corinthians, along with some of the other books of the New Testament."

"But Aristotle was pre-Christian, right?"

"Yes, by more than three hundred years."

"Why would someone put him together with St. Paul?"

Dana shrugged. "Maybe he thought the two works went together well—which, as a matter of fact they do. But, from a collector's point of view, it makes for a bit of a mishmash."

Selenka nodded thoughtfully. "Well, as I mentioned, it's not for sale anyhow."

"If you insist on keeping it, will you loan it to the Institute for study? We could pay a user's fee and give you full credit on any publications—"

"Dana, Dana, Dana. My lovely Dana. I wish I could help you. I'm afraid that it is time now for you to forget you ever saw this scroll. It doesn't exist. You dreamed me up." He chuckled, hesitating for a moment. Then he heaved himself up off the couch and lurched toward the desk.

Dana jumped up and shooed him away so she could roll the scroll properly and wrap it carefully. Selenka put it back in his briefcase.

"I thank you for your expertise, madam," he said, bowing absurdly.

"It turns out that the pleasure was all mine," she replied, hoping she wasn't pouring it on too thick. "Please, please, call me when you change your mind. Because you *will* change your mind. I know you will. Here, take my card."

He accepted her card with a winning smile. Dana winced inwardly and shook his clammy hand.

Halfway out the door, he turned. "By the way, Dana, what's *your* worst fear?"

Dana grinned. "I'll have you know that I am completely and entirely fearless."

He grinned back. "I guess that means you had either a really great childhood or a hell of a lot of therapy."

She nodded and waved cheerily, all the while hoping he would drop dead before he left the premises, leaving her to confiscate the briefcase and its precious contents.

It was after five. Time to go home. As Dana packed up her things, she was not sure how to feel about the day. On the one hand, the black market had finally reached out from the shadows and threatened her professional life. Ancient manuscript trafficking was ultimately just as dangerous as any other high-stakes, illegal enterprise. Today she had learned just how vulnerable she was—and not just in terms of her career.

On the other hand, she had handled it. Not only had she diffused the threat, she had turned it to her advantage. Dana was an excellent photographer and the owner of a recent model of Leica's best digital camera. She now possessed high-resolution, digital photos of a manuscript that could enable her to realize the Institute's vision.

Bright light, flat surface, and the shutter's almost palpable, strangely satisfying sound, snap, snap, snap!

That'll teach you to sleep on the job, Turk Selenka—or whoever you really are.

 *THE EROTICUS*

The Scene: A marketplace
The Characters: HERPYLLIS, a slave merchant
                  STRANGER, a customer

Book I

HERPYLLIS: Good morning, sir. Please allow me to show you my wares. Will you try on a silver ring?

STRANGER: Certainly. Did you make it yourself?

HERPYLLIS: Indeed, sir. In the tradition of Thrace, my homeland.

STRANGER: Although this ring is very beautiful, I like the gold one on your finger better—a linked band, set with a piece of amber. What price do you ask for it?

HERPYLLIS: The ring on my finger is not for sale.

STRANGER: I offer three times the price of the others.

HERPYLLIS: Alas, no amount of money could part me from this ring. It is a copy of the ring I gave to my own true love before he departed.

STRANGER: My dear lady, is there something wrong with all the men who remain?

HERPYLLIS: Not at all. Only that they are not him.

STRANGER: How long have you been waiting?

HERPYLLIS: Eighteen years and thirty-two days.

STRANGER: By Zeus! You have most surely discharged your duty by now. It is high time you buy your freedom and find yourself a husband.

HERPYLLIS: No, sir. I love this man.

STRANGER: Well, my lady, pardon my astonishment. I feel as though I am speaking to Penelope herself.

HERPYLLIS: Yes, I have often felt like Penelope. She is an inspiration to me.

STRANGER: It is a beautiful story. I would love to hear you tell it.

HERPYLLIS: Penelope was the wife of Odysseus, the king of Ithaca. Odysseus had to leave Ithaca to wage war on Troy. He and his men were gone for a long time and lost their way coming home.

STRANGER: Ah yes, and nearly twenty years went by. Naturally, everyone assumed Odysseus was dead. They wanted Penelope to remarry.

HERPYLLIS: Indeed. Dozens of suitors came from miles around. Penelope steadfastly refused each and every one, however, because her heart belonged to Odysseus.

STRANGER: And in time, everyone grew angry with Penelope. They demanded she choose one of the suitors.

HERPYLLIS: Penelope stalled for as long as she possibly could. Finally, she announced she would marry the man who could string Odysseus' bow.

STRANGER: Indeed. I dare say she reasoned that anyone who could string Odysseus' bow would be as great as Odysseus himself and therefore worthy of her love.

HERPYLLIS: No, sir. She reasoned that no one else would be able to do it.

STRANGER: Well, as you wish. How does the story end?

HERPYLLIS: None of the suitors could string the bow except for one man, a stranger, who looked like a beggar.

STRANGER: Ah yes, and it was soon revealed that the stranger was none other than Odysseus himself in disguise.

HERPYLLIS: Much to Penelope's relief.

STRANGER: A most excellent story! So now let us apply its lesson. If you are the very likeness of Penelope, my dear lady, then what is the test for your suitors?

HERPYLLIS: You mean what would a man have to do to win my hand in marriage?

STRANGER: Exactly.

HERPYLLIS: Well sir, he would of course have to be my long-lost love himself. You erred gravely when you suggested Penelope would have accepted any man who could string Odysseus' bow. The great and wise poet Homer wrote this story to demonstrate that true love cannot be replaced.

STRANGER: Surely it is not I but you who misunderstand the story. It is quite normal for women to remarry.

HERPYLLIS: That proves nothing at all. Losing true love is like losing a leg. One may be able to carry on. One may even be able to find new love. But one can never replace the love one lost.

STRANGER: Then why did Penelope propose the test?

HERPYLLIS: Because she knew no one but Odysseus could pass it. The bow stands for the special thing that only one's true love has.

STRANGER: And what, exactly, is that?

HERPYLLIS: Sir, your question is very deep and interesting.

STRANGER: I suppose the bow stands for the soul.

HERPYLLIS: Surely not. If the soul exists, then everyone has one.

STRANGER: True, but no one else has Odysseus' soul.

HERPYLLIS: Then the question is, why would Penelope attach herself to the soul of Odysseus as opposed to that of someone else? What is the special thing that only Odysseus' soul has?

STRANGER: It has a certain excellence.

HERPYLLIS: What do you mean?

STRANGER: I mean his strength. Clearly the bow measures strength.

HERPYLLIS: Many people have strength. Having strength fails to make Odysseus special.

STRANGER: But surely no one has as much strength or the particular kind of strength Odysseus has.

HERPYLLIS: If a particular amount or kind of strength caused Penelope to love Odysseus, then why should it not cause everyone to love Odysseus?

STRANGER: Apparently, it did. He was the king after all.

HERPYLLIS: Yes, but no one loved Odysseus the way Penelope did. What explains Penelope's love?

STRANGER: Are you asking why we love those whom we love?

HERPYLLIS: Indeed.

STRANGER: But surely there is no answer to that question. When it comes to love, we either feel it or we do not. There is no need to know why.

HERPYLLIS: I disagree completely, sir. First of all, it is always good to know why. How can there be anything that a human being does not need to know? Second, this is a particularly important thing to know.

STRANGER: How so?

HERPYLLIS: I daresay you might someday find yourself wondering whether your feeling is really love.

STRANGER: It seems to me that such wondering itself proves the negative.

HERPYLLIS: Not at all. People wonder whether the world is really a round globe without proving the negative.

STRANGER: Well, they would surely cease to wonder if they heard a proper account of the heavens!

HERPYLLIS: You are quite right. Likewise, I wish to hear a proper account of true love. Can you give me one?

STRANGER: Perhaps with the help of Plato.

Here ends Book I of *The Eroticus*.

Book II

HERPYLLIS: What does Plato tell us about the nature of love?

STRANGER: Well, according to Plato, there are two kinds of people: the lovers of wisdom and the lovers of sights and sounds.

HERPYLLIS: How do they differ?

STRANGER: The lovers of sights and sounds are interested in appearances. They trust their senses and believe things are just as they seem.

HERPYLLIS: But things are often the opposite of what they seem!

STRANGER: Exactly. This is why the lovers of wisdom ignore appearances and refuse to trust their senses. They look for the deeper truth.

HERPYLLIS: I gather Plato's successor Speusippus and his students at the Academy fancy themselves lovers of wisdom.

STRANGER: Indeed.

HERPYLLIS: Are there two kinds of love then, one for each kind of lover?

STRANGER: Well, no. In Plato's view, the lovers of sights and sounds will never know true love at all. Only the lovers of wisdom can know true love.

HERPYLLIS: So true love is always directed toward the deeper truth.

STRANGER: Indeed.

HERPYLLIS: And exactly what truth do we find behind the appearances?

STRANGER: Lovers of wisdom eventually encounter the Form of the Good.

HERPYLLIS: The Form of the Good is within my true love?

STRANGER: Not exactly. The Form of the Good is an abstract idea that transcends the physical world. Rather than existing in things, it is reflected in things. Everything in this world reflects the Form of the Good in some way because the creator god made this world in accordance with it.

HERPYLLIS: So the Form of the Good is like a pattern that I can see with my mind's eye if I look deep enough?

STRANGER: Indeed. Yet things do not reflect the Form of the Good equally. For example, in my mind's eye, I can see a perfect olive. If I go to an olive tree, however, I will find some olives growing round while others grow lopsided. A round olive reflects the idea of a perfect olive better than does a lopsided one.

HERPYLLIS: And people are the same way?

STRANGER: Except that Plato speaks not of their appearance.

HERPYLLIS: He speaks of their souls?

STRANGER: Without a doubt. Lovers of sights and sounds develop lopsided souls because they are paying attention to unimportant things.

HERPYLLIS: So a lover of sights and sounds can neither love nor be loved, at least not truly.

STRANGER: You follow me well. True love is directed toward the Form of the Good, and a lover of sights and sounds reflects the Form of the Good only a little.

HERPYLLIS: So true love exists between lovers of wisdom. Do all the lovers of wisdom love each other equally?

STRANGER: In theory they should. In practice, however, they see more of the Form of the Good reflected in some than in others. Their love is always proportional to the amount of the Form of the Good they see reflected.

HERPYLLIS: Is it really so?

STRANGER: Why should it be otherwise? The Form of the Good is the only thing truly lovable. The less you see of it the less you love.

HERPYLLIS: I know plenty of people who love bad things!

STRANGER: Only because they incorrectly suppose that what they love is good. One can love something bad supposing it to be good, but one cannot love something bad on purpose.

HERPYLLIS: I fear I do not agree with this view.

STRANGER: Yet it explains Penelope's situation. She loves Odysseus because she sees a great deal of the Form of the Good in him. Since the other suitors suffer by comparison she cannot love any one of them enough to marry him.

HERPYLLIS: And if one of the suitors reflected more of the Form of the Good than Odysseus, then Penelope would happily marry him instead?

STRANGER: Without a doubt.

HERPYLLIS: But I thought I told you true love cannot be replaced.

STRANGER: Yes, you did indeed tell me that, but I never agreed.

HERPYLLIS: You should agree, my dear sir, and I can show you why. You said we love only those things we believe to be good and never love those things we believe to be bad. But love is limitless. It can attach itself to absolutely anything. The only reason what you say seems true is because we call whatever we decide to love "good" and we call whatever we decide to hate "bad."

STRANGER: I grant that we call something "good" or "bad" depending on whether we love it or hate it. This does not imply, however, that love can attach itself to anything. For example, a child who dislikes olives will call them "bad." But this is only because he fails to understand that olives are good. Once he understands that olives are good, he will not be able to hate them.

HERPYLLIS: Some people hate olives all their lives!

STRANGER: Only because they do not understand the truth.

HERPYLLIS: You are assuming there is a truth about olives independent of our judgment of them.

STRANGER: Of course! The Form of the Good is the ultimate standard against which all things are measured.

HERPYLLIS: And, according to Plato, it implies that human beings should value each thing in accordance with how it measures up to this standard.

STRANGER: Indeed.

HERPYLLIS: Plato is easily refuted then.

STRANGER: How so?

HERPYLLIS: Well, just imagine Homer ended his story differently. In this ending, the beggar is not the only man who is able to string Odysseus' bow. Another man is able to string the bow even better than the beggar. So the beggar is sent away and Penelope marries the other man. Does that make for a better story?

STRANGER: Absolutely not! In truth, that would not have been nearly as satisfying.

HERPYLLIS: I agree. Homer would never have achieved his famous stature with such a disappointing ending. In his great wisdom, he knew human beings love each other for who they are, not for how they measure up to an abstract standard of goodness.

STRANGER: So Plato's account of love is incorrect.

HERPYLLIS: Without a doubt. Do you have any other ideas?

STRANGER: There is another school called the Lyceum where a philosopher named Theophrastus teaches. He has a theory that may help us.

Here ends Book II of *The Eroticus.*

Book III

HERPYLLIS: What does Theophrastus tell us about the nature of love?

STRANGER: As you may recall, Plato asserted that the Form of the Good is a transcendent pattern reflected to some extent in everything.

HERPYLLIS: Certainly.

STRANGER: Theophrastus asserts instead that each object in the world is made up of many different forms.

HERPYLLIS: These forms exist within the object?

STRANGER: Indeed, as its essence.

HERPYLLIS: Are all of the forms good?

STRANGER: The forms themselves are neither good nor bad. It depends on how they function in a given situation.

HERPYLLIS: What do you mean?

STRANGER: As you know, there is a merchant woman who comes to this marketplace to sell her perfumes. The one she calls "Passion" contains the essence of almond, anise, and rose. It is a good perfume to wear to a dinner party, though not so good for wearing to a funeral.

HERPYLLIS: According to Theophrastus, then, everything is a combination of essences like a perfume?

STRANGER: Indeed. Each human being first and foremost contains the essence of humanity. This is what makes us all the same. But then we also contain other essences that make us different from one another. The result is a variety of interesting characters. Odysseus' essence includes a combination of strength, courage, and intelligence, which is a perfect combination for a king, though perhaps not for a flute player.

HERPYLLIS: I see. So how do we explain Penelope's special attachment to him?

STRANGER: Presumably, she has the essence of a queen. The essence of a king and the essence of a queen naturally match perfectly.

HERPYLLIS: What about more ordinary people?

STRANGER: Well, the same principle applies. In the case of perfume, certain combinations of fragrances are complementary while others clash. Likewise, each man must strive to develop a harmonious essence within himself and to marry another with a complementary essence. When parents arrange marriages they should bear this in mind.

HERPYLLIS: It seems to me Theophrastus' account would argue against arranged marriages. Who is in a better position to judge the compatibility of one's own essence than oneself?

STRANGER: Perhaps there is something to what you say. Penelope was fortunate enough to be in a position to arrange her own marriage.

HERPYLLIS: So Theophrastus would say that Penelope rejects the suitors because their essences are not compatible with hers.

STRANGER: Without a doubt. She waits for Odysseus because only he can function as the perfect complement for her.

HERPYLLIS: Does each person have only one true complement, or are there many possibilities?

STRANGER: There are many possibilities, but they will function better or worse in different circumstances. For example, essence of rose goes with almond or with myrrh. Rose combined with almond is good for a dinner party, while rose combined with myrrh is good for a funeral. So Penelope could have married someone else had she wanted to, say, live on a farm instead of in a castle.

HERPYLLIS: Interesting. What if Penelope and Odysseus decided to leave the castle for a farm instead?

STRANGER: The result would be disastrous. Together they have the right combination only for royalty.

HERPYLLIS: So there are two different ways to go wrong in love, according to Theophrastus. First, one might choose someone with an essence that clashes with one's own essence. Second, even if one chooses a complementary essence, one might land in the wrong circumstances.

STRANGER: Well, those two factors would explain a great deal of the misery we see among couples, would they not?

HERPYLLIS: Without a doubt. One thing still worries me, however. There are only so many different essences for making perfume. Are there a limited number of essences for making human beings as well?

STRANGER: Presumably, but because each person combines different essences in different proportions and in different circumstances, the possibilities are virtually limitless.

HERPYLLIS: Yet consider the merchant woman who sells a new batch of "Passion" at this market every week. To replace the old batch she need only mix the essences according to the recipe.

STRANGER: So?

HERPYLLIS: Well, I thought I told you true love cannot be replaced.

STRANGER: You did indeed tell me that, but I never agreed.

HERPYLLIS: You should agree, my dear sir, and I can show you why. On Theophrastus' view, Penelope will accept another man with a kingly essence in place of Odysseus.

STRANGER: Oh, come now! What are the chances there would be someone else with the exact same combination of essences as Odysseus?

HERPYLLIS: It makes no difference what the chances are. The possibility alone is enough to refute Theophrastus.

STRANGER: How so?

HERPYLLIS: Since Homer's story is fiction, we can tell it however we want.

STRANGER: But some ways of telling it are better than others.

HERPYLLIS: Exactly. So let us now consider another new ending. This time, another man is able to string Odysseus' bow just as well as the beggar because they have the same combination of essences. Penelope infers from this that it makes no difference which one she marries, so she lets the roll of a knuckle bone decide between them. The beggar loses the roll and is sent away. Does that make for a better story?

STRANGER: No, my dear lady, that ending would not have been nearly as satisfying.

HERPYLLIS: I agree. Homer would never have achieved his famous stature with such a disappointing ending. In his great wisdom, he knew that human beings love each other for who they are, not for how well they complement each other.

STRANGER: I object to your assumption—made twice now—that what makes for a satisfying ending in a story must be true in real life.

HERPYLLIS: But how else do you explain a satisfying ending? A satisfying ending depicts how things ought to happen in real life. Homer is teaching us about true love—how love should be.

STRANGER: You evidently know a lot more about love than you let on at the beginning. If neither Plato nor Theophrastus is good enough for you, then give me an account of your own.

HERPYLLIS: Well, I have no account of my own, sir, but a dear friend of mine once told me some things that might help.

Here ends Book III of *The Eroticus.*

Book IV

STRANGER: What does your friend tell us about the nature of love?

HERPYLLIS: He tells us why Plato and Theophrastus are wrong.

STRANGER: According to Plato, true love is seeing the Form of the Good reflected in someone.

HERPYLLIS: Indeed. And this implies Penelope should be willing to replace Odysseus with someone who reflects more of the Form of the Good. Since this implication is clearly incorrect, we rejected Plato.

STRANGER: According to Theophrastus, true love is joining someone with a complementary essence in the right circumstances.

HERPYLLIS: Very true. And this implies Penelope should be willing to replace Odysseus with someone whose essence is equally complementary. Since this implication is clearly incorrect, we rejected Theophrastus.

STRANGER: My lady, you never tire of saying that true love cannot be replaced. You insist human beings love others "for who they are." What do you mean by this?

HERPYLLIS: Well, when one loves someone for who he is, one loves him for his own sake. That is, one regards him as an end in himself rather than as the means to some other end.

STRANGER: Surely everything is the means to some other end!

HERPYLLIS: Most things are. Consider rain, for example. We love rain for the sake of the crops, not for its own sake. Nor do we love crops for their own sake. We love crops for the sake of food, we love food for the sake of health, and we love health for the sake of happiness. But happiness is the end of the line.

STRANGER: So we love happiness for its own sake.

HERPYLLIS: Without a doubt. It is the ultimate end for any human being.

STRANGER: In fact, Penelope would likely avow that she loves Odysseus because he makes her happy. Those who are in love often say as much.

HERPYLLIS: They most certainly do.

STRANGER: Yet this implies Penelope loves Odysseus for the sake of her own happiness, not for his own sake. He is therefore only the means to another end.

HERPYLLIS: That would be true if happiness were something existing in the world like a destination to be reached. Is that what you think happiness is?

STRANGER: I confess I know not what happiness is.

HERPYLLIS: Have you ever noticed that those who seek happiness fail to find it?

STRANGER: I myself have encountered this problem!

HERPYLLIS: For good reason: you seek that which does not exist.

STRANGER: Do you mean to say there is no such thing as happiness?

HERPYLLIS: No, sir. I mean only that happiness is not something to find, but rather something to create. Happiness exists only when we create it.

STRANGER: How so?

HERPYLLIS: By falling in love.

STRANGER: I have noticed that only those who are in love seem truly happy.

HERPYLLIS: Without a doubt. Although it is possible to fall in love with an activity, a place, or an object, the best of all is to fall in love with a person.

STRANGER: Whatever you fall in love with, then, is the ultimate end for which everything else is a means?

HERPYLLIS: Indeed. Enjoying that end is how you create happiness.

STRANGER: This seems to imply, however, that true love can be replaced. Penelope could create happiness with someone other than Odysseus.

HERPYLLIS: I have already granted that it is possible to find new love. My claim is that the new cannot replace the old.

STRANGER: By Zeus! How does finding something new differ from replacing the old?

HERPYLLIS: Suppose one day you hire a worker to fix your roof. The next day you hire a different worker to finish the job. The second worker would be a replacement for the first, correct?

STRANGER: Clearly.

HERPYLLIS: Now suppose instead that, on the second day, you hire a different worker, not to finish your roof, but rather, to fix your steps. We would not call the second worker a replacement for the first in that case, would we?

STRANGER: No, my lady. We would call him a replacement only if he did the same job as the first.

HERPYLLIS: Exactly. My point is that no one could ever do the same job as Odysseus. It is not something he has but something he does that Penelope loves about him.

STRANGER: What exactly does he do?

HERPYLLIS: He makes her happy.

STRANGER: No one else can do that?

HERPYLLIS: Not the way he does. Did you notice the way the views of both Plato and Theophrastus implied that two different men can be the same? According to Plato, two different men reflect the same Form of the Good, and according to Theophrastus, two different men contain the same essential forms.

STRANGER: Indeed. On both views, all human beings share commonalities.

HERPYLLIS: Well, on my view, no two men can be the same in any way. Even if both are good, they will be good in their own way. Likewise, if both are strong, courageous, and intelligent, they will be those things in their own way. And if they both make Penelope happy, it will not be the same happiness.

STRANGER: There is no quality two men can share?

HERPYLLIS: No, sir. We speak of goodness, strength, courage, intelligence, and happiness as though these are things that can be shared. But really they are just words we use to refer to similarities we perceive.

STRANGER: How do you know this account is any more accurate than the accounts of Plato and Theophrastus?

HERPYLLIS: Well, the experience of true love proves it! If Plato's "Form of the Good" or Theophrastus' "essences" were real, then true love could be replaced. But true love cannot be replaced, as Homer's epic demonstrates.

STRANGER: On your view, then, every individual is completely unique.

HERPYLLIS: Indeed.

STRANGER: There is a good reason, however, for positing commonalities: they provide a basis for comparison. How can you compare two individuals that have nothing in common? Your view leaves us without any standard of judgment.

HERPYLLIS: If we have to create our own happiness, then we have to create our own standard of judgment as well. We create our own standard of judgment by loving some things more than others. The inevitable conclusion is that love is the ultimate measure of all things.

STRANGER: I daresay you may be right, my lady. In fact, your view is beginning to sound very familiar.

HERPYLLIS: I thought it might when I noticed the chain around your neck holding a gold ring. It is a linked band, set with a piece of amber—just like mine.

STRANGER:

> If I speak with a golden tongue,
> But have not love,
> I am only a resounding gong or a clanging cymbal.
> If I solve the riddle of the Sphinx and achieve the heights of
>   knowledge,
> But have not love,
> I am nothing.
> If I have the strength to move mountains,
> But have not love,
> I gain nothing.
> Love is patient; love is kind.
> Love is not envious or boastful or arrogant or rude.
> It does not insist on its own way:
> It is not irritable or resentful.
> It does not rejoice in wrongdoing,
> But rejoices in truth.

Love bears all things, believes all things, hopes all things,
  endures all things.
Only faith, hope, and love abide,
And the greatest of these
Is love.

Here ends *The Eroticus.*

Chapter Six

Dana rode the subway home to her brownstone in the West Village thinking about love.

Aristotle makes it sound so good. . . . But it never seems to work out that way in practice . . . . Well, at least now I have the theory. . . .

Thrilled to have photos of the *Eroticus* on her jump drive, Dana tried to think how they might be able to help her career. She could study them, of course, but how could she ever publish anything about them? A document that does not officially exist cannot be footnoted.

Nevertheless, Turk Selenka was bound to sell the scroll at some point. If he sold it to a private collector, then it might never see the light of day. But if he sold it to a publicly minded private collector or to an institution, then everyone would soon have access, and she would be that much ahead of the game.

Furthermore, purchasing it myself is still a strong possibility.

She trotted up the steps, unlocked the door, and slipped inside. Her Siamese cat, Nicomachus, sprang to his feet to greet her. Dana kicked off her shoes, dumped her bag and the mail on the hutch and swept him into her arms. He complained crossly until he had settled himself into his favorite position; she rubbed him gently behind his ears.

"You would have been proud of me today, Nico," she told him. "It was very stressful, but I think I've come out ahead."

She padded to the kitchen to get something to drink. Her answering machine was blinking, indicating a message. She set Nico on the floor and pressed the button.

"*Bonjour,* Sista!" rang out the voice of Gene Vargas, her best friend and head of the Cloisters at the Met. "Your picture was in the *Times* this morning, darling! I thought somebody should tell you since you probably wouldn't notice. Just remember, I knew you before you were famous. Hey—I was able to move up my spa appointment on Saturday, so if you'd like to head to the banquet at six instead of six-thirty, that'll be fine with me. Just let me know. Okay, talk to you later. *Adieu!*"

Dana smiled. She and Gene had taken graduate school classes together at the Sorbonne and had both ended up with jobs in Manhattan. Dana had invited him to the Institute's banquet this weekend. Going with a friend was far better than showing up alone.

That was one nice thing about being married, she reflected. *I always had a date for university functions. Still not worth it, though.*

Dana went upstairs to change into jeans, tennis shoes, and a fleece top. Then she hit the street again. Her neighbor was just returning from his customary evening walk with his Yorkie. Dana waved and headed east.

It was about six-thirty by now and almost completely dark. Traffic was thinning, but sirens screamed down Sixth Avenue. Dana crossed to Washington Square Park and bought a paper. A street performer was juggling fire sticks under the Arch. A group of giddy young tourists cheered him on and took pictures. She gazed at the buildings of New York University and thought about her position as a member of this community. She felt a bit removed, with her new office so far from the main campus. But perhaps that was a good thing.

Dana pressed onward to a quiet Italian bistro where she often had dinner. Once seated, she flipped through the pages of the newspaper until she saw a familiar face grinning at her.

Ugh! Bad picture. The article was equally disappointing.

New Institute at NYU

Woman Without Childhood Set to Restore Childhood of Western Civilization

NEW YORK—Dr. Dana McCarter, former professor of classics at Columbia University, will be the first director of New York University's Advanced Institute for the Study of Antiquity.

Dr. McCarter outlined her plan for the first year yesterday at a press conference with the president of NYU. The Institute will be devoted to developing innovative techniques and methodologies for the study of ancient manuscripts.

Dr. McCarter earned an international reputation in her field primarily for her work on the fourth-century BCE Greek philosopher Aristotle. Her plan for the Institute begins with him.

"Aristotle was a key player in the development of Western civilization," Dr. McCarter said. "The problem is that his legacy has been so manipulated by political forces throughout history that we don't have a clear picture of who he really was. The time has come to restore this crucial moment of our collective past."

During the Q&A session following her address, Dr. McCarter did not deny that her passion for restoring the past stems from the unfortunate circumstances of her own childhood. Dr. McCarter has no knowledge of her life before she was approximately five years old. She was found lying unconscious on the steps of a bookstore in Greenwich Village in 1972. When no one claimed her, the owner of the bookstore, publishing tycoon Fez McCarter, took her in and eventually adopted her. She suffered from a severe case of amnesia, unresolved to this day. Her true name and birth date are unknown.

"The past shapes the future in profound and mysterious ways," Dr. McCarter said. "The more we know about our roots, the better we understand ourselves."

The Institute will open next week.

Dana had known that the question about her childhood would end up dominating the story. In fact, it was plain as day that the story never would have merited a color photo on the front page of the education section if it hadn't been for that question.

Everyone loves a good tragedy.

She refused to credit the reporter who asked the question with having done his homework. No, there was a more sinister explanation. The NYU committee that hired her had done its homework, and her personal history had played a strong role in winning her the job. They had no doubt leaked the information to the reporter on purpose in order to get the publicity they wanted. Dana wanted to believe she landed the job because she had a stronger vision than the other candidates. Deep down, however, she feared she just had the most sensational story.

Dana was also appalled at the way the article sneakily implied that she was a psychological basket case. Self-understanding requires knowledge of roots. Dr. Dana McCarter has no knowledge of her roots. Ergo . . .

My complete blank is no worse than the incomplete and inaccurate memory everybody else has, she thought. *In fact, I may be better off.*

Dana surreptitiously studied the four other diners she could see from her table, sizing them up and comparing herself to each one in turn.

At a table by the window sat a man and a woman, still in their business suits. They were making polite conversation over dessert. The woman's face was puffy with the extra twenty pounds typical of middle-aged Americans these days. She kept on snatching glances at the action on the street.

A man at a table along the wall typed contentedly on his laptop between bites of spaghetti. He jumped when the waitress asked how his meal was, as though he'd forgotten he was in a restaurant.

A young woman who had been sitting at the bar got up and walked to the entranceway, where she stood with her purse on her shoulder and her arms folded. She tried to distract herself with the fish tank while she waited, presumably expecting a cab.

Here we all are and not a one of us wants to be here. I guess we all figure we'd be happier someplace else.

Dana decided to order takeout ravioli so that she could go back home and have a look at some of her files on Aristotle's lost dialogues. While she waited for her food, she entertained herself by speculating on the secret vices of each of her restaurant companions.

My only secret vice is my collection. Surely that's no worse in the grand scheme of things than theirs. Why should an addiction to Aristotle be any more shameful than midnight snacking or tax fraud?

When she got back to her brownstone, Dana climbed to her "museum" on the top floor, leaving her food and Nicomachus in the kitchen. The door was double-locked and sealed for climate control. Once inside, she paused to admire the eerie effect of the glowing glass boxes that housed her treasures. She pulled some files from a cabinet against the wall before crossing to her newest addition—the Aristotle letter.

"You got me in a lot of trouble today," she chided the document. Then she read it again.

Aristotle to Sweet Herpyllis, Greetings. I have not heard from you in months. Nor does anyone bring any news. I am beside myself. Where are you? How is our little boy? Have you forgotten about me? I am alone in a sea of strangers here in Athens. On the surface all is well. Yet my heart is about to crack into a million pieces. To keep myself from despair I have begun writing a series of dialogues defending Plato's philosophy. I learned today that there may be an opportunity for me to come see you next month when the weather improves. In the meanwhile, I am sending all my love to you and Nicomachus.

Dana melted every time she read it. It was more meaningful to her than any black-and-white photograph or tattered baby blanket could ever be. The letter was also historically important, however, because of its bearing on the development of Aristotle's thought.

According to the standard view, Aristotle started out as a Platonist while a student at Plato's Academy and slowly came to reject Plato's views. According to a growing minority of scholars, however, the reverse was true.

Dana originally thought the letter overturned the standard view in favor of the minority view because it was addressed to Aristotle's second wife, Herpyllis, whom Aristotle married late in life. It seemed that, if he was writing to her while writing dialogues defending Plato's views, then he must have evolved toward Platonism rather than away from it.

And that would have been so disappointing, considering that Plato has it all wrong!

Having read the *Eroticus* today, Dana was now certain that the standard view was true: Aristotle evolved away from Platonism. The letter made perfect sense if Aristotle knew Herpyllis long before he was able to marry her—just as the dialogue suggested.

Dana brought her files, her food, and a bottle of wine into the living room, making a spread for herself on the coffee table. Hours later, reclined on the sofa reading about Aristotle, she fell asleep.

Chapter Seven

 Burning sensation. In my thighs.
Burning along the inside of my thighs.
A young man. A window. I'm at the window.
I'm watching a striking young man.
He is crossing the courtyard below.
He has the face of a lynx. His eyes and hair are black as night.
I am watching and burning.
I am looking through the window at a muscular young man crossing the courtyard below.
His hair and eyes are black as night.
He moves slowly, deliberately, ready to pounce.
I know this man. I know him very well.
He doesn't know I'm watching.

The time is the third year of the 103rd Olympiad. The place is Stageira, in the northern, Macedonian region of Greece. I am Herpyllis and he is Aristotle. We are both eighteen.

The house belongs to Proxenus, the husband of Aristotle's older sister, Arimnestes. Proxenus adopted Aristotle when Aristotle's parents died around eight years ago. Proxenus bought me from slave traders around ten years ago. I am an orphan too.

I can still feel the crush of your body against mine. I can still feel you between my legs.

I was born in Thrace, a kingdom to the northeast that the Greeks consider barbarian. I have only the vaguest memory of my parents and my brothers before they were killed. Unfortunately, I can still remember the night of the invasion in graphic detail.

First, the panic spread. Then there was a great deal of shouting and commotion. Then everything was on fire. My mother hid me in a trunk. I stayed in there for what seemed like days, though it was probably only overnight. When I finally came out, my entire family was dead. Lying around in pools of blood. Flies were swarming. I knew I should run far away, but all I could think to do was go to the well for fresh water. Scavenging slave traders spotted me before I came to my senses.

After that, everything was a blur for a while. I suppose I was luckier than most of the survivors from my village. Proxenus and Arimnestes were good to me. But I was just a kid, alone in the world. I was numb. I knew very little Greek. I hardly spoke a word for two years.

Then Aristotle arrived.

Aristotle won't talk about what happened to his parents. No one other than he really knows. All I know is that, whatever it was, it must have been even worse than what happened to mine.

The first time I saw you, I recognized the hollow stare in your eyes. You looked exactly like I felt.

We were the only two children our age for miles around. Proxenus let me sit in on Aristotle's lessons. At first, I think Proxenus allowed this only because he thought company might hasten Aristotle's recovery. Proxenus began to encourage my progress, however, when he realized my aptitude. By now, he relies on me for almost all of his correspondence and record keeping. Proxenus is a successful metallurgist.

Although his specialty is casting bronze statues, he is also teaching me and some of the other slaves to make gold and silver jewelry.

Down in the courtyard, there are people milling about. It's a party. Everyone is drinking wine. Arimnestes' son Nicanor is toddling around the columns. Her daughter Hero is playing knucklebones with visiting cousins.

Aristotle has just arrived. Everyone's eyes are on him now. Even those in the midst of a conversation turn to look. It is the same way everywhere he goes. Something about him. It's not that he's pretty—it's more his energy. A certain vibrancy. The attention he draws these days still surprises him.

Aristotle and I grew up like twins. We explored the world together. Although Arimnestes was scandalized that her brother would take to spending time with a female slave, she was too busy taking care of Hero and Nicanor to bother about us much. We spent endless hours together down on the beach. Our favorite was swimming. When we wore ourselves out with that, we would fish or build fortresses in the sand. We even built a boat once. It brought us too far out into the sea before it sank. We nearly drowned.

Spending so much time outside, I was as tan and sinewy as Aristotle. When I cut my hair short, I was often mistaken for a boy.

Aristotle is pausing at the table, feeling the eyes on him. He reaches for some apples and begins to juggle. Little Nicanor is enchanted. There are "oohs" and "ahhs" from the crowd as Aristotle executes some risky moves. He seems to be in his element. His sister beams. Everyone claps.

But only I know what you're thinking right now. You're thinking that you are not one of them. You're thinking that you will never be able to keep up your end of this deal. You're thinking that, if they really knew you, they wouldn't like you at all.

I am the only one who really knows Aristotle. And it's true that his family wouldn't like him if they knew him: he has a dangerous mind.

As Aristotle and I got older, we had less time for carefree afternoons at the beach. We started making deliveries to neighboring villages for Proxenus. We talked a lot on those trips. Often we talked about religion. And here's a topic Aristotle doesn't dare discuss with anyone but me. Because he doesn't have a religious bone in his body. He never tires of ridiculing the superstitions of Proxenus and his family.

One of Aristotle's favorite pastimes is to think up pranks to send the house into a fit of religious fervor. Once, while picking berries in the woods, he and I found a freshly dead weasel. After nightfall Aristotle snuck out, retrieved the weasel, and arranged it in a provocative position on the front doorstep. Proxenus forbade anyone to leave the house for three days. It was a good way to get out of berry picking for a while!

Aristotle sometimes leaves dead birds in strategic places to influence Proxenus' decisions as well. I'm just glad when he doesn't insist on cutting open the animals we find to see how their insides work. That's another one of Aristotle's favorite pastimes.

But it's not only religion that Aristotle doesn't believe in. He doesn't believe in the king. He doesn't believe in the law. His father was court physician to the king of Macedonia. Aristotle actually spent most of his childhood hanging around the royal court. He says the king is just an ordinary man making things up as he goes along. He says Greece and Thrace are just ideas. They don't really exist. If you don't believe in them, then people aren't Greek or Thracian—they're not even citizens or barbarians, slaves or kings—they're just people.

Lover, you are a lunatic. Look at you down there having a chat with Calicles.

Calicles, who was a soldier for many years, would literally try to kill Aristotle if he knew what Aristotle thinks about Greece. But Calicles will never know because Aristotle would rather have a good time than a bad time. He enjoys finding out about all the things people believe in.

That's Aristotle's problem—everything is a study for him. He notices details that are invisible to everyone else and wonders about the most outrageous things. I'm used to it, but he has to keep it under wraps in front of others or they'll think the worst of him.

For example, just the other day he asked me how many teeth I have. He thinks males have more teeth than females. I think he just has extra. He has also asked me about my menses and other private things.

But we were never anything but the best of friends until about six months ago. We were down at the beach. We hadn't been there together in ages. We stripped off our tunics and went for a swim just like we used to. But it was windy and rough. Before long, we dragged ourselves out of the water and collapsed on the beach to dry.

You were looking at me.

This in itself was nothing unusual. Aristotle has told me a hundred times he'd cut me open to see how my insides work if only he could do it without killing me. But this time it was different. He wasn't studying me. He was taking me in. It made me feel shy, and suddenly, I knew our childhood swims were a thing of the past. Furthermore, building a sand fort was out of the question. This made me a little bit sad, but I also couldn't help feeling excited about what we might do instead.

Before I had a chance to speculate about that, he was crawling toward me, his face intensely serious. He moved slowly, deliberately, ready to pounce. And then he did.

I can still feel the crush of your body against mine. I feel your hands on my breasts and your lips on my neck. The weight of you between my legs. You stop to look me in the eye before you enter, as though to check and make sure I'm still on board. You smile at me, and I smile back, and that is all we need.

The rhythm of your thrusting . . . the sound of the sea . . . and then it's over as suddenly as it began.

We liked it. We did it again. In fact, we've been doing nothing but that whenever we get the chance. It isn't terribly often, but it's often enough to be concerned about pregnancy. At first we would just wash off in the sea afterward. But then Aristotle found out that acacia tree bark ground into a honey mixture would do the trick. So we've been using that. I let him apply it. That's one of the best parts.

I feel like a new person. I'm in love. Ari and I are one—so much so that I can't believe people haven't figured it out. But he is a master of deception. And no one pays attention to me the way they do him.

We dream of escaping to travel the world. He says he wishes he were a slave so that his escape would be noble. It would not be very noble for him to escape his own relatives, especially when they took him in and fed him for eight years.

Proxenus has high hope for Aristotle's future in metallurgy. Unfortunately, metallurgy is the one thing Aristotle is no good at. At least, he's trying to convince everyone he's no good at it. It's really just that he would rather die than become a businessman.

In the courtyard below, Aristotle is challenging his cousin Milo to a one-armed wrestling match. "Come on, Milo," Aristotle taunts, "even with one arm tied behind my back I've still got two." He strips off his toga to prove it. The crowd moans and jeers at his vulgar joke. Milo strips off his toga. They wrestle one-armed. They are well matched: Milo is bigger and stronger; Aristotle cheats. Several other neighbors and relations drift in and out of the scene, alternately chatting and cheering on the wrestlers. Now Aristotle and Milo are laughing too hard to continue.

I wish I could wave and call your name. I wish I could join you.

I think of Aristotle like I think of the constellation Andromeda, for which I was originally named (Herpyllis is my slave name). On the one hand, Andromeda is all mine. When I gaze at her in the night sky, I feel as though she sparkles just for me. On the other hand, I know that she really isn't mine at all. She sparkles for anyone who notices. And who wouldn't notice?

Aristotle is like that. When we're together, I feel like we are the only two people in the whole world. But the truth is that Aristotle makes everyone he is with feel special. He has a way of raising one eyebrow as he listens to you and responding in a way that makes what you said seem smart.

Everyone who isn't jealous of Aristotle loves him. They say he could be the next Pericles if it weren't for his stutter. It's almost as though he thinks so fast that his speech can't keep up with his thoughts. There is talk among the slaves that he fakes the stutter so he won't have to become the next Pericles or ever do anything that would get in the way of having fun. But I know it's no fake. And I know that part of him wants to change the world.

Oh, Aristotle. You should go and do that. You have to go and change the world. And maybe someday I will be able to stop crying.

It's been a very sad day for me today, Ari, because I'm sure of it now: the honey mixture didn't work. I'm pregnant, and I must tell you tonight. There will be consequences.

By Greek law, slaves are not allowed to have children. Many become pregnant, of course, often by their masters. I have heard that, in the big cities, dozens of babies are left at the gates each year, either to die of exposure or to be rescued by some kind passerby. But I've never known that to happen around here. Being so far out in the sticks, we don't always go by the law.

In fact, one of Proxenus' slaves had a baby not long after I arrived. The father is another slave here at the house. The three of them live more or less like a family, though of course there was never any official marriage. The child is now eight. Proxenus just figures he has another slave for free.

If I told Proxenus I accidentally fell asleep by the window and was impregnated by a moonbeam, he would probably believe me. But this would only be a short-term solution.

I know you. Once the baby was born, you wouldn't be able to pretend it wasn't yours. You would want to be a father.

But that isn't going to happen. Proxenus and Arimnestes will see to it. It's one thing not to follow the trade of your adoptive father; it's another to mix the family line with that of a barbarian slave.

Aristotle will be sent away. He's actually lucky. This will make it impossible for them to make a metallurgist of him. They will want him as far away from me and the child as possible. They will probably ship him off to school in Athens. With his intelligence, that's exactly what should happen anyway.

Yes, in the end, this pregnancy will work in your favor, my love. It will give you your noble escape.

I prefer not to think he planned it that way though. Surely that would be too devious even for Aristotle.

I fondle the ring in my pocket, which I secretly made out of gold scraps from Proxenus' workshop. It is a linked band, set with a piece of amber. It matches the ring on my finger.

I will give it to you tonight, Aristotle, when I tell you goodbye.

Chapter Eight

 Loud pounding woke Dana. She was still on her sofa with papers, books, and the remains of last night's dinner strewn all around her.

Pound. Pound. Pound.

At first, Dana thought the sound was coming from the party in the courtyard below.

No, no—that was just a dream, she told herself.

Someone was pounding on her front door. She sat up and rubbed her eyes. Well, at least she was dressed, she realized, looking down at her rumpled clothes. She could go make the pounding stop.

As she stood and stepped toward the door, the events of yesterday came back to her in a flash. She froze.

Why is someone pounding on my door?

Turk Selenka's shiny face came into focus in her mind's eye.

Oh, shit.

She wasn't ready for this. She would never be ready for this. She had no room in her life for thugs and threats.

Pound. Pound. Pound.

Dana glanced at the clock. Seven-fifteen. She needed to be at work in forty-five minutes.

Shit!

Dana got down on all fours and crawled to the front window, carefully peeling back the bottom corner of the curtain. A man with thick black hair stood at her door. He wore a tailored suit and good shoes. He looked southern European, probably Italian.

Hmm. There is an attractive man pounding on my door.

Suddenly feeling ridiculous, Dana stood, shuffled to the hall mirror to make sure she was presentable, and then went to the door.

"Good morning. Who's calling, please?" Dana chirped through the intercom.

"Good morning," the man responded in an Italian accent. "I would like to speak with Dr. Dana McCarter. I am Detective Domenico Conti, Vatican Police Department." He flashed his badge to the peephole.

Police! Dana's heart skipped a beat. *That rat, Selenka! He must have ratted me out.*

"May I come in, ma'am?" Detective Conti prompted.

No way. He can't possibly have a warrant already.

Dana could feel herself beginning to panic.

Wait a minute. Vatican? Why Vatican? Nothing in my collection is connected with the Vatican. What would the Vatican want with Aristotle?

"May I come in, ma'am?" Detective Conti repeated.

"Ahh, no, actually," Dana stammered. "I'm afraid I don't have time to talk to you." She winced, realizing she had just admitted she was Dana McCarter. "I can't help you. I have to ask you to leave now."

"Ma'am," he persisted, "I don't think you want to have to do this at your office."

Oh, my God.

"What is it that you want, Detective?" Dana asked.

"I'd just like to ask you a few questions."

Dana felt a wave of defeat wash over her.

Christ, if they've got me, they've got me. What am I going to do, run? I'm just going to have to hire a really good lawyer.

Dana opened the door. Detective Conti smiled politely at her.

"This will just take a few minutes, ma'am," he assured her.

"That's good, because I'd really like to get to work," she snapped, beckoning him to follow her. Avoiding the mess in the living room, she led him to the sunroom off the kitchen.

They sat down, and Dana studied him. In spite of herself, she liked his face. It was soft around the eyes but hard around the mouth, as though he'd seen a lot in his day. He was in his mid-forties, she guessed. He looked a little tired, perhaps from his flight. His bushy, black eyebrows moved expressively as he pulled a notebook out of his breast pocket and addressed her.

"Dr. McCarter, I need you to tell me about the man who came to see you yesterday."

Dana gave the detective a puzzled look. That question wouldn't make sense if Turk Selenka had ratted her out.

"I'm sorry, Detective, I don't understand," she replied.

"I'm conducting an investigation into a crime," Conti explained, "and I have reason to believe that the man who came to see you may be involved. I need you to tell me everything you can about him."

"What was the crime?" Dana asked, wide-eyed.

"Please understand, Dr. McCarter," Conti said quietly. "I am not at liberty to discuss the details of the case with you."

So! Turk Selenka stole the scroll from the Vatican. Ballsy little bugger! But what was Aristotle's Eroticus *doing there? I know the Vatican manuscript catalogue like the back of my hand, and the* Eroticus *is not in it. It's not in any catalogue anywhere—it's supposed to be lost. Was the Vatican hiding it?*

Dana got up to adjust the blinds, stalling for time to think. Then she remembered the passage from 1 Corinthians at the end of the dialogue. But she still couldn't think why the Vatican would keep such an important manuscript hidden.

"I'm afraid I can't help you, Detective," she announced finally. "I don't even know that man. I didn't invite him to my office. I'd never met him before in my life."

Conti scrutinized Dana. He nodded slightly, apparently satisfied she was telling the truth. "What is his name?" Conti asked.

"You followed him all the way across the ocean, and you don't even know his name?" Dana looked at Conti askance.

He was not rattled. He cocked his head to the side, awaiting her answer.

"I don't remember," Dana lied.

Conti shook his head. "How can that be? He stayed at your office for approximately five hours yesterday."

Dana felt her cheeks burning.

"What was he doing there all that time?" Conti asked.

"Um . . . sleeping on my couch, mostly," Dana murmured lamely.

"You let a strange man into your office to sleep on your couch?" Conti asked. He pinched the bridge of his nose as if staving off a headache.

Dana tried to resist feeling sorry for him. She needed time to think. She didn't have a plan, and she was screwing up. "Would you like a cup of coffee?" she asked.

Conti smiled gratefully and nodded. She got up and went to the kitchen to put a tray together while she thought about her situation.

Feeling no trace of loyalty toward Turk Selenka, she decided she had just two objectives: first, to avoid landing in trouble for her own collection; and second, to find a way to gain legitimate access to the *Eroticus,* either by purchasing it or by receiving official permission from its legitimate owner.

If she refused to cooperate with Conti, she would have to hope Selenka didn't get caught. If he did, then the Vatican would recover its scroll and it would go back to whatever impenetrable vault from which it came. Worst of all, she would never be able to publish any research using her photographs. To do so would be tantamount to admitting she lied to the police and conspired with Selenka.

But what if she cooperated? As long as Selenka never knew it was her who gave him up, this option may serve her better in the end. She could bargain for information about the scroll. Once she officially knew about the scroll, she could appeal to the Vatican to make it available for her research. Surely, they would agree to that.

She could see plenty of possible complications on either side, and she wasn't happy about having to choose—especially in the space of the four minutes it took to prepare the coffee. She went to the bathroom to give herself another minute.

What it came down to in the end was that, if she helped Conti, she stood a chance to gain some control of her situation instead of just having to wait to see what might befall her.

Control is always a good thing.

She returned to the sunroom with a tray of coffee and bagels, a tentative smile on her face.

Conti was ravenous. He dove into his breakfast with abandon.

"So is this your first time to New York?" Dana asked.

"Yes," he admitted. "I've always wanted to come. I just wish it was under better circumstances."

"Yes," she sympathized. "This sounds like a difficult case."

He nodded as he chewed.

"Detective Conti," Dana ventured, "I may be able to help you if you give me more information."

"Why should I give you information?" Conti queried. "It is your duty to cooperate with the law."

Dana sipped her coffee pensively. "I don't agree," she said. "First of all, I'm an American, not an Italian. Second of all, I'm not even Catholic. Your law does not apply to me. How do I know whether you're up to good or evil? I don't know much about this whole thing, but what I do know makes me think the Vatican is up to no good at all."

At this, Conti's coffee cup stopped midway to his mouth. He slowly set it back down. "What makes you say that, Dr. McCarter?" he asked, eying her intently.

"I told you, Detective," Dana persisted. "I think I deserve an explanation."

"You deserve nothing," Conti nearly shouted. "This is not optional!" He got up and walked to the window, hands on hips.

Dana was stunned for a moment. She sat back in her chair and watched him. He was clearly upset.

Is he upset at me? Partly, yes, but it seems bigger than that. Dana began to feel she was gaining the upper hand.

"Detective," she said. "This is America. We take freedom very seriously. Progress on this case is going to require some give and take."

He took his jacket off, hung it on the back of his chair, and rolled up his sleeves. "That's bullshit," he said quietly. "Everybody takes freedom seriously."

Dana shrugged defiantly and pointedly looked at her watch.

"I will share some information with you," he conceded, "and then you will tell me what you know. Deal?"

"Deal."

"A set of scrolls was stolen from the Vatican one week ago."

"A set?" Dana interrupted. "How many?"

"Five," Conti replied patiently.

"From where at the Vatican?" Dana demanded.

Conti shook his head and put a finger to his lips to shush her. "In the process of killing a guard, the thief left his own blood at the crime scene. I used our DNA database to catch the thief—Mr. Achille Benevento. We interrogated him. He had already sold the scrolls."

Conti looked out the window, debating whether or not to continue. So far, he hadn't told her anything she couldn't find out on her own.

Dana waited attentively for more.

"And then, Benevento, he . . . got away . . . and . . . turned up dead." Conti stole a glance at Dana. She looked like she wanted to interrupt again, but he plowed on. "I think I know who killed him. I caught up with this possible killer in Nantes, France. He tailed your office visitor from Nantes yesterday."

"This killer was at my office yesterday?" Dana asked.

"Just outside," Conti confirmed.

Dana shuddered involuntarily.

"Where did they go from there?" she asked.

"I don't know," Conti replied. "I lost them."

Dana felt her throat constricting. She glanced nervously out the window.

"I hope you can see that you could be in grave danger, Dr. McCarter," Conti concluded.

Dana was ready to cooperate.

"The man who came to see me called himself 'Turk Selenka'," she reported. "He had a scroll and he wanted me to identify it for him."

"Just one scroll, you say?" Conti asked, scribbling in his notebook.

"Yes."

"And what was it?"

"I think it's one of Aristotle's lost dialogues," Dana said. "It's called the *Eroticus*. It's a philosophical discussion of the nature of true love."

"Aristotle?" Conti asked. "So that would be pre-Christian."

"Yes, roughly 330 BC," Dana answered, "except that whoever copied the dialogue also included the passage from 1 Corinthians about love. You know the one: 'Love is patient, love is kind,' and so on."

Conti nodded. Then he wrote for a while, turning a page in his notebook.

"You call the dialogue 'lost.'"

"Yes," Dana said. "We know that Aristotle wrote some twenty-one dialogues, but we have only fragments of the first few and nothing but titles of the rest."

"Okay." Conti searched her face. "Why did you say just now that you thought the Vatican was up to no good?"

"Because that scroll should not be hidden!" Dana erupted. "It is a key element of the history of Western civilization. We have a right to know what Aristotle said."

Conti dropped his eyes, tracing the top of his pen along the patterns inlaid on the tabletop.

"Dr. McCarter," he said finally, "you claim you didn't know Selenka. Why did you help him?"

Dana downed a swig of coffee. "Well, I mean, it's my job."

"Your job is to help anyone off the street identify antiquities?" Conti responded, skeptical.

"Well, no," Dana admitted. "But it was evident to me that he had something important."

"Why do you think he came to you?" Conti asked.

"Well, I do have an international reputation," Dana pointed out, a little embarrassed. "Not just anyone can read these things, you know."

"Sure," Conti acknowledged. "But there must be someone in France who can. Why fly all the way to New York to ask *you?*"

"Detective, I don't know. All I know is that I was thrilled to see that scroll. I told him the Institute would be happy to buy it. He said it wasn't for sale." Dana laughed and smacked her forehead, as if amused at her own naïveté. "And by the way, his accent wasn't exactly French. I couldn't place it. Perhaps he lives here in New York."

"Perhaps," Conti granted. "But we both know that he couldn't go to just anyone to identify that scroll. Anyone who knew enough to identify it would know that it must have been stolen. So he had to go to someone who couldn't report him. What has he got over you, Dr. McCarter?"

"Nothing!" she protested.

He knew she was lying. She knew that he knew. He knew that she knew that he knew. But neither said anything. They ate in silence for a moment. Eventually, Dana broke it.

"So, you think your thief—Benevento, who is now dead—sold one of the scrolls to Selenka. What happened to the rest of them?"

"I don't know yet," Conti replied. "I'm supposed to find out and recover them."

"I see," Dana mused, struggling to contain her excitement at the thought of a whole set of Aristotle's lost dialogues.

"Do you collect antiquities yourself, Dr. McCarter?" Conti asked, taking stock of the antique decor in the room.

"No," Dana said flatly. She looked at her watch. "I'm sorry, Detective Conti. I really need to get to work now."

"Did Selenka find you through the black market, Dr. McCarter?" Conti persisted.

"That's ridiculous!" Dana blurted. She got up, putting the coffee tray together to signal that their meeting was over.

"One last question," Conti demanded as he rose. "What do you know about the cult of Dionysus?"

Dana was surprised by the question. She didn't see how it fit with anything they had been talking about.

"It was . . . well, Dionysus was the Greek god of wine," she fumbled. "The ancient Greeks worshiped him. His cult was different from other forms of paganism, though. Dionysus was a savior who died and came back to life, so the cult prefigured Christianity in many ways. It was wildly popular in both ancient Greece and ancient Rome, but Aristotle is known to have hated it. Why do you ask that?"

"It might be relevant," Conti mumbled vaguely.

They walked to the door. Conti turned and handed her his card.

"Thank you for your help and for breakfast," he said sincerely, with warm brown eyes. "I will be in New York for a while, trying to find a lead on Selenka. Please call if you think of anything else."

"Right. Okay. No problem." Dana opened the door, eager to be finished with the interrogation.

"Please be aware that you are in danger, Dr. McCarter," he warned. "The more you help me, the easier it will be for me to protect you. I assure you that my only objective is to solve this case. I am not interested in pursuing any other black market transactions." With that, he turned and sauntered down the steps to the street, his jacket slung over his shoulder.

Dana locked the door behind him and heaved a huge sigh of relief.

That was a close call. Way too close. I need to stop this madness.

Dana made a beeline for her computer to look up "Vatican theft" on an Internet search site. Dozens of web pages turned up detailing the heist of St. Paul's sarcophagus. They mentioned the murder of a guard and the escape of a prime suspect. But they did not mention scrolls.

EIGHT

Dana went to the phone and called the Institute to request that Ann order blinds for her office windows and to inform her that she wouldn't be coming in today. Then she went back to the sofa in the living room and resumed her research.

That night, she made it off the couch to her bed before she fell asleep.

Chapter Nine

 Tingling sensation. In my thighs.
Tingling along the inside of my thighs.
An important-looking man crossing the forum.
A column. I'm standing behind a column in the shadows.
I'm watching a man with a commanding presence.
He has the face of a lynx. His hair and beard are black as night.
I am watching and tingling.
I am looking from the shadows at a man crossing the forum.
His beard and hair are black as night.
He moves swiftly, boldly, as if in pursuit.
I know this man. But not as well as I'd like.
He doesn't know I'm watching.

The date is the first year of the 108th Olympiad. The place is Athens, Greece. I am a professional courtesan, and he is Aristotle. He is thirty-six and I am thirty.

I have known Aristotle since he arrived in Athens nearly twenty years ago to enroll in Plato's Academy. Plato regularly hires me and a few other girls for Academy dinner parties. The philosophers don't all like boys, you know.

I may have started out as a flute player, but I've come such a long way since then! If everything goes well, I will be running Aspasia's

School for Courtesans next year. Ah, but politics make my bid for the position so uncertain. I have a lot of networking to do before then.

Thank the gods for Speusippus! He has promised to help me. All I have to do in return is help him secure the headship of Plato's Academy. His only real challenger is Aristotle.

When Plato suddenly died two weeks ago, the Academy broke out in chaos. Such refined and sophisticated men fighting like children! Plato left no instructions about who was to succeed him, as though he thought he would live forever. As Plato's nephew and nearest male relative, Speusippus believes he has a right to the title. But all the students and not a few of the instructors are clamoring for Aristotle. Of course: the darling of the Academy.

Now Aristotle is speaking to old man Agathon, presumably buying five tickets on the next ship to Atarneus. Agathon is bartering, playing the victim. Aristotle negotiates patiently; now money is changing hands. It's a done deal. My mission is accomplished. I can tell Speusippus that Aristotle is definitely on his way across the sea.

Aristotle is so unlike other people that you can't be sure what to make of him. He seems shifty at first, but then you realize that he just doesn't see things the way other people do. He doesn't appear to be after wealth, fame, or power, like most men. He has written nine successful dialogues, but he doesn't really care. He says he wrote them for Plato and for philosophy. The dialogues provide useful propaganda for the Academy. To the public, Aristotle is one hundred percent pro-Academy, but behind closed doors he loves nothing better than to subvert everything the Academy stands for. He defends his subversions on the grounds that subversion is itself what the Academy is supposed to stand for. To Aristotle, it is the philosopher's job to be subversive.

I didn't really mind when Speusippus asked me to look for dirt on Aristotle. I knew I wouldn't find any. Last week, however, I saw a side of Aristotle I had never seen before. News arrived that King Philip of Macedonia had laid waste to Aristotle's hometown of Stageira in order to quell their rebellion against his take-over of the region. The house of Proxenus, where Aristotle grew up, was razed to the ground; there were no survivors.

Aristotle took the news hard. It was a terrifying sight. He was so angry he nearly killed the messenger.

That night Speusippus concocted a plan. The plan was to propose that the Academy send a diplomatic mission to King Hermias of Atarneus. Hermias is the only friendly ruler in a position to put a stop to Philip's advance. The diplomatic mission would include Aristotle, Theophrastus, Eudemus, Aristoxenus, and Xenocrates. Their task would be to set up council at Hermias' court to help him establish a lasting peace with King Philip. They would probably all be killed in the process. But Speusippus figures that's not his problem.

It's a shame, really, that Speusippus' plan is working. I always liked you, Aristotle. It will be hard not to miss you. You, with your absurd jewelry, and your impersonations, and your drinking songs. But I suspect you will be back. In fact, I have no doubt that you are only going along with Speusippus' plan because you have a plan of your own.

"Hello, Andromeda," says a deep voice behind me. I nearly jump out of my skin.

I turn to see Aristotle smirking at me. "Damn!"

"Did you really think I wouldn't notice such a beautiful girl on my tail?" he asks.

"But I was careful!" I complain.

"You can tell Speusippus that the boys and I will be gone in the morning," he says.

"Are you going to tell him you caught me?" I ask.

"Nah," he replies, "not unless you piss me off."

"Remind me not to do that then."

"Sure thing," he says. "Can I walk you home?"

I nod, only because I know Speusippus is at the gymnasium today. We start to walk.

"Aristotle," I venture, "can I ask you something?"

"As long as it's not about my big toe."

"Come on, I'm serious," I insist. "There's something I want to know. Is it true that you were behind that rebellion in Stageira?"

"Guilty as charged," he admits. "I've been working the resistance against Philip for years. Stageira was our stronghold."

"Why are you so bent against Philip?" I ask. "You're from Macedonia. You should be happy a Macedonian king is taking over the world."

"Andromeda," he says, "I don't think it would be good if any man took over the world, but especially not this monster."

"What makes Philip such a monster?" I ask.

"He's all caught up in the Dionysian Mysteries."

"I thought that was his wife, Queen Olympias."

"No," he counters, "Philip is actually far worse than she is. She keeps snakes—big deal. He's a raving, drunken lunatic—with a lot of power."

"I didn't mean to get you all worked up," I murmur.

"I'm already worked up, Andromeda," he replies, with disturbingly quiet ferocity. "I haven't slept in a week. I've got nothing left."

"You had close family in Stageira?"

"I had a son there."

"Oh, my god," I breathe, "I had no idea. Were you married then?"

"No, but we were planning to marry as soon as I could buy her freedom."

"She's a slave?"

"Was."

"I'm so sorry."

"Don't worry," he replies evenly, almost casually, as though we were discussing the weather. "Philip will get what's coming to him. I'm going to see to it myself."

His tone sends a shiver down my spine. I wish I could steer the conversation in a different direction.

"Aristotle?"

"Hmm?"

"Is that why you never . . . you know . . . hang out with the girls?"

"What are you talking about?" Aristotle retorted. "Just last week I had a long debate with Arete on the virtues."

"No, not like that. You know what I mean . . . never mind."

We walk in silence for a while.

"Well," I try again, "I've heard King Hermias has a daughter named Pythias who is almost fifteen. So when you're over there in Atarneus, if you play your knucklebones right, you'll have the chance to marry a princess!"

Aristotle cringes. I decide to keep my fat mouth shut for awhile.

"This is it," I announce when we arrive at my place.

He looks up at my building as though trying to remember why he is here. "This is it," he repeats, turning toward me. "Well, then, nice knowing you, kiddo."

I reach for his arm. "Are you in a big hurry to pack up and everything?"

"Not really," he shrugs. "We're all set. I was actually kind of hoping the ship would sail tonight."

"Maybe you could use a little company then," I suggest.

"Are you inviting me in?" he asks.

"Yes," I reply.

He thinks about it for a moment. Something inside him gives way. "Sure," he agrees. "Why not?"

We go up to my rooms, and before I can get any drinks poured he scoops me up and kisses me hard on the mouth. Then he makes love to me with an intensity I have never experienced before. Afterward, he holds me tight and starts to groan. I turn to look at his face to see that he is crying. He wipes his eyes and smiles gloomily at me.

"Andromeda, you caught me at a bad time," he murmurs. "I'm sorry. I'm just so——"

"Aristotle, I've wanted to do this for a long time," I reassure him, stroking his hair. "I'm glad we're friends. Maybe I can do some spying for *you* some day."

"Yes, I'll be sure to contact you if I ever need a spy," he mocks.

"But you already do need a spy."

"I do? Why?"

"To get inside the Dionysian Mysteries."

Aristotle laughs. "Andromeda, that's way too dangerous. Don't even think about it."

"No, really," I enthuse. "I've been planning to join anyway. It will be good for Aspasia's to have connections in high places. These days, participation in the Dionysian Mysteries is a requirement for any serious businesswoman. But I'll be happy to tell you all about it—even if they swear me to secrecy."

"Andromeda, don't do it," Aristotle warns, turning my chin to look me in the eye. "Those people are evil. I'm not kidding. Stay as far away from them as you can."

"Just because Philip——"

"——Andromeda, it's not just Philip," he interrupts. "I have seen firsthand the horror of this religion."

"Were you a member?" I ask.

"No," he responds in a monotone, "my father was."

"What happened?"

Aristotle closes his eyes and leans back against the wall. He groans some more and wipes his eyes again. "My father was the personal physician for Philip's father, King Amyntas. Amyntas is the one who introduced the Dionysian mysteries to the royal court. When I was ten, my father joined. My mother found out and tried to stop him. . . . They came with torches one night . . . all dressed in animal skins. . . . They dragged my mother out of the house . . . and started shredding her to pieces with their bare hands. . . . My older brother Arimnestos ran out there to try to save her. . . . My father was like a completely different person. . . . He and my brother fought. . . . Then the whole group was fighting. . . . Torches, and clubs, and knives . . .

"What did you do?" I ask, incredulous.

I ran. . . . For help, I guess—from the neighbors, a few miles away. Two people were dead when we got back and four more died within the next week.

"Your mother?"

"My mother, my father, and my brother. That's why I was sent to live with my sister Arimnestes, in Stageira."

"You poor, poor kid," I coo, holding him close.

We both fall asleep.

"Andromeda was her name, too," he suddenly announces awhile later.

"You mean your mother?" I slur, not yet fully awake.

"No, my girlfriend," he answers. "I mean, it was her real name, not her slave name."

"Well, it's a good name," I muse. "Andromeda was the daughter of Queen Cassiopeia. You see there, Aristotle, I'm a princess too, or at least named for one. Maybe I'm a royal descendant."

"Good luck tracing blood ties to a fictional character!"

"Blasphemer!" I scold, smacking his thigh.

"Well, if Princess Andromeda really existed, she sure got a raw deal," Aristotle lamented sardonically.

"I'd say! Chained to a cliff for her mother's sins."

"You forgot the part about the sea monster."

"Oh yeah," I giggle. "Chained to a cliff by the sea as a sacrifice to the sea monster for her mother's sins."

We lie there with our eyes closed, picturing it.

Then I sit up and pull the blanket down his chest. "It's kind of a sexy scenario, though, don't you think? Hey, I know!" I exclaim, "You be the sea monster and I'll be the princess—"

"Andromeda . . ."

"What?"

"I should probably be going now."

"Oh. . . . Okay."

"You take care of yourself," he instructs, rising and throwing on his toga. "When I get back, I'll look you up, and you can tell me all about your adventures."

"I'd like that," I agree, searching his eyes to see if he means it. He does.

He leans down and kisses me on the forehead. "Thanks for your company."

"My pleasure," I sigh. "Goodbye, Aristotle."

"Goodbye."

With that, he turns and walks out the door.

I go to the window to watch him on the walk below. He feels my eyes on him and turns to wave. He's smiling recklessly now, as though we are sharing some sort of inside joke with Zeus. Or maybe he *is* Zeus, dressed up as a mortal. He's playing at being human for a while, just for kicks.

Oh, Aristotle.

Who would have guessed he'd been through so much? Of course, we girls often get an earful from our clients. Somehow they feel they can tell us things they can't tell their best friends.

I turn back to the table and see that Aristotle has left me one of his bracelets. I pick it up. It is a gold wrist cuff, set with a piece of amber. Nice. Very nice. But it's a little disappointing too. I was hoping he wouldn't think of our time together as a business transaction.

On the other hand, a bracelet isn't the usual sort of payment for that. Perhaps it's just a going-away gift from one friend to another.

It's still warm, I notice, as I slip the bracelet on. It's too big for my wrist, of course, but it looks good further up on my arm. I can feel his amazing energy radiating off of it.

Philip had better watch out. I don't know what you're planning to do, Aristotle, but whatever it is, it's going to be good.

Chapter Ten

Dana woke just before her alarm, right at the end of her dream.

Andromeda, the Academy call girl, she laughed to herself. *Where the hell do I get this stuff?*

She turned off her alarm and lay with her eyes closed, considering whether the dream held any useful insights for her. She remembered the dream she had had the night before about Herpyllis and Aristotle.

Could my subconscious be connecting the dots from my research?

If only Aristotle could have returned to free Herpyllis before King Philip destroyed Stageira! The *Eroticus* is set "eighteen years and thirty-two days" after Aristotle left Stageira for the Academy in Athens. That would have been right on the eve of the destruction of Stageira. Of course, Herpyllis didn't die in the destruction, as everyone had assumed. She disappeared with the rest of the refugees, however, and Aristotle had to wait another twelve years before finally finding her again. Poor, sweet, romantic Aristotle—playing out in the *Eroticus* his fantasy of how things should have gone.

The words and images from the dream were already sliding back under the waves of Dana's mental ocean.

She got up and went for a run along the Hudson River, making a loop around Battery Park. Then she showered and rode the subway to the Institute. The lobby area was pulsing with activity. After meeting with Ann and Eva about some things that had come up while she was out the day before, she slipped into her office and shut the door.

Dana stood with her back against the door for a moment, savoring the quiet and privacy. She wondered whether she would ever be extroverted enough fill the role of Institute Director.

Yes, I can. And I will, she assured herself.

She sat down with her laptop to check her e-mail. Amidst a great deal of spam and some useless university announcements, there was a message from "Roach Rauch, Palatine Librarian, Second Life."

Dear Magenta,

Thank you for updating your file. I have recently acquired an item that might interest you. Please let me know if you are in the market for a Greek parchment scroll.

Sincerely yours,

Roach

Well, well, well, thought Dana as she typed her reply. *Hold onto your breeches, everyone, it seems we have hit the jackpot.*

"Thank you for calling me," Detective Conti said, as he stepped into Dana's office and shook her hand.

"Thank *you* for coming," Dana replied. "I'm sorry my office is in such disarray. We aren't fully moved in yet."

"It looks like it will be a nice place to work," he remarked, drawn to the windows.

It was nearly eleven o'clock; the city below was in full swing. Dana's sixteenth-floor corner office provided an excellent view of Fifth Avenue. To the left, Conti saw tourists thronging the steps of the enormous stone edifice of the Met. To the right, he saw cyclists and skaters careering along a path in Central Park. Many of the people wore coats in bright shades of red, yellow, green, and blue. Conti looked as though he was observing a festival, one he could have watched for a long time.

Dana pulled up an extra chair in front of her desk and invited him to sit. She was glad she'd dressed carefully in her taupe gabardine suit. She had been tempted to wear jeans and a sweatshirt, which would have been more appropriate for the unpacking she had planned to do today, but psychologically, she needed her professional armor. Criminals don't wear gabardine. She noticed that Conti was wearing the same suit he wore yesterday.

You don't really have time to pack anything when you're tailing a killer, do you?

Nevertheless, he looked as fresh as could be. Europeans were used to being less hygienic than Americans. They somehow managed to pull it off.

I wonder just exactly what you might smell like if I got close enough. . . .

Conti took out his little notebook.

"Unfortunately, the technicians have not been by yet to hook up my computer." Dana gestured toward a set of large white boxes on the floor. "But the monitor on this laptop has great resolution, and it's easier on the eyes. I actually prefer working on it."

She clicked and typed for a few minutes.

"There," she announced. The screen showed a vibrant, three-dimensional illustration of ancient Rome.

"It's called Second Life," Dana explained. "It's a virtual world on the Internet used by millions of people around the globe. Basic membership is free, and it allows you to select a pseudonym and an avatar to represent yourself."

"Is this you standing in front of us?" Conti asked, referring to an animated woman with her back to the screen.

"Yes. Well, it's my avatar, Magenta Mai." Dana showed him how she could move the woman with her arrow keys. She turned Magenta around to face the screen. She was a busty blond in a toga and strappy sandals.

Conti glanced at Dana, fighting back a grin.

"What?" Dana demanded. "Magenta's appearance is perfectly appropriate for Roma Redux, the section of Second Life that simulates Rome in the year 190 CE. Few people realize that the elites of the ancient world loved to dye their hair blond. Alexander the Great set the trend."

Conti just grunted, scribbling some notes.

Dana turned Magenta back around and walked her forward to an open area where several other avatars in togas were milling about. Most had exaggerated masculine or feminine characteristics. One was a large, catlike creature.

"Are those characters being run by different people?" Conti asked.

"They are avatars, yes. I can interact with them through mine."

"Is it a video game?"

"You have the right idea, but it's not really a game," Dana replied. "Many people use Second Life as a social network, but it's also used for education, artistic exhibitions, and commerce. Universities, businesses, and even governments have built virtual properties in Second Life."

"Is modern Italy there?" Conti asked.

"I don't know," Dana replied. "You'll have to check it out once you acquire an avatar."

"Me?" Conti was appalled.

"Of course," Dana insisted with a quick wink. "Roma Redux was created over a period of ten years by a consortium of scholars from around the world. It started as a computer simulation of ancient Rome and then it was merged into Second Life so that it would be universally accessible. Students and history buffs visit Roma Redux just to see what ancient Rome was like, but there is a great deal of commerce going on here too, just as there is all throughout Second Life."

"What kind of commerce?" Conti asked.

"You can make objects—like clothes or jewelry—and sell them."

"For real money?"

"Absolutely. You use a credit card to buy virtual money and then you use that to buy objects as well as property."

"And people actually do this?" Conti shook his head in disbelief.

"You mean you don't?" Dana shot back. "Millions of real dollars are circulating in Second Life."

"Why would anyone pay real money for virtual stuff?" Conti asked.

"It's a fantasy," Dana explained. "Don't you have any fantasies, Domenico?" She turned to look him in the eye and could see that he did.

Conti didn't know what to say.

Dana turned back to the screen. She guided Magenta up the steps of a stately stone building.

"This is the Palatine Library," she informed Conti. "It contains simulations of real ancient manuscripts that are for sale."

"You mean it's a clearinghouse," Conti remarked, his interest piqued.

"Bingo."

"How does it work?" Conti asked.

"You pay a fee to become a library council member," Dana replied. "Then you fill out a form indicating what kinds of manuscripts you would like to buy or sell. The librarian compiles all the forms and e-mails you if and when he finds a match. The two parties negotiate an agreement through the librarian and mail the payment and the item to him. The librarian checks to make sure everything is according to the agreement and then exchanges the item for the payment."

"What's to keep the librarian from running off with the money and the item?" Conti asked.

"Future sales," Dana answered. "He makes a cut every time. His business depends on his reliable reputation. The minute he does a dirty deal, word gets out, and he's finished."

"Why doesn't Interpol take action?" Conti wondered out loud.

"Well, Interpol may not even know about the Palatine Library," Dana suggested. "But even if they do, in order to make a bust, they would have to find a way to avoid entrapment. Interpol agents can't offer to buy or sell anything illegal without violating international law."

"I suppose the librarian is some kind of computer junkie who can hide his own identity behind endless layers of encryption," Conti speculated.

Dana nodded. "No system is immune to hackers, of course. If you knew what you were doing, you could monitor communications. But the beauty of it is that all of the communication takes place in a fictional context. Ostensibly, only virtual manuscripts are bought and sold. Therefore, any actual sales are plausibly deniable."

"And you're registered?" Conti asked.

"Yes," Dana admitted. "Becoming a council member is not a crime."

"Have you made transactions?" Conti pressed.

"That's neither here nor there," Dana retorted. "The important thing is that I'm registered for ancient Greek manuscripts. After you told me about the scrolls yesterday, I figured they would likely be sold through this site, and I wondered why I hadn't been notified. But then I realized that my specified price range was too low. I went in and eliminated my upper limit last night. Sure enough, the librarian notified me about a scroll this morning. I've already e-mailed back and forth with him a few times. He sent a partial photo. It looks like the same format as the

Eroticus. The price is set for two million dollars. The librarian denies that there are others. I suppose they've already been sold."

"Dana, if you're planning on buying that scroll, you're incriminating yourself. Why are you telling me all this?" Conti asked.

"Because I want that scroll, and I don't have two million dollars," Dana replied. "I can't buy it, but the Institute can. Although the Institute has two million easy, it can only make legal purchases. This means we need the provenance papers or some other form of authorization."

"But, Dana, you don't understand," Conti objected. "The Vatican wants that scroll back."

"I know," Dana said, "which is why we're going to give it to them."

"What?" Conti exclaimed. "Your institute will pay two million dollars to buy a scroll only to give it back to the Vatican?"

"Yes," Dana asserted, "provided the Vatican then gives the Institute the right to make digital photographs for the purpose of scholarly research. We would publish the first critical edition of Aristotle's formerly lost dialogue."

Conti pressed his eyes shut. Then he got up and walked to the window. Dana decided not to mention that she already had photos of the *Eroticus.*

"It's a sweet deal for the both of us," Dana proclaimed. "You get your scroll, we get legitimate access. What's the problem, Domenico? Everybody wins!"

Conti turned toward her. "Dana, there is a cardinal at the Vatican supervising this case. He doesn't even want anyone to know about the scrolls, much less publish them."

"Then he's corrupt," Dana snapped. "Why the hell wouldn't the Vatican want these scrolls studied? I mean, it's not as though they reveal the sex lives of the Popes or something. For Christ's sake, I saw absolutely nothing in the *Eroticus* that would warrant secrecy."

"That's not for you to decide," Conti declared, staring stubbornly out the window. "The Vatican has its reasons."

Dana studied his profile. She had run into Catholic loyalty before and it never ceased to amaze her. It was thicker than blood. How did priests do it? They could make even the most intelligent people turn off their minds when it comes to religious authority.

They got to you young, Domenico. I guess that's all it takes.

"Domenico, listen," Dana tried again. "There are two possibilities here: first, your cardinal is corrupt, in which case the Vatican will thank you for rooting him out, or second, your cardinal is in line with the Vatican as a whole, in which case the Vatican as a whole is corrupt and the world will thank us for exposing it."

"Dana, stop," Conti demanded, disturbed by how easy it was for her to jump to such a blasphemous conclusion.

"I'm willing to be optimistic," Dana continued. "And you're entitled to your faith. Here is the ultimate test for it: pitch my offer to a different cardinal at the Vatican."

"It's not so simple."

"It *is* simple, Domenico—either the Vatican is trying to hide something or it isn't. If it isn't, then they won't have any problem with the Institute publishing editions of these scrolls. If it has a problem with the Institute publishing the scrolls, then it's hiding something, and we'll go to the press with our story."

"What story?" Conti asked, growing alarmed.

"The story of what the Vatican is hiding," Dana answered impatiently. "The *Eroticus* does not provide enough information to figure out why the scrolls were buried, but I feel sure that if I can just look at this other scroll for sale through the Palatine Library, I'll be able to figure it out."

Conti simmered for a few minutes.

"But the fact remains," he finally said, taking a seat once again in his chair, "that you can't buy that scroll with Institute money without provenance papers."

"I can if I'm part of your investigation," Dana argued. "Picture the headline: 'Institute Director poses as black market antiquities trafficker to blow the lid off Vatican conspiracy.' This is just the kind of edgy work our Institute was designed for."

Conti flexed his jaw.

"Domenico," Dana persisted, "Either they release the scrolls for study or we expose them."

Conti ran his hand through his hair. "You do realize, don't you, that if we fail at this, we're finished. Both of us. Our jobs, our lives. Are you prepared to take that risk?"

"That's not the question, Domenico," Dana responded, with the serenity of a winter morning. "The question is, how could you ever go back to your job and your life knowing what you know? Face it: that ship has sailed for you and me both."

He gazed at her grimly, looking like a small boy handing over his favorite teddy bear. It made Dana feel like a psychological vandal.

Surely you're ready to let go of the Vatican, Domenico. Can't you see how it condemns you to intellectual infancy? Surely you'd rather be a lonely, old crank like me.

Dana looked at her watch. Nearly noon. "It's evening in Italy," she noted. "Is there someone you can call at this hour?"

"Of course not," Conti retorted. "This is not the kind of thing you arrange in advance by telephone. If you're serious about buying this scroll, then you're just going to have to do it. We will negotiate with the Vatican in person afterward."

Dana chewed on her thumbnail for a moment, weighing the risks. And then she flew to her laptop to make the purchase.

It didn't take long; she'd done it before. The scroll would arrive on Monday. She was to meet the courier at Kennedy Airport at noon, holding up a sign that said "Anderson."

"Let's order a pizza," Dana proposed when the deal was done. "We have to celebrate our new pact. I know a really great place just down the street that delivers."

"Yes, food is a good idea," Conti agreed. "But I can't stay much longer. I've got a seven-thirty flight back to Rome tonight."

"Oh, really?" Dana asked, disappointed. She was already on the phone to the pizza place. She held up a finger. "Do you like sausage and mushroom?" she asked.

Conti nodded, and she made the order.

"I was hoping you could stay to help me make the pickup on Monday," she continued, when she'd hung up.

"I have a meeting with our cardinal tomorrow at noon," Conti reported.

"You're kidding!" Dana exclaimed. "Does he know we're onto him?"

Conti shook his head, scowling. "We're not 'onto' anybody just yet," he corrected. "But there's something else I haven't told you. Selenka was admitted to the hospital last night, reporting that he was mugged in an alley and that his briefcase was stolen. Unfortunately, he had checked himself out and disappeared by the time I got there."

"So the killer has the *Eroticus*," Dana deduced, not knowing whether that was better or worse than Selenka having it. She got up and went to the fridge for a bottle of Chardonnay, along with a tray of carrots and celery for them to nibble on while they waited for lunch.

Conti flipped his notebook shut and tucked it away. "I'll try to make an appointment with another cardinal I have worked with before. How about next Wednesday? Will that give you enough time to have a look at the scroll and get to Rome?"

"Better make it Thursday," Dana replied. "Monday is the Institute's opening day. It will be hard enough to get away for the pickup, much less leave town."

Conti nodded.

Dana watched him select a carrot and noticed the wedding band on his finger.

Such a shame! And then there's the Catholic thing, too.

But the truth was, it didn't really matter—married, religious, psychopath, alien from outer space, you name it—it didn't really matter. Once the id was aroused from its lair, nothing else really mattered.

"How long have you been working for the Vatican?" Dana asked, uncorking the Chardonnay.

"About ten years," Conti replied.

"Do you ever get to work with the Pope?"

"Not so far. But I'm up for promotion next year. If I make chief, I'll be the Pope's bodyguard."

"So you really are Catholic, aren't you?" Dana remarked. She poured two glasses.

"You grow up with it in Italy," he confirmed. "That's how it used to be, anyway. These days, it's not the same for kids anymore."

"You have kids?" Dana asked.

"No," Conti said. He started to look uncomfortable.

"Bad marriage, huh?"

Conti looked as though he'd been slapped. "You Americans say the damnedest things."

"No, it's just me. Most Americans wouldn't have said that." Dana grinned impishly, raising her glass. "Here's to Aristotle." They touched glasses.

"While we wait for the pizza, I have to show you one more thing," Dana said.

She clicked back into Roma Redux and walked Magenta down the street from the Palatine Library to a round stone building with torches burning on either side of the entrance. The image of a bull adorned the door. There were two avatars talking on the steps. A third disappeared inside.

"This is the Temple of Dionysus," Dana said. "You asked me the other day what I knew about the cult. It was still thriving in Rome in 190 CE, the date of this simulation. The temple is a popular destination for visitors to Roma Redux. Since Dionysus was the god of wine, they do a lot of drinking."

"What good is virtual intoxication?" Conti asked, still baffled by the whole idea of Second Life.

"I'm not a member, myself," Dana said, "so I don't know what all goes on, but in the ancient world, there was a strong political dimension to the cult."

"You mean like raising money for campaigns and intimidating the opposition?" Conti asked.

"Exactly," Dana replied. "Plots were hatched and alliances were forged. Because of its secretive nature, no one knows just how influential it was."

Just then, they heard a deep male voice through the laptop speaker: "Hey baby, where have you been? I've missed you!"

Dana turned Magenta around until another avatar appeared on the screen. He approached her with his arms held out for an embrace. He was tall, buff, and dressed like a gladiator, with an attitude goatee. A text bubble hovering above him identified him as "Zen Zwanger."

"Hi, Zen," Dana said into the microphone on her laptop. The program modulated Dana's voice so that Magenta didn't sound like her. She moved Magenta in for an embrace. Zen tried for a kiss, but Magenta backed away.

"Why so shy?" Zen complained. "Are you mad at me?"

"I'm showing Second Life to a friend," Magenta demurred. "Behave."

"Oh. Hi, out there," Zen said, waving. Then he stepped closer, peering at the screen. "I can tell you're a guy. Keep your paws off Magenta's human, asshole."

"Zen!" Magenta exclaimed.

"Just kiddin', Snookums," Zen snickered. "So are you going to join the revelers tonight?"

"I just wandered over to see what might be going on," Magenta answered.

"Friday night rites!" Zen whooped. "We're going to slaughter a bull."

"Hmm," Magenta mused. "Sounds like just the thing after a long, hard week."

"I'll give you long and hard, baby," Zen purred. "Meet me at the bathhouse as soon as you get rid of what's-his-face out there."

"Ha, ha, ha," Magenta laughed sheepishly. "Catch you later, Zen." Dana clicked out of Second Life.

"So your boyfriend is a cult member?" Conti inquired.

"He's not my boyfriend!" Dana objected. "I mean, Zen and Magenta have a thing going, but that doesn't make Zen or his human my boyfriend."

"You know," Conti said, "you're going to wind up with a serious case of schizophrenia if you're not careful, Dana. This whole Second Life thing is too weird for me."

Dana smiled a little, suspecting that he might be jealous. "At any rate, if you're interested in the cult of Dionysus, get yourself an avatar and visit this temple," Dana advised. "I'll guarantee you there are world experts on Dionysus operating some of the avatars there."

Conti nodded pensively.

"What's the connection between this case and the cult of Dionysus, anyhow?" Dana asked.

"I was told that's why the scrolls were buried: 'that the cult of Dionysus be forever laid to rest.'"

Just then, there was a knock at the door. The pizza had arrived.

After they'd transferred their glasses to the table and served themselves two steaming slices, Dana sat back in her rocker and looked at Conti.

"Why do you stay with her?" she asked, feeling the wine a little more than she should.

Conti did a double take and emitted a long, low whistle. "You really don't know me well enough to ask that question."

"Sorry," Dana said. "But one of the worst things about marriage trouble is that you really can't talk to people you know well—because they know both of you and don't want to get caught in the middle. And it would be better if you could talk to someone about it. I should know. I was unhappily married once."

"Oh, really?" Conti asked standoffishly.

"Yeah," she sighed. "It sucked. I sympathize."

Conti concentrated on his pizza.

"I mean," Dana unwisely continued, "it must be especially painful, being Catholic and all."

"Being Catholic is not so bad, Dana," Conti objected indignantly. "What religion were you raised with?"

"None," Dana confessed.

"Well, *that* is certainly much worse," Conti pronounced.

"Why?"

"Because religion provides comfort."

"Only after it runs you through the wringer first," Dana rejoined.

"Everyone needs a little run through the wringer from time to time."

"You look like you're all wrung out to me."

"Do I really look that bad to you?" Conti asked.

Dana paused. *Was that a flirt?*

"No, Domenico," Dana artfully corrected, "you don't look bad at all to me. It's just that you seem like you're carrying a heavy burden."

"This case has been a strain," Conti admitted.

"Because it's making you question the church?" Dana probed. But he wouldn't bite on that, and before long it was time for him to go.

Dana was too keyed up to stay at her office and unpack boxes. She decided to go to Saks Fifth Avenue to see if she could find a new gown for the banquet. She wasn't successful, but she did find a gorgeous new necklace to go with a gown she already had: a thick gold chain, set with a piece of amber.

By the time Dana got home, it was seven-thirty. She made herself a cup of soup and a salad and plunked herself back down in the middle of the growing pile of research in the living room.

She was committed now. There was no going back. She just spent two million dollars of the Institute's money on a black market scroll. It was a decisive action that would either make or break her career.

If my plan works, she ruminated, *I will publish the most important historical document in living memory.*

But plenty could go wrong. First, she had to take possession of the scroll. Second, she needed to secure the cooperation of the Vatican.

Third, she must at all costs prevent her prior criminal transactions from coming to light.

Just three things. I can do this. I have to do this.

Picking up where she left off the night before, she read and read, until once again she fell asleep reading.

Chapter Eleven

 Draining sensation. In my thighs.
Draining along the inside of my thighs.
A distinguished gentleman, asleep on a chair.
A bed. I'm lying in a bed.
I'm watching him breathe in and out.
He has the face of a lynx. His beard and hair are black and silver.
I am looking from my bed at a man sleeping in the chair nearby.
His hair and beard are silver and black.
He breathes deeply, exhausted, a hunter after a long hunt.
I am supposed to know this man. But I don't really know him very well at all.
For once, I observe him without him observing me.

The time is the first year of the 111th Olympiad. The place is Stageira, Greece. I am Pythias, the niece and adopted daughter of King Hermias of Atarneus. He is Aristotle, my husband. He is forty-eight and I am twenty-six.

I feel something stirring in the bed next to me. It is our newborn baby girl, bundled in a blanket. A miracle! Aristotle named her "Pythias," in my honor. She looks like she would like to nurse. I don't know if I can muster the energy.

There is a steady ooze from between my legs, and the towels are already soaked again. Life is draining from me. I know I will be dead by morning.

Pythias starts to fuss. I glance apprehensively at Aristotle. He snores.

Okay, baby girl. We'll give it a try, one last time.

I painstakingly situate the baby, and then I take a good, long look at Aristotle.

I never really knew how to talk to him. Even when I practiced what I wanted to say, I would flounder under his probing gaze. He always seemed to be waiting for me to turn into something I don't know how to be. I always preferred to have conversations with him in my own head.

Was it worth it, Aristotle? I understand everything now. I may be a princess but I'm not stupid. You have been consumed by revenge since the day King Philip laid waste to Stageira, your precious hometown. Were you and your sister Arimnestes so close? Or is it your guardian Proxenus for whom you cannot cease to grieve? Maybe it was the impact of losing both of them at the same time. How would I know, since you decline to talk about it?

All I know is that you could never forgive Philip. Even when he claimed that the invasion of Stageira was the fault of an overzealous general. Even when he rebuilt Stageira so that it is now better than it ever was. You continued to interpret Philip's every action in the worst possible light.

For instance, you never believed he would honor the treaty your Academy crew brokered between him and my uncle, Hermias. I believe he would have, if only the Persians hadn't gotten wind of it so soon. Your claim that Philip deliberately leaked it to the Persians in order to get rid of my uncle is completely paranoid.

I still have nightmares about the day the Persians came for Uncle Hermias, the only father I ever knew. It was the middle of the night. Suddenly, Aristotle was in my room, yanking open the window. A sturdy trellis was conveniently available for climbing down. Soon Theophrastus, Eudemus, and Aristoxenus bolted through. Then Aristotle grabbed me, and down we climbed. Aristotle had the escape plan all worked out, as though he knew it would come to that. Thank the gods they had to go through my bedroom! I'd either be dead or speaking Persian by now. That's what happened to the rest of my relatives.

And my Uncle Hermias crucified! Witnesses said his last wish was to deliver a message to Plato's Academy: "Tell my friends and companions that I have done nothing weak or unworthy of philosophy."

After his death, Aristotle dedicated a statue for Hermias at Delphi and composed a hymn to virtue in his honor. I still like to hum it sometimes:

O Virtue,

you are the hunter's hard-won prey.

Greater than gold, nobler than name,

sweeter than sweet sleep.

O Virtue,

you are the hero's hard-won love.

Mistress of none, goddess to all,

bride of Hermias.

There is no doubt that Aristotle loved Hermias. My only question is whether he ever really loved me.

Did you marry me out of pity, Aristotle? An orphan yourself, you can't have helped feeling sorry for a twice-orphaned girl like me. But if you have so much compassion for orphans, then how can you have used Alexander so badly? Now he's fatherless too.

After we fled the palace, the Academy crew split up. Having no place else to go, I followed Aristotle and Theophrastus to the island of Lesbos.

What a pair, those two! It's a shame Aristotle isn't gay, because Theophrastus would love him better than any woman ever could. Aristotle loves Theophrastus, but only as a friend. Sometimes it seems Aristotle married me just to keep Theophrastus from suffocating him. Theophrastus never liked me much, probably because he resents sharing Aristotle's attention.

They like to study. That's all they ever want to do. They would have stayed on Lesbos forever if they could have, collecting all sorts of nasty things and writing about them in their little leather notebooks. Theophrastus can hardly interrupt his studies to eat, much less pay attention to the world around him, but Aristotle could not allow himself that luxury.

Aristotle stayed on Lesbos only long enough to arrange a meeting with King Philip's wife, Queen Olympias. He sent her some snakes he caught on the island, along with a letter detailing what he and Theophrastus had learned about them. She was intrigued. She invited him to come see her snake collection. The three of us went together to the royal court at Pella.

Aristotle charmed Queen Olympias off her feet. I wasn't jealous, though, because I could tell he was only pretending to like her. His secret objective was to become Prince Alexander's tutor.

Aristotle's a good teacher, baby girl. That's one thing even his enemies admit. But I hope he doesn't prod you into too much thinking. Thinking about things can spoil a girl for life, that's for sure! You'll be better off staying close to your nursemaid, if Aristotle ever gets around to finding you one.

Well, he'll have to once I'm gone. He refuses to admit he can't save me.

I finger the necklace around my neck—a thick gold chain, set with a piece of amber. It's from Aristotle, the only jewelry he ever gave me.

Most girls of my status would have dumped him like a rotting goat carcass when he failed to present an engagement ring. I probably should have. I'll never forget what he said.

"A necklace is more appropriate than a ring as a symbol of our engagement."

"Why?"

"Because a ring circles the finger, while a necklace circles the neck."

"True enough. But why is a circle around the neck appropriate for our engagement?"

"Well, what is the neck?"

"The stem of the head."

"Exactly. And what is the finger?"

"A branch from the hand."

"Right again. And what is the function of the head?"

"To see, to hear, to taste, and to smell."

"Yes, and what is the function of the hand?"

"To feel."

"So, now you understand. This is how it is. Let us be married and start a new life."

How do you like that for a riddle? I never enjoyed Aristotle's philosophical puzzles. But Alexander did.

Just a scrawny kid when we arrived at Pella, Alexander was already a hellion. He was far too much for his mother to handle! Aristotle's trick was to appeal to his destructive urges. For example, here is how they learned about the four elements:

1. Earth is the element whose natural motion is downward. This was proven by dropping large clumps of mud on King Philip's soldiers from rooftops and bridges.

2. Air is the element whose natural motion is transverse. This was proven by detaching King Philip's flags from all the highest poles and watching how far they flew.
3. Fire is the element whose natural motion is upward. This was proven by lighting piles of straw under King Philip's wagons.
4. Water is the element whose natural motion is stillness. This was proven by drowning King Philip's dogs.

They spent weeks on their destructive experiments, until Philip finally set up a little boarding school in an old army barracks at Mieza. Alexander and some other boys from the royal court stayed in one building, the slaves stayed in another, and Aristotle and I stayed in a third. I liked the solitude better than trying to fit in with Queen Olympias and her circle. Aristotle liked spending time with Alexander. He treated the boy like the son he never had.

That's why I have such a hard time understanding how you could at the same time conspire against Alexander's father. It's almost as though you felt like you were doing the boy a favor, fanning the flames of patricide. Only a man who hates his own father could incite a boy against his.

It wasn't hard to convince Queen Olympias that King Philip had to be eliminated. She'd wanted him dead for years. In fact, Aristotle was happy to let her think the whole thing was her idea. It wasn't hard to find an assassin either. Philip was careless and mean enough that there were always plenty of people around with bitter grudges against him. It was just a matter of paying the right man at the right time.

Both Queen Olympias and Aristotle knew that if Philip died before Prince Alexander was old enough, then someone else might seize the throne. They wanted to prevent this, believing that Alexander had great leadership potential. Olympias was already calling him "Alexander the Great." But Aristotle didn't want Alexander to become another Philip. Aristotle was determined to make a philosopher-king of Alexander instead.

I gather you were not completely successful in this endeavor, my dear. Too late now! Alexander is off to conquer the world.

While Aristotle and Olympias were fundamentally united against Philip, Aristotle tried to teach Alexander philosophical concepts that Olympias didn't know about. The main thing was superstition. Both Philip and Olympias worshiped Dionysus, and they expected their son to as well. But Aristotle says all religions are full of superstition. He thinks people shouldn't believe in superstitions because superstitions can't be scientifically tested.

Aristotle thinks everything is about science. He really has no sensitivity to the spiritual side of life. Maybe that's why he and I could never quite understand each other. I am a very spiritual person. My life has been full of adversity. The gods give me strength in my darkest hours. Like now, my darkest hour of all.

Goodbye, Aristotle. Goodbye baby Pythias, and good luck with your father, the philosopher-assassin. I never really knew him. I wish I had.

Does anyone really know you, Aristotle?

Don't go through your whole life without ever really knowing someone, Pythias. It's very lonely. . . .

Chapter Twelve

On Monday evening, in the computer lab of the main library at Istanbul University, a twenty-two-year-old computer science major named Zapher Inan sat hunched at a terminal reading his e-mail. Lanky and copper-toned, sporting two elfin ears perpetually plugged with earbuds, Zapher still passed as a teenager on campus.

And that's just the way he wanted it.

Sauntering to and from his classes in jeans and a T-shirt, forever toting the same ratty backpack, he would never give away how much his circumstances had changed over the past three years.

Maybe it was foresight and discipline that helped him keep it under wraps, or maybe it was guilt and denial. At any rate, Zapher did not have much spare time to consider the matter.

Zapher's father, Umran Inan, had been a well-loved professor of archaeology at Istanbul University. He and his young wife, Magda, had raised their only son in an apartment in downtown Istanbul. They had struggled to make ends meet on Umran's university salary.

When Umran collapsed in the middle of a lecture on Egyptian hieroglyphs and died of a massive heart attack before he even reached the hospital, Magda and Zapher didn't know how to carry on. Zapher had just finished the first semester of his freshman year at the university. He was forced to take a leave of absence. After two weeks at home with his disconsolate mother, he was firmly convinced he would never be able to return to his studies.

Magda Hassan had been an exotic dancer. Umran had met her on one of his many dig trips to Egypt. She was a runaway, without even a high school diploma. Growing up the youngest in a family of ten step-siblings in a small town south of Cairo, Magda was first neglected by her mother and then abused by her stepfather. She was tiny and graceful and had no trouble finding work in a club catering to tourists off of Talaat Harb Square in Cairo. Since her family was not far from Cairo, they could have found her if they'd tried. But they didn't try. And so, when the lumbering archaeologist from Istanbul came back to see Magda three times during her second summer on her own, it was easy for her to believe she was falling in love.

Zapher had no doubt that his mother loved his father, but she loved him more like a daughter than a wife. Sixteen years Umran's junior and arrested in adolescence, Magda needed a father more than a husband.

Hence, when his father died without life insurance, Zapher felt as though it was he and his sister, not he and his mother, who were left to fend for themselves.

Magda was too old now to make a living as a dancer, and Zapher wouldn't have permitted it even if she could. After a couple of months living off of his father's modest savings account, Zapher got a job at a Kentucky Fried Chicken in Istanbul. His mother started babysitting the neighbors' children.

Then one Friday morning in April, a bill arrived in the mail from a storage facility in the suburbs. Magda had already left for the neighbors'. Even as he held the letter in his hands that morning, Zapher knew it was going to change his life.

Before work that day, Zapher rode the bus out to the storage facility. The attendant refused to show him to his father's rented compartment until Zapher made a year's advance payment on his credit card. The compartment was locked with a padlock, and Zapher did not have the key. After a moment's thought, however, he was pretty sure he knew where to find it.

The next morning Zapher told his mother he would like to take his father's old bike out for a ride. It sat in the basement of their apartment building, locked with a cable and padlock to pipes along the wall. The tires were flat and the chain was rusty, but his mother didn't know this. She hunted up the key for him before heading to the market. Zapher got on the bus to the storage facility and returned to his father's rented compartment. Its padlock was a twin of the bicycle padlock, bought in the same package with identical keys.

Zapher opened the door. The contents of the carefully labeled boxes confirmed his suspicion: his father was a tomb raider.

How exactly did Zapher know this deep down even before he received the bill from the storage facility? That was a question Zapher could not answer.

He had never known his father very well. He often felt as though his father had conceived him as a companion for Magda. A decent man, the professor just wasn't interested in domestic affairs. But he had a sparkle in his eye whenever he spoke of the treasures of Egypt. In retrospect, it now seemed clear to Zapher that his father must have hinted at the truth on a number of occasions.

At first, Zapher felt a wave of resentment against his father for keeping the treasure trove from his family. But then again, how could Umran tell Zapher and Magda? To do so would be to incriminate them as co-conspirators.

Zapher counseled himself not to tell his mother about the storage facility for the same reason. His real reason, however, was that she couldn't be trusted. She was a child, completely naïve, without any knowledge of the ways of the world. This, of course, was also his father's real reason for not telling her.

What had his father been planning to do with his treasure trove? Was simply having these pieces of ancient Egypt enough for him, or did he have a long-range plan for how to unload them in time for a luxurious retirement? Zapher would never know. All he knew was that his days at Kentucky Fried Chicken were over.

The rented compartment contained three boxes. The first was full of broken pottery pieces. They were mostly undecorated and did not look like anything special to the untrained eye. The second box held a large assortment of scarabs, which were stone amulets ancient Egyptians carved in the shape of the sacred dung beadle. The third box held manuscripts—clay tablets and papyri.

Never having developed any interest in his father's field, Zapher didn't know the first thing about any of these curious objects. He spent the summer learning about them on the Internet at the library, while his mother thought he was still working at Kentucky Fried Chicken.

It was extremely difficult to find the necessary contacts to make a sale. At last he succeeded, and he used the money to re-enroll at the university in the fall. The next five sales followed more easily, swelling Zapher's bank account. But Zapher was keenly aware that he was now six items down. Although there were a lot more in his inventory, there was not an endless supply. He began to wonder if he could use what he'd learned about antiquities trafficking to generate a steady, renewable source of income for himself and his mother. The class he took that spring on Internet industries gave him the idea for the Palatine Library.

TWELVE

As "Roach Rauch," Zapher Inan quickly became a very rich young man. He told his mother he quit Kentucky Fried Chicken to start a computer programming business. He showed her a web page he designed as an assignment for one of his classes—a mock company called "Inan Enterprises". Magda was impressed. As she knew nothing about computers, she required no further explanation.

Zapher now had plenty of money to continue supporting his mother while renting an apartment of his own. Yet he didn't.

She just seems so vulnerable. Maybe once I finish my degree she'll be ready to let go.

"Hiya, Zafe."

Zapher jumped, clicked out of e-mail, and threw on a scowl. He knew exactly who it would be before he swiveled around: Marla, the most annoyingly beautiful girl in the world.

And he was right. There she stood under a long mop of hair, dyed blond on top and black underneath, her strawberry chiffon body wash effecting an olfactory contradiction to her combat boots and army duds. She pushed her sunglasses up onto her head, favoring Zapher with a sassy smirk. She was an American.

"How long have you been standing there?" he grumbled.

"Long enough to see that you've got a puppy for sale," the girl taunted as she slid into the chair next to his.

Zapher laughed. She had mistaken "papyrus" for "puppy."

"Get your eyes checked, girl," he advised.

"Whatever," she retorted, her attention on her own computer screen. She clicked into her e-mail and was quickly absorbed.

Zapher swiveled toward his computer terminal, but his eyes strayed back to Marla. He had met her last spring in one of his classes. She was a computer science major as well, a year behind him.

. *You're so annoying. Way too . . . skull tattoo . . . and way too . . . pink lip gloss.*

Zapher didn't have much experience with girls to begin with, and with Marla, he always felt especially inept. They had hung out a few times before she went home for winter break, but it never amounted to anything. They hadn't spent any time together outside of the computer lab since the spring semester began.

She had a small, random braid hanging behind her ear today. It was fastened with masking tape. Zapher wondered how it had gotten there. He pictured Marla sleeping over at a girlfriend's house. They would paint their toenails and braid each other's hair . . . in their bras and panties.

Man, I'd love to bend you over.

"Take a picture—it lasts longer," Marla drawled, still not looking at him.

He shook himself and got up to go, snatching a glance at her computer screen. She was in Second Life. Her avatar, Hevvee Metall, was stark naked. Lately, Marla had been taking Hevvee around Second Life without any clothes on, agitating for animal rights and vegetarianism.

"Hevvee has business in Roma Redux today," Marla announced, finally turning her heavily mascaraed eyes on Zapher.

"Oh yeah?" he retorted, feigning lack of interest and desperately hoping the action in his pants was not noticeable.

"The PETA group is staging a protest of a temple there that makes animal sacrifices."

Zapher snorted. "Like that'll do anything."

"We're anticipating a big turnout," Marla pouted.

"Yeah, but those sacrifices aren't real," Zapher argued. "Nobody makes animal sacrifices anymore in real life, so what's the point?"

"It's symbolic," Marla insisted.

"Well, for Christ's sake, put some clothes on Hevvee." Zapher looked at the screen again. "Marla, what the hell are you doing?" Hevvee was now sitting on the steps of the Palatine Library, still naked.

"Nudism is not a crime in Second Life."

"But it's completely anachronistic in Roma Redux," Zapher complained. "No woman would have gone around naked in ancient Rome. Come on, you're ruining the sim."

Zapher sat back down and clicked into Second Life on his terminal. He'd left Roach Rauch just inside the Palatine Library as usual. He copied a toga from Roach's inventory. Then he guided Roach out onto the steps and threw the toga at Hevvee.

"Ow!" Hevvee grunted. Then there was a puff of smoke and suddenly she was dressed in the toga.

"What's this?" Marla asked. "You wrote a program to reverse-assault women?"

"For stupid tourists, like you," Zapher replied. "The tourists are always dressed wrong. It's very annoying."

Marla turned Hevvee around, inspecting her new outfit. It was too big.

"Now that's a hot look," Marla crooned sarcastically. "I suppose I'll wear it, but only if you give me a copy of that puppy you're selling. Leave it on the steps for me. I've got to get to class." She clicked out of Second Life, making Hevvee disappear on Zapher's screen. Hevvee would reappear in the same place whenever Marla clicked in again.

"Later," Zapher mumbled, watching her go.

Zapher guided Roach back into the library. He needed to create some new scrolls. He worked for forty-five minutes, all the while finding it difficult to keep Marla off his mind.

I don't have time to program a puppy. I could easily buy one somewhere. But those pet programs are so annoying.

Instead, Zapher made a scroll, attached a rose to it and wrote:

Marla—
Roses are red.
Puppies go poo.
My human would like to
go out with you.
—Roach

Zapher took a deep breath. His heart was racing. He added, "P.S. Call him," at the bottom of the note, along with his cell phone number.

I know I'm going to regret this. Oh, well. She probably won't read it anyway.

He set his gift on the stairs, where Hevvee would reappear when Marla clicked in.

Just then, Roach was approached by a stranger whose name bubble read "Tyrel Seeberg."

"Hello," Tyrel said, "I'm new here. Can you tell me how to get to the Palatine Library?"

"This is the Palatine," Roach said, pointing up the steps. "I'm the librarian, can I help you?"

"Yes," Tyrel said. "I'd like to have a look at your copy of Virgil's *Aeneid* for a class project I'm working on."

"Are you with the Duke University group?" Roach asked.

"Yes," Tyrel replied.

"Follow me."

Acting as a resource for tourists and students was part of the price Zapher paid for prime real estate in Second Life. He had convinced the creators of Roma Redux to allow Roach to become the Palatine Librarian by promising to provide educational simulations of scrolls. The arrangement suited Zapher fine: perfect cover for his clearinghouse.

When Roach turned around to head back up the stairs, Zapher could see an avatar in the shape of a bull emerging from the side door of the library. It galloped down the alley away from them.

One beat later, the library exploded.

Zapher wasn't even sure what was happening at first. He watched as the building dissolved into hazy white patches. Then his screen went black for a few minutes.

When the screen came back, Roach was lying on the ground across the street. There was debris all around him, some of it burning, and his leg was bleeding. Tyrel had been thrown into an unnatural position against the wall of a building. Zapher made Roach crawl over to Tyrel and shake him. No response. Then two other avatars were running toward them, gawking at the show. The Palatine Library was on fire.

Apparently, someone had hacked in with a program to simulate a fire bomb, destroying the building and disabling the avatars in the vicinity.

Zapher couldn't believe it.

Who would bomb the Palatine Library?

Not wanting to believe his black market business was the target, Zapher desperately ran through the possibilities.

Could it be an authentic part of the simulation? Zapher knew the Palatine Library burned down in real life, but he couldn't remember when. At any rate, it seemed unlikely that ancient Romans had fire bombs.

Could it be random griefing? Second Life was, of course, full of "griefers," avatars who went around aggravating other avatars for no good reason. Although weapons were supposed to be restricted to combat zones that were used much like video games, Zapher had heard about them being used elsewhere. A handful of Second Life businesses had been bombed by activists protesting their products. Perhaps the animal rights activists were behind this bomb and it was meant for the Temple of Dionysus.

Would Marla go this far as a joke?

No. There was no way around it: someone had a grudge against the Palatine Library, and it wasn't the tourists or the students. This was an attack on the clearinghouse.

Shit.

Had he pissed someone off? He couldn't think who. As far as he knew, all of his customers were satisfied.

On further consideration, however, Zapher had to admit to himself that there was something off about his last deal.

The client had been referred to him by a previous customer in Oman. He had four ancient Greek scrolls that needed to be unloaded fast. Zapher had bent over backward to accommodate the request. He sold the first two immediately to "Gentry Wolfzhan," whom he had reason to believe was a Russian billionaire named Mikhail Durkovsky. The third he sold to Marie-Élise Toucey in Nantes, France. Marie-Élise was an eccentric recluse who had never bothered with a false identity. Zapher could tell from his exchanges with her over the years that she had a few screws loose. Still, she had been one of his first connections to the black market and had done more than anyone else to spread good word-of-mouth about the Palatine Library.

Zapher couldn't find an immediate buyer for the fourth scroll, so he bought it himself, knowing that another buyer would come along soon. And sure enough, just last Friday, "Magenta Mai" came through. He had arranged for Magenta's human to pick up the scroll from the airport in New York today.

Where did I go wrong?

The first sale went off without a hitch: Zapher had received the scrolls from the Omani contact and the payment from the Russian, checked to be sure everything was in order, made the exchange, and received confirmation of receipt from both parties.

The second sale, however, was anomalous. Zapher had received payment from Marie-Élise and the scroll from the Omani contact. Everything was in order, so he made the exchange, but he never received confirmation of receipt from Marie-Élise. He should have heard from her a week ago. While he couldn't really count on confirmations from customers he didn't know, he had dealt with Marie-Élise many times, and she'd never broken protocol before.

Did Marie-Élise turn psycho on me?

While Good Samaritan avatars loaded Roach and Tyrel onto stretchers to cart them to the hospital, Zapher shifted to the next terminal, googling "Marie-Élise Toucey, Nantes, France."

And his worst nightmare suddenly came true. Myriad articles appeared instantly, reporting the grisly murder of "Nantes' beloved eccentric."

Holy shit! Was she murdered for the scroll?

The timing was uncanny. Marie-Élise was killed the very morning the scroll was scheduled to arrive. The reports indicated that she was tied up and tortured in her home before she died. It did not seem to be a burglary. There were no suspects in custody.

Will they come for me next?

Knowing that he was in a dangerous business, Zapher had given some thought over the years to what he would do in an emergency situation. All of those plans seemed vague and unrealistic to him now.

What about Mom?

Zapher could feel himself beginning to panic. He took a mental step back. If they were going to kill him, they wouldn't bomb the Palatine Library, would they?

Maybe I got rid of the fourth scroll in time.

Chapter Thirteen

At eleven-thirty Monday morning, Dana's cab pulled up at the curb outside Terminal 1 of Kennedy Airport. She paid her driver and joined the crowd in the receiving area. The monitor told her the flight carrying her scroll was on time for arrival just before noon.

She was so excited to see the scroll she could hardly stand still. She took a sign printed with the name "ANDERSON" out of her bag and held it as she paced slowly to and fro near the window.

A few other people held signs. Everyone was watching the steady stream of arrivals coming through the door. One man stood to the side watching the watchers.

Another Anderson sign. That must be her.

Cardinal Giuseppe Torelli was relieved. His computer hacker, Tommy, had informed him that the buyer was a university professor named Dr. Dana McCarter. Tommy had monitored the Palatine Library's entire exchange with her; it was as easy as monitoring the exchange with Marie-Élise Toucey.

Marie-Élise—charming woman. Too bad my timing was off. I won't let that happen again.

When a young man in a cheap suit arrived with a sign reading "Anderson" a half-hour before, Torelli figured the man must be making the pickup for Dr. McCarter. Torelli had been disappointed; he needed to take care of some business with Dr. McCarter in person.

Torelli now knew that it was to her office Turk Selenka had led him last week. In Torelli's estimation, Dr. McCarter was the only other person who had seen the *Eroticus*. How convenient it would be to get rid of her and retrieve another scroll in one fell swoop.

Of course, it was entirely possible that the woman with the "Anderson" sign wasn't Dr. McCarter and that the man in the cheap suit was the courier pickup after all.

Damn. I should have asked Tommy to find me a photo of her. What are the chances there would be two Anderson signs on the same morning? Still, the chances that both are waiting for a courier are almost nil.

The woman was perhaps a bit too sprightly for a university professor—especially for a world-class expert in ancient Greek manuscripts. She was dressed in a magenta skirt and jacket under a tan trench coat. Pretty, in a sporting sort of way. She looked like she could put up a better fight than the man in the cheap suit.

Just then, a small blond girl, no more than ten years old, Torelli guessed, approached the man in the cheap suit. He bent down to say hello, and they walked off together toward the baggage carousel.

What an extraordinary way to pick up a child! Her parents ought to be shot, arranging for her to be handed off so carelessly. That man could be anybody. She could disappear forever!

Torelli watched the child converse with the man in complete trust as they waited for her luggage. He shook his head in disgust and turned his attention back to the task at hand.

The woman was watching the arrivals intently now.

You must be Dana.

Torelli felt the hair on the back of his neck bristle. His nostrils flared. He now had a lock on his quarry, and he was ready for pursuit.

Ah yes, the monitor shows the courier's flight has arrived.

A long time seemed to pass. People found their matches and left. New people steadily arrived. Dana McCarter checked her watch. Torelli's watch said 12:20.

At last, a young woman wearing a backpack appeared, saw Dana's sign, and approached. Dana smiled and shook her hand. The courier took a paper-wrapped parcel out of her backpack and handed it over to Dana. Dana tucked the parcel in her bag, spoke a few more words, and turned toward the door.

Torelli had hoped Dana would drive her own car to the airport. It would be easiest to accomplish his task in the parking garage. But he was prepared to follow her to the ends of the earth if necessary.

She hailed a cab at the curb. Torelli hailed the next cab and told the driver to follow Dana's cab.

Back to your office, then, my dear? That works for me.

He would leave his "Please do not disturb" sign on the door and would be long gone before anyone realized she was dead. The receptionist would remember the distinguished-looking gentleman who came to see Dana, but wouldn't be able to identify him.

Dana's cab exited from the airport and merged onto the Van Wyck Expressway, headed for the Triborough Bridge. Torelli recognized the route. It was the same route he took following Selenka to Dana's office last week.

Torelli glanced at his driver, a middle-aged Arab with a head wrap. Torelli urged him to stay close to the cab in front of him and promised to reward his efforts. The Arab gave an obedient nod and punched the gas.

"But please take no unnecessary risks," Torelli added. "We don't want anyone hurt."

Traffic was heavy with the lunch rush. Dana's cab took the Harlem River Drive exit, went south on Second Avenue and then west on

Ninety-Sixth Street. Before reaching Fifth Avenue, it slowed down, as though looking for an address. Suddenly, it pulled over in a no parking zone. Torelli's cab was forced to pass and pull over at the corner of the street.

Torelli was on alert. Where was Dana going? He had his cash out, ready to pay his driver and run after her. But she didn't get out.

A Toyota pulled up behind Torelli's cab, wanting to turn right. When the cab didn't budge, the Toyota honked.

"I cannot park here, sir," Torelli's driver said.

"Don't move," Torelli commanded, throwing a wad of twenties into the front seat.

Does she know she's being followed?

The Toyota honked again, longer and harder this time.

"Sir, if we do not move—"

Just then Dana's cab pulled away from the curb, making a harrowing U-turn back east on Ninety-Sixth Street.

Perceiving in an instant that there was no way for his cab to follow, Torelli slid across his seat and got out of the cab on the street side. Fortunately for him, the light was still red. On the other side of Ninety-Sixth Street, a woman stood with her arm raised, hailing a cab that was about to be released from the red light.

Torelli dashed across the street, shouting at the woman. "Madam! Madam, I offer you forty dollars to wait for the next taxi cab!" The light turned green just as Torelli reached the other side. The cab approached.

The woman hesitated peevishly. "Eighty," she demanded.

Torelli hastily handed her four twenties and ducked into the cab. His driver was a black man with long dreadlocks, bobbing to steel drum music on the radio. Torelli instructed him to follow Dana's cab.

Soon they were on Harlem River Drive, heading north. Dana's cab didn't slow until it reached Fort Tryon Park.

"Where are we?" Torelli asked his driver.

"Dis De Cloisters, mon. A branch of de Met."

Not comprehending a word of what his driver said, Torelli was nevertheless impressed by what he saw outside his window: a sprawling estate overlooking the Hudson River. They followed the curving stone road past graceful trees and shrubbery to a medieval fortress with a stout, square tower. It was very peaceful. Torelli felt as though he were in the Italian countryside.

"It be closed today, mon," the driver added. "Museums closed on Mondays."

Torelli pulled four more twenties out of his satchel and tossed them onto the front seat. Dana was already out of her cab and sprinting toward the entrance.

She knows.

"Please wait here for me and I will pay you more," Torelli told his driver as he swung open the door and followed her in.

Dana was in a dead panic. She flew through the door she knew would be open and down a corridor to an empty office, locking its door behind her.

Dana had given some thought to her situation over the weekend. She realized she was playing a dangerous game. Although she was accustomed to operating as an independent agent, she decided it would be foolish to proceed with the courier pickup without a backup plan.

She wouldn't be able to go to the police without implicating herself in black market trafficking. An investigation could reveal her collection and ruin her life.

She needed advice. After the Institute banquet on Saturday night, she went out for drinks with Gene and told him everything.

Gene advised Dana to take a cab to the airport and, if she was followed out, to come straight to The Cloisters. As director, he would be there on Monday anyway. They would lure the pursuer into the foyer under the video camera. Then Gene would come out and make him leave.

The moment she was sure she was being followed, Dana called Gene and told him she was on her way.

Who is the old man in the cab, and why did he follow me here? she whined to herself. *Surely he's not the killer.*

Giuseppe Torelli entered the foyer of the museum with the majestic air of a cardinal ascending to the pulpit of a cathedral. Although the door was unlocked, there was no one in sight. Torelli paused, surveying the room. Hearing a door closing down a corridor to his left, he turned to follow the sound.

Just then, another door along the same corridor opened. A stocky man in a beautiful Italian suit stepped out, converging on Torelli with an apologetic smile.

"I'm sorry, sir, the museum is closed today," he said.

"Ah, my good sir," Torelli responded. "Perhaps you can help me. I seek Dr. Dana McCarter."

Gene Vargas cocked his head as though in surprise. "I'm afraid you've come to the wrong place. No one by that name works here."

The cardinal smiled, but his face was stern. "I watched her enter just moments ago. It is a matter of extreme urgency that I see her immediately."

Gene feigned puzzlement. "Sir, there are no meetings scheduled at The Cloisters today. I'm afraid you're going to have to make other arrangements."

Torelli was becoming impatient. "Dr. McCarter!" he boomed in the direction of the corridor. "Come out here this instant!"

Gene gave a well-practiced look of shocked offense. "I'm sorry, sir, I'm going to have to ask you to leave."

Torelli ignored him. "Dana!" he called again, like a schoolmaster summoning a naughty child.

Gene pulled a slim brown cell phone out of his pocket. "I'm calling the police," he announced, shaking his head in disapproval.

"I wouldn't do that," Cardinal Torelli warned. "It is not I but Dr. McCarter whom the police will drag away to the station. And perhaps you, too, for harboring her."

Gene frowned. "I don't know who you think you are, mister," he snapped. "But this room is under video surveillance. Stalking is a crime. There is already enough evidence on tape to warrant a restraining order against you. You'll be—"

"Enough, young man!" Torelli thundered. "I am Cardinal Giuseppe Torelli of the papal curia, and I come here on behalf of the Vatican police."

Gene's mouth dropped open. He was speechless.

Torelli looked around for the alleged camera, wanting to address it directly. Not finding it, he took a theatrical step toward the center of the room, drew himself up, and began his oration. "Let it stand on record that Dr. Dana McCarter has in her possession a scroll stolen from the Vatican Library. I, Cardinal Giuseppe Torelli, have been authorized to give her the opportunity to return it immediately. If she does so, the Vatican will take no further action against her. If she does not, however, we will pursue this case to the full extent of the law, starting with a phone call to the *New York Times* divulging all that we know about her illegal dealings with the Palatine Library."

Gene could not hide his consternation. Torelli could practically see the gears turning in his mind as he scrambled to figure out a way to salvage their plan.

"Perhaps there has been a mistake, sir," Gene finally stammered. "Could you please show me some identification?"

Torelli grudgingly reached in his satchel. "Dana," he boomed. "*Finito.*"

Gene's frown deepened the moment he saw the Vatican seal on the card Torelli produced. He studied it with intense scrutiny.

"Dana," Torelli called, "I am leaving now. You have lost your chance." With that, he plucked his card from Gene's hand and turned toward the exit.

A door opened in the corridor. Both men turned. Dana emerged, a sullen expression on her face, a brown package in her hand.

"I was going to return it to you," she said with as much dignity as she could muster under the circumstances.

"Ha!" scoffed Cardinal Torelli. "I do not believe you, and neither will anyone watching this video. You are a thief and a liar." Torelli spoke calmly and factually, as though he were a prosecutor making his final summation.

"I bought this scroll in order to give it back to you," Dana protested. "All I want is permission to study it."

Torelli was unmoved. "Relinquish the stolen property at once!" he commanded, holding out his open hand.

"Please, Cardinal," Dana began. "I am the director of—"

"I know who you are, young lady," he interrupted, "and I understand what you thought you were trying to accomplish. But you have far overstepped your authority. You are in no position to negotiate. Relinquish the scroll, and the Vatican will leave you to your own devices."

"But the world has the right to know what was buried in St. Paul's sarcophagus!"

Dana's outburst surprised Torelli. He smiled a little. "I'm sorry to be the one to inform you, Dr. McCarter, that you have been misled. This scroll, it was stolen from the Vatican library. Were you told it came from St. Paul's sarcophagus? Ha! That is absurd. Who told you that?"

"I'm not at liberty to disclose my source," Dana rejoined. "However, I think the *New York Times* would find it very interesting."

"Ha!" Torelli scoffed again. "I assure you that the Vatican is not afraid of your evil slander." He advanced toward her; Gene moved to intercept him.

"It's okay, Gene," Dana sighed. She handed her package to Torelli. Torelli peered inside, turned, and left without another word.

Gene moved to the door to watch the waiting cab drive away. Then he turned and regarded Dana.

"You okay, hon?"

Dana nodded, blinking back tears of strain and frustration. He moved in and folded her in an embrace.

"I'm so sorry, Gene," she hiccupped wetly into his shoulder.

"It's all right, kitten," he soothed. "We handled it. It's all over now."

"I shouldn't have subjected you to this—"

"Hey, now," he scolded, "I'd have been mad if you hadn't let me in on this. That's what friends are for."

"But the danger, and the legal trouble—"

"Believe me, Dana," he whispered into her ear, "the tape from that camera is going right in the garbage. No one will ever—"

"No, Gene." She pulled away, gazing intently at him. "Can I keep it?"

He turned her gently, walked her down the corridor toward his office, and shut the door. "I don't think that's a good idea, Dana," he said at last. "It incriminates you."

"I know," she responded, wiping her eyes, "but it might be important."

"Don't tell me you're going to pursue this."

She didn't say anything.

"Dana?"

She raised her chin defiantly.

"Now, you listen to me," he lectured. "It's over, okay? This is as bad as it gets. You've hit bottom with this black market stuff. That's the one thing I ask of you, as a friend—that you stop taking these incredible risks. You're going to get hurt."

"Gene," Dana persisted, "I've got to get that scroll back. I just spent two million Institute dollars on it."

"So you gambled," Gene shrugged. "You gambled, and you lost. You can't always win. And you can't be blamed for trying. After all, 'bold' is the whole idea behind the Institute. Remember what they called the Institute at the banquet Saturday night—'A gutsy initiative.' Write a letter to the benefactor. He—or she—will back you."

"Gene, you don't understand," Dana fretted. "Even if the benefactor did back me, I've got a board of trustees to answer to, not to mention the president of New York University. I have to earn their respect. My appointment was controversial. Plenty of people wanted that German guy instead. I have to prove myself. I have to—"

"Dana, stop a minute, okay? Just stop." Gene put his hands on her shoulders and looked her full in the face. "You know what I think? I think you really don't give a damn about the board and the president. I think you're obsessed with those scrolls—"

"Gene—" she tried to back away, but he held firm.

"Wait a minute and let me finish, please," he remonstrated, turning her face back toward his. "I'm telling you as a friend that your obsession with Aristotle is becoming unhealthy."

"Okay, all right," she grumbled, breaking away at last. "Message received." She took a few steps back and collapsed on Gene's antique chaise longue.

He gave her a concerned frown. "Let me go get us something to eat."

While Gene trundled off to the employee break room, Dana closed her eyes and tried to clear her mind. She thought of sunshine, ocean waves, and leafy trees swaying in the breeze—all the things her therapist taught her to think about when she needed to slow her heart rate.

After she was found abandoned as a child, Dana was assigned a therapist, whom she had liked and continued to see on a regular basis into adulthood. About five years ago her therapist finally retired and moved away. Despite being referred to a new therapist, Dana had deemed it the right time to finally be done with therapy.

I can therapize myself.

After a few minutes, Gene returned with a tray holding an elegant tea set and a loaf of banana bread. He set it on the mahogany coffee table in front of Dana. She smiled. She could smell the homemade banana goodness from where she sat.

"Is Melinda on the warpath again?" Dana asked, referring to Gene's housemate, who always baked up a storm when she was between boyfriends.

Gene shook his head. "I actually bought this along with some other things at St. Mike's bake sale yesterday."

Dana suddenly realized she was famished. "Thank you, Gene," she said as she watched him take off his jacket and sit down across from her. "I really don't know how to thank you enough."

"Oh, please," Gene protested, pouring two cups. He was blushing a little under his well-tanned cheeks. He clearly enjoyed mothering her. He always had. It worked out well, because Dana needed a mother.

"Gene," she said, cutting herself a large chunk of bread, "I've been dreaming about Aristotle."

He snorted. "You need to get laid, Dana."

"No—well, okay, you may be right about that," she admitted, grinning a little. "But these dreams are amazing, Gene. They're so vivid and . . . informative. I feel like I'm finding out new things about Aristotle."

"Hold on, now—you're starting to sound like Teddy," Gene cautioned, referring to his ex-boyfriend. "He always swore he dreamed things that happened later."

"Oh, yeah," Dana recalled.

Gene nodded. "But, you know, dreams are just thoughts and memories the brain pieces together from experiences we had during the day. If you dream something that happens later, it's only because you were anticipating it."

"It's interesting you say that," Dana mused. "Because I feel like these dreams are synthesizing information from my research—showing me how it all fits together."

"But how do you know it's accurate?" Gene questioned. "You can spin many different stories from bits and pieces of information."

"True, but some stories are better than others."

"Well, what do you think these dreams are trying to tell you about your man?"

"That he was onto something very big."

"Oh, hello! Really?" Gene mocked. "Dana, we already knew that. This is Aristotle, one of the most famous and important men of all time."

"No, I mean, something other than what we thought," Dana continued. "Gene, he didn't write the lecture notes we ascribe to him. After reading the *Eroticus*, I feel sure of that. He grew away from Plato toward nominalism, and his nominalism led him to . . . extreme measures . . . that got him kicked out of Athens and got all his dialogues confiscated."

"What kind of extreme measures are we talking about here?" Gene asked skeptically.

Dana shook herself, as if from a daze. "I don't know for sure, but I'm going to find out."

Gene gave her a severe look.

"Don't worry," she said, with her most reassuring smile. "I still have the valiant Inspector Domenico Conti on my side."

"Dana, don't be an idiot."

"What do you mean?"

"I mean, who do you think tipped off Cardinal Testicles?"

"It wasn't Domenico," Dana countered. "Torelli's clearly the bad apple. Domenico said he would contact another cardinal at the Vatican to root Torelli out."

"Dana, even in America, detectives can lie to set up a bust."

"But I could tell," she protested. "Domenico wasn't lying."

"Admit it, Dana," Gene insisted. "He charmed your socks off."

"Innocent until proven guilty," she replied stubbornly.

Gene rolled his eyes. "Well, anyway, since the inspector has gone back to the hole he crawled out of, I suggest you forget about him," he advised. "Why don't you come for dinner this weekend, and I'll have Melinda invite her brother."

"He's married, Gene."

"Not for long."

"You're terrible," she grinned.

He nodded proudly.

They chatted a bit longer. Finally, Dana took her last sip of tea and smacked her knees resolutely. "I should go, Gene. I've been more than enough trouble to you for one day."

They both stood up.

"Let me drive you," Gene offered.

But Dana declined. "I'd like to walk through the park and take the A train. The fresh air will do me good."

Gene hesitated.

"I'll be fine," Dana asserted, putting on her coat.

"Much as I hate how this all turned out," he conceded, "having to give up the goods to an uptight cardinal is actually way better than there being a killer after you."

"That's definitely the silver lining," Dana agreed. "Gene?"

"Yes?"

"Can I please have the videotape?"

"No, you may not, Sassafras. However, I will keep it for you . . . for a while."

Dana smiled and bowed her head in submission. "Okay. Thanks. Thanks a million, for everything."

"My pleasure," he said. "Now, you go get some rest. Everything will look better in the morning. Do yourself a favor and give Aristotle a break. Maybe plan a little vacation or something. From what I gathered at the banquet, there won't be anything much going on at the Institute for a few weeks anyhow."

"You're right," Dana said, giving him a quick hug goodbye. Then she was out the door, bag on shoulder, camera in bag, photos of the scroll she had just lost in the camera. She was smiling to herself.

How convenient I was able to hide in the document room while Gene intercepted Torelli. Bright light, flat surface, snap, snap, snap!

Dana exited through a back door of The Cloisters and hit the footpath to the park.

Gene would be mad if he knew about the photos. But how can I tell him? They would just make him worry more. Besides, I had to take them so fast—who knows if they even turned out legibly.

The temperature had been dropping all day, and a cold wind was blowing. It looked as though it wanted to rain. Dana paused to cinch her trench coat and squint up at the sky. She had only about a half-mile to walk to the train stop. She gambled she could make it before the rain.

Gene's right, old girl. You are a gambler.

Now that her heart rate had slowed to normal and she had some food in her stomach, she was thinking clearly again. She was feeling pretty good, actually. She could sense a plan taking shape in her brain. She wasn't ready to face it yet, but she knew it was there and would thrust itself upon her before long.

A loner all her life, Dana was used to having conversations with herself in her mind. Most of the time these conversations sounded just like the conversations she had with other people. Referring to herself as "you," she would admonish herself, congratulate herself, or instruct herself to do something. Sometimes she would even recount something interesting that had happened to her as though she were telling a friend.

She often wondered if other people had similar relationships with themselves. Gene told her he had conversations in his mind, but he thought of them as a form of prayer. Although Dana had no such religious excuse, she thought her mental switchboard was relatively healthy. Her therapist had thought so, too.

Lately, however, she was increasingly aware of another presence in her mind. It didn't express itself in terms of a voice, but as a reaction or urge. She might be rambling along in her mind about how much she liked something, and then this other presence would have the nerve to flat-out contradict her, thereby causing her conscious mind to stop in its tracks and recant. The reaction could be positive as well. Someone might ask her about something she should have hated, and the presence would stubbornly assert itself with a thumbs-up, causing her to answer, "I guess I liked it, but I'm not sure just why yet." Then her conscious mind would scramble for an explanation, which was often unconvincing. The presence, her little daemon, didn't care about explanations. It just knew.

Dana wondered whether the daemon was a sign of mental maturity or mental illness. She was inclined to see it as an adaptation that stemmed from being an orphan.

Her therapist often told her that, when they are well cared for, orphans are actually better off than children with parents. Her therapist had done enough family counseling to know that most children subconsciously devote their lives to either fulfilling or undermining the perceived expectations of their parents. The same applies to children who grow up unaware that they were adopted. Orphans who know they are orphans during their formative years, in contrast, are uniquely free to set their own expectations and develop a robust self-reliance.

Dana acquired a heightened awareness of the daemon after she ended therapy. While some might argue it indicated the need to find a new therapist, Dana preferred to see it as proof she no longer had any such need.

Dana was pondering her daemon as she hurried through the park. She could feel it asserting itself—without rhyme or reason, as usual. It did not warn her about the cab parked inconspicuously on Nagle Avenue, whose distinguished-looking passenger sat feeding twenties to his reggae driver and monitoring The Cloisters' front gate, which she had completely bypassed. Instead, Dana's daemon was filling her with the urge to go to Moscow. She suspected her conscious mind would soon supply her with a justification for this rather bizarre directive, probably when she examined her photographs of the new scroll.

She returned to her office in time for a full briefing about the day's activities from Ann and Eva. They exaggerated their tribulations, clearly miffed that Dana had been inexplicably absent. Though they stopped short of complaining, Dana decided to confront them. She didn't want them to resent her behind her back. Inferring that their anger ultimately stemmed from fear of taking the wrong action while she was gone, she assured them that she trusted their judgment and would support their decisions. She told them she was grateful to have such capable staff members because she knew that, in order to do her job right, she would need to be away often. That seemed to smooth things over.

Dana shuffled through her mail as she proceeded to her office, savoring the anticipation of devouring her photographs of the new scroll. When she felt she could wait no longer, she finally plugged her camera into her laptop.

Chapter Fourteen

 *THE SYMPOSIUM*

The Scene: A banquet hall
The Characters: ARISTOTLE, opponent of religion
                     RABBI ADAR, defender of Judaism
                     ANDROMEDA, defender of the Dionysian Mysteries
                     SPEUSIPPUS, defender of the Pythagorean Religion
                     THEOPHRASTUS, defender of a Supreme Cause

ARISTOTLE: My dear friends, please gather around. It is time to begin our discussion. As you know, rumor has it that I am a godless man. I am here tonight to confirm that this rumor is true and to give you a chance to correct my erring way—if it is indeed in error. All of you have strong religious beliefs, and I would like to hear from each one of you in turn. Then I will let you know what I think.

THEOPHRASTUS: Are you willing to give us a fair hearing, or have you already made up your mind against us?

ARISTOTLE: I will give you a fair hearing, Theophrastus. I would like nothing better than to be a believer like you. Religion has many benefits, not the least of which is that it establishes a community to which one can belong. Life can be very lonely without religion. So by all means, convince me! After each of you speaks, I will tell you which religion is best.

SPEUSIPPUS: Good luck all around!

ARISTOTLE: Rabbi Adar, your religion interests me most. In recent years, we are seeing more and more Jewish people in Greece. You should be the first to speak.

RABBI ADAR: Certainly, Aristotle. We Jews believe in the existence of a single god who is perfect and who created everything that exists.

ARISTOTLE: What do you mean when you say your god is perfect?

RABBI ADAR: Well, unlike the Greek gods, the Jewish God has no body. This means he is not limited by time or space in any way. He is all-powerful, all-knowing, and everlasting.

ARISTOTLE: Does he interact with humans?

RABBI ADAR: Indeed. He listens to prayers and communicates through the prophets. Moses was our main prophet.

ARISTOTLE: I see. What message did Moses bring from your god?

RABBI ADAR: His main message concerned the Ten Commandments, which are sacred rules that all Jews must obey.

ARISTOTLE: Like what?

RABBI ADAR: Shall I rehearse them? Thou shalt have no other gods; thou shalt not make false idols; thou shalt not use the Lord's name in vain; remember the Sabbath and keep it holy; honor thy father and mother; thou shalt not murder; thou shalt not commit adultery; thou shalt not steal; thou shalt not bear false witness; thou shalt not covet.

ARISTOTLE: Interesting. I know Jews follow many other rules as well, for example, concerning what kinds of foods one may eat and how they must be prepared.

RABBI ADAR: Yes, we are a people of the law.

ARISTOTLE: Why do you have so many laws?

RABBI ADAR: The laws come from God. He rewards those who obey him and he punishes those who disobey him.

ARISTOTLE: I see. And are these rewards and punishments doled out day by day?

RABBI ADAR: Sometimes, but the prophets have foretold the coming of a messiah. At that time, the dead will be resurrected and God will issue a final judgment of each person in accordance with the law.

ARISTOTLE: I suppose that, if one is judged favorably, one is admitted to the Isle of the Blessed, and, if one is judged unfavorably, one is banished to Hades, correct?

RABBI ADAR: Correct indeed, as long as you bear in mind that our heaven and hell are not physical places, as the Greeks believe. They are spiritual states that the human soul experiences after the body dies.

ARISTOTLE: There is one thing that puzzles me about your religion: you do not seem very interested in gaining converts. In fact, people who are not of the Jewish race seem unwelcome at your temples.

RABBI ADAR: True enough. Non-Jews would be welcome at the temples if they converted, but that is a rather complicated matter. It requires a great deal of preparation, including circumcision.

ARISTOTLE: By Zeus!

RABBI ADAR: Well, the sons of Abraham are God's chosen people, Aristotle. Being adopted into this family requires many sacrifices.

ARISTOTLE: Evidently. What argument would you make on behalf of your religion? Why should I convert?

RABBI ADAR: Judaism is the only religion that both instills morality and is open to everyone. Zoroastrianism, the religion of the Persians, instills morality, but, as you may know, it does not allow converts at all. Conversely, Greek religions are open to everyone, but they do not instill morality. They may require that certain rituals be performed, but they have nothing to say about honoring one's mother and father, and all of the other values upon which civilization is built. Their gods carry on in atrocious ways, making terrible role models for humans. Moreover, their celebrations are often an excuse for sinful behavior.

ARISTOTLE: You have made some excellent points, Rabbi. And now we should hear from one of the "sinners" you have just mentioned. Andromeda, you are a maenad of Dionysus. Tell us about your religion.

ANDROMEDA: Well, I can tell you right from the start, Aristotle, that we Dionysians have a lot more fun than Jews! Our god is the god of wine.

ARISTOTLE: So your religion is basically a drinking club.

ANDROMEDA: No, no! There is much more to it than that. Dionysus is different than the other Greek gods.

ARISTOTLE: How so?

ANDROMEDA: He is half human. Zeus, our father in heaven, had an affair with a mortal woman named Semele, which produced Dionysus. Being jealous of Semele, Zeus's wife Hera hates Dionysus. Every year she sends the Titans to shred him to pieces. But every year he rises from the dead.

ARISTOTLE: Why is it good for a god to be half human?

ANDROMEDA: Because then, when he conquers death, he proves that we can too.

ARISTOTLE: How do we conquer death?

ANDROMEDA: Whenever we drink wine, Dionysus possesses us, and we become immortal.

ARISTOTLE: Interesting. But the effect of wine soon wears off.

ANDROMEDA: Well, of course. But you can do amazing things while Dionysus is within you!

ARISTOTLE: Indeed. I have heard about the amazing things you Dionysians do.

ANDROMEDA: Oh, really? What have you heard?

ARISTOTLE: I have heard you go up to the mountains where the air is thin. You drink and dance to savage drumbeats until your eyes glaze over. Then you have wild orgies involving asphyxiation and mutilation. Or you chase down animals in the woods, shred them to pieces with your bare hands, and drink their blood. Or you might even capture a human being, roast him on an iron, and eat his heart. Have you done those things, Andromeda?

ANDROMEDA: Well, you have to understand, Aristotle, it is difficult to remember exactly what happens when one is possessed by Dionysus. But one thing I know for certain is this: the good Rabbi is incorrect to accuse us of sinning during our sacred rites. Dionysus is above any human law, and whosoever he enters is above the law, too.

ARISTOTLE: Is that why you joined the mysteries, to be above the law?

ANDROMEDA: In a way, yes. Ours is the only religion that completely does away with social restrictions. It is open to people from all walks of life without any special preparation. The wine makes everyone equal, and anyone can advance to the high-ranking positions. Men trade places with women; kings trade places with slaves; foreigners trade places with citizens. One comes to realize that all of these distinctions are like masks people wear in society. The rituals invoke another world where each person can take off his mask and be himself.

ARISTOTLE: You discover your true self in the wine?

ANDROMEDA: Indeed. It is very liberating. That is why we call Dionysus our liberator.

ARISTOTLE: Tell me, then, why I should convert. What argument would you make on behalf of your religion?

ANDROMEDA: Dionysus is the god of freedom. In Judaism, following an endless number of tedious restrictions supposedly brings salvation in some distant future after we are all already dead. But Dionysus brings out the divine in all of us and saves us from tedium right now. This life can be truly inspiring when one becomes a vessel of the Holy Spirit. Why wait to find paradise?

ARISTOTLE: Thank you, Andromeda, for your candid explanation of the Dionysian mysteries. Speaking of wine, I believe it is time for an interlude, after which we will hear from our other two guests in turn.

Here ends Book I of the *Symposium*.

Book II

ARISTOTLE: Let us gather around again, my friends. It is time to hear from Speusippus and Theophrastus. So far, we have heard two individuals without any philosophical training defending ancient religious traditions. Rabbi Adar commends the most organized and documented form of worship known to man, namely Judaism, while Andromeda commends an explosively popular alternative, namely, the worship of Dionysus. We turn now to the philosophers. How does training in the art of intellectual inquiry affect one's view of faith?

SPEUSIPPUS: Well, Aristotle, I would like to defend the Pythagorean religion. Although our practices are sometimes called "mysteries," we Pythagoreans are very different from Dionysians.

ARISTOTLE: How so?

SPEUSIPPUS: We do not worship Pythagoras, nor any man nor deified image of man. Pythagoras was a great mathematician who realized that everything is made of numbers. Those who learn the mathematical formulas of things will come to understand a deep, mystical truth.

ARISTOTLE: Is this deep, mystical truth a god?

SPEUSIPPUS: Well, yes, in the sense that it is the ultimate principle of reality. But you must not think of it as a father figure who takes care of us. It is more like an abstract pattern that the soul must aspire toward.

ARISTOTLE: Ah, yes. I believe Plato called it the "Form of the Good" because he believed it was the only thing truly lovable.

SPEUSIPPUS: Indeed. Plato was a Pythagorean.

ARISTOTLE: Why do you believe in the Form of the Good?

SPEUSIPPUS: The Form of the Good explains all human knowledge. Tell me something you think you know.

ARISTOTLE: How about this: that the inside angles of a triangle always add to 180 degrees.

SPEUSIPPUS: Good. Now, how do you know this? Surely not by measuring the angles on all the triangles that exist in the world! In fact, you have never even seen a true triangle with your bodily eye, because every so-called triangle in this world is imperfect—lopsided and irregular. You could never conclude anything by examining them. Your knowledge of triangles is not acquired through your bodily eye at all but through your mind's eye—by conceiving of the perfect, abstract triangle.

ARISTOTLE: The perfect, abstract triangle is part of the Form of the Good?

SPEUSIPPUS: Absolutely. The Form of the Good is nothing but ideal proportion: the sum total of all mathematical truth.

ARISTOTLE: Interesting. Does your religion welcome converts?

SPEUSIPPUS: Indeed. Anyone with sufficient intellectual ability for abstract reasoning may join us.

ARISTOTLE: And why would I want to join you?

SPEUSIPPUS: The Form of the Good is divine. The more you learn about it, the more it becomes part of your intellect, and the more divine you yourself will become.

ARISTOTLE: I suppose achieving a measure of divinity does wonders for one's self-esteem!

SPEUSIPPUS: Don't be glib, Aristotle. People who accuse the Pythagoreans of arrogance and elitism are just lazy. Our religion requires sustained mental effort, and there is nothing wrong with taking pride in the results.

ARISTOTLE: Thank you for enlightening us, Speusippus. Theophrastus, would you say that your religion requires mental effort as well?

THEOPHRASTUS: Indeed. My religious belief arises through the desire to understand the universe.

ARISTOTLE: Do you agree with Speusippus that mathematics is the key to this understanding?

THEOPHRASTUS: Not at all. Although Pythagoras' formulas make for amusing exercises, they have no connection to reality. As Speusippus said himself—you will never find a perfect triangle in this world. So why spend so much time studying perfect triangles? My religious belief is based on the principle that explains what we actually see and hear around us.

ARISTOTLE: And what principle is that?

THEOPHRASTUS: It is nothing other than the principle of cause and effect. Everything that happens is caused by something prior to it and causes something posterior to it. Causality is the ultimate link between all things; it is the fabric of reality.

ARISTOTLE: Your view seems more like science than religion.

THEOPHRASTUS: Although it is less mystical than the other views we have heard tonight, it does posit the existence of God.

ARISTOTLE: How so?

THEOPHRASTUS: Well, think about it. Everything around us is a link in the great causal chain. A is caused by B; B is caused by C;

C is caused by D; and so on. But this sequence cannot go on forever. Something had to start it all. Clearly, this something is God, the Supreme Cause.

ARISTOTLE: What makes God different from all the other links in the chain?

THEOPHRASTUS: God is an eternal force that causes everything without itself being caused by anything else. This force is unlike the links in the causal chain we see around us because they work through motion. For example, a wave can move the sand only because it is itself moved by the wind. Likewise, Speusippus walks across the forum only because he hears Plato calling him. Everything around us is a moved mover in this way. God alone is the unmoved mover.

ARISTOTLE: How can a force move something else without itself moving?

THEOPHRASTUS: Through the principle of attraction. After all, a beautiful boy can attract admirers from far and wide without budging an inch, simply by being beautiful.

ARISTOTLE: Interesting. Does your religion welcome new members?

THEOPHRASTUS: Well, Aristotle, it is hardly a religion, at least so far. Those who believe in God as Supreme Cause have no weekly meetings or secret handshakes. In fact, I don't really feel like I'm part of any group at all. We believers in the Supreme Cause are just a few scattered individuals right now.

ARISTOTLE: If you were to become an organized religion, what would your main activity be?

THEOPHRASTUS: We would devote ourselves to contemplation. All things on earth are attracted toward the divine force in their own ways. The human attraction is contemplative; we draw nearer to God by thinking about how the universe works.

ARISTOTLE: Well, I am not sure you will have much luck in spreading this religion, since contemplating causality is a bit on the dull side for most people.

THEOPHRASTUS: I suppose you are right.

ARISTOTLE: On the other hand, so is doing math problems! I do declare it a toss-up between you and Speusippus for excitement value. But fear not! I never intended to determine the winner of this contest based on number of converts. The winner will be the religion that best accomplishes the true purpose of religion. Now leave me alone for a while so that I may consult my notes and make my final determination.

Here ends Book II of the *Symposium.*

Book III

ARISTOTLE: My dear friends, you have all had the chance to make your case. It is growing late and high time for me to announce the results of your efforts.

Since Speusippus and Theophrastus are the philosophical heavyweights, I had the highest hopes for them. They each base their argument on a false premise, however, namely, that the purpose of religion is explanation.

Speusippus, you posit divinity to explain knowledge, while you, Theophrastus, posit divinity to explain causality. Each of you therefore supposes we need a divine realm in order to explain the natural realm. If this were the case, then what would explain the divine realm? Presumably, some realm higher than divinity, which in turn would require another realm higher still, and so on, and so on, *ad infinitum!*

No doubt you will try to block this absurdity by saying that the divine realm needs no higher explanation. But that answer defeats you—why then does the natural realm need a higher explanation in the first place? Clearly, if we are diligent, we can explain both knowledge and causality in purely natural terms.

So, you philosophers, may you take your seats in shame!

The palm goes to Rabbi Adar and Andromeda. Although they may not be trained in the rigors of intellectual inquiry, they both know the true purpose of religion, namely, to make people happy. While neither of their religions is acceptable by itself, together they make the most excellent religion of all.

THEOPHRASTUS: But Aristotle, how can Judaism and the worship of Dionysus be combined? They are the exact opposite of one another!

ARISTOTLE: You are quite right, Theophrastus. Judaism gives its followers a sense of control. If one learns the rules and follows them carefully, one will be rewarded. Meanwhile, Dionysus gives his followers the ultimate freedom. Once one has imbibed his spirit, the sky is the limit and anything goes. But there is no contradiction in working both of these elements into the same religion. As a matter of fact, this is exactly what people seem to need.

SPEUSIPPUS: How so?

ARISTOTLE: Well, in virtue of the fundamental obstacle to human happiness. Do you know what that is?

RABBI ADAR: No, Aristotle, tell us.

ARISTOTLE: It is none other than akrasia.

ANDROMEDA: What is akrasia?

ARISTOTLE: Akrasia is weakness of will: when you know the better but choose the worse.

SPEUSIPPUS: What? Surely there is no such thing, Aristotle. It seems to me people always choose whatever seems better to them at the time.

ARISTOTLE: Not at all, Speusippus. How many times have you eaten a food that you know is bad for you? How many times have you said something that you know will land you in trouble? How many times have you put off until tomorrow something you know you should do today? We vow to ourselves to stop doing something or to start doing something, but then we fail to follow through. This is akrasia.

THEOPHRASTUS: How can akrasia be the fundamental obstacle to human happiness? It seems like a fairly minor problem.

ARISTOTLE: It would be minor if it only happened occasionally. In my observation, however, people constantly act against their own better judgment. The cumulative effect of this, which reflective individuals often notice, is that we are not the people we want to be. I have written a poem about it.

My own behavior baffles me:
I fail in what I truly love;
In what I loathe, I find success.

Yet, in loathing what I do,
I prove my heart is right.
Who then is it, what then is it, that goes wrong?

I have the will to do the right,
I lack the power, strength, and might.
The good I see I cannot do.
I seek the evil I reject.
If it is I who rejects, is it me who pursues?

When I face a moral choice,
I keep the right and give the wrong.

In my mind is one principle;
In my members is another one.

I am at war.
I am a prisoner.
Oh, agony!
Who can rescue me from the clutches of myself?

SPEUSIPPUS: Aristotle, you are suggesting that we are our own worst enemies!

ARISTOTLE: Exactly. When we realize how often we let ourselves down, we come to hate ourselves. Come now, Theophrastus, tell us the truth. Are there things you do not like about yourself?

THEOPHRASTUS: Indeed, I suppose there are.

ARISTOTLE: Why, then, do you not change?

THEOPHRASTUS: Well, let me see. Sometimes I try, but I always seem to end up more or less where I started.

ARISTOTLE: Just as I suspected. Human beings are creatures of habit. We develop habits before we even have the chance to decide whether or not we approve of them. The patterns we learn as children become ingrained in us and carry on a life of their own even when we grow up and want to change.

SPEUSIPPUS: What does this problem have to do with religion?

ARISTOTLE: Such a big problem requires a big solution. People pray to the gods to help them because they know they cannot succeed alone. They need an ally in the war against themselves.

RABBI ADAR: Jews succeed by following the law.

ARISTOTLE: But they can never follow the law perfectly. So they are fraught with guilt and anxiety.

ANDROMEDA: This is precisely why we Dionysians give up trying and let the divine take over.

ARISTOTLE: And as a result you become irresponsible—secretly horrified by your excesses.

THEOPHRASTUS: It seems to me that both of these religions are too extreme.

ARISTOTLE: Well, severe problems call for extreme solutions. My proposal is that both extremes are needed at the same time to balance each other out. Give people a religion that expects people to follow the law but at the same time grants that they cannot do it by themselves. It should offer to wipe away the past and make anything possible. This will be extremely attractive to people who are tired of themselves, frustrated with being slaves to their own bad habits.

SPEUSIPPUS: How would such a combination of religions ever come about?

ARISTOTLE: There are two central components: a god who judges, setting the high expectations, and a god who redeems, embracing failure. These two gods have to be very closely related so that they provide unified purpose, but at the same time, they must be distinct, so that the failure does not erode the high expectations.

ANDROMEDA: How about the father and son team of Zeus and Dionysus?

ARISTOTLE: Well, the problem with that suggestion is that Zeus has lost his credibility. He has been committing adultery far too long to be accepted as a moral authority. Instead, I believe Dionysus needs to be born into the family of Abraham. He would be the son of the Jewish God and a mortal Jewish woman, and he would conquer death, thereby providing all humans with a path to salvation. He would tell people that they should try to obey the father, and that they will fail, but that the son will help. Only by embracing his spirit will one win the battle against oneself.

THEOPHRASTUS: And this will solve the problem of akrasia?

ARISTOTLE: It will not eliminate akrasia by any means. But it will acknowledge it, so that people will at least understand what the problem is. And they will feel better knowing that everybody else has the same problem. They will continue to fail but they will cease to hate themselves because the son of god has validated their failure.

ANDROMEDA: But will there still be orgies?

ARISTOTLE: No, Andromeda. The orgies and the criminal activities have to stop. They cause too much harm. But you do not need them anyway. They were just symbols of the real liberation Dionysus provides: a taste of divinity. This is what everyone craves. They want their very bodies to be sacred temples for the Holy Spirit.

RABBI ADAR: But each culture wants their own religion so they can hold their own sacred festivals, preserving their own distinctive values and identity.

ARISTOTLE: No, Rabbi. The religion I envision would assimilate every culture to promote unity among the entire human race. If we are all prone to the same problem with akrasia, then the same solution should suit us all. Think about it: my religion has the power to take over the entire world!

THEOPHRASTUS: Hold on! Stop right there, Aristotle. You are mocking us. Your sudden religious zeal flies in the face of your most cherished belief: that every human being is fundamentally unique. Since when have you ever thought people could be or should be the same in any way?

ARISTOTLE: Well, done, Theophrastus. You have seen through my act. My true view is that everything existing in the world is an absolute individual. While I do think most human beings are prone to the problem of akrasia, I think each can overcome it in his or her own way. I have also come to the conclusion, however, that this is not what people want to hear. They want to hear that they are doomed to failure so that they have to be saved.

SPEUSIPPUS: I gather you have no intention of joining this religion yourself.

ARISTOTLE: In some ways, I wish I could. But it would be hard for me to have faith in my own fabrication! I suppose that, since this religion would seem to make people happy, I should at least try to promote it. But I am not enough of a politician to engage in such shenanigans! Perhaps someday someone else with sufficient ambition for world domination will do the job. As for me, I fear I shall have to be content to lead a hopelessly godless life.

Here ends the *Symposium*.

Chapter Fifteen

Dana never made it home that night. She was riveted to her desk, reading the scroll, double-checking all the crucial words. Around three-thirty in the morning, she slumped back in her chair to close her eyes, just for a minute. The next thing she knew, her phone was ringing and it was eight-thirty.

She sat up, alarmed, but let the call go to voicemail. Then she woke up the sleeping screen on her laptop to be sure she hadn't dreamed the photographs.

They were still there. Nothing less than astonishing. The *Symposium:* a dialogue in which Aristotle invents Christianity.

In fact, the poem about akrasia Aristotle wrote for the *Symposium* had made it straight into the New Testament—the well-known and well-loved seventh chapter of the book of Romans, by St. Paul.

Evidently, St. Paul was the "someone with more ambition" whom Aristotle had foreseen as the promoter for his new hybrid religion. Like Aristotle, St. Paul was originally against cults, but when he saw that Christianity had all the ingredients Aristotle predicted for world domination, he converted and became its mastermind.

As a Jew educated in Greek literature, Paul was in an ideal position to take Aristotle's proposal seriously. Furthermore, as a citizen of the Roman Empire, Paul would have had access to the Palatine Library in

Rome, where Aristotle's dialogues were rumored to have been stored before they disappeared.

Now I know why the Eroticus *contained the "love is patient, love is kind" text. It wasn't copied in later. Aristotle wrote it as the ending for his dialogue, and Paul lifted it for his first letter to the Corinthians—just like he lifted Aristotle's poem about akrasia for his letter to the Romans.*

So St. Paul was a plagiarist. How many more of his contributions to the New Testament were stolen from Aristotle's lost dialogues?

Of course, there was no concept of intellectual property back in those days. In fact, copying was considered a form of tribute. It would have been nice for Paul to cite his source, as was often done even in those days. But perhaps he did—and the medieval churchmen who prepared Paul's letters for insertion into the New Testament left the reference out in order to downplay their connection to paganism.

Either way, discovering Aristotle's role in the New Testament was a historical revelation. *For a Christian,* Dana mused, *it would be kind of like finding out who your real parents are after not even realizing you were adopted.*

Dana considered her own feelings about being adopted. At the recommendation of her therapist, Dana had participated in an orphan support group during high school. While Dana had known from age six that Fez and Maxine McCarter were not her real parents, many of the other orphans in the group had not been told until much later. Finding this out seemed to have a profound impact on their self-image. On the other hand, it didn't necessarily change anything. Some of the kids rebelled for a while. But how much of that was just hormones looking for any excuse to rebel? Most of the kids continued loving their adoptive parents all the same.

Dana wondered to what extent the analogy would hold. No doubt, most Christians would be disturbed to learn their religious lineage traced through Paul to Aristotle. For those who were already dissatisfied with the faith, this revelation might provide the impetus to finally abandon it. For others, however, it wouldn't change anything. They would go on believing in the same way.

So the question was, why did the Vatican insist on hiding these scrolls? Dana was sure that, if she were a cardinal—*Now that's a good one!*—she wouldn't even attempt a cover-up. So what if some of Christianity's most profound doctrines came from Greek philosophy? To Dana, the revelation seemed benign.

But I'm not a believer. It's hard for me to know what it would be like. Dana tried to picture what Gene would say. She would have to ask him.

The shocking part, I guess, is not so much the plagiarism, but the fact that Aristotle dreamed up the core concept of Christianity by combining Judaism with the cult of Dionysus. Tracing your religious lineage to the cult of Dionysus is kind of like finding out your biological mother was a psychopath.

Of course, scholars often remarked on the striking resemblance between the cult of Dionysus and Christianity. Christian patriarch Justin Martyr, writing in the second century CE, argued that the devil must have read the Old Testament prophesies of the messiah and sent Dionysus as a decoy before Jesus arrived on the scene.

Looks like Aristotle was in cahoots with the devil.

But does the fact that Christianity was anticipated by earlier developments undermine its credibility? Do believers really think it sprang up out of the blue? A completely new concept that no one had ever thought of?

Surely not.

Dana's phone rang again, stirring her from her reverie. This time, she cleared her throat and picked it up.

"This is Dana McCarter," she said into the receiver.

"Dana, it's Domenico."

Dana stiffened. During the night, Gene's mistrust of the inspector had slowly soaked into her, like dew on a doormat. She hadn't yet figured out how to handle it.

"So what's your game, Inspector?" Dana ventured, almost flippantly, as though she had the upper hand. Although she didn't really have the upper hand, she did have photographs of both the *Eroticus* and the *Symposium*—neither of which he knew about.

There was silence on the other end of the line.

"What are you talking about?" he finally asked.

"You know exactly what I'm talking about," she answered.

"No, I don't," he countered. "Dana, are you all right? Tell me what happened."

She sighed and held the phone away from her ear.

I should just hang up.

She almost did.

"Dana, don't shut me out, dammit. We had a plan. What's going on?"

Dana kneaded her forehead with her free hand.

If he sicced that cardinal on me, why would he be calling? He wouldn't have any reason to call, would he?

"Dana, are you still there? Talk to me. Please."

"Why did you tell that cardinal about my courier pickup?" she finally asked. "That was not in the plan."

"I didn't," he answered indignantly. "What cardinal? Cardinal Torelli?"

"Yes," Dana said, swallowing a sob before it gave her away. "Is he the one who told you not to tell anyone about the scrolls?"

"Yes."

"Well, he took it."

"He took the scroll you bought? Dana, tell me what happened."

The concern in his voice was not to be resisted. Dana's defenses gave way. She wanted an ally. She wanted him for an ally. She just plain wanted him.

She told him the whole story from beginning to end—including the photographs. He probed gently. She kept herself from falling apart by folding a memo on her desk into a tiny football.

"I was so close, Domenico," she concluded. "I had it in my hands." She flicked the football toward the window. It fell behind her desk.

"Dana, I'm so sorry," he said. "Torelli must have hacked into the Palatine Library."

"But how did he even know about it?" Dana asked. "You told him, didn't you."

"No, Dana. Torelli cancelled the meeting we were supposed to have on Saturday."

"Who else could have told him?"

Conti was silent.

"You know, don't you, Domenico," Dana accused.

More silence.

"Now look who's holding out," she complained. "I tell you everything, and you tell me nothing."

"Dana, I'm trying to keep you out of harm's way."

"By keeping me in the dark?" Dana got up to pace.

"By ending your involvement," he retorted. "You need to go back to your work and forget this ever happened—"

"Like hell I will!" Dana exploded. "Domenico, I sank two million dollars into this thing."

"Losing two million dollars is better than losing your life."

"The killer is not in the picture anymore, Domenico," she snapped. "He was after Turk Selenka for his scroll, and he got it. He doesn't know about the Palatine Librar—" Dana cut herself off. Suddenly the pieces of the puzzle began fitting together in her mind. "Unless, of course, hacking into the Palatine Library is how the killer found Selenka."

Conti was silent.

"That's why the killer killed the sarcophagus thief, isn't it," Dana hypothesized, talking more to herself than to the man on the other end of the line. "The killer went after the sarcophagus thief to find out where he sold the scrolls. He got the thief to identify the Palatine Library before he killed him. Then the killer hacked into the library and began monitoring transactions. As soon as Selenka bought the *Eroticus,* the killer hunted him down. Why then didn't the killer hunt me down for the *Symposium?*"

"Dana—"

"Oh, my god, he did!" Dana erupted. "Torelli is the killer. He would have killed me yesterday if he could have. Wouldn't he, Domenico!"

"I don't know," Conti admitted. "All of this is outrageous speculation."

"But Torelli is the one you followed to New York. The one who was following Selenka."

"Yes."

"Goddammit! Why didn't you tell me? I could have been killed." She was shaking now.

"I did tell you—far more than I ever should have," he objected apologetically. "My mistake was telling you five scrolls were stolen from the sarcophagus. If you hadn't known that, none of this would have happened."

"No, I'm glad you told me," Dana countered, somewhat mollified. "Otherwise, I wouldn't have photos of the *Symposium*. Those photos alone were worth the risk."

"Dana, you have to forget about those photos. You can see that now, can't you?"

"Torelli would kill me for them."

"Someone would," Conti amended. "We can't jump to conclusions about Torelli. He has an alibi for the night Achille Benevento—the sarcophagus thief—was killed."

"Yeah, well, Torelli isn't doing the computer hacking himself, either," Dana surmised. "Come on, Domenico. You know very well Benevento didn't 'escape.' He was interrogated and killed by Torelli, or one of Torelli's minions. Torelli probably has a whole army of minions working for him. "She paused. "Domenico?"

"Yes?"

"How do I know you're not one of them?"

"One of who?"

"One of the minions."

"Because I wouldn't have called you if I were."

"Why did you call me?"

"To see if you were all right."

"Really?"

"Yes."

"I'm all right."

"I'm glad."

Dana tried for a moment to convince herself that they were lovers only pretending to be involved in an international conspiracy. It didn't work.

"I'll just go to Interpol and demand protection until they arrest Torelli," she suggested.

"But there is no evidence against Torelli."

"There's the videotape from The Cloisters."

"That implicates you, not him."

"Well, okay, but you witnessed him following Selenka."

"But I didn't witness the assault."

Dana sighed. "You just want it to be somebody else so that you don't have a scandal in your church."

"I want justice. In Italy, justice means 'innocent until proven guilty.'"

"Fine. So how are you going to prove Torelli guilty?"

"I don't know yet."

Neither of them spoke for a moment.

"I feel like we still only have half of the picture," Dana reflected. "Why would a cardinal kill to recover these scrolls? Granted, the two scrolls I've seen would cause a revolution in biblical scholarship, but since when has biblical scholarship been a matter of life and death? The worst these two scrolls can do is undermine the faith of someone who was already prone to disbelief. The logical strategy would be to try to defend the faith through further biblical scholarship. Why is Torelli willing to kill?"

"He, or whoever did this, may just be a religious fanatic out of control."

"Or he has some further stake in those scrolls. I bet if I could see the rest of them I could figure it out—"

"Dana, no. Your role in this is over. It's too dangerous."

"Domenico, don't you see?" Dana heard her own voice as if someone else were speaking. "It's too late to back out. Torelli can't afford to let me live. He may not know about my photos, but he knows I know too much. He's probably waiting for me at my house right now. Either I go to Interpol, or I nail Torelli myself."

"Dana, you don't have a case. Interpol will rip you to shreds."

"I know. That's why you have to help me," Dana begged. "We have to figure out what Torelli is up to, catch him at it, and bring him down. He wants me dead. I can't go on with my life until he's locked away."

There was an extended pause on the line.

Finally, Domenico spoke. "Dana, why don't you just take a long vacation somewhere and come back when I have this case solved."

This is the second time in the last twenty-four hours that I have been urged to take a vacation. Maybe I should listen.

Dana looked out her window at cold rain battering the street below. *How about a trip to the Caribbean?* Dana pictured herself on the beach—pacing.

Then she pictured the bulbous spires of Moscow's Kremlin, and she had a plan.

"I'm not backing out," she told the inspector. "You need me to help you solve this case. Torelli's secret lies in those scrolls, and you will never find them without me."

"Dana, I have a well-trained professional team—"

"Domenico, shut up, okay? I know who bought the other scrolls."

"You do?"

"Meet me at the Medea Hotel in Moscow. I'm leaving for the airport immediately. I'll take whatever flight I can get. I know you want those scrolls, mister. Believe me, I'm your best lead. Get there as fast as you can."

Chapter Sixteen

Zapher Inan sat looking across a large veneer desk at a heavyset professor with thick, round glasses. The professor's name was Dr. Basim Al-Dahadha.

Zapher had come to Muscat, Oman, to find the client who contacted him to broker the sale of the four cursed scrolls. He could still hardly believe he was here. But what choice did he have? Extreme times called for extreme measures.

He told his mother he was going on a camping trip. Much as he hated camping, he wished what he said was true.

About an hour after the Palatine Library was bombed, Zapher clicked back into Roma Redux to see about retrieving his avatar, Roach Rauch, from the hospital. Instead of lying on a bed in the hospital, Roach was chained to the wall of a dimly lit cave. On a nearby cart were a variety of grisly surgical tools. Hovering over them was "The Surgeon," an avatar dressed in accordance with his name. The surgeon had somehow abducted Roach from the hospital and was now preparing to torture him for information concerning the whereabouts of "the last of the five ancient Greek scrolls."

It didn't matter that Zapher knew of only four ancient Greek scrolls. The surgeon would not listen and would not answer any questions. In fact, Zapher soon realized that the surgeon was not being operated by a human. The surgeon was an avatar robot programmed to execute and repeat coercive behavior. In spite of himself, Zapher had to admire the 'bot; whoever designed it clearly knew what he was doing.

The surgeon instructed Roach to produce the fifth scroll by the end of the week. As he spoke, the surgeon pounded pins into Roach's arms, splattering a great deal of blood.

It was a horrifying thing for Zapher to witness.

Nevertheless, it was not the slow and painful-looking demise of his virtual alter ego that prompted Zapher to track down Dr. Basim Al-Dahadha. It was the fact that the surgeon referred to Roach's human, "Mr. Zapher Inan of Istanbul," by name. Whoever programmed the surgeon knew exactly who Zapher was. Zapher had to assume it was only a matter of time before the pins and the blood were real.

Zapher inferred that the client who sold him the four ancient Greek scrolls must have kept the fifth for himself.

As he sat in front of Dr. Al-Dahadha, Zapher tried to penetrate his mind. He supposed that this man was Qaboos University's counterpart to his own father, Umran Inan. Watching the professor as he called to his secretary for coffee, however, Zapher was not reminded of his father at all. Dr. Al-Dahadha was not a fatherly man.

First of all, Zapher's father would probably never have conducted business in Second Life. He was deeply suspicious of computers and downright scornful of computer games. Although Second Life wasn't a game, it looked enough like a game to provoke a snide remark from Umran whenever he saw Zapher messing around with it. This was years ago when Second Life was brand-new and Umran was still alive.

Second, Zapher's father would certainly never have vamped around Second Life as a female avatar. Dr. Al-Dahadha was "Bambi Babad" in Second Life, a substantial landowner and creator of a popular virtual amusement park called "Bambiland." In addition to the usual Ferris wheel, roller coaster, fun house, and the like, Bambiland was famous for its prophesy tent. Every Friday, Bambi herself would appear in traditional Persian costume to tell avatar fortunes using a virtual deck of Tarot cards. People flocked to Bambi to learn the fate of their virtual alter egos. Apparently, Dr. Al-Dahadha fancied himself some kind of mystic. Umran would have called him a "homo."

No one but Zapher knew about Dr. Al-Dahadha's virtual transvestitism, of course, and Dr. Al-Dahadha didn't know that Zapher knew. If Zapher were just a student of Dr. Al-Dahadha's, he might never have guessed that there was a girl—a voluptuous young temptress, no less—inside the professor, clamoring to get out.

Zapher cast another surreptitious glance at the professor as the coffee arrived and was served. Was there something about the way he pursed his mouth at the end of his sentences? Zapher scanned for signs of girlishness. He knew there had to be an intimate connection between the man and his avatar. There always was.

Zapher was not a religious person. Though Magda had tried to raise him in the Muslim faith, he never really took it seriously. Nevertheless, he firmly believed in the existence of the soul. He further believed that Second Life was a venue in which people unleashed their souls.

Marla was a case in point. Her avatar, Hevvee Metall, looked exactly like her.

This is because, deep down, Marla is exactly who and what she is on the surface. Annoying as she can be, at least she's not a fake. She's just herself. Completely uninhibited.

Unlike me.

Zapher had named his avatar after Charles Millhone Rauch, the greatest Horace scholar who had ever lived. Zapher had encountered the ancient Roman poet in his college Latin classes. Horace was the one who coined the phrase "*carpe diem*" in one of his poems.

Seize the day.

Zapher found the saying very moving every time he thought of it. He had it inscribed over the entrance of the Palatine Library. He was also considering having it tattooed on his left shoulder. If Zapher ever ran across an ancient scroll containing Horace's "*carpe diem*" poem, he would buy it for himself for any amount of money.

Zapher liked to think he had the soul of an ancient poet, just like Charles Millhone Rauch did. Zapher believed that the heavy metal music he listened to all the time was very poetic. He even liked to write lyrics himself sometimes. Unfortunately, he couldn't carry a tune. Since he had no future in music, he hoped he had the soul of a poet. He supposed his avatar proved that he did.

". . . why you've come." Dr. Al-Dahadha was looking expectantly at Zapher.

Fortunately, Zapher could understand Dr. Al-Dahadha's Arabic perfectly well. Magda, being from Egypt, had never really learned Turkish, and the Inan family always spoke Egyptian Arabic in the home. Although it was not the same as Omani Arabic, it was close enough for the two to communicate.

Upon arriving at Dr. Al-Dahadha's office, Zapher had presented himself as "Abdul Hassan," a student at Cairo University interested in joining Dr. Al-Dahadha's archeological expedition to the protohistoric site known as "Bat," which lay near a palm grove in the interior of Oman. According to the advertisement Dr. Al-Dahadha posted on the web page of Qaboos University's history department, Bat formed the most complete collection of settlements and necropolises from the third millennium BCE in the world. Zapher spoke to Dr. Al-Dahadha so enthusiastically about Bat that he almost convinced himself he actually wanted to go.

SIXTEEN

It was time now to get down to business. Zapher could feel his palms sweating.

"While the expedition is the main reason for my visit," Zapher lied, "I also wanted to talk to you about the Palatine Library."

At this, Dr. Al-Dahadha choked on his coffee and had to cough violently into a napkin. He stood up. "What are you talking about?" he finally managed to say.

Zapher put out his hands, fingers outstretched, as though calming a spooked horse. "It's okay," he said. "Don't worry. I work for Roach Rauch."

"I don't know what you're talking about," Dr. Al-Dahadha spat, crossing his arms. He glanced furtively at the door, as though considering making a run for it.

Zapher didn't move. He put on the sad little smile that he used on Magda when he really needed to get his way.

"Dr. Al-Dahadha," Zapher implored, "it's okay. No one knows I'm here. It's just that there's a problem at the Palatine Library and I thought you should be warned."

Dr. Al-Dahadha glowered at him. "I know nothing about this 'Palatine Library' of which you speak."

"I know it's all supposed to be anonymous and everything," Zapher continued. "But I do all the tech support, so I was able to trace you through your account."

"Let me get this straight," Dr. Al-Dahadha said coldly. "You came all the way here from Egypt pretending to be interested in my expedition so that you could accuse me of . . . of something?"

"No, no," Zapher soothed, shaking his head. "It's the opposite. I'm trying to do you a favor. There's big trouble at the Palatine. I admire your work and I don't want you to get caught up in it."

Dr. Al-Dahadha was alarmed again. "What trouble?"

"Didn't you see? The library was bombed."

Dr. Al-Dahadha's eyes grew large. He reclaimed his chair, turned to his computer screen and opened up Second Life. His avatar, Bambi Babad, was in the prophesy tent at her amusement park. He teleported her to Roma Redux and found nothing but wreckage where the Palatine Library used to be.

The professor sucked air through his nostrils. Then he snatched his glasses off his face and rubbed his hands over his temples. The earpieces of the glasses had left indentation marks in his pudgy skin. For a moment, he seemed to forget Zapher was there. Finally, he turned back to the young man. Without his glasses on, his face looked distorted and weak.

"Who has done this?" he demanded.

"We don't know," Zapher replied.

Dr. Al-Dahadha slid his glasses back on. "So the Palatine Library is based in Cairo?"

"Yes," Zapher lied. While Zapher may never have been a very bold person, he was a good liar. He considered lying a virtue as long as it was for the greater good—or at least for his own greater good. He attributed his flair for lying to his years of experience with Second Life, which taught one how to eliminate the distinction between fantasy and reality.

Dr. Al-Dahadha leaned back in his chair and folded his arms over his belly. "What's going to happen?"

"Well," Zapher improvised, "there was a strategic planning meeting at the head office. The prevailing theory is that it was just a random hit. But a few of us are convinced it was deliberate. We're getting out while we can."

Dr. Al-Dahadha nodded. "Is there time?"

"Yes, if we act fast. The records have not yet been compromised. I've put in my two weeks' notice. I'm deleting myself from the system as soon as I return. While I was here, I thought I'd find out if you'd like to be deleted from the system."

"Will they allow that?"

Zapher shrugged grimly. "It's a huge database. By the time they figure it out, if they ever do, it will be too late to do anything about it. In my view, they have no right to keep our information under the circumstances."

Dr. Al-Dahadha nodded again, looking somewhat relieved. "Yes, I'd like to be deleted. Thank you."

"It is an honor for me to be of assistance to you."

Dr. Al-Dahadha studied Zapher. "Where did you come across my work?"

Zapher was ready for this one. "I spent a semester at Istanbul University and took a course with Dr. Umran Inan. Did you know him?"

Dr. Al-Dahadha cocked his head and looked to the upper left corner of his visual field. "I think I met him at a conference once. He writes mostly about Egyptian hieroglyphs, right?"

"Did, yes. He's deceased now."

"Oh, what a shame."

"Yes. At any rate, he was a big fan of yours and gave me your book on ancient Persian burial practices."

"Really?"

"Yes. For me, ancient history is more of a hobby, since my major is computer science. But I'm hoping to find a career that combines the two."

"The technology of archaeology is a burgeoning field. I'm sure you won't have any trouble finding work." Dr. Al-Dahadha was warming up again.

"My experience at the Palatine Library has been enormously valuable. I hate to leave, but I think staying is too much of a risk now."

"Who do you think is behind the bombing?"

Zapher shrugged. "You would know better than I."

"I would?"

"Sure. You know what's in the manuscripts. I only work the data-base. I see titles, and authors, and even photos from time to time, but they don't really mean anything to me. There must be something in the recent inventory that someone doesn't want people to read."

"Oh, really?" Dr. Al-Dahadha asked. "I was assuming the bomber was Interpol or some other policing agency."

"Oh, no. Believe me, the last thing they would do is bomb a clear-inghouse. They'd much rather infiltrate the system and make a bust. In fact, Interpol regularly tries to hack into our database."

"It does?" Dr. Al-Dahadha looked worried again.

"Sure. But the Polies are amateurs when it comes to programming. I can firewall them in my sleep." Zapher grinned conspiratorially. "The fun part is feeding them bogus data to send them in the wrong direction when they think they're making progress."

The professor scowled. "What if they let you think you're sending them in the wrong direction while they monitor transactions without you knowing?"

"It can't happen," Zapher declared, with the confidence of a lion tamer. "I always knew the real threat would come from some religious or activist group. . . ."

"You think a religious or activist group is responsible for this bombing?"

"Yes," Zapher confirmed without hesitation, taking another sip from his tiny *kahwah* cup. "I bet it wouldn't be hard for you to figure out who it was."

Dr. Al-Dahadha put the tips of his fingers together and examined them for a moment. Then he licked his lips and started riffling through the papers on his desk. He looked at his computer, then back at Zapher.

"What's wrong?" Zapher asked.

Dr. Al-Dahadha hesitated briefly. Then he made up his mind. "Abdul, do you know the software Paleofonts?"

"Of course." In fact, Zapher did not know this software. Working at the computer help desk at school, however, he learned never to admit ignorance in computer-related matters. Besides, he sensed he was getting closer to the information he needed.

"I've been using it with Persian cuneiform for nearly two years now," the professor continued. "But I can't make it work right for ancient Greek. It freezes every time I ask it to retrieve a file."

"It's probably your Linux distro," Zapher asserted, assuming his most unyielding computer geek expression. "Just reconfigure your GRUB."

Dr. Al-Dahadha nodded, visibly withering under the weight of Zapher's incomprehensible instructions. He selected a *halva* confection from the coffee tray and popped it into his mouth.

"Listen, Abdul," he finally confessed. "I need your help."

Zapher looked at his watch. "I'm afraid I really have to be going."

"Abdul, it's important," Dr. Al-Dahadha persisted. "I know who bombed the library."

"You do?"

"Absolutely. It was the Christians."

"The Christians?"

"Abdul," Dr. Al-Dahadha continued, "what I'm about to tell you is a sacred secret that must not leave this room. I'm telling you only because I need help and I now see that you have been sent by Allah himself to help me."

Zapher sat up, listening attentively. He congratulated himself for having the foresight to greet Dr. Al-Dahadha in the traditional Muslim fashion Magda had taught him. Fortunately, the professor was not a conservative Ibadi Muslim, who would never have been fooled by a *Kafir* like Zapher.

"I am ready to serve Allah with my very life," Zapher vowed.

"I can see that, young man, and I give thanks." Dr. Al-Dahadha laid both palms on his desk and looked Zapher in the eye. There was a sesame seed stuck at the corner of his mouth.

"Abdul," he began, "In a matter of days, a very important event will occur and you have a very important role to play in it."

Zapher nodded vigorously.

Dr. Al-Dahadha went on, gaining momentum. "A Persian manuscript I recently procured revealed the hidden location of five ancient Greek scrolls that prove Christianity to be a fraud. Naturally, I reported my discovery to the Omani government and we arranged to acquire the scrolls. We were only able to keep the most decisive scroll, however. Against my vigorous protestations, the other four scrolls were sold through the Palatine Library. Clearly, the Christians have bombed the Palatine Library for its treachery against their faith."

Zapher considered the professor's theory. Bombing in retaliation for religious offense seemed more like something Muslims would do. On the other hand, maybe the Christians were finally beginning to fight fire with fire. He vaguely recalled that Marla was a Christian. He would have to ask her whether she knew of any radical Christian activist groups.

Marla.

Zapher realized with a start that the message Roach left for Marla on the steps of the library had probably been incinerated in the blast.

The moment this nightmare is over, I'm going to ask Marla out in person. I'll tell her what I've really been doing at the Palatine Library, and she will understand.

Dr. Al-Dahadha cleared his throat.

"So you have the last of the five ancient Greek scrolls here?" Zapher queried.

"Yes, and I need to finish my translation for the big event. I am falling behind schedule thanks to this confounded Paleofonts program."

"What's the big event?" Zapher asked.

"My son, I have already told you more than you need to know. Time is wasting. I beg you to fix my program so I can finish my work." Dr. Al-Dahadha sprang from his chair and gestured for Zapher to come over and sit down.

"Of course." Zapher moved around the desk. "First of all, why don't you show me what it's doing wrong. . . ."

Thus began an hour of phony technical assistance during which Zapher pretended to fix the problem while instead loading a time bomb into Dr. Al-Dahadha's files. The time bomb would cause the files to self-destruct in four hours, when Zapher was long gone.

The professor was working from high-resolution digital photos of the scroll.

"Did you notice that the pixel partitioner has degraded your photos?" Zapher asked.

"It has?"

"I think so. To be sure, I would need to compare the original."

Dr. Al-Dahadha squinted at the screen, trying to see what Zapher saw. "Those letters at the bottom of the page look smudged," he agreed, "but they might be that way in the original."

"Let's have a look at the original then." Zapher stretched nonchalantly. Butterflies were flapping madly in his stomach.

Dr. Al-Dahadha waddled to a closet in the back of the room pulling a ring of keys from his pocket. First, he unlocked and opened the door to the closet. Next, he unlocked and opened the top drawer of a filing cabinet inside the closet. Standing on tiptoe to reach in, he withdrew a thin black box and unlocked it. Finally, after returning to the desk, he carefully lifted the scroll from the box.

Seize the day.

Zapher got up from his chair, picked up a ceramic paperweight, moved behind the professor, and slammed the paperweight against the back of the professor's head with all his might.

The professor's knees gave out. Zapher caught him and pulled him into the chair. Then he gently laid the scroll back in the box, stowed the box in his carry-on bag, and strolled out.

Chapter Seventeen

 Dana examined the tag on the blouse, regretting for the seventeenth time that day that she had never learned Russian.

How pathetic is it that I can't even figure out the difference between "large," "medium," and "small"?

Dana was good at languages. With reading knowledge of Latin and ancient Greek along with fluency in Italian, French, and German, she could function comfortably in most countries throughout Europe. But not Russia. Russia and the entire continent of Asia were linguistically beyond her, which is why she usually avoided traveling there. She didn't like feeling helpless and dependent.

She took her Blackberry out of her purse, looked up "medium" in Russian, and selected a blouse to try on.

Dana was at Okhotny Ryad Shopping Center in downtown Moscow. After she'd hung up with Conti the previous morning, she scooted straight to JFK Airport for the first available flight to Moscow. It ended up not leaving until six-thirty that evening. Yet, she did not go home to pack, for fear Cardinal Giuseppe Torelli would be waiting for her there. This is how it came to pass that she was still wearing the magenta suit she'd put on Monday morning. She had now slept in it twice: Monday night, slumped in her chair at the office, and Tuesday night, on a plane. She felt ready to burn it. Hence, she stopped at Okhotny Ryad on her way from the airport.

Dana had been to Moscow once before. She was hoping that, on her second visit, the city would be more accessible and inviting than it was on the first. It wasn't. Everything seemed gray, from the sky to the buildings to the people. She felt like she had landed in a sprawling metropolis of raw clay, neither hard nor soft, just unfinished, and hopelessly indeterminate.

Dana knew, however, that this impression had more to do with her mood than with the city itself. She hadn't had a decent night's sleep in days.

I need a nap.

She intended to have one just as soon as she bought a few days' worth of supplies. But shopping was taking longer than she expected. Part of it was the language barrier. The other part was that she was being too particular. It shouldn't be necessary to find matching bras and panties in her color and in silk. But it was. And Dana knew why.

If he decides to come, and if things go well . . .

Dana was only somewhat ashamed to admit that she liked married men. She wasn't as ashamed as most women would be, because she wasn't religious. The divine prohibition against adultery had absolutely no hold on her; she felt no fear of hellfire.

She wasn't even ashamed of being a "home-wrecker." In her experience, which was considerable, married men didn't make themselves available unless they were coming from an already wrecked home. Nine times out of ten, a brief, uncomplicated affair was just what they needed to repair their situation. Dana had sent several men back into the arms of their wives—sometimes with the wives knowing what had happened, sometimes not.

The way Dana saw it, evolution built men with the drive to sow wild oats from time to time. She was happy to oblige. Married men were less demanding and more grateful than single men. They were also a lot of fun.

The smidgeon of shame she felt in connection with her predilection had to do with the fact that it left her without a sustained social life. As Aristotle said, "Man is a social animal." He believed one could not live a fully human life without genuine relationships. Dana supposed that a "genuine relationship" was deep and long-lasting. Since the failure of her five-year marriage ten years ago, Dana had become an underachiever in this regard. Although she got along with just about anybody, she tended not to take it to an intimate level. Her only close friend was Gene, whom she saw a few times a month. She knew she needed more, but she didn't yet care enough to do anything about it.

Aristotle would not approve of my complacency.

Dana's "I'm on the rebound from a failed marriage" excuse had stretched pretty thin by now. She figured she still had another forty years or so to come around, however. Her goal was to be able to write a last will and testament like Aristotle's. With a tenderness truly rare in ancient literature, he had made generous provisions for his family and friends, demonstrating that he was surrounded in the end by people he loved.

Dana suspected social relations hadn't come easily for Aristotle. As a natural born genius, he was always ten steps ahead of everyone he ever met. Nevertheless, he found a way to forge meaningful bonds.

Yes, Aristotle. I know. I need to get a life. But in the meantime, it helps to have nice underwear.

Having finally found most of what she wanted, Dana bought a bowl of borscht from a vendor and sat watching the clay figures around her as she ate it. Then she slogged back to the Medea, finally stripped off her poor magenta suit, and crashed naked on one of the two twin-sized beds in her room.

Dana awoke to the sound of her telephone ringing. The clock read 18:03. She had slept for nearly three hours.

Crap!

She fumbled for the receiver.

"Hello?" she said, trying unsuccessfully to sound wide awake.

"Hello, Dana. I'm here." It was Conti. "Are you sleeping?"

"No—I mean, not anymore. I was."

"Sorry. You asked me to call."

"Yes. I'm glad you're here! Um . . . how was your flight?"

"Uneventful."

"That's good."

"When are you going to tell me what this is all about?"

"Let's have dinner. I'll meet you in the lobby in an hour."

Dana was still feeling a little groggy as she swept down the staircase in her new Russian dress. Although she hadn't been so sure when she bought it, she was beginning to really like it. It had a tiered skirt slung low on the waist and a tight-fitting bodice that laced up the front. The pattern was whimsically floral, in shades of brown, black, and dusky rose. It was velvety soft, though Dana wasn't sure exactly what it was made of since she couldn't read the damn label.

She found Conti at the bar. He was having what looked like vodka on the rocks and studying a map.

Sensing her approach, he turned to look at her. *"Ammazza,"* he approved. "You've been here less than a day, and you've already become a gypsy."

"Well, I couldn't go home for clothes," Dana shrugged. "I figure this way, if I'm overcome with the urge to pilfer a wallet or two, I'll be dressed for the part."

"Good thinking."

"Thank you for coming, Domenico," Dana added sincerely. "I promise I will make it worth your while."

"I'm going to hold you to that."

They smiled at each other.

"Are you hungry?" Dana asked.

"Yes, and I spoke to the bartender about possible restaurants." Conti held out his map, folded open to the Red Square district. "He recommends the Godunov, which is here," he pointed.

Dana examined the map. "That looks walkable," she pronounced.

"I agree. Let's go then." Conti helped Dana put her coat on. Shrugging into his own coat, he reached for her elbow and steered her out.

It was wintery cold out. The wind quickly whipped the remaining cobwebs of sleep from Dana's mind. She felt invigorated.

He came to meet me in Moscow! I'm so amazed. I wonder what he's thinking.

They walked briskly without speaking. Lamps lit the street. An earlier smattering of rain had left a shimmering sheen on surfaces. A noisy group of Russians exiting a bar crossed their path; Dana listened to their incomprehensible chatter.

"Do you know any Russian?" she finally asked.

"Not a word."

"Me neither," Dana lamented. "I was really hating it today—not understanding what anything meant."

"But that's why people travel," Conti asserted. "To be someplace completely different."

"I travel a lot for work."

"I like to travel when it's not for work," Conti said. "It gives you new perspective." As he stopped speaking, they turned a corner and arrived at Red Square.

It was truly stunning. They stood and stared for a moment before continuing through the gate. The Kremlin was all lit up, its bulbous spires making Dana feel like an ant in an exotic mushroom patch. The sheer size of the space made all of her problems seem small and insignificant. She felt happy, almost as though she were an ordinary person on vacation.

Live gypsy music escaped through the doors of the Godunov as they approached.

"They must have been expecting you," Conti quipped.

"My peoples!" Dana enthused.

The hostess showed them to a table for two. There was a heavy haze of smoke in the dark, oaken room. They were seated along the wall, a group of four Japanese men on one side and an older, Russian couple on the other.

After removing their coats and sitting down, Dana handed the wine list to Conti. "Why don't you order us a bottle?"

"*Con piacere.*"

As Conti examined the list, the waiter arrived, bidding them good evening. Conti ordered an Italian red.

When the waiter had gone, Dana asked, "Missing home already? What happened to going someplace completely different?"

"I'm not on vacation," he replied. "I'm working." He looked at her pointedly.

He's uncomfortable. He's uncomfortable because he feels like he's on a date. Is that a good thing or a bad thing?

"Okay," Dana conceded. "Let me fill you in so that you can relax." She smiled reassuringly at him. "A Russian billionaire named Mikhail Durkovsky bought the first two of the stolen scrolls."

"Just two?"

"Yes. I still don't know what happened to the fifth scroll. We know Selenka had the *Eroticus* and I had the *Symposium*. Torelli has both of those now. But I know who has two others."

Conti reached into his jacket pocket for his notebook.

"Domenico." Dana put her hand on his arm. "We may be working, but we're not going to turn this into an interrogation."

He pulled the notebook out and slapped it onto the table. They stared each other down. He looked away first. Thankfully, their wine arrived at that moment. They watched the waiter serve in silence, then spoke politely about the wine for a few minutes.

Finally, Conti said, "I'm going to need a summary of all of this for my records."

"I'll type it up for you on my laptop later and e-mail it," Dana offered.

"Fine."

He looked exhausted all of a sudden, as though they'd been fighting about this all night. Dana realized she'd accidentally tripped the "wife wire." It was the same with all married men eventually. They unconsciously transferred long-standing issues with their wives onto their new girlfriends. It didn't usually happen this fast. Once again, Dana wondered if it was a good sign or a bad sign. At any rate, she knew what to do about it.

"Even better," she announced, "I'll jot all the key points down now."

Conti looked surprised. Whatever battle she'd blundered into, he was used to losing it.

Dana wrote: *Russian billionaire Mikhail Durkovsky bought first two scrolls from Palatine Library.* She also drew a few flowers and happy faces and then showed him.

He smiled grudgingly. The wine was helping.

Dana reached for a piece of bread. "Wow! All this work is making me hungry. Let's figure out what we want to order."

The waiter returned to tell them about the specials and appetizers. Dana ordered a salmon salad; Conti ordered *studen*, a jellied pork dish served with horseradish, and a plate of calamari for them to share.

"Okay, tell me how you figured out that this Russian billionaire bought the first two scrolls," Conti said.

Dana grinned smugly. "Remember how I was alerted about the *Symposium* right after I changed the budget on my Palatine Library account to 'no upper limit'?"

Conti nodded.

"I realized that whoever was already registered for no upper limit must have gotten the first notification. And I know of only one person with no upper limit for ancient Greek manuscripts, namely, Mikhail Durkovsky. You see, library members only register for exactly what they want and exactly what they are able to pay, because the librarian charges for every notification."

Conti's expressive eyebrows shot up.

"It's a safety feature," Dana explained. "The more information is flying around willy-nilly, the greater the chance of a breach."

Conti nodded thoughtfully, pouring himself another glass of wine.

"The only reason I know Mikhail Durkovsky is registered for no upper limit on Greek manuscripts is because he is the one who introduced me to Second Life three years ago. I met him at a paleography conference."

"Paleography?"

"The study of ancient writing."

"How does a paleographer become a billionaire?"

"Oh, Mikhail's not a paleographer."

Their calamari arrived. They dug in enthusiastically.

"Mikhail made his money in Siberian oil, of course," Dana resumed. "He's just not your ordinary oil tycoon. He's a humanist, and a dilettante, and a womanizer, and, well . . . a lot of other things."

"A womanizer, huh?"

Dana paused and wrote *WOMANIZER!* in block letters in Conti's notebook. She underlined it and made an arrow to where she had written Mikhail's name.

"And he collects ancient Greek artifacts," Dana finished. "As I recall, his mother is Greek."

"Sounds like maybe you womanized him."

"I just e-mailed him and told him about the situation. He said he would sell the Institute the two scrolls if I could get—"

"Hold on," Conti interrupted. "Back up. You told him about the situation?"

"Well, not about St. Paul's sarcophagus or anything," Dana amended. "Just that the Institute wants to publish his scrolls."

"And he's just going to hand them over."

"Sure. I wouldn't even be surprised if he refused payment." Dana shrugged. "I'm a friend with a worthy cause. He's a billionaire. It's like an ordinary person giving a hundred dollars to the United Way. If he keeps the scrolls, they will rot away unseen in his private museum because he doesn't have provenance. Selling them to the Institute will be like giving them to the world, because we'll publish them."

"But you can only do that if you get provenance."

"Right."

"How are you going to get provenance?"

"Domenico, it's the same plan as before! We go to the Vatican and offer to return the scrolls in exchange for the right to study and publish them."

In his notebook, Dana wrote, *See notes from last Friday for plan*. Then she drew stars all around the sentence.

Conti was absorbed in the calamari. "Dana," he finally said, "as I recall, Friday's plan didn't work so well."

"That's only because I didn't know Torelli was the killer," Dana protested with a mouth full of calamari. She paused to swallow. "If I had known that, I'd have dared him to go ahead and call Interpol. He never would have done it, because he's in worse trouble than I am. Once Interpol starts looking into his activities for the past few weeks, he's finished." She took a swig of wine and set her glass down a little too hard.

Domenico put a hand out to calm her. "First of all, we don't know he's the killer. Second of all, even if he is the killer, he may have been very careful to cover his tracks."

"Okay, so Torelli is still somewhat of a risk," Dana conceded. "But we're not going to run into him again anyway. We're going to pick up the scrolls tomorrow and take them straight to Rome before he even knows what we're doing."

"And in Rome?"

"Well, did you contact the other cardinal you said you were going to contact?"

Conti nodded. "Cardinal Freppe."

"Great. We'll pitch our offer to him. Then he'll consult the Pope or whoever. Either they agree, or they don't get their scrolls back."

"But what if they just sic Interpol on you?"

"Then we go straight to the press."

"If you go to the press, you implicate yourself in illegal antiquities trafficking. Are you—and Durkovsky—prepared to go down for this?"

"Domenico, I'm only *posing* as a trafficker to aid in your investigation," Dana reminded him. "And I'll just keep Mikhail out of it."

"Yeah, good luck with that."

"He has the best lawyers," Dana said. "He knows the risk and is prepared to accept it for the cause." Dana waited for Conti to look her in the eye. "The only real question is whether *you* are prepared to accept the risk."

Just then, their dinners arrived, and their conversation turned to places they had traveled.

Finally, over coffee, Conti asked, "Of all the places you've been, what was your favorite?"

Dana thought for a moment. "Florence," she answered decisively.

"Really?"

"Yes." Dana laughed, remembering. "My parents rented a castle near there for the summer of their twenty-fifth anniversary. I stayed with them. I was fifteen years old. It was a dream. Everything seemed to be in Technicolor. We went to the vineyards and the olive orchards and the museums. And we had a castle all to ourselves. It was rather absurd, really. But perfect for a fifteen-year-old girl. I felt like a princess. All grand and lonely. . . ."

Conti was watching her closely. "You would make a good princess," he said in Italian.

She did a double take, unsure whether or not he was kidding. He wasn't.

Surely he knew that was an insult?

But she never found out because it was time for their argument over the bill, and then restrooms needed to be visited, and by the time they hit the street, the moment was gone.

They decided to see the sights around Red Square before heading back to the Medea. The buildings were both stately and mysterious. Dana loved the giant cannons best of all. They made her feel like one of the toy soldiers she played with as a child. She wanted to take her camera out and snap some pictures; she wanted pictures of Dana and Domenico together. But she knew that was out of the question.

They paused in the sheltered nook of a building to view the Kremlin.

"Dana," Conti said, when they'd run out of exclamations, "why did you bring me here? It would be much easier for you to accomplish your mission alone. You go to this Russian tomorrow, he gives you the scrolls, and then you fly to meet me and Cardinal Freppe in Rome." He stopped and turned her toward him.

"Well," Dana replied, "there's something I haven't told you yet, Domenico."

He waited.

"It's not going to be quite as easy as that." She bit her lip.

"Getting the scrolls?"

"Right," Dana admitted. "You see, Mikhail's wife has thrown him out of the house again. He says this time it may be for good. Anyhow, the scrolls are in his private museum at the house. But his wife is there, and she has a restraining order against him. He's actually in New Zealand right now—yacht racing or some such."

"Great." Conti cast his eyes at the sky. "So how—"

"Well, that's why you're here." Dana poked his chest to punctuate her words. "You have to go to Ivana and persuade her to hand over the scrolls."

"Oh, my god." Conti ran his hands through his hair. "Why me?"

"Because a woman on the verge of a divorce from a philandering husband is not going to hand a few million dollars' worth of ancient artifacts over to me. She'll think I'm one of the, you know—"

"Are you?"

"No. Not—I mean, not lately."

He snorted. "What makes you think she'll hand them over to me?"

"Because she's Catholic and you're with the Vatican police."

Conti took a few steps out from the nook and turned his back to her. He put his hands on his hips.

Is he angry with me?

Dana hugged herself in the nook and looked helplessly at him.

Dammit. He's angry.

She studied the cobblestones on the street, wondering what to do now.

After a few minutes, she felt his hand on her shoulder. She looked up at him. He was smiling. At that moment all she could do was crush herself against him in the biggest hug she had shared in a long time.

He laughed and rocked her back and forth a little.

"What an adventure you are," he said into her hair.

She pulled back and smiled at him. "Thank you, Domenico, for— you know—putting up with me."

"Hey, I'm not doing this for you. I'm doing it for Mikhail. We oppressed husbands have to stick together, you know."

Dana laughed, and then stopped abruptly and nodded sympathetically. She brushed a little tear from the corner of her eye.

I thought I'd lost you for a minute there.

Domenico studied Dana's face thoughtfully.

"It's cold," he said. "Let's go back to the hotel."

She nodded.

They walked briskly without talking, their heads bent against the wind. They finally entered the yellow light of the Medea lobby. There were a few people milling about.

Conti hesitated.

Dana waited.

"Would you like a nightcap at the bar?" he asked.

She glanced toward the bar and then back at him.

"Why don't we have a nightcap in my room?" she countered, with a winning smile.

Without another word, he took her hand and led her to the elevator, where they joined another couple waiting. Up they went to the ninth floor, eyeing each other covertly, just like teenagers. When the doors opened, Dana slipped away and dashed down the hall, fumbling in her purse for her key. He was close on her heels, catching her around the waist before she could get the door open.

She turned around in mock outrage. "What do you—"

But then his mouth was on hers and he was pressing himself against her body. She felt her thighs melting. She closed her eyes and breathed him in. There was no more silliness.

He took the key from her hand and took charge of everything from there on. He was completely absorbed and single-minded, like a painter completing a masterpiece. He undressed her slowly, allowing her to help from time to time, never taking his eyes off of her. Then they tumbled into the bed she'd already slept in and made love.

Afterward, they lay close together on the narrow bed, Dana on her back and Conti on his side. He traced the tip of his finger along the shadows on her skin. At her neck was a leather string with a pendant attached.

"What's this?" he asked, lifting it to the moonlight.

"It's the necklace I was wearing when they found me as a child."

"What do you mean?"

"I'm an orphan," she explained. "They found me unconscious on the steps of a bookstore in Greenwich Village when I was five years old. No one knows who my parents are."

"But how is that possible? Weren't you registered somewhere?"

"No. They think I was born in someone's home. I have no memory of my parents. They think the trauma of the abandonment gave me amnesia."

"You were talking about your parents earlier."

"The owner of the bookstore, Fez McCarter, and his wife, Maxine, adopted me."

Conti nodded, examining the pendant. It was a small rectangular tray engraved with a circular design:

Dana held it up for him. "It's based on the alchemy symbols for the four elements: earth, air, fire, and water."

Conti moved his thumb over the jagged left edge of the tray. "Is it broken?"

"The hinge," Dana confirmed. "It's actually the back half of a locket."

"Ah." Conti laid it gently in the hollow of her neck. "So I guess the front half is still out there somewhere."

"Perhaps." Dana laced her fingers through his.

They were silent for a few minutes.

Then Conti spoke again. "Aren't earth, air, fire, and water Aristotle's four elements?"

"Wow," Dana exclaimed, turning her head to look at him. "What are you, some kind of closet Aristotle scholar?"

"I've been researching Aristotle ever since you told me about the *Eroticus* last week."

"Really? What have you learned?"

"Well, mostly I was looking into the connection between Aristotle and nominalism, since you said that's what the dialogue attributes to him. I was trying to figure out why it would be such a big deal if Aristotle were a nominalist."

"Nominalism has always been the pariah of the intellectual world," Dana explained. "It's not so much what nominalism says, but what it implies."

"All it says is that everything that exists in the world is an absolute individual," Conti said. "There are no real commonalities between things, only perceived similarities."

"Right," Dana said, "and that alone is enough to blow all the ideologies people hold near and dear right out of the water."

"Why is that?"

"For example, people make a big deal out of nationality—being an American or being an Italian—as though fellow countrymen have something real in common. Nominalism says the only thing they have in common is a name. Likewise for marriage. It doesn't signify any real unity. Likewise for humanity itself. We are all radical individuals. So nominalism ultimately destroys just about any religion—especially Catholicism."

"It seems like a very lonely view," Conti reflected.

"I don't know," Dana returned. "I see it as liberating. Individuals can still choose to forge connections. But it's always a choice. It's never metaphysical."

"Hmmm," Conti mused. "Do you consider yourself a nominalist?"

"Sure," she ventured. "Why not? I mean, I just can't take that metaphysical stuff seriously. It's so obviously made up to force people to act in a unified way."

"But if people didn't act in a unified way," Conti objected, "there would be sheer chaos. It would be every man for himself."

"Domenico, it already *is* every man for himself. And that wouldn't be such a bad thing if we would just admit it, and learn how to do it considerately, instead of operating under the lie of a thousand nonexistent unities."

Conti didn't respond.

"I don't believe in unity," Dana continued. "Do I seem like an especially chaotic person? Of course not."

"Umm . . ."

"Oh, come on!" she unlaced her fingers and punched his shoulder. "Okay, so I'm not an especially conventional person, but I'm not dangerous—"

"Umm . . ."

"Hey!" Dana protested. "You're the one with the killer cardinal, mister, not me." This time she shoved his shoulder, and he nearly toppled out of the bed.

When he recovered himself and they stopped laughing, he sat along the side of the bed and smoothed back her hair. "I'm going to go to my room now, princess. Just give me the Russian's address, and I'll phone you tomorrow when the job is done."

"The address is on a piece of notepaper on the top of that folder on the desk." Dana pointed without getting up.

Conti put on his boxers, walked over to the desk, and looked at the paper. "What are these codes you wrote below the address?"

"Oh, yeah," Dana recalled, suddenly yawning uncontrollably. "The first is the code to unlock the museum, and the second is the code to unlock the box in which the scrolls are displayed. Mikhail said Ivana wouldn't know the codes."

Conti nodded appreciatively, "This should actually be very helpful in convincing her to cooperate."

"Yes, just don't say anything about illegal trafficking," Dana warned. "She could use it against him in court—if it comes to that."

They went over the important details again as he got dressed. Then he tucked her in, said goodnight, and was gone.

But Dana lay awake. Talking about the plan had given her a second wind. She got up, put on her new sweat suit, and dug in her handbag for her cell phone.

She decided she'd better check her voicemail to make sure her neighbor, Diedre Hill, got her message about feeding Nicomachus while Dana was gone. There were just two messages waiting for Dana: one from Ann about the blinds for her office windows, and another from Diedre.

"Miss Dana," Diedre squealed, "I have terrible news. I got a call from your security service just before noon. They were responding to the alarm at your house. Somebody fired a gun at your back window. It must have been street kids, scared away by the alarm, because it doesn't look like anything was stolen. But Miss Dana, Nicomachus was by the window. He's dead, Miss Dana! Please call when you can and let me know what you want me to do."

Dana listened to the message again in disbelief.

"Poor Nico!" she moaned aloud, collapsing on the bed.

Street kids, my ass, she thought to herself bitterly. *This is Torelli's doing all right. Was he trying to get in through the widow, or was he just trying to send me a message?*

Since it was already after eight a.m. in New York, Dana called Diedre and made arrangements for disposal of the body and repair of the window. Then she called the police department. They said they would send her the report. There was nothing else she could do, short of going home, which of course was exactly what Torelli wanted her to do.

Dana thought of Nico, soft and silvery white. Aloof like most cats, but also quirky and playful. Her faithful companion since the divorce.

Fuck you, you evil bastard! I am going to get those scrolls and nail you to the wall.

Dana was having a hard time calming down. She pulled a book about Aristotle out of her laptop bag and tried to read. An hour later, she finally fell asleep.

Chapter Eighteen

 Freezing sensation. In my thighs.
Freezing along the inside of my thighs.
A man. A coffin.
I'm in a yard looking at a man lying in a coffin.
He has the face of a lynx. His hair and beard are silvery white.
I am watching and freezing.
I am in a yard at a funeral, looking at a dead man.
His beard and hair are silvery white.
His face and body are contorted, as if objecting to the end.
I know this man. I know him better than he knew himself.
This is the last time I will ever see him.

The time is the third year of the 114th Olympiad. The place is Chalcis, Greece. I am Herpyllis and he is Aristotle. We are both sixty-two.

We are in the yard of a country estate belonging to Aristotle's maternal uncle, not far from Athens. Dozens of friends and relatives are gathering for the funeral.

Next to me, Aristotle's niece, Hero, wails with grief. But I'm not crying anymore. I am beyond tears. I feel like all my life, I have been saying goodbye to this man.

Looking around at the multitude of mourning faces, I can still hardly believe I am Aristotle's wife. Aristotle's daughter, Pythias, and our grandson, Nicomachus, are sitting quietly nearby. They are both fourteen.

When Aristotle learned King Philip destroyed Stageira, he assumed our son Nicomachus and I were killed. This lit a fire in him that was not extinguished until Philip was dead twelve years later.

But Nicomachus and I weren't killed. We fled to Thrace, where I still had relatives, and tried to make a life for ourselves. It was not to be, however. The moment Prince Alexander succeeded Philip as king, he invaded Thrace. This time, Nicomachus didn't survive. Nor did his wife or the other relatives. Only I made it out alive, along with Nicomachus' infant son, named for him.

Aristotle nearly fainted when I showed up on his doorstep in Stageira with our grandson in my arms. Having heard Stageira had been rebuilt, I returned, hoping to find refuge with some old friends or neighbors. I never expected to find Aristotle there, suffering from a stomach illness, with his wife Pythias freshly buried and an infant daughter to take care of. Theophrastus was staying with Aristotle.

After the initial shock of the unexpected reunion, becoming a family seemed like the most natural thing in the world. I put the house in order and nursed Aristotle back to health. He and Theophrastus were able to resume their studies. Xenocrates was now running Plato's Academy, after Speusippus' disastrous stint. Aristotle and Theophrastus hatched a plan to summon Eudemus and Aristoxenus and start a school of their own—the Lyceum—in Athens.

What happiness we found at the Lyceum for twelve years, my love! But we were robbed of so much of our lives.

Suddenly, a trumpet sounds and the crowd hushes. A soldier enters the courtyard, announcing the arrival of Antipater, the great Macedonian general, whom King Alexander put in charge of all of Greece. Aristotle and Antipater have been friends for a long time. Everyone turns to look as Antipater strides through the gate in full regalia.

I feel a hand on my shoulder. It is Andromeda, an old friend of Aristotle's. She is holding Pythias' hand. We are Aristotle's girls, his three princesses, and we each have a piece of him to prove it. I have the gold ring with the linked band, Andromeda has the gold wrist cuff, and Pythias has her deceased mother's necklace, a thick, gold chain. Each is set with a piece of amber: yellow with black flecks, the eye of the lynx.

They say the lynx has such keen eyesight that it can see through walls. It was always Aristotle's dream to catch one alive to see if this is true. But he was never able to catch one alive.

Since Aristotle does not believe in the afterlife, we won't put our jewelry in the casket. He wouldn't appreciate the gesture. I almost wish he would. I can't bear to look at my ring. I fear that for the rest of my life, it will slay me whenever it catches my eye. But Andromeda says that, in time, I'll be glad to have it as a reminder. I suppose she's right.

Instead of offering our jewelry, we three women lay daffodils around the casket. Daffodils grow in barren soil, elegant symbols of death. I ordered a dozen buckets full of them because I knew Theophrastus would want plenty to fry, a delicacy for the funeral feast.

A tall, thin, balding man with large drooping eyes and a drawn face steps to a podium at the center of the yard and begins his oration.

Friends, philosophers, countrymen: lend me your ears!

I am Theophrastus of Lesbos. It is my lamentable duty to address you today at the funeral of our most noble compatriot, Aristotle.

Aristotle's father was Nicomachus, personal physician to King Amyntas of Macedonia, who was the grandfather of Alexander the

Great. Aristotle's mother was Phaestis, who was born and raised here, at the most splendid estate in all Chalcis. Due to the early deaths of his parents, Aristotle was raised in Stageira by his worthy sister Arimnestes and her eminent husband, Proxenus, who was my uncle.

In addition to being my cousin through marriage, Aristotle was my colleague, as co-founder of the Lyceum school in Athens. More than that, however, he was my best friend, the very best friend any man could ever have.

Aristotle published twenty-one illustrious dialogues and was known far and wide for his uniquely outstanding virtuosity as a teacher. There is no doubt that he could have published ten times what he did had he not devoted himself with such enthusiasm to the philosophical development of others. No one in all of Greece has more beneficially influenced the minds and hearts of the next generation than has Aristotle. Today, the world says goodbye to a truly great—yea, extraordinary—man, far too early, and under the most unfortunate circumstances.

Aristotle died of a long-standing stomach illness, an illness that was well under control until its embers were stoked and its flames fanned by the stress to which Aristotle was subjected over the past year. This stress was due entirely to Eurymedon, hierophant of Dionysus, who brought charges of impiety against Aristotle.

Could we allow the Athenian senate to try, convict, and execute Aristotle the way they tried, convicted, and executed Socrates eighty years ago? No, we could not. We sent Aristotle here to Chalcis, against his own valiant protestations, hoping that Eurymedon would take his evil elsewhere. But he did not, and with Aristotle's death, he has received his wish. In addition to receiving his wish, may Eurymedon someday soon receive what he deserves.

But I come to bury Aristotle, not his enemies.

Let it be known that I shall assume sole leadership of the Lyceum now that Aristotle is gone forever.

I have thought long and hard about our situation. As most of you know, Eurymedon points to Aristotle's recent dialogues as the cause of his offense. These dialogues contain powerful criticism of religious belief and practice. Following Aristotle's lead, I, myself, and other Lyceum members have begun engaging in similar criticism. As concerned citizens, we cannot help but want to expose a public menace. Nevertheless, the Lyceum is located in Athens, and it has become abundantly clear that we are fools to trust the Athenian people. The worship of Dionysus is already well entrenched and growing among them. It is they who give Eurymedon his power and indeed they who cheered him on when he persecuted Aristotle.

I have therefore decided to call a moratorium on all anti-religious writings and lectures. The Lyceum is committed first and foremost to the advancement of science and logic. We cannot any longer afford to jeopardize our studies by provoking public disdain.

Hear me, ladies and gentlemen, hear me well: not only will the Lyceum sponsor no more anti-religious writings or lectures, it will retract all of Aristotle's recent dialogues. This includes any work about the worship of Dionysus as well as any work propounding the doctrine that everything in the world is an absolute individual. All such works by Aristotle or any other member of the Lyceum shall be removed from circulation immediately and destroyed.

I deeply regret it has come to this, especially since I know Aristotle was inclined to oppose such reactive measures. Nevertheless, I have determined that we have no choice. The Lyceum shall not become a casualty of religious war.

Moreover, in an effort to restore its reputation, the Lyceum shall commence the most ambitious lecture compilation project ever attempted. Over the next several years, I shall supervise a system of official note taking at all the special lectures of the senior instructors. These notes shall be compiled and edited with the goal of publishing a comprehensive record of what the Lyceum is really all about. Rest assured that Aristotle's legacy as premier scientist and logician will shine brightly through the result.

And so, all regular courses and other Lyceum activities shall resume as normal as soon as possible. . . . I say "as normal" on a false note, of course, because nothing will ever be the same again without our beloved Aristotle. . . .

Theophrastus chokes up and cannot continue. Aristoxenus helps him through the crowd, and they disappear into the house.

As soon as they are out of sight, there is a raucous reaction to Theophrastus' speech. There will be resistance to his decision to suppress Aristotle's work. In the end, however, Theophrastus will have his way.

Although I am very disappointed by Theophrastus' decision, I am not surprised. He and Aristotle had argued about it. Aristotle felt that if we don't fight this religion now, it will grow into a monster; meanwhile, Theophrastus feels that fighting only feeds its growth. Aristotle finally let Theophrastus win the argument. A dying man should not ask others to carry his torch.

Now Eudemus steps up to the podium. "May I have your attention please!" he shouts several times. "I am Eudemus of Rhodes. It is my honor to read Aristotle's last will and testament."

May things turn out well. In the event that something should happen to me, however, I wish it to be known that I have made the following arrangements.

Antipater shall serve as the general executor of my estate, while Theophrastus serves as guardian of my family and trustee of all my property. Aristomedes, Timarchus, Hipparchus, and Dioteles shall be of assistance when Theophrastus is off mucking about in the marsh.

After my daughter Pythias marries Nikanor, Nikanor shall become my chief heir. If, heaven forbid, anything should happen to Pythias or Nikanor before the wedding, then any arrangements Nikanor has made in his will shall stand until my grandson Nicomachus comes of age.

I snatch a glance at Pythias. She smiles wistfully. Her betrothed, Nikanor, is one of Antipater's generals, off fighting abroad and unable to attend the funeral. She hopes for his return in two months and would like to be married then. Although I feel she is too young, I wouldn't want to interfere.

Eudemus continues reading from Aristotle's will:

I ask that my executors take good care of Herpyllis, remembering how well she has loved me. If she be inclined to take a husband, then they shall approve anyone she deems worthy. In addition to all that has already been given her, Herpyllis shall receive a talent of silver. She may keep the three maidservants if she pleases, along with her current handmaid and her handmaid's son, Pyrrhaeus. If Herpyllis would like to stay at Chalcis, then she shall have the house by the garden. If she would like to move back to Stageira, then she shall have the house of Proxenus. Whichever of these houses she elects shall be furnished with everything she and the executors see fit.

I can hardly bear to listen. I close my eyes, feeling the weight of Aristotle's devotion upon me. I hear whispering in the crowd behind me. No doubt many people are scandalized by Aristotle's lavish bequest to a former slave. I already knew about it. Aristotle and I discussed his will together, just as we discussed everything of importance.

Eudemus continues reading the will for a while. It specifies how the executors should see to the other members of the household. All of the slaves will be freed when they are ready. At last, Eudemus reaches the end:

Finally, I ask that my executors take care of the memorial statues I commissioned Gryllion to make. The statues of my adoptive father, Proxenus, of his wife, who was my sister Arimnestes, and of their son, Nicanor, should be erected in Stageira. The statue of my brother, Arimnestos, who died childless, should be erected in Chalcis. The statue of my mother, Phaestis, can be erected in Stageira or in Chalcis, whichever my executors see fit. And if they bury me in Chalcis, they should transfer the bones of Pythias from Stageira, so that they lie with mine, as she herself requested.

I also commissioned Gryllion to make a stone lynx, four cubits high, to stand guard at the city gates of Stageira. Nikanor may announce his role as my chief heir by dedicating this statue during Stageira's annual festival of Zeus and Athena. May we all aspire to the greatness enshrined in Homer's myths, and may this aspiration save us all.

Having finished reading, Eudemus steps down. Andromeda signals the flute players to begin.

The Chalcis relatives are no doubt the most surprised by the contents of the will. They would, of course, prefer to bury Aristotle here at the estate. But no one is going to want to go and dig up Pythias' bones.

And so, even in death, my love, you will have your way, but only with the utmost diplomacy and charm.

I will, of course, accompany Aristotle's body back to Stageira, the place where it all began. And I will bring my own parchment copies of Aristotle's recent dialogues. Theophrastus would never allow this, but he needn't know. The scrolls will be safe with me and with those who survive me, until the world is ready for them.

Chapter Nineteen

The next morning Conti woke at six and was in a taxi on his way across town an hour later. Dana had made an appointment with Ivana Durkovsky for him at eight.

The city was awake, and traffic was already heavy. It was an oppressively bright morning. Conti wished he hadn't forgotten to pack his sunglasses. With one hand shielding his eyes, he gazed at the stained glass windows of a church as the taxi inched by. He was feeling a strong urge to go to Mass.

Conti thought about the night before, trying to convince himself it was only a dream. After all, it may have been a dream. He'd had vivid sexual dreams many times before. Perhaps he was still dreaming now and he wasn't really in Moscow at all. He wished this were true, but he couldn't quite convince himself.

I've broken the seal, as they say. Nineteen years of marriage and I never strayed. Now this. What next?

He'd been proud of his record of fidelity, especially considering that he and Carina had been separated three times in the last five years, the third time being this month. She was staying with her sister.

There were a whole slew of supposed issues they'd been hashing out in therapy. He was completely convinced, however, that they really had only one, single, irrevocable problem: their inability to have children.

When it first began to dawn on them that they were infertile, Carina secretly resented him for it, until they went through a battery of tests that determined he was not the problem. He was relieved, thinking that, if it wasn't his fault, she would be content to carry on with him without children. But that was a miscalculation. Although she found things to do, nothing ever filled the emptiness she felt. She was just killing time, waiting for a miracle.

Carina is fundamentally and hopelessly unfulfilled. There is a lifelessness about her. Everything is a chore. I cannot make her happy.

Before he met Dana, Conti had a hard time imagining a woman without children somewhere in the picture who could be so engaged in life. Usually, children were at the center of everything for women. But not for Dana. She was so much like a man.

It's unnatural.

Conti pictured the stained glass window of the Madonna and child back at his own neighborhood church in Rome.

That is the essence of womanhood. How can you deny it? How can you deny there are common essences?

Conti had run into atheists before. His impression was always that they were in denial of the truth that was written on their hearts. They were running from the inevitable, like dogs fighting the leash.

Naturally, Conti fantasized about leaving his wife, leaving the church, leaving Rome, escaping all the binding ties at once. They were all connected. He never got very far with the fantasy, though. Who would he be without those things? It would be like peeling off the layers of an onion until there was nothing left. He couldn't picture himself in his own fantasy.

Who could stand to be so completely alone?

It's unnatural.

He thought again about going to Mass. He wanted to go to confession and then take communion. He wanted to eat the flesh and drink the blood.

I should be able to finish my business this morning in time to make it to a noon Mass somewhere.

Before long, Conti's taxi pulled up at the gate of Mikhail Durkovsky's mansion on Chernigovsky Lane in the Zamoskvorechye district. It was an enormous, seventeenth-century colonial with red brick and white pillars. Not exactly Conti's style, but impressive nonetheless.

Conti presented his identification to the guard at the guard shack and was admitted. From close up, Conti saw that the mansion was showing its age. He suspected it wasn't the most comfortable place to live. Durkovsky probably bought it more as a place to house his museum and entertain high society than as a place to live. It felt like an institution rather than a private residence. There was a caterer's truck parked near the front door.

Conti was beckoned through the front door by a waiting butler who never quite looked him in the eye. He said something to Conti in Russian that must have meant, "Follow me, please."

The atrium was covered in plush red carpet. Its high ceilings created a cavernous space dimly lit by a few long, narrow windows. Swords and other military paraphernalia hung along the stone walls.

Two women in matching black uniforms were hanging silver, bell-shaped decorations from the banister of a magnificent curving staircase that led to the second floor. A third woman, dressed elegantly in an ivory suit, emerged from one of the back rooms speaking on a cell phone and carrying a coat. Her hair was professionally hennaed and her face was artfully made up. Without giving Conti so much as a glance, she strode out the front door.

Conti stopped and looked after her. He had a sinking feeling she was Ivana Durkovsky. He wondered whether it would be too rude to go after her.

Realizing Conti had stopped, the butler doubled back and spoke the same Russian words, this time more forcefully.

"I'm sorry," Conti said to him in English. "Was that Mrs. Durkovsky?" He pointed toward the front door.

"Yes, sir," the butler answered dispassionately.

"Will she be back for my appointment?"

"Yes, sir," the butler said again, growing uncomfortable.

Conti sighed and nodded for the butler to continue on. They walked down a corridor to a door that opened onto what looked like the antechamber of an office. A beefy, middle-aged woman in a white uniform was already sitting there. She glanced at Conti and smiled primly as he sat down.

Conti glanced around for something to read. No luck. He ran through the contents of his briefcase in his mind. He needed something to help pass the time. The last thing he wanted to do was sit here with nothing but his thoughts of Dana and Carina.

He had a sudden vision of himself mounting the back staircase, finding the museum and simply letting himself in.

Would anybody notice? Would they care?

Would I go back for Dana at the Medea then, or would I just take the scrolls straight back to the Vatican myself?

Conti hadn't had a chance to consider the idea until now.

Why take the scrolls back to Dana? They are stolen property. They should be returned to their rightful owner.

On the other hand, I would never have found them without Dana's help. Surely that's worth something.

Conti didn't trust his own judgment in this matter. He suspected he may have let Dana talk him into more than he should have because he was so attracted to her.

It isn't too late to extricate myself. I could take the scrolls back to Rome and sic Interpol on her.

Although the idea held some appeal, he knew he wouldn't do it.

After all, Dana could retaliate. She could tell Carina what happened last night.

But that wasn't why he wouldn't do it.

Suppose Dana were a man. Or better yet, suppose Dana were this beefy woman sitting here in this waiting room with me. Would I take the scrolls and turn her in? Would I betray a less attractive woman?

In his years on the police force, Conti had done plenty of dirty dealing. He'd never thought twice about lying to a criminal before.

But he didn't want to do it to Dana. And it wasn't exactly because she was attractive.

It's because she likes me. And I don't want her to stop liking me. She really seems to like me.

It was such a good feeling. Conti tried to remember the last time he had felt that a woman liked him. Carina hadn't liked him in years.

And the truth is that I like Dana.

He really did. He didn't quite approve of this fact, but it was a fact nonetheless.

Dana is a friend. That's why I won't betray her. It isn't right to betray a friend, not even in the line of duty.

This last judgment, that true friendship supersedes duty, seemed right to Conti. But was Dana really a true friend?

Conti felt a trickle of sweat run down his back. He took his coat off and laid it on the chair next to him. He thought again about going to confession and unburdening his soul. He didn't know how long he could stand to sit here and wait. He knew he would feel better after Mass. Everything would be clearer.

He glanced back at the woman in the white uniform. She smiled primly again and glanced at her watch.

"Are you waiting for Mrs. Durkovsky?" he asked, pronouncing each word carefully in English.

"Yes," she answered with a heavy Russian accent.

He nodded. "Me, too. Unfortunately, I think I saw her leave when I came in."

The woman gaped at him for two beats and then exploded with a stream of Russian. At first she sat erect, chopping the air with her arms. As she wound down, she slumped in her chair.

Conti looked at his shoes, embarrassed.

"Sorry," she finally said.

"I sympathize, ma'am, I really do."

"It is only that I am up to my wits with her," the woman ranted.

"You've been waiting a long time already?"

"All day yesterday and last week too I try. I cater party here tomorrow night. Two hundred people! Nothing is decided. Last time I work for her I say, 'Never again!' But I need business, you know? Is outrage, how she treat me."

Conti nodded sympathetically.

"Already I should make zakuski." She folded her arms over her chest and shook her head morosely.

"Perhaps it won't be much longer," Conti offered lamely. He got up and reached his hand out to shake hers. "I am Domenico Conti."

She grasped his hand and shook it firmly. "I am Vera Kupre."

"If you'll excuse me, Ms. Kupre," he said, "I'm going to go find a restroom."

"Down hall this way," she instructed, waving to the left.

"Thanks."

Conti ambled down the corridor. He found the restroom. Rather than entering, he shot a glance back down the hall to be sure Vera wasn't watching, and then continued down the corridor.

When he got to the end, he found a door behind which were two staircases: one leading up to the second floor and the other leading down to the basement.

He went up.

At the top of the stairs, he opened the door a crack and peeked out into another corridor. It appeared to be empty. He ventured out, looking at each of the doors he passed for signs of the museum. They all looked the same. None had a keypad lock.

After four or five doors on each side, the corridor opened out onto the upper landing of the curving staircase he had seen from below. The maids were apparently finished decorating the banister. Conti peered over the balcony. No one was in the atrium below at the moment.

Where's that damn butler?

Conti strode purposefully across the landing to the other side of the corridor. The house was basically a long, thin, symmetrical box. Continuing on, he passed more identical doors. At the end of the corridor was a door that led to a staircase going down. He knew from seeing the house from the outside that there was a third floor as well. It did not extend quite as far as the first two floors. Where were the stairs leading to it?

Conti went back to the balcony landing. Observing from behind the wall, he saw the butler cross to the front door and open it for a man in coveralls carrying a toolbox.

I hope they're not headed for the waiting room.

The butler led the man to the wing opposite the waiting room.

As soon as their backs were to him, Conti carefully tried the double doors at the center of the landing. Behind the doors was a spiral staircase.

Hearing nothing above him, Conti climbed the stairs. There was no door at the top. Instead, he emerged into a large sunlit studio space with hardwood floors. This portion of the mansion had clearly been entirely remodeled. Straight ahead was a full bar. To his left was a glass wall, behind which lay a set of modern fitness equipment and a racquetball court. To his right was a lounge area. Beyond it, under a skylight and near a large window overlooking the back garden, stood three easels holding amateurish paintings in progress.

There were no doors along the walls. Conti was quite sure he could see the entire floor from his vantage point.

Where is this alleged museum?

Either it was behind one of the matching doors he had passed on the second floor, or it was on the first floor in the wing opposite the waiting room.

But wait. Where are the kitchen, the dining room, and the living room?

Probably in the wing opposite the waiting room.

Conti silently descended the spiral staircase. At the bottom, he took a deep breath, opened the door, and advanced toward the unseen wing without even looking to see if he had been noticed. Since no one tried to stop him, he continued down the corridor until he came to the staircase at the end. He descended slowly along the edge, where there was less give in the old boards. This time, as he reached the bottom, he heard voices and other noises on the other side of the door.

The kitchen.

Beyond that would be the dining room. In the center, the living room, or some sort of "grand hall." There would be no room on this floor for a museum.

Conti tiptoed as lightly as possible back up the creaky steps. At the top, he closed the door carefully behind him and then headed for the opposite staircase, once again not even so much as glancing down to the atrium when he passed the balcony. He reached the door to the stairs without incident, went through, and started down. Before he turned at the bend, however, he heard a door below him open.

Conti froze.

Stop? Go back? Keep going?

He decided he must have been seen crossing the balcony. He would have to keep going. When he turned at the bend, he found the butler leaning through the door, glaring up at him in disapproval.

"Ah, good," Conti said with a confused smile. "I'm looking for the restroom."

The butler scowled. He held the door to the stairwell open and pointed toward the restroom, as though sending Conti inside for a time out.

"Oh," Conti exclaimed, brushing past him. "Do you mean *this* door?"

"Yes, sir."

"How stupid of me. Thank you very much." Conti entered the restroom and locked the door behind him.

His heart was racing. He hadn't done this kind of investigatory work in years. He smiled a little to himself.

After using the toilet and mopping the sheen of sweat from his forehead, Conti returned to the waiting room. Vera was still there. She was speaking on her cell phone. When he came in and sat down, she got up and went out to the corridor, continuing her conversation as she paced back and forth.

Conti began thinking about the basement.

Can I risk it? Being caught out of place once is excusable. But twice is pushing it. I cannot afford to be thrown out. . . .

After another fifteen minutes, the door to the inner office suddenly opened and Mrs. Durkovsky appeared. Conti was startled. He hadn't heard her enter through another door. He sprang to his feet.

"Hello," she purred in English. "You must be Inspector Domenico Conti from the Vatican."

"I am," Conti responded, reaching out his hand to shake. She was slightly taller than he was, probably just over six feet. He didn't dare to check whether she was wearing high heels. "And you are Mrs. Durkovsky?"

"Yes. I am so sorry to keep you waiting." She smiled disarmingly. She was a very beautiful woman.

"It is kind of you to see me," Conti said.

"My pleasure. It is just that I am in the midst of preparing an engagement party for my daughter." She rolled her eyes. "It has been such a nightmare."

"I won't keep you long," he assured her.

"Won't you come in, then?"

She turned, drawing him into her office.

Conti hesitated. "Actually, Mrs. Durkovsky——"

She looked back inquiringly.

"Someone else is waiting to see you. It's . . . ah . . . your caterer." Conti couldn't remember the name. "I think her business is quite urgent."

"Vera?" Mrs. Durkovsky peered back out into the antechamber without seeing anyone.

"She's in the hall." Conti held up a finger indicating that Mrs. Durkovsky should wait a moment. Conti stepped into the hall. Vera was at the end, by the door to the staircase. Her back was to him, and she was still on the phone. He approached her, hovering within range of her peripheral vision to catch her attention.

She broke off mid-sentence and turned to him. "What's wrong?"

"Mrs. Durkovsky has arrived," he reported.

"Thank you!" she exclaimed, already in motion. Muttering a hasty goodbye into the phone, she disappeared through the door to the waiting room.

Conti heard the two women exchange artificially cheerful greetings in Russian, and then the door to the inner office closed. He sauntered back into the waiting room and parked himself on his chair.

He could hear nothing from behind the door.

After another half-hour, the butler appeared from the corridor.

"Mrs. Durkovsky asks me to say she is need leave now."

Conti put a hand to his temple. "When will she return?" he asked.

"Yes, sir," the butler answered, uncomprehendingly.

"No," Conti said, pointing at his watch. "When will Mrs. Durkovsky come back?"

The butler hesitated and began to look extremely uncomfortable.

Suddenly, Conti could hear the two women's voices in the atrium. He charged past the butler and hurried toward them. They were putting their coats on.

"Mrs. Durkovsky!" he called.

She turned. "Ah. Inspector. I do apologize. I must go. Can you come back tomorrow?"

Conti glanced at Vera. She frowned guiltily.

"I'm afraid I have an appointment back at the Vatican tomorrow," Conti lied. "I could come back later today. . . ."

Mrs. Durkovsky looked at her watch, gasped, and shooed Vera outside. "Okay, Inspector. Let us say five o'clock. I will be back. I promise. I do apolo—" The door slammed shut before she finished.

Conti closed his eyes and shook his head. Then he looked at his watch: 10:47. Perhaps he could make it to Mass. With unnecessary courtesy, he told the butler he would be back at five. Then he walked out the door. On the street he took out his phone to call for a taxi. Then he changed his mind.

I think I'll walk to church.

Chapter Twenty

Eight hours later, Conti was back at the bar at the Medea, sipping a vodka on the rocks. He'd earned it—not because the day had been a success, but because its lack of success was enough to fray even a Stoic's nerves.

After he left the Durkovsky mansion, he had walked for more than an hour, asking people he met along the way for the nearest Roman Catholic church. There were not many in Moscow. The people directed him to the city's cathedral. He stopped for a cabbage pie and ended up having to take a taxi the rest of the way. He didn't make it by noon, but it didn't matter because there was no noon Mass. The building was open, and the security guard did not object to his entering. There were a few other visitors lighting candles in the alcoves. Conti slumped into a pew with a good view of the stained glass windows and tried to pray.

He didn't actually pray. As he sat there, trying to pray, he realized he hadn't prayed by himself for a very long time, perhaps since he was a child. He always let the priest pray for him. When the priest prayed for him, he felt like he was praying. But today, alone in the church, he realized how different it was trying to pray by himself. He felt self-conscious, even a little silly. It never felt that way when the priest and all the people were there.

Instead of praying, he studied the stained glass windows. He found them incredibly beautiful. After about a half-hour, he walked out of the church feeling better. Something about the images, the colors, and especially the symbols reassured him.

Sitting at the bar now with his vodka, he wondered wryly whether his commitment to Catholicism really had anything to do with God. All he really needed was a sanctuary. On the one hand, it seemed that the Catholic aesthetic was alone enough to satisfy him. On the other hand, how could this aesthetic afford any satisfaction if there were no God behind it?

Conti had always been a pacific man. He wondered if his current bout of inner turmoil and bad behavior qualified as a bona fide midlife crisis.

Why not? Everyone has to have one at some point, right? Perhaps I should just sit back and enjoy it while it lasts.

The vodka was encouraging him in this direction.

Before he could give it any further thought, Dana appeared, in a brown jumper and tights. She paused, shy at first. Then, when they made eye contact, he smiled, and she bounced toward him for a hug. He didn't have time to get up from his stool. She just pressed against him and rumpled his hair.

Conti looked around, embarrassed. He unconsciously reached up to straighten his hair. Dana's eyes twinkled. She knew she was unsettling him.

"Are you hungry?" she asked.

"Yes, and I have a place on the square picked out, if you're game."

"You bet."

Off they went into a mild, moonlight night. She didn't dare reach for his hand, though she would have liked to.

Conti glanced sidelong at Dana. He had called her cell phone around eleven to cancel their lunch date and arrange to meet for dinner instead.

Over the phone, she told him about what happened to her cat and about the dream she had concerning Aristotle's funeral. Conti wasn't sure which had disturbed her more. They were somehow both part of the same thing in her mind. Evidently, she had set it aside for the time being, however, since she seemed in good spirits.

"So tell me everything," she prompted, trying to assume the right facial expression for a woman risking her career on a cockamamie scheme. "Did you speak to Mrs. Durkovsky?"

"I did. She came back as promised at five."

"What did she say?"

"No dice."

Dana looked at him, disappointed. His face was set in stone.

"No dice at all?" she queried. "Did you tell her—"

"I told her everything," Conti interrupted. "I tried every trick in the book. Once she found out I wanted to remove some property from the estate, she wouldn't even listen. Apparently Mr. Durkovsky has already tried to sneak some things out—a car and some paintings, among other things. She has a lawyer. She gave me his card and dismissed me."

"Shit," Dana sighed.

"Well," Conti mused, "now we know why your old friend Mikhail was so cooperative. He figured we might hammer a chink in her armor for him."

Dana shook her head. "That's not why. He wants to help."

"Not very helpful to send us into a brick wall."

"Come on. He clearly figured your Vatican credentials would budge her."

"Maybe."

"Well," Dana offered with new optimism, "at least we know he would approve of our next step."

"Our next step?"

"Domenico, we need to go in there and get those scrolls. We have the codes. She'll never miss them."

Conti cleared his throat and stared into the distance. "Dana, we do not have a warrant. What you're proposing would land us in a Russian prison."

"Only if we were caught, which we wouldn't be."

"Which we would be! There's a butler and a bunch of other house staff. And I couldn't find the museum anyhow."

"You snooped around?"

"A little."

"Good boy!" Dana patted Conti's shoulder. "You see? You were already thinking along the same lines as me."

"If the museum were easily accessible, your proposal might be in the realm of possibility," Conti conceded. "But it isn't. I couldn't find it. You can't steal something if you don't even know where it is."

"But where didn't you look?" Dana pressed.

"I looked everywhere."

"Domenico, you can't have looked everywhere. If you had, you would have found it. Come on. Where didn't you look?"

Conti didn't say anything, hoping she would back down. She didn't. She just kept looking at him.

Conti let his eyes follow a silver Bentley Continental passing on the street. *I feel so conflicted. Should I just see where this goes?*

"The basement," he finally admitted.

"Well, there you have it," Dana pronounced. "We need to get into that basement."

They arrived at Red Square and were distracted by a noisy street performer. Then Conti spotted the Café Bosco. They made their way in. It was completely packed. Dana gave Conti a withered look. They had no reservation, and there was already a crowd of people waiting for tables.

Conti steered Dana out. "I guess the weekend starts on Thursday in Moscow too," he remarked. "Or maybe it's the nice weather. We're not likely to get a table anywhere without a wait."

They stood for a moment, looking around the square.

"Do you like sushi?" Conti finally asked.

"I do," Dana answered. "And I am a fiend for edamame."

Conti looked around the square to get his bearings. "We passed a Japanese place on our walk yesterday. Maybe they would make us a take-out order if they're full."

"Brilliant!"

Conti's plan worked, and before long they were in his room at the Medea with a delicate, Japanese feast spread before them on the coffee table. Conti sat on the couch, leaning, dipping, and trying unsuccessfully not to drip soy sauce on his lap. Dana, sitting cross-legged on the floor, tidily popped edamame into her mouth until her lips stung with salt. They'd made cocktails for themselves from the mini bar.

"Domenico, can I ask you something?" Dana blurted.

Conti braced himself. "Sure."

"Why did you go to that church today?"

"What church?"

"The big cathedral."

He threw her a sharp look. "You followed me today?"

She nodded.

"How?"

"I rented a car from the airport when I arrived yesterday because I thought we might need it."

Conti glowered at her. "I can't believe you followed me."

"I was there in case you needed help. Not to spy."

"But you did spy."

"Only because you canceled our lunch date. I thought you might be walking out on me."

"I considered it," he admitted.

"I thought you might." She grinned. "But you didn't."

"No."

"Did you go to that church because you feel bad about what happened with us last night?"

Conti chewed his sushi carefully, swallowed, and took a drink before answering. "I just have a lot of things to sort out."

"Did it help? Going there, I mean."

"Somewhat. It was beautiful, but they didn't have Mass."

Dana cocked her head to one side. "I could see myself enjoying the architecture."

"Yeah." Conti saw the church again in his mind's eye. "I love stained glass windows."

"I wouldn't be able to sit through the Mass though," Dana mused. "I'd be just like a kid, wanting to get up and wander around."

"Have you ever been to a Mass?"

Dana frowned, thinking. "Well, I've been to Catholic weddings and to a few Protestant services. I don't think I've ever been to a proper Sunday Mass, no."

"They wouldn't let you take communion anyhow," Conti said. "You have to be Catholic."

"Bunch of snobs." Dana took a long sip of her Jack and coke.

"Yeah. Too bad for you because the Eucharist is the best part—the whole point of it, actually."

"Really?"

"Absolutely."

"Come on, those wafer thingies are for old ladies, Domenico."

Conti's brow shot up. "You clearly have no idea what those 'wafer thingies' are."

"Sure I do. They're supposed to represent the flesh and blood of Jesus Christ."

"No, no, Dana." Conti shook his head in disappointment. "That's the Protestant version. For Catholics, they *are* the flesh and blood of Jesus Christ."

"Oh, yeah." Dana smacked the palm of her hand to her forehead. "Excuse me for making your religion seem slightly less laughable than it actually is."

He winced.

I always have to go one step too far, she thought to herself, as she got up to get another cocktail.

At last, Conti broke the silence. "Dana, have you ever killed something? I mean something bigger than a mosquito."

"Well, sure. For example, there's fish in this sushi." She pointed her chopsticks toward their tray. "I eat meat all the time."

"No, that's not what I mean," Conti said. "I mean have you yourself ever *killed* something?"

"Hmm." Dana chewed thoughtfully. "Okay. When I was about eight or so I went with some of my buddies down into the sewer. We caught some salamanders, put them in a box, and kept them in the backyard. Over the next few weeks it got really cold and they died one by one. I suppose we killed them, because if they'd been in the sewer they would have survived."

"Well, that's closer," Conti granted, "but it still isn't what I mean. Most modern people have no idea what it's like to kill something or even what it's like to be present when something is killed."

"Yeah, it's called 'civilization,'" Dana sneered sarcastically. "Most humans have outgrown such primitive urges."

"It's not the killing per se I'm interested in," Conti continued, ignoring her tone. "It's what happens right afterwards."

Dana narrowed her eyes at him, wondering how she'd gotten herself into this distasteful topic of conversation.

Conti plowed on. "Being on the force, I've seen my fair share of fresh kill. Especially before I transferred to the Vatican, when I was just a rookie working inner-city Rome. First, there were the weekly murder victims. Then there was a fellow cop shot dead while covering for me and my partner during a riot. Plus, I shot and killed two criminals. One died right in front of me . . . mid-sentence. . . ."

Dana grimaced. "Domenico, I'm trying to eat here. What are you saying?"

"I'm saying that everything has a life force in it." Conti looked into the distance behind Dana. "And you can feel it coming out of them when they are killed. If they die a slow, natural death, then you don't really feel it because it's so weak by the time they die. But when something is suddenly killed, you feel it coming out. You really do."

"Life force," Dana repeated uneasily.

At the sound of her voice, he broke from his trance and suddenly seemed a little embarrassed. "That's what the Eucharist is about. That's why it has to be flesh, not just a metaphor."

Dana drummed her fingers on the coffee table. "Domenico, you are an intelligent man. Surely you see that no matter how many Latin words a guy in a gown mumbles over a wafer, he can't change it into flesh."

"You're thinking about it the wrong way around, Dana. If life force is the ultimate reality, then it is all-powerful and omnipresent. It's not so much a question of how the wafer becomes life force; it's more a question of why everything else doesn't."

That idea stopped Dana in her tracks. She felt like she was looking at the optical illusion that changes from a vase to two faces, depending on how you look at it. She gazed around the room—at the lamp, the TV, the pillows on the bed—picturing them coming to life. She shivered.

"Things lose their life force. People lose it. We're all dying. It leaks out of you. . . . " Conti lifted his hands and examined them, scowling a little.

Dana leaned her elbow on the table and put her head in her hand. "So you eat the wafers to feed your life force."

He nodded and shrugged. "It's fresh flesh."

Dana laughed. "Is that what they teach you in Sunday school?"

"Not exactly," Conti admitted. "But I didn't make it up. It's the true story behind the ritual. True Catholicism is not for the faint of heart."

Dana smiled slyly. "Domenico, you make even church sound racy."

He shrugged again.

Dana carefully peeled the label off her cocktail bottle. "I must admit, I find your explanation intriguing. Of course, if it's true, I'm in deep trouble, right? I must be just about out of life force by now."

"That's the part I don't understand. Because you're not. You're so full of life force, I'd like to rip your heart out and eat it raw——"

"Oh, my god! You didn't tell me you were into kink!"

"Actually, I would love to open you up and see what's inside—if it didn't kill you." He smiled congenially.

Dana started to laugh but then stopped, suddenly overwhelmed by a sensation of déjà vu.

Conti frowned at her. "I was just kidding."

"I know," she said. "It's just that I feel like . . . did we talk about this before?"

"Dana, I assure you that I've never talked to anyone about this before."

"Hmm . . ."

"Anyway," Conti rambled on, "you're throwing a monkey wrench in my system. That's what it comes down to. That's what makes you so . . . that's why I have such a hard time—umph."

While he spoke, Dana had gotten up from the floor and crept predatorily over to the couch. She put his plate and napkin on the table and then straddled his lap. She leaned forward until her lips were next to his ear. "I'll be you're little monkey wrench any time you want," she whispered.

He set his drink on the end table so he wouldn't spill it. "Ah, Dana?"

"Mmmmm?"

"Dana, hang on. Hold up." He grasped her shoulders and pushed her off of him. We have a problem to discuss, remember? We have no scrolls."

She leaned back against the side arm of the couch, all business again. "It's not a problem, it's just Plan B."

"Plan B?"

"That's right. Don't worry, I've got it all figured out. I'll explain it to you in the morning. We've done enough work for one day." She leaned back toward him again. Conti caught a glimpse down the front of her blouse. She began kissing his neck.

Conti opened his mouth to protest. Then he changed his mind.

They didn't say much of anything else the rest of the night. They made love on Conti's double bed. Afterward, when Dana got up to go back to her room, he asked her to stay instead. She did, and she slept the deepest, most dreamless sleep she had slept in a long time.

Chapter Twenty-One

At seven the next evening, Dana and Conti were careering through the streets of Moscow in a white minivan. They were wearing white uniforms. Dana was at the wheel; Conti was riding shotgun with a map.

"I said turn left. Take a left here!" Conti shouted.

"Okay, okay. I've got it." She turned to look at him. He was upset.

He noticed her look. "I'm sorry. I didn't think you heard me."

"Domenico, it's been a stressful day. Are you sure you don't want to stop for some coffee or something before we do this?"

"We don't have time. The guests will already be arriving by now. We need to slip in before everyone is settled or we'll be caught."

In the back of the van were two long, flat boxes containing an assortment of rolls—black rye, caraway, and sourdough. Dana and Conti were ready to penetrate the Durkovsky mansion disguised as caterers. But it had taken them longer than they expected to gather the supplies. With both of them ignorant of Russian, everything was more difficult.

First, they called around to car rental companies for a white van. They were lucky to find one without a reservation. After picking up the van, they stopped at a bakery for the bread. Next, they found a uniform store and purchased two chef's uniforms, which they hoped were close enough for caterers. Finally, back at the hotel, they convinced the concierge to teach them a few Russian phrases. Dana had originally planned to paint the logo of one of Moscow's catering companies on the side of the van, but they ran out of time. Conti said it wouldn't matter.

What really mattered, in Dana's view, was that they hadn't had time for dinner. They'd managed to find cabbage pies for lunch while they were out and about. But that was around two. Dana knew Domenico was hungry, and she knew this was not a good thing.

At the next light, she cranked on the emergency brake, slid out of the van, and circled to its rear to pop the hatch. She could hear Conti shouting her name in escalating panic from the front seat. With the hatch up, she hastily broke the tape on one of the boxes and reached in for a handful of rolls. In the corner of the box was a bag of individually wrapped pats of butter. She grabbed it, too. Before she had the hatch back down, the light changed and the cars behind her began to honk. She slammed the hatch, flew back to the driver's seat, tossed her prizes into Conti's lap, and put the car in motion.

"*Che cavolo?*" Conti demanded.

"Domenico, we have a complicated job before us, and we need fuel."

"I'm not eating this."

"Fine. Give one to me." She accelerated onto the highway.

"You're not going to eat while you're driving."

"Yes, I am. Just break it open and smear some butter on for me."

"I don't believe this!"

"We've got a good fifteen minutes to go on this highway. What do I have to do to get some food around here?"

Conti sighed. He broke open a caraway roll.

"This is my body, broken for you—" Dana intoned.

"Not funny," Conti snapped.

The roll was fresh and soft. Dana could smell it from where she sat. She herself felt too nervous to eat, and didn't really need to. But she knew that Conti did, and that if she did, he wouldn't be able to resist.

He opened the butter bag, took out a pat and smeared it onto half of the roll, but not without getting it all over his fingers. He looked around in vain for a napkin.

"Just wipe it on your uniform," Dana advised. "It will make you look more authentic."

Conti handed Dana the buttered half of the caraway roll. She bit in and moaned approvingly. Conti stared stubbornly out the window for a minute. Then he smeared butter on the remaining half of the roll and took a bite.

"In my bag in the back seat is a bottle of water," Dana mumbled through her last mouthful.

Still sullen, Conti reached for the bottle and handed it to her. She took a swig, sneaking a glance at him. He was devouring his half of the roll. She placed the bottle in the cup holder between them. He took a swig and then began buttering the black rye. When he offered her half, she declined; he took a bite. Dana smiled triumphantly.

Soon they spotted the sign for their exit. While Conti finished his roll, Dana took a slip of paper out of her pocket and began rehearsing her lines.

"Special delivery for Mrs. Durkovsky," she said in Russian. "We're caterers. My name is Svetlana Ibanov. It's an emergency." Her pronunciation was atrocious, she knew. But she hoped it wouldn't matter. There must be caterers in Moscow with heavy American accents just as there were caterers in New York with heavy Russian accents.

Conti followed their progress on the map. He was returning to himself again. He snorted at her linguistic efforts, correcting her as though he knew better.

When they arrived at the mansion, there was a line of cars waiting to enter the driveway. It looked as though the occupants of the cars were showing their invitations to the guard at the gate and then giving their keys to valets at the front door. When it was her turn to pass the guard, Dana shouted her lines at him. He peered hastily into the windows of the minivan and then pointed her toward a drive disappearing behind the right side of the mansion. Dana nodded professionally and proceeded in that direction.

Two vans and a car were already standing by the service entrance. Dana had to double park.

"It's all right," she said, "we shouldn't be here long."

Conti pulled his gun out of his coat and tucked it in the glove compartment. They clipped their cell phones to their belts. Then they got out and went to the back of the van.

Dana opened the trunk, and they each hoisted out a box full of buns. Conti knew from his earlier foray into this region of the house that they would have to pass the door to the kitchen on their way down to the basement.

There was no one in sight. Without a word, Conti charged into the service entrance. Dana took a deep breath and followed close behind.

The door to the kitchen was straight ahead. They could smell food and hear the clatter of dishes, pots, and pans.

Conti opened a door to the left and disappeared behind it.

Dana was having trouble with her box. It was flimsy, and because she had broken the tape for their impromptu snack, it wanted to sag wherever she wasn't holding it. She propped it on her hip and held it in one arm while catching the door with the other.

Behind the door it was pitch black. She hesitated. Conti reappeared, impatiently grabbing her arm to pull her in.

The bottom fell out of the box. Rolls spilled onto the floor in every direction.

Conti flashed Dana a look that could have frozen water in midstream.

Dana glanced over her shoulder in terror. There was no movement at the door to the kitchen. She dropped to her knees and began shoving rolls through the doorway.

Having set his box down, Conti bent and scooped handfuls into Dana's box, which was now torn. When he was satisfied the passageway was clear, he pulled Dana in so he could close the door.

It was very dark and very quiet. They could hear themselves panting from the sudden, unexpected effort.

They both instinctively reached for their flashlights. They were in a stairwell with one flight leading up and another down. Leaving both boxes on the floor, they plunged downward.

The stairs creaked loudly with every step. Though Dana was afraid the sound would give them away, she knew the kitchen had to be much noisier.

At the bottom of the stairs was another door. Locked.

Damn.

They examined the knob. There was no place to enter a code. Mikhail had given them one code for the door to the museum and another for the case that held the scrolls. There must be an inner electronic door. What they needed here was an old-fashioned key.

Conti wrenched the knob and slammed his shoulder against the door. Not even a budge.

What now?

Conti sank back against the door. He knew there was another identical stairwell on the other side of the building, but it was likely to be locked as well. After all, both stairwells led directly to the outside.

Conti inspected the door. There was a layer of grime on the top side of the knob, and cobwebs hung from the doorjamb above.

He pulled Dana close and spoke into her ear. "This door hasn't been used in years. There must be another staircase in the interior."

Conti reviewed his tour of the house. *Of course!*

The spiral staircase he took from the second floor to the third floor had led down to the first floor as well. Did it continue down into the basement?

It was their only option.

"There's a spiral staircase in the center of the house," Conti whispered. "It may go down to the basement. We can get to it from the second floor."

Conti led Dana up two flights to the door through which he had accessed the stairwell the day before. This time, however, it was locked tight.

Damn!

"We're going to have to go through the kitchen," Conti rasped.

Dana's eyes grew wide. She set her jaw and nodded back.

They retraced their steps to the first floor, where they'd begun. Conti hoisted his box and gave it to Dana. Leaving her ruined box on the floor, they cracked the door to the passageway and peered toward the kitchen. Conti ushered Dana through the door and closed it quietly behind them.

He gestured for Dana to wait. Putting his ear to the door, he listened intently. At last, he yanked open the door and motioned Dana through.

"*Doora!*" he shouted, shaking his fist in frustration at her.

Dana did not have much trouble feigning fear as she stumbled past him into the kitchen. Heads turned. Conti shut the door and strode in authoritatively, beckoning Dana to follow him. He headed for the door on the other side.

One of the women in white uniform looked around, puzzled. Then she called a question to them in Russian which, of course, neither of them understood.

"Ah, ah, ah," Conti responded waving his hands at the woman without breaking stride. He opened the door for Dana, and they both passed through. The woman decided not to pursue them.

Leaving the kitchen behind, they hurried down a corridor. It opened to the left into the large atrium leading to the front door. Straight ahead was the magnificent curving staircase the maids had been decorating. To the right, the corridor continued behind the staircase toward a large set of double doors, one of which stood propped open. They could hear voices and the tinkling of silverware on the other side of it.

Conti figured they had two options. *We can either try to find an entrance to the stairwell somewhere near the dining room, or we can ascend the curving staircase from the atrium and enter the stairwell where I entered it before, this time going down instead of up.*

Conti did not deliberate for long. He leaned into Dana. "We can access the spiral staircase from the second floor."

Dana nodded and they went to the left.

Before they got to the base of the curving staircase, however, they were spotted and intercepted by an old man with a moustache.

Christ! It's that same damn butler, thought Conti.

The butler seemed spryer tonight than he had the previous morning. He called to them in a stern voice and pulled a walkie-talkie off of his belt. When he reached the bottom of the stairs he questioned them in unintelligible Russian.

Conti was trying his hand-waving trick again. "Ah, ah, ah!" he shouted, as he began mounting the stairs, barely looking at the man. Dana followed meekly behind, hanging onto her box of buns as though it were a life raft.

But the trick didn't work this time. Evidently taking Conti and Dana for Germans, the butler called, "Halt!" Then he said something into his walkie-talkie. Conti froze and turned back.

"Where do you think you are going?" he asked in German. Although Dana understood him perfectly well, she hesitated to respond since she was playing subordinate to Conti.

"Don't you remember me?" Conti asked slowly, in English. "I was here yesterday. I have to deliver supplies."

The butler did not fully understand. He rapidly translated his confusion into anger. "The gathering is only on the first floor," he barked in German. He pointed toward the dining room.

Just then, the front door swung open and two security guards marched in. They were tall, young men dressed in black and armed with guns.

The butler fired a stream of Russian at them. They nodded mutely. One gestured for Conti to put his hands on his head and began to pat him down. The other took Dana's box away from her, set it on a nearby table, and opened it. His hands were dirty. Engine grease, probably. He started pawing through the box. Dana cringed as though someone were actually going to be eating those rolls.

Conti protested in English. The guards probably understood English perfectly well, but they did not let on.

Dana finally appealed to the butler in German. "Please, sir. There has been a misunderstanding. We are delivering supplies for Mrs. Durkovsky. We were told to take them upstairs."

But Dana's decision to reveal her knowledge of German was a mistake. The butler began firing questions at her. What were their names? Who did they work for? Where were they going with the box? What were their instructions? He was clearly enjoying his chance to play gestapo. This was probably the most interesting thing that had happened to him in a long time. He demanded to see some identification.

Just then, however, a short woman in a white uniform appeared from the direction of the kitchen. She stood with her arms folded over her ample bosom. Her small, dark eyes darted from one figure to another, assessing the scene before her.

Conti saw his chance. "Thank god, Vera!" he called out. "Please tell these gentlemen who I am."

Vera Kupre looked irritated. "I don't understand. What is the problem?"

"My assistant and I are here to set up Mrs. Durkovsky's studio for tomorrow morning—the easels and canvases and so forth. All this should have been done yesterday, of course, but, as you may remember, I did not have the opportunity to meet with Mrs. Durkovsky when I was supposed to. . . . "

"Ah," Vera remembered, throwing down her arms as though she were dumping a load of firewood on the floor. Then she began bellowing at the butler and the guards in Russian. An argument ensued. In the end, Vera conceded to compromise.

"Okay," she said, turning to Conti. "This is how it must be. You go up with this one guy here." She indicated the guard with the dirty hands. "He's good guy," she said, smacking him on the shoulder. "It will be good. Is good?"

Conti nodded gratefully and shook her hand. Dana went to retrieve her box. Vera eyed the box suspiciously as Dana passed, but made no move to inspect it. Dana, Conti, and the guard trailed up the curved staircase, through the door on the landing, and up the spiral staircase within.

Conti led the way to the studio on the right. Scanning quickly, he located a supply cabinet.

"Okay, Ms. Weber, you know the drill," Conti said to Dana, rolling up his sleeves. "I need you to clear some space over there for mixing the paints. These easel configurations are all wrong. Your box goes right here on the counter." He smacked the counter with confidence. Then he opened the cabinet and pulled out various old, paint-stained trays.

"Oi!" he exclaimed. "These trays are unacceptable. Did you bring the turpentine?"

Dana shook her head, looking stricken.

"Oi!" he exclaimed again. "Okay, you're going to have to go fetch some turpentine at the shopping center." He glanced at his watch. "If you hurry, you should be able to make it before they close. Buy the gallon jug. We're going to need it."

Dana nodded and turned for the stairs. Conti glanced at the guard. He had clearly followed their conversation. Still, he looked torn for a moment. Should he stay and make sure the Italian man didn't steal anything, or should he escort the German woman out? Dana was through the door and flying down the stairs before he could decide.

"She will be back," Conti explained in loud, slow English.

The guard nodded uneasily.

Fifty-five minutes later, Dana returned empty-handed. Conti was working industriously on a broken easel he'd pulled out of the cabinet. He had been careful to undo everything he did as he went along so that Mrs. Durkovsky would not notice the intrusion—if she ever even came up here anymore. Judging by the decrepitude of the supplies, he suspected she didn't. Perhaps painting was a phase her daughter went through at some point in the past.

Conti looked up in relief when he heard Dana approach. The guard was already eyeing her.

Dana shrugged helplessly under their gaze. "I could not find any at all," she said in English with a German accent.

Conti smacked the table in front of him angrily.

Dana winced. "The store we need was already shut!"

Conti got up and looked around the studio. "Well, I have everything ready except those filthy trays and this broken easel. We're simply going to have to come back in the morning."

"Oh, no!" Dana complained.

Conti ignored her and addressed the guard. "We must go now."

The guard nodded and got up from the couch he'd been lounging on. He almost looked sorry to leave the studio. It was probably better to be stationed here by himself than outside in the cold with his obnoxious partner.

Conti put the easel back in the closet, and the trio trooped downstairs. The only remaining sign of their intrusion was the box of buns. Conti wondered whether they would be discovered before they moldered.

When they emerged from the door on the landing at the top of the curved staircase, they caught sight of a small group of people by the front door downstairs. Ivana Durkovsky was among them. She was bidding farewell to some early-departing guests.

Conti stopped in his tracks. Mrs. Durkovsky glanced up, midsentence, to see who was coming down the stairs.

"Forgot something!" Conti gasped, abruptly turning around and heading back through the door. *Did she see me? Is it too late?*

Dana and the guard followed him back up. The guard was becoming impatient now. Conti stalled for as long as he could, looking for an imaginary sheet of paper on which he had supposedly written the measurements for the broken easel. But the guard had already initiated radio contact with his partner. Before long, he hurried them out without their measurements.

Ivana Durkovsky did not come upstairs to investigate, and she was no longer in the atrium when they arrived once again on the landing. They made their way down to the atrium and around to the corridor unmolested. Carts stacked with dirty dishes were parked along the wall now. Two servers rushed past them with coffeepots in each hand.

Dana, Conti, and the guard passed through to the kitchen. Vera Kupre was deep in conversation with two of her assistants on the far side. She did not notice their departure.

The guard watched them climb into the van. Without a word to Dana, Conti took the wheel, carefully backing out of their tight parking space. The guard at the gate scarcely looked up as they passed, having been informed by radio that a white van would be leaving.

Conti and Dana did not speak until they were out of sight of the mansion.

"Please tell me you got them," Conti murmured.

Like an overfilled helium balloon that was released before it could be tied, Dana broke out in an elated whoop. She unbuckled herself and dove into the back seat before Conti could stop her. Poorly hidden under the floor mat were three identical metal canisters.

Conti glanced over his shoulder. "Three? Why three?"

Dana giggled gleefully. "Oh, I might have taken another one while I was at it."

"Dana!"

"What? It's our little gift of gratitude to Mikhail. Remember, Mrs. Durkovsky is likely to win his entire museum in court."

"She won't get the whole thing."

"Still."

"What is the third scroll?"

"Marcus Aurelius's *Meditations*." Dana checked Conti's eyes in the rearview mirror to see if he recognized the name. He didn't. "It's second-century stoicism," she explained, "which is nothing but a lot of pretentious drivel to me. But the scroll looks like an original. It's Mikhail's best piece—that is, in terms of its value on the market."

Conti nodded. "Was there a lot of stuff?"

"Hell, yes." Dana revisited the museum in her mind, wishing she could have rescued more of its languishing prisoners. The collection was a lot like her own: glowing glass boxes containing all manner of ancient secrets.

Conti interrupted her reverie. "How did you get them to the van?"

"The side door we tried from the outside opened from the inside."

"Is Mrs. Durkovsky going to know you were down there?"

"I don't think so," Dana replied. "I replaced these babies with some photographs from a desk drawer. To anyone but Mikhail, they'll look like part of the exhibit." She jiggled the latch on the canister she was holding.

"Dana—don't take them out now."

"I just thought I would find the Marcus Aurelius and tag its canister with this twist-tie from the butter bag so we would know—"

Suddenly, there was a loud "Crack!" and the van jolted forward. Dana, who didn't have her seatbelt on, was thrown against the front passenger seat. Fortunately, she'd been crouching sideways on impact, or she might have been thrown between the front seats and into the windshield.

The van squealed over the median line as Conti fought to regain control of the wheel. An oncoming car veered out of the way, blaring its horn.

Dana shook herself, trying to register what was happening. She was sprawled sideways on the floor of the back seat. She had wrenched her back and bruised her elbow.

Ow . . .

"Someone's ramming us!" Conti shouted in Italian. "Fasten your seatbelt!" He punched the gas.

Dana tried to brace herself. She was puzzled by this turn of events and felt vaguely cheated. She had been so happy just moments before.

What was it that she'd been so happy about? All she knew is that she didn't like the way the van was lurching from side to side. She needed to get back into her seat.

Slowly untwisting her body, she pulled herself up off the floor. As she reached for the seatbelt, however, the van suddenly swerved, knocking her over again.

Ow . . .

From the floor Dana sat up and peered out the rear left window. A black SUV was barreling down on them, forcing them off the road.

The sight snapped Dana's brain back into place. She could see the driver as clear as could be. It was a woman.

Conti had no choice but to veer further right, off the road. The van bucked wildly as they hit the grass. Dana turned to the front windshield in horror. They were hurtling down a steep embankment toward the Moscow River.

"Domenico, stop!" Dana cried. "Stop the van!"

Conti hit the brakes. Before they came to a stop, the SUV hit them from the rear left with a bone-rattling crash. The airbags in the front seat instantly inflated. Dana was thrown forward into them. Then the van rolled upside-down, dumping Dana on the ceiling, unconscious.

Chapter Twenty-Two

Dana woke up moments later to the sound of glass shattering. Broken glass littered the ceiling of the van where she lay. And now it was coming through the window at her. Someone was breaking a back window from the outside.

Dana pulled a floor mat over her face for protection. She lay still, hoping the person would think she was dead. Was it the woman she had seen driving the car? Though she wanted to look, she didn't dare. She heard rustling and broken glass crunching.

What the hell is going on?

Oh, my god—the scrolls. She's come for the scrolls.

Dana very nearly sprang up at the thought, and probably would have, if she didn't hurt all over. Her uncooperative body afforded her time to think.

Someone who rams a van off the road is also going to have a gun.

I need to get to Domenico's gun.

Oh, my god—Domenico. Is he dead? I have to call an ambulance.

Dana looked down at her belt to see if her cell phone was still clipped to it. No such luck. She looked around a little without moving.

Who knows where it might have landed!

I can use his phone.

Straining her ears, she could no longer hear the woman in the back. She peeked out from under the floor mat. No one.

Just then Dana heard an engine start. The SUV.

She's got the scrolls, and now she's making her getaway.

Dammit! I've got to stop her.

Dana twisted around toward the front of the van. The passenger-side airbag completely obscured the glove compartment. She would never be able to get to the gun.

The SUV started rolling forward.

Suddenly, Dana saw motion from the driver's side of the van. Still pinned upside-down behind his airbag, Conti raised his right arm, aimed through the broken window, and shot at the SUV's right rear tire. The sound was deafening. He kept on shooting until the tire was shredded and the SUV lurched to a stop.

"Domenico, are you okay?" Dana croaked.

"I'm calling for help," he replied. He sounded fine, though he made no move to extricate himself from his seat. "Hello? I need to report an accident . . ."

"I'm going after her," Dana announced. She was already halfway out the window. She did not wait for his response.

The woman jumped out of the SUV and took off running toward the river. She was dressed all in black and carried two metal canisters.

Dana tested her legs, and found to her surprise that they held. She took off running after the woman.

"Stop, or I'll shoot," Dana screamed, though she had no gun. The woman didn't even look back.

Dana's adrenaline propelled her forward. She felt a searing pain in her left knee with every step. But she didn't care. She was gaining.

The woman was heading for a bridge over the river. There was no place else to go.

The occasional motorists passing on the road were apparently uninterested in the chase. Anyone who noticed the women probably took them for two joggers, one carrying two oversized water bottles.

Dana could hear her heart pounding in her ears. She had no idea what she would do when she caught the woman. She could only hope instinct would take over.

They raced onto a pedestrian sidewalk running along the side of the bridge. It was protected from the road by a concrete wall, obscuring motorists' view of them.

It's now or never.

Dana flung out her arms and grabbed a firm hold of the woman's collar. She yanked downward hard, while driving her knee into the woman's kidney.

The woman turned to the right, aiming her right elbow at Dana's face. Dana ducked and lunged forward, tackling the woman against the railing of the bridge. The canisters clattered to the sidewalk.

Dana knew that if she bent to get them, the woman would have time to go for her gun, presuming she had one.

I'm going to have to knock her out.

Up close, the woman looked astonishingly young to Dana. But she didn't look innocent. She had short, jet-black hair and a long, jagged scar down her left cheek. Her mouth curled in a cruel sneer.

Dana took a roundhouse swing at the woman's face. The woman saw it coming a mile away, blocked it with one arm, and moved in with her other for two sharp jabs into Dana's abdomen. Dana curled her body under and kicked at the woman's knee with all her might.

The woman cried out and fell back against the railing of the bridge.

Dana gasped for breath, clutching her stomach without taking her eyes off the woman, who still did not go for a gun.

She must not have one. Of course not. If she did, she would have shot me and Domenico point-blank back at the van.

Dana squatted and grabbed one of the canisters. She would clock the woman over the head with it.

The canister made a fairly good weapon. It was heavy steel, designed to protect its contents from a nuclear holocaust if necessary.

The woman had recovered her balance. With a quick glance at Dana, she knew she was out-weaponed. She faked a turn, as though she was going to try to run. Just as Dana came slamming down with the canister, she spun backward and upward, both arms raised to intercept the blow.

The collision happened in slow motion. Dana was taken completely by surprise. The woman knocked the canister out of Dana's hands. Dana heard herself screaming "Noooooooooo!" as the canister flew over the railing and down into the river.

They both watched it go in disbelief. It would be hard to say who was more devastated. The water swallowed the canister up like a tasty treat.

An instant later Dana heard a bullet ricochet off of the railing nearby. Her response was immediate and unhesitating. Though she had no time to think about it at the time, she would often think about it later, wondering what it meant.

Dana's back was to the shooter so that she was positioned between the shooter and the woman. Her immediate response was to grab the woman and swing her around so that the woman would block further shots while Dana took off across the bridge.

The questions Dana would ponder later were as follows: *Did I do this because I knew the shooter would stop shooting if the woman was in the way, or did I do it to get the woman shot? And if I did it to get the woman shot, was this the same as shooting her myself? Granted, she had just run me off the road. But it was now I who was chasing her. Perhaps my action could be construed as self-defense, executed in the attempt to retrieve stolen property. The only problem is that I'm the one who stole the property in the first place. . . .*

Dana's instinctive response was to use one enemy as a human shield against another. She liked to think she would not have done the same to an innocent woman who happened to be standing on the bridge. But the whole thing happened so fast and so thoughtlessly that it was hard to tell.

One way or the other, the strategy worked. With one hard swing, the woman stumbled toward the shooter while Dana took off across the bridge.

"Stop shooting!" the woman shrieked in Italian. "I'm hit."

The roar of the river drowned out anything else the woman might have said. Dana didn't dare look back until she made it to a concrete lamppost at the middle of the bridge. She dove behind it and peered out.

A man in a black trench coat and black hat was helping the woman into a black sedan parked in the grass. The woman was favoring her right leg.

Will he come back for me?

Dana pulled herself to standing and prepared to start running again. Just then, she heard a siren in the distance.

The man paused to look in its direction. Then he hurried around the car and slid into the driver's seat. Although Dana couldn't see him very well, she knew exactly who he was. And he was holding the silver canister that had fallen to the sidewalk.

After the car sped away and crossed to the other side of the river, Dana began shuffling back toward the van. The siren continued to grow louder and then stopped.

As she passed the spot on the bridge where the ill-fated canister had taken its dive, she searched the waves below in the vain hope of seeing it bob to the surface.

Gone! Two more scrolls slipped through my hands!

With adrenaline draining away and depression setting in, Dana hardly felt able to drag herself any further. Her injuries asserted themselves more forcefully with every movement.

But then she had a new thought that put some spring back into her step.

We lost only two of them. There is still another scroll in the van!

As she gained speed, drawing closer to the red and blue flashing lights, Dana thanked her lucky stars for the greed in her heart that had prompted her to take an extra scroll.

Which one did the woman leave behind?!

Fortunately, the police who arrived on the scene were fairly fluent in English. Conti told them he lost control of the wheel. He said he and Dana were trying to find their way back to their hotel from a cooking class. He was reaching for a road map when they hit some sort of bump. That was all he could remember.

"I bet I hit the same thing that SUV hit," Conti said, pointing to their assailant's abandoned vehicle. "Looks like it blew a tire out."

When both Conti and Dana passed the breathalyzer test, the police lost interest in their case. They did not ask about the silver canister Dana held tightly on her lap, assuming it was some kind of Thermos from the cooking class. They did not ask about Conti's gun, because he had chucked it into the woods before they arrived. They helpfully called a tow truck for the van, found Dana's cell phone, and handed Conti over to paramedics.

Conti's left wrist was broken.

Dana rode with him in an ambulance to the hospital. She was treated for a number of superficial cuts and bruises. The doctor said he thought she might have some cracked ribs. She looked like a complete wreck.

Conti, on the other hand, looked as fresh as a rose, without a visible nick on him. Nevertheless, by three in the morning, when they were finally discharged, a fat, white cast immobilized his left hand and forearm.

Dana filled Conti in on what had happened at the bridge. He did not dispute her assessment that the man and the woman were Torelli and one of his minions. They decided not to return to the Medea, in case someone was waiting for them there. Instead, they took a taxi to a nearby Radisson. Agreeing not to discuss anything further until morning, they tried to convince themselves they were home safe and crashed in a room with two queen-sized beds.

Dana's plan was to lie down until Conti fell asleep and then sneak a look at the scroll. The canister had been impounded at the hospital, and she hadn't yet had a chance to figure out which scroll it held. As soon as she hit the pillow, however, she drifted off into a blurry sleep. The four pain pills she had taken were no doubt to blame.

The next thing Dana knew, light was streaming in through the window between the curtains they had neglected to draw.

Conti was gone. So was the canister.

Dana was not terribly surprised. Over the next few minutes, as she stared at the spot on the bureau where the canister had stood, she felt a series of emotions course through her veins: disappointment, anger, sadness . . . but not so much surprise. In fact, now that she gave it some thought, it made sense. A major trauma like the one they'd just suffered was liable to send him running back to his safety zone.

Of course, you may have been planning to betray me all along, baby. But I don't think so. I think you really wanted to escape the grip of your religion. At least part of you did. I knew from the beginning I only had about a fifty-fifty chance. That's why I took photos of the scrolls before I removed them from Mikhail's museum last night. Bright light, flat surface, snap, snap, snap!

Dana patted the pocket of her baggy chef's pants where her camera still nestled. She hadn't even bothered to strip her clothes off before climbing under the covers last night.

Time for Plan C.

Dana was pensive, almost vacant, as she checked out of the Radisson. One question bothered her most: *How did Torelli find out about our raid on Mikhail's museum?*

There were three possibilities. First, Torelli could have followed Dana from New York to Moscow, summoned the woman, and then lain in wait while Dana and Conti did the dirty work for him. Second, the woman could have traced the scrolls to Mikhail through the Palatine Library and summoned Torelli to Moscow where they stumbled upon Dana and Conti doing the dirty work for them. Third, Conti could have summoned Torelli to Moscow, only to be betrayed after doing the dirty work for him.

Dana considered each possibility in turn.

The first one seemed unlikely. *If Torelli was on my tail the whole time, then who shot my cat? The disturbance at my house was reported just before noon on Tuesday, by which time I was already in the frequent flyer club at the airport trying to arrange a flight to Moscow.*

The third possibility seemed unlikely as well. *If the three of them were in cahoots the whole time, then why the demolition derby? Torelli could more easily turn on Domenico after Domenico presented the scrolls.*

The second possibility seemed the most likely. The woman had traced Mikhail's purchase through the Palatine Library and informed Torelli sometime on Tuesday afternoon. They had met in Moscow and caught on to their rival's scheme in time to take advantage of it.

But what about Domenico? Dana wondered. *What's his plan?*

Perhaps he judged that Torelli and the woman were winning this war. He could use the scroll to convince them to let him join their team.

Dana's daemon affirmed this last hypothesis as the truth before her conscious mind had time to think up a more charitable explanation. But Dana urged her conscious mind to challenge the daemon anyway.

How could Domenico go crawling back to a man who nearly got him killed? Surely he's mad as a hornet at Torelli by now.

Just then it occurred to Dana, however, that Conti might just be mad enough to try to blackmail Torelli to secure his all-important promotion to papal bodyguard.

Dana didn't know exactly what Conti would do next. It would depend, she supposed, on which scroll he'd scored.

One of Mikhail's scrolls had gone to the bottom of the Moscow River, another to Torelli, and the third to Conti. But which one was which?

In her mind, Dana saw a magician placing pennies under two of three walnut shells and sliding them around on the table until no one but he knew which shell was empty.

Who had the Marcus Aurelius? It made all the difference in the world. If Conti had it, he wouldn't be able to cut a deal with Torelli. If he had one of the Aristotles, however, he would.

No one was waiting to ambush Dana back at the Medea. She wondered whether Conti had tried to steal her laptop before he checked out. It probably wouldn't have been too hard for him to find an obliging maid to let him into her room or even to pick the lock himself.

This was one thing, however, that did not worry her. She had brought the laptop with her in her rental car when she tailed Conti to the Durkovsky mansion the day before.

Good thing I left it in the trunk!

There was no sign anyone had been in her room, but who could tell? After a quick, painful shower, Dana checked out and drove her rental car back to the airport. She had just enough time for a late breakfast at one of the airport restaurants before the flight she'd called ahead for was boarding.

Dana was going to Rome.

And I'm not going to Rome to chase after you, Inspector. I'm not even going to tell you I'm there. I'm letting go of you.

What Dana really wanted was to go someplace quiet and safe where she could recover from her injuries and examine her photos of the two lost dialogues she'd just found and then lost again.

She wanted to read them so badly she'd almost fetched her laptop from the car at the Medea. But she caught herself in time. If she'd done that, she would not have checked out, and she'd still be there now, like a sitting duck.

She not only *wanted* to read them, she *needed* to read them. She needed to build a case against Torelli before he shut her up once and for all. And she needed a safe place to do it.

Time to regroup. This war is not over yet.

Dana was going to Rome to stay with her old therapist, Dr. Gloria Wynch.

Chapter Twenty-Three

Cardinal Giuseppe Torelli was laughing. He had a rich, melodious laugh, the kind that spreads contagiously when others hear it. He glanced over his shoulder self-consciously, but there was no one around to hear him now.

Torelli sat at the desk in his cluttered study. The lamp was on, and there was an ancient manuscript spread across the blotter before him.

He had placed his magnifying glass in front of the first column of letters on the parchment. He instantly saw the name "*Nerinthus.*" It was in Greek lettering, of course, but he knew enough to decipher it. And this is what made him laugh.

"Aristotle," he shouted out loud. "You old devil!"

Torelli had already read a copy of the *Nerinthus.* The Pope's most secret library held translated copies of all five of the dialogues buried in St. Paul's sarcophagus.

This is a good one to have back.

Torelli laughed again, remembering the look on Dana McCarter's face when the other canister went over the rail into the Moscow River. It was a dead match for the look on the face of his assistant, Tomasina Ferri.

Girls, girls! It's okay. The river is as good a place for that scroll as any.

He cleared his throat, trying to control the giddy levity welling up inside him.

The young man who has not wept is a savage, and the old man who will not laugh is a fool.

Torelli found himself laughing uncontrollably rather often of late, and he liked to repeat this quote in his mind to make himself feel better about it. The quote was from the great philosopher George Santayana, of course.

Torelli communed with George more and more often as he aged, as he grew to be just like the old man he remembered.

Torelli had known George Santayana personally. In fact, he had lived with the philosopher for eight years and was George's best friend in the world when he died in 1952.

Torelli and Santayana were both residents at the Convent of the Blue Nuns on the Celian Hill in Rome. Santayana had retired there at age seventy-nine. He had no family to take care of him. And so, when he was too old to take care of himself, he went to the city he loved best and consigned himself to the care of the sisters.

Torelli had arrived in 1944 at the tender age of eight. He was a sickly child. His father was a colonel in the Italian army that invaded France in June of 1940. His mother cared for their only son as best she could by herself for four years. When she died in an air raid in 1944, young Torelli was sent to the Convent of the Blue Nuns. By the time he saw a proper doctor, he had rheumatic fever.

During his convalescence, Torelli spent a great deal of time with the slowly dying Santayana. He was a truly extraordinary man, especially to an adolescent boy with a weak heart.

They would walk, when they could, slowly, around the grounds. No one but Torelli could walk as slowly as George Santayana. George did not believe in exercise.

The need of exercise is a modern superstition, my dear boy, invented by people who eat too much and have nothing to think about.

Though George hated exercise, he loved nature, and the paths around the grounds were too uneven for a wheelchair.

It was George who first introduced Torelli to Aristotle.

How about a little reading, my dear boy, eh?

Torelli would never get very far, stumbling over the big words, before George would start expounding on his own ideas, often only tenuously connected to the text. Although the activity was an incomprehensible word game for Torelli when he was ten, by the time he was sixteen, it was an education.

Torelli leaned back in his desk chair, seeing George in his mind's eye as clearly as he saw the magnifying glass in his own hand. George had bright black eyes that crinkled around the edges when he thought of a good idea. While his craggy, aristocratic face was always supremely serene, there was extraordinary drama in his hands.

George's gnarled hands came alive when he spoke, pinching words and shuffling sentences, kneading the difficult points and pushing away inanities. Torelli was fully convinced that, if George's hands were ever tied down, the man would not be able to speak at all.

My dear boy, believe me when I tell you that Aristotle knew all the secrets of nature.

What exactly were those secrets? Torelli wished he had had enough foresight to keep a journal of his conversations with the great philosopher. As a boy, of course, he didn't even know the old geezer was a great philosopher. It wasn't until George Santayana finally expired and Torelli read the obituary articles that he realized he had been convalescing with a famous man: a man educated at Harvard with other great men, the author of philosophical treatises, poetry, and a successful novel.

George Santayana died in obscurity because his philosophy was out of fashion.

His philosophy, in Torelli's carefully considered opinion, boiled down to the thesis that there is only nature, and nature is beautiful in its savagery.

One day, when the old man and the boy were painstakingly walking the grounds, they came upon a praying mantis feeding on a baby bird. The bird quivered under the insect's squeeze. They watched the mantis position his victim with his front legs and rip into its throat with his snapping jaws.

George was transported. He was struck dumb. When the insect finally dragged the bird under the brush for more private dining, George turned around without a word and walked back to his room. He wrote furiously in his notebook for the rest of the afternoon. But then he burned the notebook in the fireplace that very night.

Torelli asked him about it later. George just smiled beatifically and said that the point of what they had been so fortunate to witness was self-evident. It was a sacred revelation. Nothing he could ever say or write would do it justice.

Beauty, as we feel it, is something indescribable; what it is or what it means can never be said.

From then on, Torelli was subconsciously on the lookout for praying mantises whenever he walked in the woods. Later, when he entered the priesthood, he came to appreciate that the insect was named for its prayer-like stance. But he never saw one again.

The nuns at the convent regularly tried to lure George back to the Church. He refused. He received no last rites in the end and specifically requested that he be buried in unconsecrated ground.

There's no such thing as spirits! Nature has no room for God or the devil.

Despite his atheism, George loved the Church. He chose, after all, to spend the last ten years of his life at a convent. His love, however, was purely aesthetic. With its rituals and parables, spires and stained glass windows, the Church had somehow successfully captured the true sense of beauty.

George was just like Aristotle. Both men were so much in love with nature and so much in love with myth that they could not bear to combine the two.

Torelli was with George when he died. His last coherent words before he fell asleep and drifted into oblivion seared a hole through Torelli's heart.

Why shouldn't things be largely absurd, futile, and transitory? They are so, and we are so, and they and we go very well together.

Even as a boy, Torelli knew it was true.

That day, the day George died, was the saddest day of Torelli's life. It was sadder than the day his mother died because he had been only eight then, too young to really comprehend. And he never knew his father, the Italian colonel, well enough to be sad when he died twenty-three years later. When George died, on the other hand, Torelli was sixteen—an introspective boy, swimming in a sea of adolescent passions.

When George died, the earth moved. Torelli knew what he had to do.

The very next day, he told the sisters he was leaving the convent to enter the Jesuit order. He was determined to find the truth underlying the poetry of Catholicism.

Torelli was an outstanding Jesuit novice. He threw himself into its rigorous studies with zeal. When he realized he was such a natural for the priesthood, he vowed to become Pope someday. Alas, he never quite made it that far.

Oh, it's still a possibility, I suppose. If the political winds were right and the opportunity presented itself, I certainly wouldn't spurn the invitation.

The papacy didn't matter much to Torelli, though, because in his own mind, he had already risen to the top of the true church: the Church of Nature.

It was George who had taught him that all of the Church's talk of spirits was symbolic, not meant to be taken literally. "God" is just a name for the life force in all living things. There is nothing bigger or more powerful than that.

The Greeks knew this truth; their knowledge of it was reflected in their cult practices. Then the Romans hijacked Greek religion, stripping it of its raw vitality, feminizing it with ethereal concepts and otherworldly metaphors, and institutionalizing Christianity.

Torelli preferred the raw form. Correction: he was devoted to the raw form, like a drone to the queen bee.

The crucifix he knelt before every morning portrayed fresh meat—a man just killed—bleeding the life right out of him. Offering himself up for the taking. The sacrificial lamb.

You have to take life in order to live. Think about it, my dear boy, it's true: you have to take life in order to live.

This was the ultimate secret of nature. It was therefore the true religion, the true meaning of salvation.

Torelli was the head of the true church because he was the head of the cult of Dionysus. And the cult of Dionysus was the interior core of Catholicism itself.

As head of this cult, Torelli would do anything necessary to protect it. Over the years, this had not been much of a challenge, since the cult was revered within the closed ranks of the Catholic hierarchy as a legacy of sacred history.

Not until St. Paul's sarcophagus was raided had the danger of exposure presented itself.

Why did Emperor Theodosius bury St. Paul's library in his sarcophagus instead of simply destroying it?

It was a great puzzle, and yet it made perfect sense.

Torelli understood it firsthand now.

It's for the same reason I cannot bring myself to destroy the scrolls I've just recaptured: because they contain the truth. Because those in the inner circle deserve to know who they are. We have a right to the record of our history, to the proof of our origin, even if that proof can never see the light of day.

Torelli felt that protecting this truth was his special purpose in life. He was born for the role. It was both an honor and a pleasure.

He glanced at the ceramic plaque over his desk on which was inscribed Santayana's famous "Animal Creed":

That there is a world.
That there is a future.
That things sought can be found.
And things seen can be eaten.

He laughed out loud again, this time with unrestrained joyfulness. He felt so lucky to be in the inner circle. To know what things meant.

But he had work to do.

Although the fiasco of St. Paul's sarcophagus was mostly taken care of, there remained three crucial tasks: to find the fifth scroll; to bring Domenico Conti back into the fold; and to eliminate the McCarter woman.

The first task was up to Tommy.

Dear girl, taking a hit for the cause yesterday!

Oh, it was just a flesh wound. It transformed her from trusted assistant into war hero. She's loving every minute of it.

And Tommy could afford a few days of rest. She already had the black market dealer pinned to the wall through some sort of Internet arrangement. This dealer would produce the fifth scroll. It was just a matter of time.

The second task, bringing Conti back into the fold, was up to the Inspector himself. After the "accident" in Moscow, he was at a psychological disadvantage for further resistance. His little rebellion had never really amounted to much anyway. Torelli preferred to regard it as deep-cover spy work. Conti would have no choice but to come back.

It would be one thing if Conti had succeeded in obtaining the scrolls. After all, he was clearly in the grip of the McCarter woman. With evidence at his disposal, he may have been foolish enough to pursue his experiment in autonomy a bit longer.

But he did not succeed in obtaining any evidence.

I have the Nerinthus, *and the other scroll is at the bottom of the Moscow River.*

Without evidence, Conti has no leverage. He will fall back under the weight of his own religious belief.

I will welcome the prodigal son with open arms.

Torelli knew Domenico Conti was a kindred spirit. He had learned all about Conti long before they had ever met.

About eleven years ago, when Torelli was just beginning his charity work with inner-city youth recreation facilities, he received a visit from Gabriella Mantini. Gabriella was a social worker at a free clinic in the worst neighborhood in Rome. She was a wreck. There had been an incident.

The evening before, Gabriella got a call from Tomasina Ferri, a thirteen-year-old girl who had been referred to the clinic by her school nurse on suspicion of domestic abuse. Gabriella had been meeting with Tommy on and off for nearly a year. They weren't making any progress.

Tommy made and kept appointments at the clinic only to receive the food stamps it offered for mental health patients who followed through with treatment programs. She wouldn't talk about herself. She wouldn't talk about anything.

Gabriella had investigated the flat where Tommy lived with her father. It was a rat-infested hellhole. The entire building would have been condemned if the corrupt and incompetent health inspectors even knew it existed. Tommy's father, Vito Ferri, was a former Marine and an alcoholic. Tommy's mother had been dead since Tommy was a baby. There was no question in Gabriella's mind that Vito was molesting Tommy sexually and had been for a very long time.

Despite her situation, Tommy was running the household. While Vito spent his monthly disability checks on booze, Tommy supported herself by babysitting and delivering newspapers. She was the smartest and bravest young lady Gabriella had ever met. Unfortunately, she was also the hardest to reach.

"Gabriella? I need your help."

Gabriella was surprised to hear Tommy's voice on the other end of the telephone line. Tommy had never called for anything but appointments, and she had recently begun missing the few appointments she made. Gabriella figured it wouldn't be long before Tommy was walking the streets at night and doing drugs—dead by fifteen, if she was lucky. But now, suddenly, Tommy was on the phone, calling for help.

"It's my father. He's going to kill me. I don't want to die."

Tommy begged Gabriella not to call the police. Tommy would meet Gabriella on the corner for a ride to the clinic where she could stay for a while.

Although she didn't like it, Gabriella did as she was asked. Just as she feared, Tommy was not at the prearranged pickup point. Gabriella waited. Then she got out of her car and used the phone at a convenience store to call the Ferris' flat. She got a busy signal; the phone was off the hook. It was five-thirty on a January night, dark and cold. She called the police and made her way into the building.

Gabriella could hear Tommy shrieking and crying before she even reached the door to the flat. Why no one else in the building could hear her, or why they failed to respond, she would never understand. Gabriella pounded on the door. Although she was breaking every rule in the official handbook of social work, she had to do something.

Vito opened the door and yanked her inside without a word. He was raging drunk. There was blood spattered on his grimy T-shirt, and he had a coat hanger in his hand.

Tommy was on the bed, bleeding to death.

Vito screamed at Gabriella to fix Tommy and started tossing her around the apartment when she didn't cooperate.

Although it seemed like an eternity, it couldn't have been more than fifteen minutes before the police started banging on the door. When Vito didn't open it, they broke it down.

The first officer who entered the room absorbed the horrific scene before him in a flash. He didn't say a word. He simply drew his gun. Vito started to say something, but before he could finish his sentence, the officer shot him straight through the heart.

That was how Tommy came to work at Cardinal Giuseppe Torelli's first inner-city youth recreation center. She was, in fact, the single most important factor in its success. And that was how Domenico Conti came to be transferred to the Vatican violent crimes unit rather than being fired. He never knew Torelli was involved behind the scenes.

Well done, Domenico Conti. Yes, indeed, you are a prime candidate for induction to the inner circle, my son. Delay no longer and come home!

Torelli's third task, eliminating the McCarter woman, would require a concerted effort on his own part. She was a slippery one, all right. But Torelli was glad she had so far escaped her fate. He wanted it to be special. One must never underestimate the importance of ritual. The most significant day of the year was just around the corner—the Feast of the Lamb. Torelli had decided that Dr. Dana McCarter would play a key role in the celebration.

To knock a thing down, especially if it is cocked at an arrogant angle, is a deep delight of the blood.

Torelli laughed. No one was more arrogant than Dr. Dana McCarter. Meddling thief. Academic fraud. Philistine unbeliever. First-class bitch.

To knock a thing down, my dear boy, to knock a thing down.

He thought about Dana's Siamese cat—the way it looked down on him so haughtily from the window. It never ceased to amaze Torelli how much people resembled their pets. He only wished he'd had the opportunity for a more personal kill. His shots, while good, were so distant, so cold. He couldn't get a whiff of the life force escaping. He'd had to depart in haste.

Because people don't understand.

Why is it so hard for people to understand the necessity of nature?

Tommy understands.

Dear girl!

Tommy reminded Torelli so much of himself as a young man. Tommy, like himself, was a bona fide ugly duckling, beginning life with the deck stacked against her.

But I will see to it that you receive your college degree, my dear girl. A degree in computer hacking, if they have that.

Torelli laughed.

Then he turned his attention back to the scroll on his desk to see if he could pick out the passages of *The Nerinthus* that had been immortalized in the New Testament.

Chapter Twenty-Four

 *THE NERINTHUS*

The Scene: The Temple of Dionysus in Athens
The Characters: NERINTHUS, High Priest of Dionysus
                 ARISTOTLE, concerned citizen

ARISTOTLE: Nerinthus, people tell me you have made a remarkable journey through life. You started out as a farmer. Then one day you came across Plato. You were so impressed that you left the farm to study at his Academy in Athens. But soon you grew dissatisfied with philosophy, and now you are a high priest of Dionysus. Is all of this true?

NERINTHUS: It is indeed, Aristotle.

ARISTOTLE: Moreover, you have found great success. The worship of Dionysus has become widespread under your leadership and is growing every day. It is an extraordinary phenomenon. There are a number of things I would like to ask you about it.

NERINTHUS: I am happy to speak with you, Aristotle, because I believe you would make an excellent priest for us. My hope is that I can help you see the light. But you must promise me one thing: that you tell no one what I tell you today.

ARISTOTLE: My good sir, I cannot promise you that, but I can promise you that I will never slander your religion.

NERINTHUS: Even the truth will be a kind of slander to the ears of those who do not understand.

ARISTOTLE: Then help us understand. What are your main beliefs?

NERINTHUS: We believe that the race of mankind is united by a single essence or spirit, and that this common nature is corrupt.

ARISTOTLE: You believe that God made us with a corrupt nature?

NERINTHUS: No, we believe that God made the first man pure, but that he sinned against God and thereby passed his sin to all of his descendents.

ARISTOTLE: Normally, if a man commits a crime, it is he alone who is punished for it.

NERINTHUS: You speak of human law, Aristotle, which is superficial. God's law treats one for all and all for one because he knows that, at the deepest level, we are all the same.

ARISTOTLE: I see. What makes you believe in this deep commonality among us?

NERINTHUS: It is evident when you look around and see that the human race is miserable. Even those who do not admit they are miserable really are. They do not understand why they are miserable because they do not understand that they share a corrupt nature.

ARISTOTLE: What are the consequences of this corruption?

NERINTHUS: The wages of sin is death.

ARISTOTLE: You mean, because the human race is jointly corrupt, it is jointly sentenced to death?

NERINTHUS: That is correct. It would be unjust for God to let those who sin against him live. But Dionysus, the son of God the father, offers the human race redemption.

ARISTOTLE: How will the human race be redeemed?

NERINTHUS: Listen, and I will tell you a secret. We shall not all die, but suddenly, in the twinkling of an eye, every one of us will be changed as the trumpet sounds! The trumpet will sound and the dead shall be raised beyond the reach of corruption, and we who are still alive shall suddenly be utterly changed. For this perishable nature of ours must be wrapped in permanence; these bodies which are mortal must be wrapped in immortality. When the perishable is lost in the permanent, the mortal lost in the immortal, this saying will come true: "Death is swallowed up in victory! O death, where is your sting? O Hades, where is your triumph?"

ARISTOTLE: Hold on, Nerinthus, you are leaving me behind! How do mortals become immortal?

NERINTHUS: By believing in Dionysus.

ARISTOTLE: What does that involve?

NERINTHUS: We baptize with water to symbolize that Dionysus washes away our sin, and then we gather regularly to eat the flesh and drink the blood of Dionysus.

ARISTOTLE: Interesting. How does that work?

NERINTHUS: After we bless the sacrifice, Dionysus comes to dwell within it. Therefore, when we consume the flesh and blood of the sacrifice, Dionysus comes to dwell within us. It is important that the flesh be consumed while it is still freshly quivering and the blood while it is still warm, before the spirit of Dionysus departs from it. We repeat the following sacred invocation:

> Close the door you uninitiated!
> The Lamb of God is nigh!
> The Lamb of God takes away the sins of the world.

Have mercy on us.
The Lamb of God takes away the sins of the world.
Grant us peace.
The Lamb of God takes away the sins of the world.
Feed our spirit.
Come Dionysus, enter our skin.
Come Dionysus, enter our bones.
Come Dionysus, enter our hearts.
Let the feast begin!

ARISTOTLE: What kind of sacrifice do you use in this ritual?

NERINTHUS: There are three different levels of sacrifice corresponding to the three official ranks within our religion. Dionysus is half human, so human sacrifice is best. Only the high priests, however, are allowed to take part in human sacrifices. For the middle ranks, we use Dionysus' sacred animal, the bull. For the vast number of non-ranking participants, we substitute the use of bread and wine.

ARISTOTLE: Why do you use bread and wine?

NERINTHUS: Because Dionysus himself instructed us to do so when he appeared to the Persian people, who call him "Mithras." According to the Persian scripture, when Mithras returned to his father in heaven, he had a last supper with his twelve disciples. After he had given thanks he broke the bread and said, "Take, eat, this is my body which is being broken for you. Do this in remembrance of me." Similarly when supper was ended, he took the cup, saying, "This cup is the new covenant in my blood. Do this, whenever you drink it, in remembrance of me." This can only mean that whenever you eat this bread or drink of this cup, you are proclaiming that the Lord has died for you, and you will do that until he comes again.

ARISTOTLE: Does Dionysus appear in different forms all around the world?

NERINTHUS: Indeed. For example, he was Osiris in Egypt and Attis in Phrygia.

ARISTOTLE: How is the resurrection of the dead achieved? No one has ever seen anything dead come back to life.

NERINTHUS: Now that is talking without using your mind! In your own experience you know that a seed does not germinate without itself "dying." When you sow a seed you do not sow the "body" that will eventually be produced. Rather, you sow the bare grain of wheat, for example, or one of the other seeds.

ARISTOTLE: So our earthly bodies are seeds?

NERINTHUS: Indeed. God gives the seed a "body" according to his laws—a different "body" to each kind of seed. Likewise, in this world, all flesh is not identical. There is a difference in the flesh of human beings, animals, fish, and birds.

ARISTOTLE: After this body dies, a new body grows from it?

NERINTHUS: Exactly. There are bodies that exist in this world, and bodies that exist in heaven. These two types of bodies are not, as it were, in competition; the splendor of an earthly body is quite a different thing from the splendor of a heavenly body. The sun, the moon, and the stars all have their own particular splendor, while among the stars themselves there are different kinds of splendor.

ARISTOTLE: So this life is really just a waiting period, until we are born again.

NERINTHUS: Yes, born again! The body is sown in corruption; it is raised beyond the reach of corruption. It is sown in dishonor; it is raised in splendor. It is sown in weakness; it is raised in power. It is sown a natural body; it is raised a spiritual body. As there is a natural body, so will there be a spiritual body.

ARISTOTLE: It seems you are saying that the evil of this life is necessary to the growth of the spiritual being, just as the dirt in the ground is necessary to the growth of a plant.

NERINTHUS: I am. That is why we Dionysians are fond of saying that all things work together for good for those who love God.

ARISTOTLE: But why do some human beings experience more evil than others?

NERINTHUS: At present we are men looking through a glass darkly, Aristotle. The time will come when we shall see reality whole and face to face! At present, all I know is a little fraction of the truth, but the time will come when I shall know it as fully as God now knows me!

ARISTOTLE: Is it your goal to spread this religion to the entire world?

NERINTHUS: Of course. One day soon it will be impossible to escape the reach of Dionysus. We will prove that every other religion is either false or just another way of expressing the one true faith.

ARISTOTLE: Why, then, do you operate with such secrecy? And why are you concerned about what I might tell?

NERINTHUS: Because history has shown that, in order to succeed, religion requires an inner circle and an outer circle. The inner circle consists of special people who understand that true belief is a kind of madness. It is our responsibility to continue practicing human sacrifice and the other divinizing rituals. Meanwhile, in order to spread as far and wide as possible, we create an outer circle of ordinary worshipers. Unable to achieve our madness, they are permitted to experience divinization vicariously.

ARISTOTLE: Nerinthus, it seems to me that you are aiming for world domination.

NERINTHUS: Well, Aristotle, that would be the wrong way to put it. We are simply spreading the good news. You are correct, however, that, in the end, we will triumph over all.

ARISTOTLE: What makes you think so?

NERINTHUS: In face of all this, what is there left to say? If God is for us, who can be against us? He that did not hesitate to spare his own son but gave him up for us all—can we not trust such a God to give us, with him, everything else that we need?

Here ends *The Nerinthus.*

Chapter Twenty-Five

Dana sat back on a lounge chair and sipped from a glass of Chianti. It was sunset, and she was on the patio of Dr. Gloria Wynch's Italian villa. It was an exceedingly pleasant evening for March. By rights it was still too cold for sitting outside. But with her jacket on, tucked in a corner away from the wind, her body warming from the inside with the wine, it was heavenly.

What a treat, to watch the stars come out. I wish I had a place with a patio where I could see the stars.

Every Christmas since she'd retired five years ago, Gloria had sent Dana a card, insisting that she come for a visit. Dana had put it off, not sure whether she was comfortable making the transition from professional to personal relationship with her former therapist. Four days ago, however, when the need for a refuge in Rome arose, she finally decided to take the plunge. After all, Dana had developed friendships with former students, and it wasn't awkward at all. This shouldn't be much different—especially after five years. She'd rather be in a supportive environment right now than simply squatting in another hotel.

When she called the villa from the plane in Moscow just before take-off, however, she immediately regretted it. Beatrice Dalton answered the phone.

Dana had met Beatrice a few times over the years. Beatrice was Gloria's lifelong best friend. Although Beatrice had raised a family, her children were now long grown and scattered, and her husband was dead. Although immigrating to Italy had been Beatrice's idea, she never could have afforded it without Gloria. At her retirement party, however, Gloria tearfully avowed that she never would have had the courage to make the leap without Beatrice. They were quite a pair.

It wasn't that Dana didn't like Beatrice; on the contrary, she suspected she could develop a friendship with Beatrice much more easily than she could with Gloria. Rather, it was Beatrice's news that took the wind out of Dana's sails.

Gloria was sick. The headaches had started about two and a half years after they arrived in Italy. Less than a year later, she was diagnosed with an inoperable brain tumor on her frontal lobe. She was treated and was in remission until about four months ago. First, the headaches started again. Gloria didn't tell Beatrice, determined to die quietly without suffering through another round of treatment. But before long she was slurring her words and having trouble walking. She became belligerent and paranoid. In desperation, Beatrice slipped a sedative into Gloria's tea and brought her to a clinic. There was nothing they could do but keep her comfortable at home until the end. A visiting nurse now stopped in each day to tend to her. The doctors gave her anywhere between a day and a year to live.

Naturally, Gloria never mentioned any of this in her Christmas cards. She used a lot of herbal remedies and alternative medicines. She strongly believed she could recover and carry on as before.

Dana was ashamed to admit that her first thought upon hearing all of this from Beatrice was, *Forget it! This is the last thing I need right now.* But it was too late. She'd already called. How could she back out now? How could she explain to Beatrice that she had just survived an attempt on her life and that she was on the verge of uncovering the scandal of the century at the Vatican?

She couldn't. Her plane was about to take off. She told Beatrice she would come for dinner but that she had someplace else to stay.

Gloria wasn't even close to being able to join them for dinner. She lay in a rented hospital bed, attached to an IV, unresponsive and almost completely unrecognizable. Dana had to cover her shock at the sight of her former therapist. Beatrice had aged more than she should have as well, from the strain.

Beatrice served a lovely Italian dinner, clearly grateful for the company. The two women drank wine and talked well into the night. Dana told Beatrice she was working on a project involving some Vatican scrolls, without getting into any details.

Beatrice said Gloria still had moments of clarity from time to time and that they could try to talk to her again tomorrow morning after her first round of medications. Dana agreed to stay the night.

But Gloria was no better in the morning.

Over lunch, Beatrice convinced Dana to work on her photos at the villa instead of going to a hotel. Dana did not hold much hope that she would have any meaningful interaction with Gloria, but the villa was a quiet and peaceful place. She really had no reason to leave.

Dana had enjoyed a lot of time to herself over the last few days. This evening, Beatrice was out, taking advantage of a rare opportunity to have dinner with friends. Dana didn't mind staying with Gloria. The visiting nurse had been by to tend to Gloria's needs.

Dana felt more or less recovered from the car crash by now, and she just finished reading the *Nerinthus.*

So the cult of Dionysus is the source of the most sacred rites and symbols of the Catholic Church. Is this the secret Torelli is willing to kill for?

Dana found herself wondering again just how devastating such a revelation would be to the average Catholic.

If I were Catholic, would the Nerinthus *cause me to lose my faith?*

The *Nerinthus* was certainly more damaging than the *Eroticus*. The *Eroticus* only showed that St. Paul lifted some of Aristotle's poetry. The *Nerinthus* was probably also more damaging than the *Symposium*, which showed that Aristotle anticipated the concept of Christianity three hundred years before the birth of Jesus. Domenico was Catholic, and he hadn't seemed too shaken by the *Symposium*—even when taken together with the *Eroticus*. His religious crisis had more to do with his wife and with Cardinal Giuseppe Torelli.

And with me.

Or did it? Perhaps Domenico was more troubled by the contents of the dialogues than he let on.

What would Domenico—or Gene for that matter—say about the *Nerinthus*? It showed that, not just the poetry, not just the concept, but also the sacred rites and symbols of Christianity were stolen from pagans. Not even from Aristotle, but rather *through* Aristotle from a barbaric pagan cult.

Does that rock your world, Domenico Conti? Dana taunted, picturing him squirming.

She wondered what revelation the fourth and fifth dialogues held. Could it get worse for the believer? Did they hold incontrovertible proof against Christianity? What would such proof be?

Dana couldn't wait to dive into her next set of photos. She was having trouble, however, downloading them from her camera. Although she'd downloaded the *Nerinthus* without any trouble, her laptop stopped retrieving files about halfway through Marcus Aurelius's *Meditations*. Since she could see that the files from all three of Mikhail's scrolls were in her camera, she wasn't overly concerned. But she didn't know how to fix the problem.

I'll have to bring my equipment to a computer shop first thing in the morning.

Dana knew there was a computer shop at the mall near the villa; she'd noticed it when she'd stopped at the mall on her way from the airport to buy a nice bottle of wine for Beatrice as well as some comfortable clothes for her stay in Rome.

Dana sipped her wine, watching stars wink into existence. She looked to the northern sky, easily locating Cassiopeia. She could barely make out the outline of Cassiopeia's daughter, Andromeda, the princess in chains.

I wonder what Gene would say about the symbolism in my Aristotle dreams? I wonder what Gloria would say?

Dana could see her breath in the moonlight. Soon she realized, even through her alcohol-induced haze, that she was cold.

She got up and went in through the sliding glass door. It was 7:15. She wandered to the fridge, pulling out some hummus and celery sticks. There was a box of crackers on the counter. She stood in the kitchen, paging through an Italian magazine while she ate.

Dana was just pouring herself another glass of wine when she heard a noise coming from Gloria's bedroom.

She froze, listening. Then she grabbed the notepad with the phone numbers Beatrice had left in case of emergency and went to her purse for her cell phone. By the time Dana entered the bedroom Gloria was moaning quite loudly. She was twisted onto her side facing the wall with her fists clenched.

"Gloria, what is it?" Dana asked. "Are you all right?"

At the sound of Dana's voice, Gloria was silent. She cocked her head.

"Gloria? It's me, Dana." Dana laid a hand on the bedrail. "I'm here from New York. I don't know if you remember me saying 'hi' before . . . because you weren't feeling well. I'm in Italy on business, you know, so I thought I'd finally take you up on your invitation for a visit." Dana could see that, as she spoke, Gloria was unclenching her fists. "Beatrice is out for dinner tonight, so it's just me. Can I get you something?"

Gloria was slowly starting to twist her body so that she could face Dana. Dana wondered if she should help. She didn't really know how, and Gloria had stopped moaning, so she just pulled up a chair and sat down.

"I was hoping you might be up for a chat." Dana smiled brightly and patted Gloria's hand. "I'm so sorry you haven't been well. Are you feeling better tonight?"

Gloria seemed to hear her but was still completely engrossed in the effort of repositioning herself so that she could look at Dana.

Dana cringed inwardly at a note of condescension hanging in the air from the tone of her last question. It was so easy to slip into baby talk with sick people.

I have to watch my tone.

Gloria was a shrewd woman. In fact, it was her "cut the bullshit" philosophy that had made her such a success as a psychologist. During the '70s and '80s, the new breed of female therapists had the tendency to mother their patients to the point of undermining their progress. Not Gloria. She had made her name by putting honesty before comfort, sincerity before sweetness, and insisting that her patients do the same. If she was listening now, as she clearly seemed to be, she would not appreciate being coddled.

Dana pictured Gloria suddenly turning to her and saying, "Oh, cut the bullshit, Dana," just the way she always used to. Dana almost laughed.

"It seems you are feeling a little better, huh? Well, I wanted to tell you how much I love your villa. . . . " Dana went on for a little while, since Gloria seemed to like hearing her voice. She told her about the new job at the Institute, without, of course, getting into her recent adventures. In her Christmas card, Dana had sent Gloria a clipping from the newspaper about the anonymous benefactor.

Finally reaching the position she wanted, Gloria tried to focus on Dana's face.

"How about a pillow? Would you like another pillow so you can sit up for a while?" Dana had seen Beatrice insert and remove pillows a number of times over the past four days. She went to the closet and brought one over.

"What do you think about this one?" she asked.

Gloria seemed to try to lean forward. Dana reached around her shoulder and pulled her forward enough to wedge the pillow behind her back. It wasn't hard. The woman was skin and bones.

"There!" Dana was genuinely proud of herself. Not being a mother, and growing up as an only child, she had rarely ever had to take care of someone. Her adoptive parents were in their seventies now but still healthy, and so active that she hardly ever saw them.

Dana sat down and patted Gloria's hand again. Gloria was looking at her intently. Her eyes were bright and watery. Dana continued smiling bravely, as though they were just having an ordinary chat.

"Is there anything else I can get you? Perhaps you'd like a drink. . . ." Dana trailed off, looking around the room. She knew Beatrice gave her a drink from time to time, but she didn't have any idea how to go about it.

"Is there a special cup you like to use?"

She looked at Gloria for a clue, by now wishing she hadn't brought it up. She was in luck. Gloria was in motion again—this time, her arms. She was reaching up toward her head. She moved her mouth as if to speak, but no sound came out.

Dana leaned in attentively, trying to figure out what Gloria was up to. She was reaching for her neck. Her fingers raked weakly along her collarbone as though she had an itch all along it. Then she was fumbling with the top button of her blouse, or gown, or whatever it was.

"Is it too warm in here?" Dana asked. She herself thought it was too warm—and stuffy, too. "Maybe I could open a window or turn down the heat." She looked around the room again, wishing a thermostat would magically appear on the wall.

Dana stood up, thinking she might venture out to the hall to find a thermostat but she paused when she saw Gloria pulling heroically at her collar.

"Would you like some help unbuttoning your top?" Dana asked.

At this, Gloria stopped, dropped her hands, and looked at Dana, opening her mouth.

Dana took this for a "yes."

Dana moved in and gently unbuttoned the top two buttons of Gloria's top. She had some kind of slip on underneath.

"How far do you want it unbuttoned?" Dana asked.

Gloria reached up and made the raking motion again until her finger caught in a gold chain. Her eyes grew wide and she pulled on it. Then she brought her other hand up and pulled on the chain with both hands.

Oh, boy.

Dana was growing tired of playing nurse. Gloria clearly was not as lucid as she at first seemed. She probably had no idea who Dana was, or who she herself was for that matter. There was no point trying to have a conversation with this woman. She wasn't really Gloria anymore.

I hope the end comes soon for you.

Dana shook herself, hoping Gloria couldn't tell what she was thinking. All she wanted now was to go in the living room, have another glass of wine, and check her e-mail on her laptop.

"I bet that necklace is uncomfortable," Dana said. "How about I take it off, and then you can get some sleep."

Gloria instantly stopped pulling, looked at Dana, and opened her mouth just as before.

"Does it go over your head, or is there a clasp?" Dana asked, untangling the chain from Gloria's fingers. She pulled one side around Gloria's neck until she saw a clasp. Then she undid the clasp and pulled the necklace off of her.

There was a pendant on the chain. Dana did not see it at first because it had fallen behind Gloria's back.

Gloria moaned and lay back looking at the ceiling. Her fists started clenching again, but Dana didn't notice.

Dana was examining the pendant in disbelief. It looked just like hers. It looked like the other half of her four elements locket.

"Gloria, this looks like the other half of my locket." Dana looked from the locket to Gloria. Gloria was twisting back onto her side, facing the wall again.

"Gloria," Dana demanded, "Is this the other half of my locket?"

Dana could feel an electric flood of emotion in her veins. She grasped Gloria's arm, hoping to prevent her from turning any further.

"Gloria, why do you have the other half of my locket?"

Gloria moaned, still turning. Dana let go of her arm. She stopped moaning and reached the position she wanted. Her eyes were closed.

"Gloria, do you know who my parents are? If you know who my parents are, you have to tell me. How long have you had this pendant? How long have you known?"

Dana gripped the side rail of the bed. Gloria had shut down.

What the hell is this? What the fuck is going on?

Dana turned and stomped out of the room.

When Beatrice got home nearly two hours later, Dana was passed out on the couch, an empty bottle of Chianti on the coffee table.

"That's the spirit, hon," Beatrice rallied, "I'm ready to join you."

Dana did not stir.

Beatrice unbuttoned her coat and turned the light on in the dining room. As she set her purse on the table, she caught sight of Gloria's necklace.

Beatrice looked from the necklace to Dana. She eased her way toward the door, shut off the light, and began backing out of the room.

"I want to know *now,* Beatrice," Dana slurred. She had opened her eyes.

Beatrice jumped. "I thought you were asleep."

"Nope." Dana slowly sat up. "I'm waiting for you to get your ass in here and tell me what the fuck is going on."

Beatrice frowned. "You found the necklace."

"Found it?" Dana asked. "I wouldn't quite put it that way. It was more like she practically ripped it off her neck and threw it at me."

"Was she lucid?" Beatrice folded her arms over her chest and leaned back against the wall. Dana's state of intoxication was beginning to make her nervous.

"Fuck if I know," Dana spat. "She's probably pretending the whole thing, for all I know."

"You're drunk," Beatrice pronounced disapprovingly.

Dana put her hands to her head as if to steady herself. "Fuck!" she groaned. "I know. I'm sorry. Just . . . just come in here and sit down and tell me."

"Maybe this should wait until morn—"

"No! Goddammit, Beatrice, I have the right to know."

Beatrice cocked her ear toward the bedroom for sounds from Gloria. Then she turned back to Dana. "Keep your voice down."

"Get in here and sit down." Dana's voice was ice-cold.

"I don't owe you anything," Beatrice whispered. "This is not my problem."

Dana's hands clenched in her lap. She pressed her eyes tight shut in an effort to gain control of the raging lightning storm in her body. Then she started to cry.

Beatrice sighed and came over to the couch to sit down next to Dana. She took the quilt off the back of the couch and threw it over Dana's shoulders.

"It's all right, baby girl," Beatrice said. She pulled Dana against her considerable girth and rocked a little.

"You still cry just like you did when you were a baby."

Dana stopped crying and turned to look Beatrice in the eye. "How would you know that?" she asked pointedly.

"Dana, what I'm going to tell you is going to come as a shock—"

"Just tell me already!"

"Dana, Gloria is your birth mother."

"Oh, my fucking god." A dam broke somewhere inside Dana. She cried out and began to sob uncontrollably. Reaching for a pillow, she bent forward and buried her face in it.

The rest of the night was a bit of a blur. Beatrice told Dana the whole story. Dana sat next to her, fighting nausea and trying not to cry.

Beatrice had met Gloria in 1965, when Gloria moved into the commune in Greenwich Village where Beatrice was living. They became fast friends. It was the height of the hippie era. Beatrice was doing a lot of drugs and making psychedelic jewelry to sell on the streets. Gloria was working at a bookstore and attending classes part-time at NYU.

When Gloria got pregnant in 1967, the members of the commune were supportive. Everyone wanted to help raise the love child. With assistance from a medical student Gloria knew, they delivered the baby at the commune and never registered her.

Gloria named her daughter "Andromeda Sky." It was a truly transformative episode in the history of the commune. They thought no human being had ever been born so naturally in such an ideal environment.

Gloria never revealed who the father was because she didn't want him involved. People moved in and out of the commune. Over time, Beatrice was the only one who stuck by Gloria. They managed pretty well and loved Andromeda very much.

When Andromeda turned five, Gloria was finishing her master's degree in psychology. It was 1972. The commune was falling apart and the sun was setting on the era of free love. Gloria was keen on pursuing a PhD. Beatrice was battling a heroin addiction. Neither was prepared to homeschool Andromeda. Gloria was beginning to think her daughter would be better off in a conventional family setting. But what could she do with a child who didn't officially exist?

Gloria knew of a couple who wanted a child very much: Fez and Maxine McCarter, the owners of the bookstore where she worked. But how does one approach a couple of millionaires and say: "Would you like to adopt my daughter?"

Even more importantly, what would Gloria say to her daughter? How could she ever make little Andromeda Sky understand that she wasn't really cut out for motherhood?

Gloria thought long and hard about it, growing increasingly desperate. Finally, she hit upon a solution. Though outrageous on the surface, to someone who had lived in a netherworld of anarchy and radical idealism for years now, it seemed creative and life-affirming.

While completing her master's degree, Gloria worked as a research assistant for a world-renowned German hypnotist who held a visiting professorship at NYU. Gloria arranged for him to hypnotize Andromeda so that she would forget her entire past. During the trance, the hypnotist gave Andromeda the necklace with the back half of the locket. If, and only if, she ever fitted the locket back together again, would she remember life at the commune.

The hypnotist left Andromeda in a deep sleep. Gloria laid her on the steps of the bookshop, precisely where Fez McCarter would find her when he arrived, as he always did, at six o'clock that morning.

Amazingly, Gloria's solution worked. Of course, "the case of the abandoned bookshop girl" received a great deal of media attention for a while. But Gloria had sheared off Andromeda's long brown locks during the hypnotic trance and, because Andromeda had led such an insular life at the commune, there was little chance anyone would recognize her. Gloria told the handful of stoners who remained at the commune that Andromeda had gone to live with her father.

Gloria followed the case of the abandoned bookshop girl with care. When Andromeda was processed through child services, becoming "Dana," Gloria presented herself with her NYU credentials and volunteered to help. She claimed she was researching orphan psychology and wanted some hands-on experience. The little amnesiac took to Gloria without recognizing her. Once the McCarters adopted Dana, it was not hard for Gloria to convince them to continue sending Dana to her for therapy.

Despite occasional bouts of guilt and regret, Gloria firmly believed her solution was best for everyone. Dana adjusted well and enjoyed an enviable childhood. The McCarters finally had the daughter they had always wanted. Gloria went on to a PhD and an illustrious career. Beatrice kicked her heroin addiction, got married, and had children of her own. What more could anyone ask for?

By the end of Beatrice's story, Dana was paralyzed with conflicting emotions. She sat gaping at Beatrice, wondering if there was any way this woman could have simply made the whole thing up. It was preposterous.

Of course, Dana knew all along that, if she ever did find out the truth, it would be preposterous. It would have to be. How else but through extraordinary circumstances did a child appear in the world *ex nihilo*?

But I don't want Beatrice's story to be true. I don't want Gloria to be my mother. Gloria isn't at all like how I imagined my mother—especially not now that she's wasting away.

Dana got up without a word to Beatrice, tottered over to the dining room table, and pulled the front half of her locket off of Gloria's chain.

"I actually made that locket, Dana," Beatrice murmured.

Dana ignored her.

She moved through the kitchen to the mirror in the entranceway and fit Gloria's half of the locket into place on the half hanging from her own neck.

Dana looked at herself in the mirror with the reunited locket in place. Suddenly, images of much younger versions of Gloria and Beatrice came tumbling into her mind.

Then she fainted.

Chapter Twenty-Six

 Dana woke the next day feeling woozy and disoriented. She was in bed, but she couldn't remember how she got there. The clock on the bedside table read 12:06. She could see daylight filtering through drawn curtains.

But where am I?

Whose room is this?

Looking around, Dana spotted a familiar carry-on bag on the floor. Pulling the covers off her, she noticed she was dressed in a pair of jeans and a turtleneck.

I bought these clothes in Rome. . . .

Then she realized she was at Gloria's villa, and the events of the night before came crashing back to her. She bolted upright and reached for her necklace. The locket was intact. So, she hadn't dreamed it; Gloria was her birth mother.

Dana closed her eyes and breathed deeply.

Gloria's abandonment of me was criminal. Is there a statute of limitations on such crimes?

Dana felt a strangely detached sort of outrage, the kind of outrage people feel when they hear about a human rights violation on television. They think, *That's terrible! Somebody should do something. I should do something. . . .* But the enormity of it makes them tired, and so they soon turn their attention to something else.

Dana padded to the bathroom. As she went through the reassuring motions of using the toilet, showering, and putting on fresh clothes, just one thought pressed on her mind: Domenico.

I want to see him.

I want him back.

When Dana finally opened the bathroom door, she could hear voices in the kitchen. Beatrice was talking with the visiting nurse.

After silently gathering her coat, her purse, and her laptop bag, Dana waltzed out the front door. She waved affably as she passed the women in the kitchen to prevent Beatrice from coming after her. Before long, Beatrice would find a sticky note affixed to Dana's closed bedroom door saying, "Gone to computer shop at mall."

It felt good to breathe fresh air. The day was damp and foggy, the kind of weather most people, especially tourists, really hate. It would make all their photos of the eternal city turn out spectacularly dreary. But Dana reveled in it. Cool and comforting, it created a blanket of protection from the frenetic energy of the sun.

She walked briskly in her tennies, almost having to hold herself back from a jog. With such strong momentum propelling her away from the villa, she decided she must be suffocating there.

What am I doing bunking with a couple of crazy old ladies? While I'm out, I'll find a hotel and transfer my things tonight.

It took nearly an hour to reach the mall on foot. After leaving her laptop and camera at the computer shop, Dana ducked into a bistro for lunch. As she sat slurping spaghetti and meatballs, she considered her next step.

It's Thursday. Domenico will be at work. I will simply show up there, and when he sees me he will be glad. I will forgive him for abandoning me in Moscow, and he will come around.

I know you want to, Domenico.

I know you want me.

We have to give this thing a chance.

After she finished eating, Dana took a taxi to Vatican police head-quarters. She was informed by the receptionist, however, that Inspector Conti was out of the office. He would not be back for the rest of the day. Dana gave the receptionist her name and cell phone number, and requested that the inspector call her as soon as possible. She did not mention she was planning to be back first thing in the morning.

Then Dana walked to the nearest hotel, the Piccolo Mondo. The momentum she'd felt earlier was flagging. She would need a boost before returning to the computer shop for her equipment. She got a room at the Piccolo Mondo and headed straight to the coffee shop next door.

The Tazza Infinita was a cozy little retreat. It held a jumble of overstuffed furniture in addition to a few wooden tables and chairs. Half-read newspapers and magazines were scattered about. The patrons spoke in low voices over a subtle stream of classical music. Dana ordered a cappuccino, scooped up a copy of *La Repubblica*, and sank into the armchair facing the fireplace.

The next thing she knew, a waitress was shaking her. "*Scusilo, signora. Scusilo. Il sonno non è permesso.*"

Dana opened her eyes, disoriented for the second time that day. She apologized to the waitress for falling asleep and looked at her watch. Nearly six.

Christ. What's wrong with me? I slept until noon today. How much more sleep do I need?

Dana went to the restroom. In the mirror she caught sight of the locket hanging from the leather string around her neck. She paused to look at herself.

Hello, Andromeda.

She considered the etymology of the name. From ανδρός (*andros*), meaning "man," combined with μήδομαι (*mēdomai*), meaning "to think about or be mindful of."

I am she who thinks of a man.

Well, I guess Gloria had me pegged for my obsession with Aristotle from the very beginning, didn't she.

But how can that possibly be my real name? It's the same as the real name of Aristotle's second wife. The mother of his son, Nicomachus. His one true love. The princess in chains. . . .

Dana tried to remember when she first learned Aristotle married a slave whose real name was Andromeda.

She shivered.

It was in a book about ancient Greece Gloria gave her when she graduated from high school.

Dana left a generous tip on the table near her chair and pushed through the heavy door into the evening.

She turned right onto the sidewalk and then right again at the corner, hoping she remembered correctly that there was a busy street not too far up where she could hail a taxi to take her back to the computer shop. She fished the shop's card out of her pocket and punched the numbers on her cell phone as she walked.

"*Calcolatori de Venezia.*"

"Hello," Dana said in Italian. "I dropped off my laptop and camera earlier for express service. I'm calling to be sure they're ready for pickup."

"Your name?"

"Dana McCarter."

"One moment, please."

Dana listened to a tinny recording of Italian pop music for a minute.

"Ms. McCarter, your daughter waited here for your equipment and took it with her when it was finished."

Dana's heart stopped. "My what?"

"Your daughter. She paid for the service."

"Sir, I do not have a daughter. Can you please check for my equipment? There must be a mistake." Dana's daemon told her instantly that there was no mistake.

She backed against a storefront and watched the street in agony as she waited for the clerk to come back to the phone.

"I'm sorry, ma'am. Someone named 'Ugolina Romano' signed for your equipment."

Dana slowly closed the phone. She felt like throwing up.

Stupid, goddamn, irresponsible clerk! How can he just give my equipment away? I should have known better than to trust him! He was clearly as high as a kite. . . .

Dana fought back her anger and tried to focus.

Torelli's girl. . . . Her gunshot wound must not have been very bad. . . . Can I track her down? . . . But "Ugolina Romano" is obviously a fake name. . . .

A wave of defeat washed over Dana.

I don't have any other copies of my photos! My only link to the scrolls, my only evidence against Torelli, is in that laptop bag.

Dana felt like she was hanging by a thread that was hanging from a rope that was hanging over the edge of a cliff. She had reached the very limit of hope. All of her strategies had unraveled one by one. She was almost in freefall. She had just one thread left.

Domenico, only you can save me now. And that's only if you drew one of the Aristotles instead of the Marcus Aurelius.

Dana seized that thread and forced herself to think clearly.

I need to go back to the villa to get my carry-on so I will be ready to confront him first thing in the morning.

With heroic effort, Dana put one foot in front of the other, and before she knew it, she was walking once again toward the main road where she could hail a taxi.

I can't believe I've gotten myself into this situation. But how did Torelli's girl find me? How did she know I would leave my laptop bag at the mall? She must have somehow followed me.

A spike of fear sliced through Dana. She whipped around and scanned the street behind her.

Was it just her imagination, or did a tall, thin man slip hastily into a doorway so she couldn't see him?

Unable to tell, and not wanting to investigate, she turned and started jogging up the street. If she was being followed, this would be a good way to find out.

She wanted to keep running and believe that what she could not see could not harm her. But she knew this wasn't true. She had to turn and see whether he was coming after her.

I have to turn and look.

Dana did not want to turn and look. She was breathing heavily by now. She didn't want to break her stride.

I have to turn and look.

Dana twisted her head to the left and tried to make sense of the shapes and shadows she glimpsed behind her. In the process, she nearly plowed into a plump old woman walking her chihuahua. This earned her a string of angry expletives. But she did not stop.

I have to stop and turn around.

Dana jogged on for another block. At the corner, she grasped the light post she was passing and used it to swing around for a full view of the street behind her. The tall man she had seen earlier was just twenty feet away, caught in mid-turn toward the nearest shop window.

Shit!

Dana swung full circle and accelerated to a run. She was panicking now. There was no way he could be that close unless he'd been running too.

But who is he?

He wore a black leather coat and a Greek fisherman's cap pulled low on his forehead. He didn't look the least bit familiar.

Dana could see the bright lights of the main road ahead. If she could get there in time, she would be safe.

I can make it!

Dana ran as fast as she could. She veered around planters and sidewalk signs, pushing past startled pedestrians.

She was still a good thirty feet from the finish line, however, when two hands clamped down on her shoulders, jarring her to a halt.

"Help!"

"Dr. Dana McCarter?" the man asked in heavily accented English. "Please stop. I'm not going to hurt you."

Dana was breathing hard. She pivoted around to escape the man's grasp and looked at his face. He was young. Incredibly young. She had never seen him before.

"Dr. McCarter, my name is Zapher Inan. I am here to help you."

A couple passing by stopped and stared. Zapher stepped back.

"Are you okay, miss?" The man asked in Italian.

Dana looked at the couple, then at Zapher. She decided she was okay.

"Yes, I'm fine, thanks." She flashed some teeth, hoping it would pass for a smile. "He was . . . we were . . . just goofing around."

The woman glared at Zapher. The man shrugged disapprovingly. They continued on their way.

"Who the hell are you?" Dana rasped at Zapher.

The woman walking away looked back over her shoulder.

"Please," Zapher said, motioning for Dana to continue up the street with him. "I didn't mean to scare you. I couldn't tell from the picture whether it was you." He unfolded a computer printout of the front page of the education section of the *New York Times* in which Dana's picture appeared along with the article about the Institute.

"That's a terrible picture," Dana snapped. "What do you want?"

"I need to speak with you. It's about the scrolls. I . . . am Roach Rauch." Zapher cringed, hearing his Second Life name out loud. Until now, Marla was the only other person in the world who knew Zapher was the Palatine librarian.

Dana's mouth fell open.

How can the Palatine librarian be so young?

On the other hand, why wouldn't he be? Philip Rosedale was only seventeen when he founded the company that eventually led to the creation of Second Life.

"How did you find me?" Dana stammered.

"Your credit card," he apologized. "Your online statement showed you bought a ticket to Rome. But then I lost you for a few days, until you checked in at the Piccolo Mondo."

Dana studied him. If he was in fact Roach Rauch, then he could have accessed her credit card number from purchases she'd made at the Palatine Library.

"Let's sit down someplace where we can talk," Dana suggested warily. They proceeded without speaking until they reached the street they had been racing toward.

She led him to the closest restaurant, the Porta Bella, a colorfully decorated building that was already half-full of hungry tourists. A bleached-blond waitress seated them and brought them coffee.

It would have been a great pleasure for Dana to meet the human behind Roach Rauch under different circumstances. As it was, however, she was in no mood for pleasantries.

"Okay, what's going on?" she asked.

"Well," Zapher put his fist to his mouth to cover a small cough, "someone is . . . threatening me."

"Who?"

"I don't know." Zapher's eyes darted around the room. "First the Palatine Library was bombed. And then a robo-avatar called 'The Surgeon' abducted Roach. . . ."

Dana shook her head trying to picture this. She didn't know such things were possible in Second Life. She thought of Magenta Mai, wondering if she was safe. *That's the last thing I need right now—to be chasing after my avatar. . . .* "What does the surgeon want?"

Zapher's hands groped the table as though wishing they had a keyboard to anchor them. "The surgeon says he wants 'the last of the five Aristotle scrolls.'"

Dana leaned forward, her eyes glittering at Zapher in the candlelight. "Do you have it?" She uttered the question slowly, as though not sure whether or not she could bear the answer.

"No," Zapher lied. He had made the one error, however, that can thwart even the best of liars: he wanted to tell the truth. He wanted to tell her, and he didn't hide it fast enough.

"I think you do," Dana countered.

"No, I don't."

Dana folded her arms across her chest impassively. "Well, I don't have it either. What do you want with me?"

"I thought you could help me figure out who the surgeon is."

"How would I know?" Dana asked, growing irritated.

"Because he's after you, too," Zapher replied. "He has to be. He already got to Marie-Élise."

"Who's that?" Dana demanded.

Zapher swallowed. This interview was not going the way he wanted it to. He had pictured himself interrogating her, not the other way around.

She looks a little like Marla, Zapher realized, scanning Dana's face. *An older Marla. Marla's mother, maybe.* Zapher had never met Marla's family. Accessing his memory banks, he discovered he knew absolutely nothing about them, and this suddenly seemed to him like a fatal mistake. He wanted nothing more at this moment than to turn time back to the morning before the Palatine Library was bombed. *Marla came to the computer lab because she knew I was there. If she just wanted to check her e-mail, she could have used any other computer terminal on campus. I cannot believe I didn't talk to her . . . let her know how I feel . . . or at least ask her out. Now I'll probably never get the chance. . . .*

"Marie-Élise bought the *Eroticus,* and now she's dead, isn't she," Dana probed.

Snapping back to the present, Zapher nodded. "How did you know?"

"A man named Turk Selenka came to me with the *Eroticus* about two weeks ago," Dana said.

"What did he want?"

"He wanted to know what the scroll was," Dana recalled. "I couldn't figure out why he would buy it from the Palatine Library or steal it from the Vatican when he knew so little about it."

"Who is he?" Zapher asked. "Do you think he could be the surgeon?"

"I don't know who he is," Dana answered. "But I don't think he's the surgeon because someone else was chasing him."

"Who?"

"Cardinal Guissepe Torelli."

Zapher registered no recognition of this name. "Did Torelli get the *Eroticus* away from Selnik?" he asked.

"It's Selenka," Dana corrected. "Yes. He did."

"Did Torelli come after you?"

"Yes. Twice."

Zapher was already convinced Torelli was the surgeon. "So he has the *Symposium* too?"

Dana nodded unhappily. "Torelli has the *Eroticus,* the *Symposium,* and probably one of the two scrolls bought by Mikhail Durkovsky."

Zapher was surprised Dana knew about Mikhail. "Does Mikhail still have the other?" he asked.

"No," Dana replied. "At least, as of last Saturday, it was either in the hands of Domenico Conti or at the bottom of the Moscow River."

Zapher grimaced. "Who's Domenico Conti?"

"He's a Vatican detective who may or may not be working with Torelli."

"So this Torelli has at least two of the scrolls and at most four."

Dana shot Zapher a cold, hard look. "Are you going to give him the fifth?"

"I told you, I don't have it."

"Well, I don't believe you," Dana challenged. "Come on. 'Fess up, Zapher. I've given you a lot of information for free. Either you return the favor, or I'm gone."

"Dr. McCarter, please. My whole life is on the line here." Zapher blinked hard.

Dana was unmoved. "So is mine. Zapher, why did you track me down?"

"To warn you."

"Bullshit." Dana got up and reached for her coat.

"No, don't go," Zapher pleaded.

Dana paused with her hand on her hip. She arched her eyebrows expectantly.

"I tracked you down to find out who the surgeon was."

Dana grudgingly took her seat. "But what's your plan?"

"Well, the surgeon promised he would leave me alone if I just returned the fifth scroll. So I went and got it from the guy who sold me the other four."

"And who's that?"

"An Omani professor. The Omani government stole all five of the scrolls from someplace."

"They were in St. Paul's sarcophagus," Dana supplied.

"Here in Rome?" Zapher asked.

Dana nodded. "At St. Paul's Basilica, just outside the walls of Rome."

"Well," Zapher continued, "this Omani professor figured out their location from a Persian manuscript I sold him a while ago. According to the Persian manuscript, the fifth scroll proves Christianity is a fraud. So the Omani government was going to use it to win their religious war."

Dana sipped her coffee. "But you stole it from them."

"Yes," Zapher confessed. "And I was going to hand it over to the surgeon. But the more I thought about it, the more I realized this would be stupid. . . ." Zapher trailed off. Though he was trying to be brave, he could feel his stamina wearing thin. He'd put everything he had into the trip to Oman. But it still wasn't over. He still wasn't home. "I'm thinking the surgeon is planning to kill me."

"You're probably right about that," Dana agreed. She saw a vulnerable young man before her. A boy, really. Although she tried to show concern, she felt almost completely indifferent, as though they were discussing whether he should take art history or astronomy next semester. Like Zapher, Dana was already beyond her crisis limit.

Zapher cleared his throat and drank some water. He did not touch his coffee. Too weak for a native of Turkey. "The surgeon will take the scroll and rub me out."

"So," Dana repeated, "what's your plan?"

Zapher lowered his voice. "I thought, if I knew who he was, I could kill him."

Dana scoffed. Then she swallowed hard. He was serious. "So your plan is to hunt down and kill Cardinal Giuseppe Torelli."

"Yeah." Zapher slumped back in his chair and tried to look tough. "I've killed before; I can kill again."

Dana rubbed her forehead and signaled the waitress. She had finished her coffee, and she was starving.

When the waitress appeared, Dana said, "We'll take a couple of burgers and fries. That okay with you, Zapher?"

Zapher nodded.

Dana watched impatiently as the waitress painstakingly recorded their order in her little book.

"Okay, and how would you like your burgers done?" the waitress asked.

This seemed like an outrageously tedious question to Dana under the circumstances. They each answered it, along with a few more, until the waitress finally scampered off to the kitchen.

"Who did you kill, Zapher?" Dana reluctantly inquired. The restaurant was noisy enough that there was no danger of being overheard.

Zapher blanched. "The Omani professor," he answered. "I don't really know if I killed him, actually. I mean . . . I left him for dead. After hitting him on the back of the head . . . really hard . . . with a heavy . . . thing." Zapher stopped abruptly and unconvincingly resumed his tough-dude look.

Dana resisted the temptation to roll her eyes. *I cannot believe I am being pressed into service as teen counselor on top of everything else I've been through this week. I'm simply not up to it.*

"Is anyone after you?" she asked with the utmost forbearance.

"Nah. I'm a pro." He grinned, but it didn't last.

"You probably didn't kill him."

"I probably did."

"Okay, listen to me, Zapher," Dana reasoned. "You can't hunt Torelli down and kill him in cold blood."

"Why not?"

"Because this is not a video game."

Zapher threw her a nasty smirk.

Dana tried again. "Think of it this way: if you get caught, your life is ruined."

"Gee," Zapher sneered sarcastically, "that's exactly the same thing that happens if I don't kill him."

Dana sighed.

"You got a better plan?" he asked.

"Yeah," Dana answered. "We take your scroll to another cardinal at the Vatican and convince him that Torelli is corrupt."

Zapher processed this input. "But any cardinal would kill us for this scroll," he objected. "It's a threat to their religion."

"Zapher, normal Catholics don't kill to protect their religion. Torelli is the leader of a bloodthirsty cult. When the Church finds out what he's been up to, he's finished."

Zapher checked Dana's face for signs of deception. *She's making it sound so easy. Like there really may be hope.* "But we don't have any proof," he pointed out.

"We don't, but Domenico Conti does," Dana clarified. "Or at least, he can get it."

"I thought you said he might be working with Torelli."

"I think we can win him over."

"Is he a Catholic?"

"Yes, but he's not a member of the cult."

Zapher frowned. *How can she go running to a Catholic?*

"Dr. McCarter," Zapher ventured, "it seems like maybe I didn't explain the situation right. This fifth scroll I have contains decisive proof that Christianity is a fraud. We can't trust a Catholic to help us. I mean, if you were Catholic, what would you do?"

"Well, I'd examine the proof, Zapher, and then I'd make up my mind whether or not to believe it. Do you think Catholics don't care at all about the truth?"

"But this isn't about the truth," Zapher retorted. "It's about which team wins. Islam is taking over the world. A discovery like this, whether it's true or not, would be devastating to Christianity. The Catholics are not going to lie down and let that happen."

Dana was appalled to find herself rising to the defense of the Catholic Church. She might not be a believer, but she certainly didn't see all Catholics as corrupt. In Zapher's mind, Christianity and Islam were like two rival high schools whose student body would stop at nothing to win the homecoming game.

He's so young.

Just then, their burgers arrived, giving Dana a chance to consider how to convince Zapher of her plan.

"Zapher, think of it this way," she finally proposed. "What could possibly be in that fifth scroll that would constitute decisive proof that Christianity is a fraud?"

Zapher chewed thoughtfully for a moment. "I have no idea," he admitted.

Dana washed down a mouthful of burger with a gulp of soda. "Well, let's suppose—I don't know—let's suppose it were a letter written by Jesus himself saying that he is not the son of God, that all his supposed miracles were bogus, and that he was taken off the cross before he died so that it would seem like he rose from the dead. He says he wants to come clean, but the disciples won't let him because they want to start a new religion." Dana paused to inhale a few fries, liking the scenario she'd painted. "Okay, suppose that's what the letter says, and suppose you're a Catholic. What would you say?"

Zapher responded without hesitation. "I'd say we have to hide the letter and kill everyone who knows about it."

"No, no, no!" Dana couldn't help laughing a little. "Only a psychopath or a teenager would say that. Pretend for a moment that you're a reasonable adult, Zapher. What would you say?"

Zapher scowled and tore into his burger.

In a moment he was ready to try again. "Okay, I'd say the letter was a fake," he pronounced. "Even if tests proved it dated back to Jesus's day, it could have been forged by one of Jesus's enemies. Or someone might have forced Jesus to write it."

"Okay, right," Dana concurred. "You would find a way to explain the whole thing away. This is what the average Catholic is going to do—explain it away. Oh, there will be a media circus for a little while, and a few doubters might jump ship, but it won't make any difference to the loyal majority."

Zapher took a long draw on his soda. "So like I said, it's about making sure your team wins. It's not about the truth."

"Well, all right," Dana conceded, "I see your point. But my point is that people at least have to *pretend* to take the evidence into account. Hiding it is just . . . medieval. It's not accepted within the mainstream anymore."

Zapher buoyed up with new hope. "So you think that even though Torelli is medieval, the majority of the Catholic Church is mainstream. And they will make sure Torelli is put away where he can't come after me."

Dana almost applauded. "Yes. That's exactly it. We just have to find the right cardinal. And I think Domenico will help us."

"But wait," Zapher balked. "If we bust Torelli, he'll bust the Palatine Library—"

"Believe me, Zapher," Dana interrupted. "the Palatine Library is already a lost cause. But, with a good lawyer, and with the main witness against you going down for murder, you could be free of all of this in no time."

Soon the waitress came back to check on them. Having finished his burger and fries, Zapher ordered a piece of chocolate cake. He was beginning to relax. His belly was full, and he had a new ally.

"It's kind of cool how Christianity can deflect such a heavy blow," he mused.

"Yeah, well," Dana muttered, rummaging through her purse for her cell phone, "to some of us, that's actually the whole problem with it."

Zapher watched her closely, trying to guess what she meant.

Dana felt his eyes and looked up from her purse. "All good theories are falsifiable," she informed him.

He still didn't compute.

Dana lay her phone on the table and tried to think of a way to explain what she meant. "Okay. Suppose we hear noises coming from the stairwell. And my theory is that there's a dragon in the basement. So you volunteer to test my theory. You go down there, look everywhere, and you don't see any dragon. So you come back up and tell me my theory is wrong. Rather than accepting your refutation, however, I say that the dragon must be invisible. So you go back down and look for signs of an invisible dragon, but all you come up with are signs of a burglary. Well, this should convince me to admit I was wrong, but instead, I just say that my invisible dragon is trying to make it look like a burglary. . . ."

Zapher nodded perceptively. "No matter what I find, you won't change your view."

"Right." Dana waded up her napkin and tossed it on her plate. "And that's not intelligent. Intelligence corrects itself in light of the evidence. Intelligent people say, 'Here's our theory, and here's the evidence you would need to prove it false, and if you find that evidence, we will gladly admit we're wrong.'"

Zapher thought about it. "But there must be some form of evidence Christians would recognize as proof that they're wrong. There must be something that would convince them."

"I don't think so, Zapher," Dana said as his chocolate cake arrived. "That's faith. And that's exactly the problem."

Chapter Twenty-Seven

Before they left the Porta Bella, Dana and Zapher exchanged cell phone numbers. Then Zapher walked Dana back to the Piccolo Mondo. He was staying at another hotel not far away. Dana said she would call him just as soon as she was able to set up a meeting with Domenico.

A few things were still bothering Dana about her assessment of the situation. If Torelli was using the Palatine Library to track the scrolls, the fifth of which he still had not located, then why would he suddenly bomb it? Was he really so psychotic as to undermine his own investigation? And if Torelli killed Marie-Élise for the *Eroticus*, how did Turk Selenka get his hands on it?

Who is Turk Selenka, and how does he fit into the picture?

Hopefully, by now, Domenico would have more information.

Dana went up to her room at the Piccolo Mondo and was surprised for a moment to find it empty. The events of the evening made her forget that her carry-on was still back at the villa. They also made her forget about her stolen laptop and camera. She sat down with a thud on the stiff mattress of her bed. It was almost nine. She wanted her photos back so badly she felt like crying.

At least I didn't have to have another fight with Torelli's girl tonight. She must have gotten what she wanted. But how the hell did she find me? Not even Zapher could find me at the villa.

The image of Zapher versus Torelli's girl on a whiz-kid game show suddenly flashed into Dana's mind: "Alex, I'll take 'Hacking' for six hundred, please. . . ."

Dana used the room phone to call the front desk for a taxi back to the villa. Then she listened to the four voicemail messages she'd noticed when she entered Zapher's number in her cell phone.

The first was from Gene the day before: "*Bonjour,* Sista! It's me. I just called your office, and Ann said you were off gallivanting about in Europe somewhere. This better be you taking my advice about a vacation. We don't want any more trouble now do we? Give me a jingle when you have a minute. I have some hilarious news about Richard. . . . It's too funny." He laughed. "Okay. Call me, baby!"

The second was from Beatrice, at 12:56 that afternoon: "Dana? It's Beatrice. Why did you leave today without saying anything? You could have taken my car. I'm worried about you. This neighborhood isn't a good place to be walking around with a laptop. There's been a string of muggings, especially near the mall. Please call me."

The third was from Beatrice again, at 1:22. "Dana? Listen. There's no way you can walk all the way to that mall and back again with that heavy bag. I'm sending Leena after you. Just stay at the computer shop. She will be there in a few minutes. Come home and let's talk, Dana. I realize you've been through a lot. . . . I want to help. Please call. . . . Bye."

Dana looked hard at her phone. *Who the hell is Leena?*

Oh, my god, the visiting nurse. Oh-my-god-oh-my-god-oh-my-god. Ugolina? Ugolina Romano? Please tell me you picked up my equipment!

That had to be it. Her supposed daughter wasn't Torelli's girl, it was Gloria's visiting nurse.

Dana could barely steady her hands enough to punch the call-back button.

"Hello?"

"Beatrice, it's Dana."

"Jesus, Dana, thank God. We've been so worried about you."

Dana wondered who Beatrice meant by "we." Her and Gloria? Her and Leena? Or maybe it was just a turn of phrase.

"I'm fine, Beatrice, thanks. Look, I'm sorry I took off by myself today. I just needed the exercise." As she said this, Dana realized that, to an overweight woman in her seventies, choosing to walk such a distance for exercise was a sign of mental instability.

"Honestly, Dana—"

"Listen, Beatrice, did Leena pick up my laptop and camera?"

"Yes, I have the bag right here on the counter. Don't worry, you can pay me back. Have you eaten? Where are you?"

After a huge sigh of relief, Dana felt a surge of anger at Beatrice's meddling. But she didn't want to start a fight. "Yes, I've eaten. I actually had a very busy day. I've arranged to do some work at the Vatican Library. So, I got a hotel nearby. I'd like to come and pick up my things, if that's okay."

"Dana, you can't run from this."

"Gloria—" Dana shook herself. "I mean, *Beatrice*—it's just not a good time right now. I came to Rome on business, remember? I'm really grateful for your generosity, opening your home to me and everything. But I have to get down to work now."

There was silence on the line. "Okay, Dana. Whatever you need to do."

"Thank you, Beatrice, for understanding." Dana looked at her watch. "I'll try to be there before ten."

They signed off. Dana was about to close her phone and go downstairs for her taxi when she remembered her fourth call.

It was from Domenico, at 8:10 that evening.

"Dana? It's me. My secretary told me you stopped by the office today. I can't believe you're in Rome. I'm . . . *ah, merda.* I guess you're probably mad at me for leaving you in Moscow. . . . I thought maybe . . . I thought maybe we could talk. Please call me when you get this."

Dana pressed "repeat" and listened to the message again.

"Contrite" would be the word that comes to mind.

Dana remembered Gene warning her about Domenico. She pictured how outraged Gene would be when she told him Domenico took the scroll and left her in Moscow. But it was no use. Dana's heart ached.

She called Domenico back. He knocked on the door of her room fifteen minutes later.

When she opened the door, she was surprised for a moment to see his arm in a cast.

"I forgot about your broken wrist," she remarked, stepping aside so he could enter. "How are you feeling?"

"The pain has mostly subsided," he reported, moving past her.

"Have a seat. What can I get you to drink?"

"A beer would be nice."

Dana went to the mini-bar and pulled out two cans of beer. Then she selected a can of peanuts from the snack tray and brought every-thing over to the coffee table.

Despite his cast, Domenico looked good. Dana remembered the first time she saw him, knocking on the door of her brownstone in New York. Although it had been only two weeks, it seemed like an eternity ago. When she looked at him now, she felt the same little thrill all over again, as well as the same apprehension.

Who is this man, really? Do I know him as well as I feel like I do?

He was wearing a suit, presumably what he wore to work today. *Don't you ever relax?* Dana felt scruffy by comparison in jeans and a sweater.

"How are *your* injuries?" Conti asked, opening his beer. She opened hers and sat down on the opposite end of the couch.

"I still have some pain in my ribs," she admitted, "but the cuts and bruises are healing nicely." She pulled back the sleeve on her right arm to show him her worst scrape. It was scabbed over.

Conti inspected Dana. She still had a faint ring of purple under one eye. Her hair, normally pulled up in a French twist or swept stylishly behind her ears, was a bit wild.

She seems lost, like a lamb in the woods. She always talks big, as though she has everything under control, but she's really just a wobbly little lamb.

Dana observed Conti observing her. *I wonder what he sees.* She straightened her sweater self-consciously.

They sipped their beers.

"That night was so awful," Dana recalled.

He nodded soberly.

"But we still had a scroll and a plan," she reminded him. She set down her beer, suddenly feeling a little queasy. "Domenico, why did you leave?"

Conti issued a heavy sigh. "I wasn't ready for you, for what happened. It was too much."

Dana watched him trace a pattern on the couch with his finger in the same way he had traced shadows on her naked body in the moonlight.

He's not wearing his wedding ring.

"So are you back with your wife now?" she asked.

"No," he answered. "My marriage is over. She's been staying with her sister. We were supposed to have an appointment with her therapist on Monday, but I called and told her I can't do it anymore."

"I remember the day I told my husband that," Dana sympathized. "It's hard."

"Yeah. On the bright side, however, I don't have to listen to that damn therapist anymore." He chuckled, but without much mirth.

"There are many bright sides to the end of a bad marriage," Dana assured him.

"I know." Conti stretched his arm out, resting the cast on the back of the couch, and flexed his fingers.

Dana tipped her head to the side and smiled tentatively at him. Then she reached her arm along the back of the couch until she touched his fingers.

He smiled gently at her and got up to look out the window.

Dana watched him go, swiveling around on the couch to face him. "What did you do with the scroll?" she asked his reflection in the glass.

"I'll be honest with you, Dana," he answered with his back still turned. "My intention, on leaving Moscow, was to take it straight back to Cardinal Torelli." He had his hands on his hips, and he spoke authoritatively, in the same voice he used to admonish rowdy children and drunk drivers.

Dana shook her head in disbelief. "How could you go back to him when he sent his assistant to kill us?"

Conti turned from the window and leaned an elbow on the high back of the parlor chair. "We can assume Torelli told her to get the scrolls from us, but we have no evidence that he authorized lethal force." He cast a sharp glance at Dana. "Torelli can legitimately claim he was just trying to defend Tommy when he fired those shots at you on the bridge."

"Tommy?" Dana asked.

"Hmmm?" Conti was confused for a moment.

"The girl's name is Tommy?"

"Oh. Yeah. . . . I did some checking. She's just a street kid. He hired her through his inner-city youth program."

"I can't believe you're still defending that psychopath!" Dana exclaimed.

Conti sat down in the parlor chair and gave her another gentle smile. "Dana, I'm just trying to tell you how your case looks from the point of view of the law."

"So you're going to turn the scroll over to Torelli?"

"I said that was my intention—because that would have been the right thing to do."

"But you didn't?" Dana prompted hopefully. She perused Conti's face, summoning all her powers of concentration to understand him.

Domenico, I can't tell whether you came here tonight to make up with me or to arrest me.

Conti reached across the coffee table for the peanuts. He read the can as though trying to decide whether or not they met his standards.

"I didn't take the scroll to Torelli," he finally said, "because I want to find out once and for all what he's up to."

Conti selected a single peanut from the can and tasted it. Then he indiscriminately grabbed a handful and popped them in his mouth.

Dana moved his beer to a corner of the coffee table he could reach from his chair. She didn't dare speak.

I just have to be patient. He's wound so tight. I just have to let him unwind in his own way. She ate a few peanuts and waited.

Conti rubbed the thumb and fingers of his good hand together to brush off the salt. He glared at the can of peanuts, as though dissatisfied with the quality of his snack.

"I met with Cardinal Freppe," he announced.

Dana's eyes widened. She wanted to ask when, but she remained silent.

"I told Freppe about Torelli's . . . interest . . . in my investigation."

Dana nodded, encouraging him to continue. But he wasn't looking at her.

"Freppe indicated that he has had his own concerns for some time about Torelli's clandestine service."

Clandestine service—would that be the cult of Dionysus?

"The clandestine service is an ancient Vatican tradition that no one knows much about. Freppe thinks it involves illegal activities. Torelli could be hiding the scrolls to prevent any investigation. If so, he's in deep. His only way out would be to deny that he ever even knew about any scrolls."

Dana was too excited now to hold back. "So how are you going to find out what he's up to?"

Conti's face jerked toward Dana, as though he had almost forgotten she was there. She wished she'd kept her mouth shut.

They sipped their beers.

Then Conti leaned forward and looked intently at Dana. "There's really only one way to proceed." He looked very serious, as though he were about to read Dana her rights. "Cardinal Freppe would have to present the scroll to Torelli and insist that it earns him membership in the clandestine service. They are holding some sort of major celebration this weekend. With Freppe on the inside, it won't be hard to obtain all the evidence we need."

Dana lit up. "That's great! I've already got the third scroll translated. It's called the *Nerinthus,* and it's all about the sacred rites of the cult of Dionysus. I think it will be very useful in building our case."

Conti stared at her. "Are you telling me you took photos of Mikhail's scrolls?"

"You bet your ass I did. Before I brought them up from the basement. I have photos of all but the fifth scroll." Dana was galvanized.

With the cult purged, she knew the Vatican would grant her permission to publish. It didn't matter whether Torelli kept or destroyed the scrolls he recovered. As long as she still had one scroll, her photographs of the others would be accepted by the academic community.

"Don't get too excited, Dana," Conti cautioned. "Cardinal Freppe says the scroll I have is the Marcus Aurelius."

Dana suddenly felt like an overripe plum. She fell off the tree with a splat on the hard ground. "Shit."

Conti finished his beer.

"Wait a minute, Domenico, wait a minute!" Dana lit up again. "We're okay. We still have a scroll. We have the fifth scroll."

"We have the fifth scroll?" Conti pulled his little notebook out of his breast pocket, balanced it carefully on his knee with his cast, and began paging through it, as though he had overlooked some vital clue.

"I know who has it." Dana blurted. "He's here. In Rome. He wants to cooperate, because Torelli is threatening to kill him."

"Slow down, Dana," Conti urged. "Start from the beginning."

"Okay," Dana said, taking a deep breath. "Do you remember the Palatine Library?"

"Yes."

"Well," she continued, "Zapher Inan is the man behind its librarian, Roach Rauch. Roach was recently abducted by someone called 'The Surgeon'—who is, no doubt, Torelli's assistant, Tommy. The surgeon is threatening to kill Zapher if he does not produce the fifth scroll."

Conti awkwardly jotted a few notes. "And Zapher has the scroll?"

"Yes." Dana could hardly contain herself. "He got it from the Omani Muslims who bought it. They were going to use it to discredit Christianity."

"What does Zapher intend to do with the scroll?"

"He wants to use it to bust Torelli so that Torelli can't hunt him down and kill him." Dana smiled triumphantly. "I told him you would set him up with a good cardinal."

Conti looked up from his notebook and blinked at Dana. "So we're in business after all. We should meet with Freppe as soon as possible."

"Finally!" Dana exclaimed. She could hardly believe the turnaround. Three hours ago, she had been on the verge of despair. Now she had her photos back, a viable plan for catching Torelli, and an attractive Italian man sitting in her hotel room.

I knew you'd come through. I knew we could do this!

Dana beamed at Conti and grasped his good hand.

He smiled sheepishly.

"We're such a good team," she declared.

Conti shook his head in wonder. "I figured I'd never see you again."

Dana slid closer, adding her other hand to his. "I will admit that, on Saturday morning when I woke up alone, I tried to leave you behind. But I just couldn't. I really like you, Domenico."

Conti looked for a moment as though he'd been slapped in the face. Then he reached for Dana and kissed her.

They made love. Conti's cast created some comic moments. After it was over, however, they lay in each other's arms, just as though last Saturday morning had never happened.

Dana felt that the entire room was humming happily, celebrating their reunion.

Conti's good hand stroked Dana's back. She nuzzled his neck, taking in the scent of him. Her locket fell onto his shoulder. He propped himself up on his elbow to look at it.

"I thought you said your birth mother had the other half of this locket," he demanded.

Dana grinned. "Not much gets by you, does it, Inspector."

Conti waited in silence for her explanation.

"It's . . . I know this is going to sound crazy." Dana laughed. "I found her. My birth mother. She gave me the other half of the locket the other day. Actually, it was just last night."

Domenico furrowed his brow. "Where did you find her? Here in Rome?"

"Yes."

"That's amazing. What happened?"

"Well, when I arrived on Saturday, I went to stay at my old therapist's villa. You see, I had the same therapist ever since they found me when I was a kid. But she retired about five years ago and moved here. She has cancer now, and she's very ill. But she gave me this, and her housemate Beatrice told me the whole story."

"Let me get this straight," Conti probed. "Your mother gave you up for adoption and became your therapist?"

"That's right. Weird, huh." Dana smiled uneasily, hoping he wouldn't decide she was damaged goods.

But Conti was glancing around the room. "So that's why none of your stuff is here."

"Yeah, I'll get it in the morning."

"Are you sure you're up for this meeting with Freppe?"

"Of course."

Conti lay back to face the ceiling. "And here I thought *I* had problems."

"No, it's all right." Dana patted his shoulder. "I mean, I'm all right. I have great adoptive parents. Gloria, my birth mother, she's dying. She can't even speak any more. So it's not as though I suddenly have a new person in my life to deal with. Really, it's just a chance to forgive her and say goodbye. I haven't quite gotten to that point yet, but I think that's what it will be."

Conti nodded, doubting that any woman could handle such a dramatic development so rationally. "At any rate, I suppose you're glad you finally know."

"Yeah," Dana agreed. "It's so important to know the truth about the past."

"'He who does not remember the past is condemned to repeat it.'"

Dana cocked her head. "I've heard that aphorism before. Who said that?"

"George Santayana."

Chapter Twenty-Eight

 The next morning, Dana woke up alone just after seven. Conti had once again snuck out without her hearing him.

Oh, no.

But this time there was a note on his pillow, scribbled on a piece of paper from his little notebook.

> D—
>
> I'll pick you up at 9.30 to meet with Freppe. Bring Zapher and the scroll.
>
> —D

Dana jumped out of bed. She had a lot to do.

First, she called Zapher and told him the plan was a go. He should be in the lobby of the Piccolo Mondo with the scroll at nine-thirty.

Next, she called Beatrice. No answer.

Damn! Well, I'm just going to have to find a way into the villa to get my laptop.

Dana rang the front desk to request a taxi. Then she showered, threw on the same clothes she had worn the day before, and dashed downstairs.

Dana instructed the taxi driver in Italian to take her to Gloria's villa as fast as he could. It was already eight o'clock. Traffic was not too bad since it was Saturday morning. But the villa was more than a half-hour away, and there would be more traffic on the way back.

Crap! I might not actually make it by nine-thirty.

Dana pulled out her cell phone and called Zapher.

"Hi, Dr. McCarter," he answered.

"Hi, Zapher. I have to run an errand, and I'm not sure if I'll be able to make it back to the Piccolo Mondo by nine-thirty. If I'm not there, you should go ahead with Inspector Conti to the meeting with Freppe."

"Can't your errand wait?" Zapher sounded nervous.

"I'm afraid not," Dana replied. "I'm picking up my laptop and camera. They have photos of the scrolls. We may need them."

Zapher was silent.

"Okay, Zapher?"

"Yeah," he allowed. "Hurry up, though."

"I will. Just be cool. Domenico will be there. He's really nice, and he's looking forward to meeting you. Bye, Zapher."

Dana grew increasingly carsick as the taxi made its speedy journey to the villa. She was sorry she'd eaten the remainder of the peanuts from last night for breakfast.

When they finally arrived at the villa, Dana gave the driver some money and asked him to wait for her. He nodded and slumped under his cap.

She ran up to the front door and knocked.

No answer, just as she expected. She had called again three times in the taxi on the way over. At first, she was merely annoyed that no one answered the phone. Then it occurred to her, however, that someone should always answer the phone at the villa. If Beatrice herself wasn't there, someone else should be there to watch Gloria. Dana was not just annoyed anymore; she was alarmed.

Dana dashed around to the back of the villa and climbed the steps to the deck. She knew she hadn't locked the sliding door when she came in from stargazing the other night. Hopefully, Beatrice hadn't noticed.

When she got to the top of the stairs, however, she saw that the glass panel on the door was shattered.

Dana stopped, pressed herself against the wall, and sucked in air.

Holy fuck! The door is broken.

Why is the door broken?

You have to go in there.

Dana stealthily moved up the stairs, grabbing a fist-sized stone from the herb garden as she passed. When she got to the broken glass door, she called Beatrice's name. There was no answer.

Dana gingerly stepped over the threshold. Everything in the living room looked just as she had left it. The blanket Beatrice had thrown over her shoulders the other night was still lying in a rumpled pile on the couch.

"Beatrice?" Dana called again. Keeping her back to the wall, she moved through the dining room toward the kitchen.

Then she saw her.

Beatrice was lying on her back on the floor, her left arm above her head and her neck twisted at an unnatural angle. There was no blood, but her eyes were wide open in a dead stare.

Dana clamped her hand to her mouth, stifling the urge to scream. She looked around wildly.

Oh, my god. Where is my laptop?

Oh, my fucking god—they killed Beatrice for my laptop!

Dana backed into the dining room until she couldn't see Beatrice anymore. Then she turned and sprinted out the broken door through which she'd entered. She hit the stairs too fast and almost tumbled down them, catching herself in the nick of time on the railing. She clung to it and gulped in deep breaths of air.

You have to pull yourself together!

Dana straightened her shoulders and continued down the stairs at a normal pace. Rounding the corner, she strode back to the taxi in the most businesslike manner she could muster. Folding herself into the backseat, she asked the taxi driver to take her back to the Piccolo Mondo.

As the taxi backed out of the driveway, Dana realized she still had the stone from the herb garden in her hand. Setting it on the floor by her feet, she reached in her purse for her phone.

Torelli finally found me. I have to warn Domenico.

But before she punched the button, she stopped herself.

How did Torelli find me?

Dana tried to think how Torelli could have learned she was staying at the villa. Zapher never figured it out, savvy as he was. Dana hadn't told anyone she was at the villa. Not even Ann back at the Institute. Not even Gene.

But Beatrice called my cell phone from the villa yesterday. Could someone have traced that call? Could a computer whiz kid do that? All Tommy would have needed was the phone number. Then she could look up the house it belonged to in a reverse directory.

But how would Tommy get the number? The phone company?

Actually, all she would have to do is look at the call record on my cell phone.

But how could she have seen my cell phone?

Dana's mind flashed to an image of Tommy hiding under the bed while she and Domenico made love in her room at the Piccolo Mondo.

That's ridiculous.

Before Dana could come up with anything else, her daemon supplied the answer: Domenico.

No way! No fucking way!

It was too late. Dana's mind flashed to an image of Domenico flipping her phone open in the dark while she slept last night.

Not again. No, no, no, no, no.

Dana clamped her hand over her mouth when she realized she was speaking out loud. The taxi driver cast her a curious glance in the rearview mirror.

Dana tried to look casually out the window as she realized she told Domenico both that she was staying at the villa and that her stuff was still there.

You are a very stupid, evil person, Dana. You've once again lost your hard-earned photos of the scrolls. You slept with the enemy, got a nice old lady killed, and left your mother at a crime scene without even so much as checking on her. Oh, and you just sent a brave young man to his death as well.

Dana snatched up her phone and dialed Zapher's number.

It rang.

Come on!

It continued ringing

Zapher! Answer the phone, goddammit!

Dana looked at her watch.

It's only nine o'clock. Why aren't you answering your fucking phone!

Then Dana heard a recording saying she should try her party later.

She snapped the phone shut and bit her lip. *Can I make it in time to stop Zapher from handing the fifth scroll over to Domenico?* She looked in frustration at the bumper-to-bumper line of cars in front of her taxi. They weren't at a standstill, but they were slowing and still miles away. She leaned forward and told the driver she would pay him double if he could get her there in half an hour.

Suddenly Dana's phone rang. She dropped it in horror as if it were a scorpion. Then she grabbed it up and looked at the caller ID. It was Domenico.

Dana groaned. She couldn't possibly answer it. But of course, she had to answer it.

Just play it cool.

She opened her phone and put it to her ear.

"Hello?" she chirped.

"Dana? It's Domenico. Where the hell are you?"

"I'm, ah, . . . shopping," Dana improvised. "I just . . . couldn't bear to wear a dirty pair of jeans to our meeting with the cardinal."

Silence on the other end of the line.

"Don't worry," Dana continued. "I'll be there in time. I still have a half hour."

"Where exactly are you?" Conti asked.

"I'm in a taxi. I'm . . . just a minute . . . I can't read the street sign." Dana waited. She had no intention of telling him where she was.

"Dana," Conti said irritably, "never mind. Listen, I'm here with Zapher at your hotel."

Dana looked at her watch again. "But it's only nine. I told Zapher to come at nine-thirty."

"I know," Conti said. "I picked him up instead. Freppe has another engagement this morning, so he wants to get started now. I tried to call you but your line was busy—"

"Domenico," Dana interrupted, "how did you hook up with Zapher?"

"You gave me his phone number last night."

No I didn't, you son of a bitch. You took it from my phone.

"Oh, yeah," Dana said nonchalantly. "You know, I was actually just trying to call Zapher. He must have turned his phone off. Could I talk to him?"

"Now?" Conti asked. "Why?"

"Because," Dana answered, "he . . . asked me to pick up something up for him. A toothbrush. I need to ask him which size. And whether he wants floss and stuff."

More silence on the other end of the line.

"Dana," Conti growled, "we have much more important things to worry about right now."

"Please?"

"Just a second."

"Hello?" Zapher said. He sounded strained.

"Zapher," Dana hissed, "pretend I'm talking to you about a toothbrush you wanted me to buy for you. Say, 'I want a medium, along with waxed floss.' Say that right now, Zapher."

"I want a medium, along with waxed floss."

"Good." Dana tried to sound calm. "Listen. You need to get away from Domenico Conti right now. Do not give him the scroll. When we hang up, tell him you have to go to the bathroom and then get the hell out of there. Say 'yes' if you understand me."

"Yes."

"Good." Dana took a deep breath. "You'll be fine if you go *now*. Meet me back at the Porta Bella where we ate dinner last night as soon as you can. And Zapher?"

"Dana?" Conti was back on the line.

"Jesus, Domenico," Dana complained, "I was trying to talk to Zapher."

Conti ignored her. "How soon can you be here?"

"Maybe about twenty minutes," Dana estimated.

"That's too long for us to wait. You'll have to meet us at the Vatican Library. Go around back to the entrance marked 'Employees Only' and call me."

As Conti was speaking, Dana realized that, when she called Zapher earlier, she told him she was going to the villa to pick up her laptop.

Did Zapher relay that information to Domenico?

"You know," Dana added, "I was going to swing by the villa to pick up my laptop, but I guess I don't have time. I'll be there as soon as I can."

"Good," Conti said, and he hung up.

Dana closed her phone. Chewing on her knuckles, she stared out the window in desperation.

Did I convince him? It would be a miracle if I did. That was the lamest pack of lies anyone ever told. There aren't any clothing stores open in Rome at eight-thirty on a Saturday morning. And Zapher could have bought a toothbrush in the gift shop at his hotel. I should have just said I was stuck in a traffic jam on my way to the villa.

Shit!

Dana held onto the door of the taxi as it swung precariously around a stalled car. She felt sick again. She leaned forward and told the driver to take her to the Porta Bella instead of the Piccolo Mondo.

And of course, the Porta Bella won't be open either.

Dammit!

She clenched her stomach in an effort to keep herself from vomiting. *How could he do this to me? How did I not see it?* Dana felt the betrayal like an anvil in her chest, pressing the air out of her lungs.

As she curled up in her seat, the image of Beatrice lying dead on the kitchen floor pushed its way into her mind. Her neck had clearly been broken. Someone must have given her head one fast, hard twist. Those eyes in shock, as if she knew she was dead.

Dana couldn't help wondering how likely it was that she would be arrested for fleeing the scene of a crime. She didn't think anyone saw her, though. And they would not be able to trace her through the taxi if she paid in cash.

On the other hand, Domenico knew she had been staying there.

Is that his plan? To pin the murder on me?

But wait a minute. If Domenico wanted the laptop, it would have been far easier for him to let me retrieve it and then grab it at the meeting with Freppe. He could even have written "Bring your laptop" in the note he left for me.

So then it must have been Tommy who broke in and killed Beatrice after all! I bet she could hack into my cell phone account online.

Dana flushed, elated with her new explanation.

She still had enough of her wits about her, however, to be suspicious of her own reaction. The new explanation enabled her to go on believing in Domenico. It conveniently ignored the fact that Domenico had lied about her giving him Zapher's cell phone number. She felt sure she could come up with a creative explanation for that, too. But she was equally sure now that she was deluding herself. She was committing the fallacy of believing what she wanted to be true rather than what was most likely to be true.

The most likely explanation is that Domenico reasoned as follows: if I write "Bring your laptop" on my note, Dana will make copies of the files on a jump drive and drop it in a mailbox, addressed to some friend in New York or something. Whereas if I retrieve the laptop before she returns to it, there's a good chance she won't have made copies yet.

Dana had a jump drive, of course, on which she scrupulously backed up all of her files. It wouldn't do her any good now though, since it was in the stolen laptop bag. She had bought a new jump drive the day before at the computer shop when she had dropped off the equipment. She had planned to make another copy of everything and mail it to Gene. The new jump drive was in her purse, still unopened.

Domenico probably even saw the unopened jump drive in my purse when he went for my cell phone. Ha, ha, ha! Dana was beginning to feel hysterical. *What now?*

I have to think. I haven't lost yet. Surely there is still a way to win.

She thought back to what Conti had said last night. He said that if the cult were exposed, the only way out for Torelli would be for him to deny that he ever even knew about the scrolls, much less killed for them.

But there's still the video footage of Torelli at the Cloisters taking the Symposium *scroll away from me and lying about it being stolen from the Vatican Library. This might be enough to undermine his defense.*

Dana accessed the Internet on her cell phone and located Rome's Interpol office. After she found it, she looked at her watch: 9:39. It had been over twenty minutes since she had spoken to Zapher. That was more than enough time for him to escape to the Porta Bella. He was either there or he wasn't. If he was there, she would pick him up, and they would go straight to the Interpol office together. If he wasn't there, she would have to go without him.

Dana dared to believe Zapher would be there until another question occurred to her: *Why would he have turned off his cell phone?*

The taxi slowed, and Dana recognized the street. Though it had been lit up and full of life the night before, it was almost completely dead now. In the daylight she could see how dirty it was. A stray dog ambled across the road to an ugly pile of garbage on the curb. Storefronts hid behind security gates sprayed with graffiti. The desolation outside the taxi seemed surreal to Dana, a projection of the landscape of her mind.

As the taxi approached the Porta Bella, Dana scanned the sidewalk for a tall man in a leather coat and fisherman's cap.

Come on, Zapher.

Come on!

Then she saw him, standing in the doorway, with his hands deep in his pockets.

Dana's heart leapt.

She rolled down the window and called to him. His eyes found hers, but he made no move.

Suddenly, he jumped out from the building, shouting, "Go, go, go!" He made large sweeping gestures with his arms as if to push the taxi on its way.

Dana heard shots.

The next thing she knew, her whole world was falling apart. First, she saw Zapher go down. Next, the taxi veered crazily onto the sidewalk and crashed into a lamppost. Dana, having unfastened her seatbelt in order to slide over for Zapher, was thrown violently against the front seat. After that, she was vaguely aware of being dragged from the taxi.

And then the lights went out.

Chapter Twenty-Nine

 When Dana regained consciousness, she found herself in the dark. She blinked groggily, seeing absolutely nothing. Her head felt swollen.

She was lying on her back on a slatted surface.

She was sore all over.

I sure hope I'm in the hospital.

Dana looked around, trying to determine where she was. As she did so, she realized that the reason it was so dark was because she had some kind of cover over her head.

She tried to sit up and found she couldn't. Her arms and legs were tied down.

Dana struggled, beset with a terrible panic. She tried to cry out and found that something was fastened over her mouth. She began hyperventilating through her nose.

She laid her head back down and tried to calm herself.

I'm all right.

I'm not seriously hurt.

I'm going to be okay.

She could hear voices. Mostly a single, male voice, echoing as though in a large, vaulted chamber. The words were not quite Italian. Latin. The man was speaking in Latin.

Dana tried to think where she might be. The last thing she remembered was riding in the back seat of a taxi in Rome. She had been looking for Zapher Inan. When she'd finally seen him, he was shot. Then the taxi had crashed.

I was taken from that taxi. . . . Torelli's got me. . . . But why?

Dana was sure she had nothing left for him. He had the scrolls now as well as her laptop and camera.

Why didn't he just shoot me in the taxi?

Dana felt cold fingers of fear creeping over her. She lay limp, too upset to cry.

She was freezing. As she shifted uncomfortably, she realized with a new jolt of horror that she was naked.

The Latin chanting droned on relentlessly. It seemed distant and muted, as though coming from another room.

I will not give up.

I'm going to get out of here.

Dana concentrated on listening. The words were distorted, and she couldn't make them out. Then suddenly many voices joined together in a Greek chant that Dana recognized instantly.

Come, Dionysus, enter our skin.
Come, Dionysus, enter our bones.
Come, Dionysus, enter our hearts.
Let the feast begin!

Oh, my god!

Domenico said there was going to be a major cult celebration this weekend. The other cardinal—Cardinal Freppe—was going to gather evidence. Clearly, that was a lie. Does Cardinal Freppe even exist? Domenico no doubt knew about the cult celebration because he was planning to be there himself.

Dana's fists clenched in anger as she thought of Domenico.

Suddenly, she heard echoing footsteps. A door opened, and she was no longer alone. Soon the surface on which she lay was moving.

Meanwhile, Interpol Agent Marco Rossi screeched to a stop at the curb a block away from St. Paul's Basilica, just outside the walls of Rome. In the back of the van were six men prepared for a stealth operation. It was 7:48 p.m. At eight o'clock, they would penetrate the basilica and capture the suspects.

They had a Polish agent named Turkowsky on the inside. According to him, there would be approximately fifteen individuals in the church, several of high profile, engaged in a cult initiation ritual involving a human sacrifice. The ritual was part of a clandestine celebration known to the cult members as Liberalia, "the Feast of the Lamb." It took place annually on March seventeenth, the supposed birthday of the Greek god Dionysus.

The cult had always been careful to cover up its ritual killings. But when a set of scrolls that contained incriminating evidence about the cult had been discovered a few weeks ago, they had grown reckless. They had killed the scroll thief, Achille Benevento, as well as Marie-Élise Toucey, a woman in Nantes who had bought one of the scrolls from Benevento.

Tonight's operation promised to yield a major bust for Interpol as they finally cornered the leader *in flagrante,* as it were. It had taken the better part of a year to arrange.

Timing was of the essence. If they arrived too soon, they could walk away without sufficient evidence of murderous intent; if they arrived too late, the victim would be dead.

Agent Rossi was nervous. It had been a long time since he had coordinated a mission like this. Although he felt excited, he also felt flabby. He solved too much crime at his computer keyboard these days.

Through his headset, Agent Rossi signaled to his unit that they had arrived.

"Initiate one-minute countdown to execute protocol Beta-Zed," he commanded.

He looked over at his colleague, Rick Valerio, in the passenger seat next to him. Rick nodded. They put on their hats, took the safety off their handguns, and unfastened their seatbelts. A moment later, eight Interpol agents were creeping through the shadows toward the back of the basilica.

Rossi anticipated difficulty entering the building without alerting the cult members inside. What he did not anticipate was colliding with ten Omani special forces agents about to execute their own version of protocol Beta-Zed.

The Omani agents did not look like the tattered mujahedeen fighters often seen on the television news. They wore fitted black bodysuits and black face masks with holes cut for the eyes and mouth. Five of them kneeled along the shrubbery with automatic rifles. Their job was to provide cover while the other five scaled the wall to the roof for undetected entry through a ventilation duct. They did not plan to interrupt the sacrifice; instead, they had brought audiovisual equipment to broadcast it live on al-Jazeera.

Poised to commence their climb, the Omani agents heard the Interpol agents coming a mile away. They were ready. Marco Rossi went down almost without a sound. Thanks to the quick reflexes of Rick Valerio, however, the rest of the Interpol agents took cover. An exercise in mutual annihilation ensued.

Dana was taken to the apse behind the high altar of the basilica, an arched alcove where Mass was regularly celebrated.

Compared to the monumental proportions of the basilica as a whole, the apse was intimate, its ornate ceiling painted with familiar figures from the New Testament. At the back of its semicircular recess, the apse had its own impressive altar with stairs leading up to it.

A carpet had been laid in the area in front of the altar as well as down the center aisle of pews to mark the ritual space. The space was lit with candles alone; everything beyond lay in shadows and darkness.

The stretcher of wooden staves to which Dana was tethered was laid against the stairs to the altar at a forty-five-degree angle. Then the covering on her head was removed. She blinked at the candlelight and found herself looking at twelve men kneeling in a semicircle around her. Dressed in brown robes, each held a long wand with a pinecone on the tip. Dana recognized the symbol immediately: the Dionysian phallus. Large, drooping hoods on the robes made it impossible for Dana to see the men's faces.

Another man, dressed in a purple robe with a laurel crown instead of a hood came down from the altar. A leopard skin was draped over his shoulders. It was Giuseppe Torelli. His hands gripped a large, silver flaying knife.

Torelli smiled ever so slightly when he caught Dana's eye. He was pausing for effect, allowing his new initiates to absorb the obscenity of the scene.

A naked woman lay bound and gagged before them. In moments, Torelli would make a long, deep slice down her torso and invite them to take and eat with their bare hands.

They would devour the warm, quivering flesh together.

Before that, however, their hoods must be removed, exposing them to each other and to themselves.

The moment would transform them, making them divine.

Torelli began speaking again in Latin. He was extolling the beauty and innocence of the lamb.

"*Ecce Agnus Dei, ecce qui tollit peccata mundi . . .*"

Dana shuddered.

Torelli approached the first man in line.

"Brother Domenico Conti," he charged, "see and be seen." He pushed the hood back onto the man's shoulders.

Conti looked up and received a kiss on each cheek from Torelli. When Torelli moved to the next man, Conti locked eyes with Dana. His face was completely expressionless.

Dana squeezed her eyes shut and screamed. Although the sound was muffled by the tape on her mouth, it was still loud enough to be heard. It sounded animal.

Everyone looked at her.

This is a nightmare.

This cannot be real.

This is a nightmare.

Dana was ready to be done. The problem was that the end was not coming soon enough.

If someone would just put me out of my misery now, I would be happy. Who knows what else I will have to endure?

The thought enraged Dana. Her heart was racing. But there was nothing she could do.

Soon Torelli reached the last man in line. When Torelli pushed his hood back, Dana did a double take—it was Turk Selenka.

Dana gazed uncomprehendingly at Turk. As Torelli turned away from him, Turk seemed to wink at her.

At first Dana was revolted. Then she began to wonder if it was a sign. She could not figure out how Turk Selenka fit into the big picture.

TWENTY-NINE

Who are you? Whose side are you on?

Torelli stood in front of Dana and faced the initiates, telling them it was time now to imbibe the eternal wine. He summoned Conti, who retrieved a large, silver chalice from a side table and set it on the steps to Dana's left.

Conti moved methodically, immersed in his own private prayer. *Almighty father, praise be your name! I have been through the valley of the shadow of death. I was wandering in the wilderness. I couldn't see you. I couldn't speak to you. Now I know you were there all along, never leaving my side. Everything that happened was part of your plan. You were showing me the way. You were preparing me for my ultimate purpose. You have exalted an unworthy man! I am forever your grateful servant. . . .*

Conti carefully untied Dana's left arm and held it in an iron grip over the chalice.

Torelli knelt down before Dana and drew his knife across her upper arm. A bright stream of red immediately began to flow down to her elbow and then from there in a neat arc through the air into the chalice.

Searing pain ripped through Dana's arm. She moaned and fought futilely, like a fish in a net on the deck of a boat.

At Torelli's signal, Conti tied a red scarf around Dana's wound and then retethered her arm to the staves on which she lay. She tried to catch his eye. He looked at her serenely. He was a paramedic assisting someone he had never seen before in his life.

Conti's mouth moved ever so slightly. "Lamb of God, you take away the sins of the world." He presented the filled chalice to Torelli and resumed his place in the semicircle.

Dana was overcome with a wave of nausea.

What will happen if I throw up behind this tape? Will I suffocate?

Torelli droned on in Latin. Dana felt faint. Her ears were ringing, and she could not hear what he was saying. She had to fight to keep her eyes open.

Soon Torelli gave Conti a drink from the chalice and moved on down the line. Dana watched, transfixed in disbelief, as each man drank her blood.

Back at the beginning of the line, however, Conti started coughing, gripping his throat. He rose to his feet and then faltered as though dizzy, collapsing onto the floor.

It was just what Dana was wishing would happen, as though she had somehow managed to will her blood to poison him. Then the next man followed suit. General pandemonium erupted and instantly wilted as each man in turn fell under his own weight.

Meanwhile, Torelli had reached the end of the line. Rather than drinking from the chalice, Turk grabbed it from Torelli's hands. Rising from his knees, he deftly swung the heavy square bottom of the chalice at Torelli's head, knocking him to the floor.

Oh, my god! He's on my side! He's going to save me! Dana's system reached overload. Her eyes rolled up and her head fell back.

Turk lumbered toward her.

"Dana, can you hear me?" he briskly patted her cheeks to rouse her. "I am Interpol Agent John Turkowsky. I came to your office as Turk Selenka two weeks ago and I've been . . . interacting . . . with you as Zen Zwanger in Second Life."

Turk tore the tape off Dana's mouth. She started coughing uncontrollably.

"Sorry," he said. Then he held her head and looked closely at her pupils. "Are you all right?"

Dana nodded. She tried to stop her teeth from chattering.

Turk's stubby fingers tore at the knots on the tethers. Once Dana's right arm was free, she was able to help.

"I laced that chalice with sleeping dust," he explained, "but my backup was supposed to be here by now. Something must have gone wrong. Can you walk? We have no time to lose."

Dana tried to walk. The room spun. She closed her eyes and reached out her arms to keep from falling. Turk clasped her hand.

Then Dana heard a loud thud. Turk's hand slipped from hers, and he tumbled to the floor.

Torelli stood behind him with the chalice in his hand.

Dana screamed.

Torelli lunged for her. Turk grabbed his ankle just in time, pulling Torelli to the floor with him.

Torelli had the energy of a man half his age. He began kicking Turk in the gut.

"Stop," Dana cried, casting about for a weapon. She caught sight of Torelli's flaying knife on the side table. She took a step, unsteady at first, and then hobbled over to the table as fast as she could.

Meanwhile, Turk had rolled away from Torelli and gotten to his knees, but Torelli sprang to his feet and charged him. Both men sprawled on the floor again, taking shots at each other.

By the time Dana got back to the two of them, Torelli was choking Turk. Dana ran at Torelli with the knife, but he moved at the last minute, and she delivered only a glancing blow to his shoulder blade.

Before she could recover, Torelli grabbed the knife and pushed her to floor.

Turk pulled himself into position to lunge at Torelli. But then he caught sight of the knife and froze.

"Don't like the knife, my boy?" Torelli taunted.

Turk shrank back in terror.

Before Turk could move, Torelli stabbed the knife forcefully into his chest. Turk made a deep grunting sound and fell back on the floor, writhing.

Torelli turned to Dana, brandishing the knife.

"Stop!" she screamed. "You're not going to get away with this."

Dana backed slowly down the center aisle of the pews with her hands in front of her, as though they could shield her naked body.

Torelli moved steadily toward her, limping. His face was a mask of fury.

When she reached the end of the pews, Dana turned and ran, her bare feet slapping on the cold marble floor.

Torelli was right behind her.

Dana ran through the blackness toward another cluster of lights in the distance. She could see as she approached that it was St. Paul's sarcophagus. Faithful visitors had left votive candles, flowers, signs, cards, stuffed animals, and pictures all along the edge of the construction zone. It was the usual detritus of public mourning that probably had to be cleared daily.

Dana stooped to grab a dried-grapevine wreath and slid behind a pillar.

Torelli skidded to a stop in front of the pillar.

They were both panting from their sprint.

"Dana," Torelli sang. "Come out now. There is no place for you to go."

"Wait," she gasped. "It's not too late for you to turn this around. You don't need to kill me."

Torelli was undaunted. He crept around the edge of the pillar, holding the knife in striking position. "Oh, but I do."

"No."

Torelli laughed. "Before you contradict an old man, my fair friend, you should endeavor to understand him."

"You're a killer," Dana spat. "Tell me what I don't understand." She was stalling for time, a plan forming in her mind.

Torelli's leopard skin had fallen off his shoulders, and his laurel crown was askew. "What you don't understand is that I need your flesh. We must take life in order to live."

While he spoke, Dana dipped her wreath into the flame of a candle. The glue affixing silk flowers to the grapevines acted as an accelerant. The decorated half of the twisted circle exploded in an angry flame.

Taking a deep breath, Dana swung the flaming wreath at Torelli with all her might. He stabbed at it with his knife, reeling backward in surprise.

Dana kept swinging, backing him into the construction zone. Achille Benevento's dynamite had torn a deep hole in the floor, and rubble was still strewn all along its edge.

Torelli's foot missed its purchase, sending him sideways onto the knee that had been making him limp. As it gave way, he tumbled backward into the hole in the floor, hitting his head on the bottom.

He lay in the hole without moving.

Shaking and still grasping her impromptu torch, Dana ran back to the apse. As she drew closer, she could see that Turk had moved to prop himself up on the steps to the altar. She also heard groaning among some of the initiates collapsed in front of the first row of pews.

Are they waking up?

Dana grabbed Torelli's leopard skin from the floor at the end of the center aisle, where it had fallen from his shoulders. As she moved up the aisle, she used her wreath to light the leopard skin on fire. Then she threw it and the wreath in the general direction of the initiates, hoping the diversion would buy her enough time to save Turk.

She knelt by Turk's side and took his hand.

Blood was burbling from his mouth.

"Turk," she panted. "We need to get out of here."

"Dana . . ." he murmured, not comprehending what she was saying.

Dana put her arm around his shoulders and tried to pull him up. "Come on," she urged.

But she couldn't lift him, and her efforts just made more blood ooze from his mouth.

"Dana . . ."

Releasing his shoulders, she took his hand again and tried to calm herself.

He was struggling to focus on her face. "Dana. I . . . I bombed the . . . Palatine Library."

"You?" Dana kneaded his hand in hers. It felt like rubber. "Why?"

"To save you." He finally found her eyes. "I figured out . . . Torelli . . . was using it to track you . . ."

Dana's face crumpled. *I had no idea I had an ally all along.* She wiped her eyes and smiled at him. "That must have been some pretty fancy programming," she sniffed.

He smiled.

"How did you get the *Eroticus* from Marie-Élise?"

"It came . . . by courier . . . to her house . . . the day after Torelli killed her. . . . I was working the crime scene. . . . I didn't know Torelli was waiting for it. . . . He followed me to New York. . . . I never meant to drag you into this . . . I just wanted . . . to meet you . . . in real life."

"Turk, it's okay." Dana thought of Zen Zwanger.

How could this chubby little man be Zen Zwanger? How could Zen Zwanger be dying?

Just then, Dana smelled smoke. She glanced nervously back toward the pews. The carpet had caught on fire. It was spreading fast.

"Dana . . ." Turk could not keep his eyes open.

Dana turned back to her virtual friend. "Turk, I'm really glad you brought the *Eroticus* to me." She fought back tears. "I got to read three of the scrolls. It was worth it."

Turk's eyes fluttered open suddenly and gazed intently at Dana. "I . . . told Interpol . . ." he sputtered.

Dana lifted his heavy head in her hands.

"That Torelli," he continued, "got the *Eroticus* . . . away from me."

"You told Interpol that Torelli got the *Eroticus* away from you?" Dana prompted, waiting for more.

Turk nodded with the last of his strength, and then went limp.

Dana started to cough at the smoke. She heard sirens.

She shook the man in front of her. "Turk! They're coming for us. Hang on!"

But it was no good. His tongue lolled over his lower lip. He was gone.

Traveling along the carpet, the fire had reached the initiates. As Dana rose to her feet, she saw one man's robe burst into flame. Two of the men appeared to be awake, but they were still barely able to move.

Dana spotted Conti, lying farthest from the fire.

Poor, deluded man.

Crouching underneath the smoke, she moved toward him and peered at his face. He slept on, beatifically.

Dana felt alone. Completely alone.

The sirens grew louder.

Dana hugged herself. *Should I stay and turn myself in, or should I make a run for it?*

I have absolutely no evidence of anything except my own black market crimes. Would anyone believe my story?

Dana wasn't sure she believed it herself.

Bending over Conti, she pulled his robe off of him and put it on. Then she stumbled her way to an emergency exit and out into the night.

Chapter Thirty

 Two weeks later, Dana was sitting by Gloria's bedside, holding her hand. Gloria had stopped breathing ten minutes before.

Dana hadn't budged.

She was sure she could feel the hand growing cold as the minutes ticked by, but it may have been her imagination.

Gloria is dead.

My mother is dead.

My long-lost mother is dead.

Although Dana was trying to think all the right thoughts, she had the feeling she would never be able to achieve the right reaction—the reaction of a normal daughter under normal circumstances.

The circumstances are not normal.

And I am not a normal daughter.

I am Andromeda Sky.

Dana felt content, thinking about her last week at the villa.

With Beatrice dead, she could hardly run back to New York. Someone had to stay with Gloria to the end. The doctor predicted it wouldn't be long. According to Leena, the visiting nurse, Gloria never regained consciousness after the night she gave Dana her necklace.

The last week wasn't enough time to make up for a lost childhood, but it was enough time to find a certain peace.

Peace is good. I think I'll work on staying out of trouble for a while.

Dana's mind flashed back to the horrific end of her quest for Aristotle's lost dialogues.

When she escaped from the fire at St. Paul's, it was after nine o'clock on a Saturday night. She was barefoot and dressed in a monk's robe, with a serious gash in her arm. She had no money and no identification. She wasn't even wearing any underwear. Dana had never felt so vulnerable. The only remnant of dignity she possessed was her four elements necklace, which Torelli had perversely left around her neck.

Putting her monk's hood up, she found the nearest phone booth and made a collect call to Gene in New York. Then she walked back to the Piccolo Mondo.

The journey took over an hour. Since it was a Saturday night, most of the people she passed had a few drinks in them, and therefore didn't pay much attention to her. The worst was at the beginning, when she had to ask for directions. The first few people she stopped pointed vaguely and hurried on their way. When she finally got her bearings, she tried to keep her head down and her pace up. On a sports bar strip, men shouted *"Forza Roma! Forza Lupi!"* mistaking her for a soccer mascot. She had to stop a few times to warm her bare feet.

On finally arriving at the Piccolo Mondo, she told the front desk clerk she was at a costume party and forgot her purse. Although he clearly didn't believe a word she said, he recognized her and grudgingly gave her a new room key.

Dana then collapsed on her bed. She did not wake until nearly noon the next day. Her room phone was ringing. It was Gene. He was downstairs in the hotel lobby.

From there she began the slow process of reconstructing her life—from her arm, to her credit cards, to her passport, to her sanity. After four days, Dana sent Gene home with the deepest gratitude and moved into Gloria's villa, prepared to stay as long as it took. Ann and Eva would be fine holding up the Institute without her for awhile. Besides, Dana wasn't ready to tell the board that her first official act as director had been to squander two million Institute dollars.

If only I had a scroll, any one of them, to show for it!

On the bright side, maybe the anonymous benefactor will be so angry he'll call to ream me out himself, revealing his true identity.

News reports of the debacle at St. Paul's said only that thirteen people had been attending a private service when a fire broke out. There were no survivors.

Dana didn't feel bad at all about causing the death of Torelli and his initiates. Unlike her fight with Tommy on the bridge in Moscow, her action in the basilica was clearly self-defense. She had been abducted, humiliated, terrorized, and wounded. She would surely have been murdered if Turk hadn't saved her. Although Torelli was the instigator, his initiates were accomplices who were prepared to violate her dead body.

Surely, one is entitled to self-defense to avoid being eaten.

Meanwhile, police assumed that the assault on Beatrice at the villa was a random burglary. Her body was repatriated to Iowa, where her oldest son, Walter, lived. Dana contacted Walter about sending Beatrice's personal effects and about selling the villa. Gloria had named Beatrice and Dana as her sole heirs in the will she left in an unlocked fireproof file box on the floor of her closet. It was a modest inheritance. Dana would let Gloria's lawyer handle the details.

In between all the logistics, Dana had plenty of time on her hands to reflect.

She finally knew her own origins, and she could not deny that it explained a lot about the person she had come to be. Without even realizing what she was doing, Gloria had planted tiny seeds of ancient philosophy in her daughter that grew and dominated her lifelong development.

Now that I know who I really am, will anything change?

Will I finally find happiness?

In the *Eroticus*, Aristotle argued that happiness is not something to be found but something to be created. He claimed we create happiness by falling in love.

My recent experiment in love was an abysmal failure. I never really knew Domenico Conti. How could I, when he didn't even know himself?

Dana pondered long and hard the question of why she fell so hard for the Vatican inspector. According to Sigmund Freud, women fall for men who remind them of their fathers. Dana could see no resemblance whatsoever between Domenico Conti and Fez McCarter. She wondered whether it were possible that Domenico somehow resembled her biological father. Gloria would, of course, deny that Dana's biological father had any influence over her psyche. But how could Dana know he didn't, when she didn't even know who he was? Now that Gloria was dead, she might never know.

Perhaps Dana's attraction to Domenico was triggered by the fact that he was a mystery to be figured out, just like her biological father—and just like Aristotle.

The truth is that my love for Aristotle is stronger than my love for any living, breathing man has ever been.

In the *Eroticus,* Aristotle wrote that, while it is best to fall in love with a person, one can also fall in love with an activity, a place, or an object. Dana decided she was an activity-lover.

People are too difficult. They change on you in all sorts of disappointing ways.

What Dana truly loved was investigating history. All along, she had thought this activity was just the means to an end—that once she knew the truth, she would lay history aside with a sigh of relief and have a real life.

She now understood that the activity had been an end in itself to her from the beginning. She was in love with Aristotle, a name that, in her mind, stood not really for a person, since he was long gone, but for a process, the process of learning the truth.

I am a lover of truth.

Dana might have welcomed learning that her happiness lay in her chosen career if it weren't for the fact that all of the progress she'd made in the past month had cruelly disappeared.

Dana ran through the inventory of scrolls in her mind one more time, as though by recounting their fate, she might somehow be able to summon them back to her.

The *Eroticus* was bought by Marie-Élise, but intercepted by Turk and then snatched by Torelli on the street in New York. The *Symposium* was bought by Dana, but snatched by Torelli at the Cloisters. The *Nerinthus* was bought by Mikhail, but snatched by Torelli at the bridge over the Moscow River. And then there were the two whose titles Dana didn't know. One was bought by Mikhail, but dropped to the bottom of the Moscow River. The other was bought by the Omani, but stolen by Zapher and then snatched by Conti and handed over to Torelli.

Torelli came out the big winner, having bagged four of the five scrolls. Now that he was dead, where would they end up?

Although Dana had managed to escape with her life, she felt like the big loser. She had no scrolls. She had seen three, but she didn't even have any photos by which to remember them.

The worst part of all was that she may never see the two unknown scrolls.

Perhaps all the scrolls will come back to me someday. But will I have to wait for twenty years, like Penelope?

Dana wished she could pop into Second Life and hang out with Zen Zwanger for a while, just like she used to before everything happened. There was no one like Zen for dispelling heavy thoughts.

Dana tried to erase from her memory the image of Zen's human, Turk Selenka, dying in her arms. She now knew what it was like to feel the life force escaping from fresh kill.

At least I know I'm not cut out for the cult of Dionysus—I never want to feel that again.

What still bothered Dana more than anything else about her night at St. Paul's Basilica were Turk's last, dying words.

He looked at me with such urgency and said he told Interpol that Torelli got the Eroticus *away from him. What did he mean?*

Dana studied Gloria's lifeless hand.

I have your hands, Gloria. I don't see a bit of me in your face, but this hand of yours is definitely my hand, twenty-some years later.

At last, Dana laid Gloria's hand down.

Pulling out her new cell phone so she could call the doctor, she found a message waiting for her. It was a secretary at Rome's Interpol office.

"This is a message for Dr. Dana McCarter. The late Agent John Turkowsky, a.k.a. Turk Selenka, has left a package for you to claim."

Dana felt a familiar thrill rising in her loins.

Afterword

Black Market Truth: **Fact and Fiction**

"During his life, Aristotle published twenty-one dialogues. While fragments from the first half of them have been found, the others have vanished without a trace, except for the titles. The complete works attributed to Aristotle today were precariously compiled from a set of lecture notes in the library of the Lyceum where Aristotle taught. They were never intended for publication. Is Aristotle even the author of those lectures? Why did *they* survive while his dialogues didn't? These are the questions we are trying to answer."

Dana McCarter, the lead character of *Black Market Truth*, speaks the above words at the beginning of an adventure that leads her to find the last dialogues Aristotle wrote before he died. The facts Dana reports in the passage are true and her questions are real. It was learning these very facts and asking myself these very questions that prompted me to write the novel.

In the novel, it turns out that Aristotle's friend and colleague Theophrastus wrote the lecture notes in question based on courses taught at the Lyceum by all the senior instructors, including Aristotle. When Theophrastus took over the Lyceum upon Aristotle's death, he buckled under pressure to remove Aristotle's last dialogues from circulation because of their radical, anti-religious content.

I want to make it completely clear that I do not mean to present this story as a historical thesis. The story is consistent with the historical evidence we have and is even to some extent suggested by it. Nevertheless, in so far as I intend the novel as anything other than pure entertainment, I intend it, not as a historical thesis, but rather, as a philosophical thought experiment.

A thought experiment is an imaginary scenario designed to test our intuitions on a controversial issue. Philosophers have used thought experiments throughout Western history to advance our understanding of ourselves and the world. For example, Albert Einstein, who was a great master of the thought experiment, raised the question: What would happen if you were traveling on a rocket ship at the speed of light? Einstein did not intend to assert that such a trip could or should actually be made. Rather, he aimed to find out what would be true under certain conditions.

Likewise, my aim in this novel is to find out what would be true under certain conditions. The lost dialogues Dana finds landed Aristotle in trouble because they constitute an attack on the dominant religion of his day, namely, the cult of Dionysus. But the dialogues also make shocking revelations about the dominant religion of our day, namely, Christianity. Dana discovers: (1) that Saint Paul plagiarized the best passages of the New Testament from Aristotle; (2) that the central concepts and rituals of Christianity were stolen from the cult of Dionysus; and (3) that the cult of Dionysus is still alive and well within the Catholic Church today.

The thought experiment, suggested throughout the novel, is this: Suppose Dana's three discoveries were actually true: Should it make a difference to believers? Is there anything that can falsify faith? If so, then exactly what would it take? If not, then how is belief different from prejudice? These are very deep questions. The novel invites readers to find their own answers.

Philosophical thought experiments can be as fanciful as you like. However, they tend to be more compelling when grown from a few kernels of truth. For example, if there were no such thing as rocket ships and we didn't think light travels at a constant speed, then Einstein's thought experiment would be meaningless. It therefore seems like a good idea for me to explain the kernels of truth upon which my thought experiment is based.

I owe the majority of my understanding of the issues surrounding Aristotle's lost dialogues to Anton-Herman Chroust's painstaking study: *Aristotle: New Light on His Life and on Some of his Lost Works*, Vols. I and II (University of Notre Dame Press, 1973). In this work, Chroust launches a bold and impressive effort to make sense out of the sparse and confusing historical data. While I disagree with his interpretation of the data in the end, I am greatly indebted to him as well as to the other scholars cited below.

I. Aristotle's Life

We do not know much about Aristotle's life and what we do know is less than one-hundred percent certain. This is not unusual: Aristotle lived more than two thousand years ago, in an age when record keeping was unreliable.

The Greek historian Dionysius of Halicarnassus wrote a biography of Aristotle in the first century BCE that is widely accepted to be roughly accurate. He writes:

Aristotle was the son of Nicomachus. . . After his father had died, he went to Athens, being then eighteen years of age. Having been introduced to the company of Plato, he spent a period of twenty years with the latter. On the death of Plato . . . he went to Hermias, the tyrant of Atarneus. After spending three years with Hermias . . . he repaired to Mytilene [i.e. the capital of Lesbos]. From there he went to the court of Philip . . . and spent eight years there as the tutor of Alexander. After the death of Philip . . . he returned to Athens, where he taught in the Lyceum for a space of twelve years. In the thirteenth year, after the death of Alexander . . . he retreated to Chalcis where he fell ill and died at the age of sixty-three.[1]

Based on this and other biographical evidence, historians infer that Aristotle was born in 384 BCE in Stageira, a coastal town in the northern region of Greece known as Macedonia. Because his father was physician to the king of Macedonia, Aristotle probably spent some of his early years at the royal court. Aristotle's parents died when he was around ten, prompting him to live with his sister Arimnestes and her husband Proxenus in Stageira until, around age eighteen, he left for Athens to study at Plato's Academy.[2]

This outline of Aristotle's life leaves us with a number of important questions. The one that interests me most is this: What was Aristotle doing for three years in Atarneus (which is in Turkey) at the court of the "tyrant" Hermias?

The dominant hypothesis, accepted by Chroust, is that Aristotle and a group of his colleagues from the Academy were sent there on

---

1 Dionysius, of Halicarnassus, *The Critical Essays*, Vol. II, ed. Stephen Usher (Cambridge, MA: Harvard University Press, 1974–1985), p. 315–317.

2 For a standard biography of Aristotle, see: W.D. Ross, *Aristotle* (London: Routledge, 1995), pp. 1–20.

a diplomatic mission.[3] The problem with this hypothesis, however, is that we don't know what Aristotle and his colleagues might have been trying to accomplish. Given that Aristotle was a Macedonian, it has been easy for some scholars to assume that Aristotle was working for King Philip of Macedonia, who was aiming to expand his empire into Turkey. However, the other members of the group from the Academy were not Macedonian and we have no reason to believe that they or Aristotle were ever in favor of Philip's expansionism.

Moreover, before the group from the Academy left Hermias's court, Philip betrayed Hermias to the Persians, who proceeded to assassinate him—by crucifixion. Chroust prefers to think Aristotle simply forgave Philip for precipitating the travesty:

> Although this incident might have caused a brief personal alienation between Aristotle and King Philip—an alienation which probably induced Aristotle temporarily to withdraw from all public or political activities on behalf of King Philip—we may conjecture that soon afterwards Aristotle once more began to play an important role in the diplomatic schemes of the Macedonian king. Presumably, he assumed an active, if not decisive, part in a number of political negotiations which took place between Macedonia and some of the Greek states, including Athens . . . In any event, throughout his mature life, Aristotle seems to have been actively associated with many of Macedonia's diplomatic moves or manoeuvres."[4]

What makes it difficult to accept Chroust's speculation is that Aristotle met Hermias when they were both students at Plato's

---

3 A.-H. Chroust, *Aristotle: New Light*, Vol. I, p. 44.

4 A.-H. Chroust, *Aristotle: New Light*, Vol. I, pp. 253–254.

Academy. They became personal friends. In fact, Aristotle married Hermias's adopted daughter Pythias and wrote a touching hymn to Hermias upon his death.[5] Aristotle was definitely deeply involved in the affair between Philip and Hermias, but whose side was he on?

Lack of sufficient information leaves the door open for my suggestion, explored in the novel, that Aristotle and his colleagues were offering aid to Hermias *against* Philip's advance. It is possible that Aristotle hated Philip from the beginning. After all, Philip razed Aristotle's hometown of Stageira when it resisted his domination.[6] I don't see any reason to suppose that Aristotle maintained loyalty to Philip under these circumstances.

Of course, such a loyalty would readily explain Dionysius's claim that Aristotle tutored King Philip's son, the boy-prince who was to become Alexander the Great. But this claim is less telling than it seems. The sources claiming that Aristotle tutored Alexander are no more or less reliable than other sources claiming that Aristotle conspired in the assassination of Alexander's father Philip.[7] The truth may be that Aristotle did neither. For the novel, however, I chose to imagine that he did both: tutoring Alexander was Aristotle's pretext for being at the royal court, which eventually enabled him to avenge the murder of his friend Hermias.

Aristotle's love-life is only somewhat less murky than his politics. As mentioned, he seems to have married Pythias, the adopted daughter of

---

5 I present an impressionistic translation of the hymn in Dana's dream about Pythias in *Black Market Truth*. For a literal translation, see: Aristotle, *The Complete Works of Aristotle*, ed. J. Barnes, (Princeton, NJ: Princeton University Press, 1984), Vol. II, p. 2463.

6 C.M. Mulvany, "Notes on the Legend of Aristotle," *The Classical Quarterly*, Vol. 20, No. 3/4 (1926), p. 162.

7 C.M. Mulvany, "Notes on the Legend of Aristotle," p. 158.

Hermias. Pythias bore Aristotle a daughter, also named Pythias. After the mother died, Aristotle took up with and probably married a slave named Herpyllis, who bore him a son named Nicomachus.[8] We do not know when either of Aristotle's marriages occurred and we do not know when the children were born. It is likely that Aristotle married Pythias after the death of Hermias, and that he took up with Herpyllis after the death of Pythias. In the novel, I completely invented the idea that Aristotle and Herpyllis actually first fell in love as teenagers and produced an illegitimate child. This is just a bit of harmless fun.

In the biography quoted earlier, Dionysius mentions that Aristotle spent some time in Mytilene, which is the capital of Lesbos, an island off the coast of Turkey, and the birthplace of Aristotle's closest friend from the Academy, Theophrastus. There is some evidence that Theophrastus was related to Aristotle's sister's husband, Proxenus. Theophrastus seems to have had a home in Mytilene where he and Aristotle pursued botanical and zoological studies at some point. At any rate, it is clear that the two men did a great deal of studying together. After Aristotle finished tutoring Alexander, he and Theophrastus seem to have worked together again in Stageira for awhile before they moved back to Athens to found the Lyceum. Theophrastus took over the Lyceum when Aristotle died.[9]

There is no question that Theophrastus was a formidable scientist in his own right and a prolific author. He wrote an important work on minerals.[10] He wrote about the strange physical phenomena of

---

8 C.M. Mulvany, "Notes on the Legend of Aristotle," p. 156.

9 For an overview of Theophrastus's life and works, see: *Encyclopedia Britannica*, Eleventh Edition, article "Theophrastus."

10 Theophrastus, *On Stones*, trans. E.R. Caley and J.C. Richards (Columbus: Ohio State University Press, 1956).

sweat, dizziness, and fatigue.[11] He also wrote the first treatise on perfume, cataloguing different kinds and discussing their effects.[12] This is why I use perfume as an illustration when developing the view of Theophrastus in the *Eroticus*.

Despite their friendship, Theophrastus and Aristotle strongly disagreed about some things. For example, Theophrastus was a vegetarian while Aristotle was not.[13] I believe Aristotle and Theophrastus also disagreed about religion. In particular, I think Theophrastus was inclined to believe in God as an impersonal force, far removed from the pantheon of squabbling superheroes that uneducated Greeks worshiped. This impersonal God is traditionally ascribed to Aristotle as well. But I think Aristotle went much further than Theophrastus, denying the existence of God altogether.

We know Aristotle was forced to leave the Lyceum for Chalcis just after Alexander died and one year before his own death. But we are not certain why. Chroust suspects that it was because of his politics. He writes that Aristotle's

> status as a 'Macedonian resident alien' and his close ties with the Macedonian royal house as well as with Antipater, the lieutenant of Alexander in Europe, made him immediately suspect in the eyes of the Athenians who considered him a philo-Macedonian, if not a Macedonian 'political agent' stationed in Athens to report on the political developments throughout Greece.[14]

---

11 Theophrastus, *On sweat ; On dizziness ; and, On fatigue*, trans. W.W. Fortenbaugh, R.W. Sharples, and M.G. Sollenberger (Leiden: Brill, 2003).

12 Theophrastus, *Enquiry into Plants*, Vol. II (*Libellus de odoribus*), trans. A.F. Hort, Loeb Classical Library, 2 vols. 1916.

13 A. Taylor, *Animals and Ethics* (Broadview Press, 2003), p. 35.

14 A.-H. Chroust, *Aristotle: New Light,* Vol. I, p. 22.

I have already given my reasons for rejecting the view that Aristotle was loyal to Macedonia. Would Aristotle have been *perceived* as loyal to his Macedonian roots even if he wasn't? This too is doubtful in my view. When Alexander left on his campaign to conquer the world, Aristotle arranged for his nephew Callisthenes to accompany Alexander as military reporter. The arrangement ended badly. Three different sources report that Alexander had Callisthenes brutally tortured and killed for allegedly plotting against him.[15] (More about this incident in the second volume of this Dana McCarter trilogy!) When news of this travesty got back to Athens, few would think that Aristotle had much loyalty left for Macedonia.

Unlike Chroust, I put my stock in the official story, according to which Aristotle left the Lyceum for Chalcis because of a pending charge of impiety. Aristotle is reported to have said that he chose to leave Athens rather than face the charges, lest Athens should "sin twice against philosophy."[16] He is here referring to the fact that Socrates was executed by the Athenians on a charge of impiety just over seventy-five years earlier.

Chroust rejects the claim that Aristotle was charged with impiety because he prefers to believe that Aristotle was a deeply religious man. Chroust cites passages from Aristotle's "Complete Works" as evidence of Aristotle's reverence for the divine. As we shall see in the next section, however, there is good reason to believe that these works are attributable to Theophrastus and others at the Lyceum rather than to Aristotle.

---

15 T.S. Brown, "Callisthenes and Alexander," *The American Journal of Philology*, Vol. 70, No. 3 (1949), pp. 225–248.

16 Most biographers accept the official story. See, for example, W.D. Ross, *Aristotle*, p. 6. For a translation of the letter, see: Aristotle, *The Complete Works of Aristotle*, p. 2461.

Furthermore, Chroust reads a great deal of significance into one of Aristotle's final quotations: "The lonelier and the more isolated I am the more I have come to like myths."[17] While Chroust interprets this quote in terms of religion, I read it more literally, as an appreciation for the epic poetry of Homer. This is why I used the story of Odysseus and Penelope as the setting for the *Eroticus*.

Toward the end of his life, Aristotle did a number of strange things that could be interpreted as religious or sacrilegious.[18] In the end, I think Chroust prefers to see Aristotle as a religious man because Chroust himself was a religious man. Committing the same fallacy, I prefer to see Aristotle as an atheist. But I believe that my fallacy is more justified than Chroust's for the following reason.

The Lyceum was an empiricist school. Empiricists believe that all knowledge comes from the evidence of the five senses. Empiricist philosophers throughout history have been known for irreligion because the five senses provide no evidence of God. Theophrastus himself criticized superstitious rituals.[19] Theophrastus's successor as head of the Lyceum, Strato of Lampsacus, went even further. Strato was one of the first philosophers on record to promulgate a truly atheistic worldview, according to which there are no transcendent forces. According

---

17 A.-H. Chroust, *Aristotle: New Light*, Vol. I, p. 231. It should be noted that J. Barnes translates "story" where Chroust translates "myth." See Aristotle, *The Complete Works of Aristotle*, p. 2461.

18 For example, Aristotle was accused of worshipping a statue of his wife dressed as the goddess Demeter. See C.M. Mulvany, "Notes on the Legend of Aristotle," p. 157. Needless to say, I see this as an example of Aristotle's "mordant wit" (see below).

19 W.R. Halliday, "'The Superstitious Man' of Theophrastus," *Folklore*, Vol. 41, No. 2 (1930), pp. 121–153. As a vegetarian, Theophrastus was especially opposed to the animal sacrifice involved in cult practice.

to Cicero, who was an avid reader of philosophy in the first century BCE, Strato

> denies the need to appreciate the work of the Gods in order to construct the world. All the things that exist he teaches have been produced by nature . . . Strato, in fact, investigating the individual parts of the world, teaches that all that which is or is produced is or has been produced by weight and motion. Thus he liberates God from a big job . . .[20]

Strato was a highly impressionable eighteen-year-old when Aristotle died. It is possible that he represents Aristotle's true legacy, a legacy that did not sit well with the Athenian public. Upon his own death, Theophrastus tried to bequeath the Lyceum to an instructor named Nelius. But Nelius lost the vote of his peers and they appointed Strato instead. The Lyceum began its decline under Strato's leadership. (More about this drama in the third volume of this Dana McCarter trilogy!)

I think that the most plausible interpretation of the situation is this. The members of the Lyceum, as empiricists, were generally irreligious, some more so than others. When Aristotle was charged with impiety, Theophrastus realized that the Lyceum would need to tone down its irreligion if it wanted to be allowed to continue its scientific studies. Caring more about the continuation of science than he did about social reform, Theophrastus tried to name the harmless scholar Nelius as his successor. But the rebellious spirit of the Lyceum could not be repressed: Strato was elected instead, thereby vindicating Aristotle and at the same time tolling the death knell of the Lyceum.

---

20 Cicero, *Academica priora (Lucullus)*, excerpted in G.A. Reale, *History of Ancient Philosophy* (SUNY Press, 1985), p. 103.

Overall, then, I have tried to base the novel's portrayal of Aristotle upon his biography, filling the gaps liberally with what I consider to be genuine possibilities. I have incorporated authentic details wherever possible, such as the fact that Aristotle had a mordant wit, a speech impediment, and a penchant for jewelry.[21] Lacking much information about Aristotle's personality, I modeled my character after a philosopher I worked with in graduate school. His lovably crafty demeanor is not the least bit unrealistic for a person of true genius! I think people have tended to picture Aristotle as a stodgy pedant because stodgy pedants have been casting him in their own image for so long. I refuse to see the ancient world in stiff Victorian terms. The ancients were every bit as stylish and sexy as we are today—all the more so, in fact, because they predated the rise of Christianity.

It is not my goal, however, to revise history. On the contrary, my goal is to raise a philosophical question and this comes, not from Aristotle's biography, but from his work.

II. Aristotle's Work

While the questions surrounding Aristotle's life are not unusual or unexpected, the questions surrounding his work are. Knowing about Aristotle's political involvement, one can easily see that he may have had enemies who tried to censor his publications. But Plato was politically active in controversial ways as well and yet he left us a plethora of manuscripts for his dialogues. Why didn't Aristotle? Although the ancient period was unreliable and careless with historical record, Aristotle's case is downright mystifying. As R.D. Masters puts it,

---

21 A.-H. Chroust, *Aristotle: New Light*, Vol. I, p. 28.

One of the most puzzling questions that can be posed in the history of "classical" thought concerns the apparent disappearance of Aristotle's [dialogues]. Of course, many works that were well known in antiquity have not survived to modern times. But some of these lacunae are more difficult to explain than others . . . Aristotle presents us with the paradox of an author whose works directed to a public audience—the so-called "exoteric" dialogues for use outside the Lyceum—have disappeared, whereas the lectures destined for his students (and called "esoteric" for this reason) have survived. Moreover, the now lost, public writings were well known to exist in antiquity, because they are mentioned both in the surviving lectures and in literary histories.

Why, then, should dialogues written for a general audience by a thinker as famous as Aristotle have simply disappeared?[22]

This, in my view, is an excellent question that may warrant a fairly imaginative answer.

The ostensible reason for the disappearance of Aristotle's dialogues is that his library was badly managed after his death. Aristotle presumably left his books at the Lyceum, which he turned over to Theophrastus. Presumably, Theophrastus guarded Aristotle's books carefully until his own death. Upon the death of Theophrastus, Strato took over the Lyceum, as mentioned earlier. Yet Theophrastus left the Lyceum's library, not to Strato, but to Neleus, who brought it to Scepsis (in Turkey).

In all likelihood, Theophrastus left the library to Nelius because he didn't expect that his colleagues would appoint Strato instead. But,

---

22 R.D. Masters, "The Case of Aristotle's Missing Dialogues," *Political Theory*, Vol. 5, No. 1 (1977), p. 31.

having been entrusted with the library, why didn't Nelius leave it at the Lyceum for his colleagues to use? It seems there must have been some bitterness about the succession of leadership at the Lyceum. Nelius, having been selected by Theophrastus but not elected by his peers, left in a huff with the library.[23]

Upon the death of Nelius, the library passed to his heirs who didn't give a damn about philosophy and didn't know how to take care of books. They buried the books in a damp tunnel where they deteriorated to the point of irreparable damage. A century later, the damaged books were dug up and sold to a wealthy book collector named Apellicon of Teos. Then, in 84 BCE, the Roman dictator Sulla despoiled Apellicon's entire library, transferring it to Rome. Shortly thereafter, an editor named Andronicus of Rhodes cobbled together what remained from the Lyceum. The result soon became known as the "Complete Works of Aristotle." Chroust writes,

> The long and confusing wanderings of this library, which lasted for more than two centuries, the several futile as well as inept attempts to recover and restore it, and the many capricious efforts to implement, correct and edit its essentially unidentifiable remnants, make it impossible for us to ascertain with any degree of certainty which parts were composed by Theophrastus and by Theophrastus' associates and disciples. It is quite possible and, as a matter of fact, very likely that after its recovery (c. during the first decade of the first century BC by Apellicon of Teos, or c. the middle of the first century BC by Andronicus of Rhodes), this whole library simply came to be known as 'the works of Aristotle.'[24]

---

23 J. Barnes and M. Griffin, "Roman Aristotle," *Philosophia Togata: Plato and Aristotle at Rome* II (Oxford: Clarendon Press, 1992), p. 8.

24 A-H. Chroust, *Aristotle: New Light*, Vol. I, p. xiii–xiv.

Aristotle was known to have been a great collector of books. But books in those days were scrolls which, when damaged, are hard to identify. There were dozens of other talented instructors and students at the Lyceum. Yet few of their works have been preserved. This may be the explanation: they actually have been preserved—under the name of the "Complete Works of Aristotle."

There are other reasons for doubting that the "Complete Works" were written by Aristotle. First of all, it is disturbing that there are almost no autobiographical reports in these works, even where such reports would be wholly appropriate.[25] Second, according to Arthur Hort, the style of Theophrastus' own separate publications is the same as the style of the so-called "Complete Works" of Aristotle.[26] Third, if Aristotle was as politically active as it seems, when did he have time to write these voluminous works? Theophrastus, on the other hand, avoided politics and lived to be eighty-four years old. Theophrastus assumed such a prominent role at the Lyceum that some ancient reporters call Theophrastus rather the Aristotle its first scholarch.[27]

The last and perhaps most important reason for doubting that the "Complete Works" of Aristotle were written by Aristotle is that they contain a range of views that contradict each other. In particular, the *Metaphysics*—the single most definitive work in the collection, which lays the foundation for all further theorizing—defends both immanent realism and nominalism.[28] These are two mutually exclusive positions on the problem of universals.

---

25 A.-H. Chroust, *Aristotle: New Light*, Vol. I, p. xxiv.

26 A.F. Hort, "Introduction," *Theophrastus: Enquiry into Plants,* Loeb Classical Library, vol. I, 1916, pp. xxi–xxii.

27 A.-H. Chroust, *Aristotle: New Light,* Vol. I, p. 256.

28 For an overview of the relevant texts, see: J. Barnes, "Metaphysics," in J. Barnes, ed., *The Cambridge Companion to Aristotle* (Cambridge: Cambridge University Press, 1995), pp. 89–101.

The problem of universals raises the question, what makes two different things members of the same kind? According to immanent realism, individual members of the same kind share a common essence. For example, each human being shares the universal essence of humanity. According to nominalism, however, there is no such thing as a common universal essence: every individual is absolutely unique. Common terms, such as "humanity," which we use to call two different things members of the same kind, indicate nothing more than perceived similarities according to nominalists.

A man as logical as Aristotle could not possibly have held both immanent realism and nominalism.[29] The *Metaphysics* is traditionally interpreted as favoring immanent realism. In the novel, however, I propose that Aristotle was actually a nominalist, both because it is the logical companion for atheism and because William of Ockham, one of the greatest interpreters of Aristotle who ever lived, reads Aristotle as a nominalist.[30]

My interest in the lost works of Aristotle has been sustained by fifteen years of research on Ockham, who is a fourteenth-century logician. Ockham was himself a committed nominalist and he derives his view from Aristotle. Ockham writes,

Past ages have begotten and reared many philosophers distinguished by the title 'sage'. Like shining lights they have illumined with the splendour of their knowledge those who were plunged in the dark

---

29 George Santayana, who was no logician and who embraced Aristotle's "Complete Works" as authentic, tried to maintain both. See G. Santayana, *Realms of Being* (New York: Cooper Square Publishers, 1972), p. 72, n. 93.

30 For a comprehensive overview of Ockham's interpretation of Aristotle, see: M.M. Adams, *William Ockham* Vol. I (Notre Dame, IN: University of Notre Dame Press, 1987).

night of ignorance. The most accomplished man to have appeared among them is Aristotle, outstanding as a man of no slight or insignificant learning. With the eyes of a lynx,[31] as it were, he explored the deep secrets of nature and revealed to posterity the hidden truths of natural philosophy.

Since many have tried to explain his books, it seemed to me, and to many earnest enquirers, desirable that I should write down for the benefit of students what I thought to be the mind and intention of Aristotle. None but the envious should object to my desire to communicate ungrudgingly what I regard as probable opinions on this work of the great philosopher. For my aim is investigation pure and simple, and not obstinate quarrelsomeness nor ill will; and without any rash assertions I proceed to an explanation of what Aristotle's labours disclose. . .

Properly speaking, the science of nature is about mental contents which are common to such things, and which stand precisely for such things in many propositions, though in some propositions these concepts stand for themselves as our further exposition will show. This is what the Philosopher means when he says that knowledge is not about singular things but about universals which stand for the individual things themselves.[32]

---

31 Although Ockham probably did not know this, Diogenes Laertius describes Aristotle's eyes as "μικρόμματος." In the novel, I interpret this as lynx-like. See Διογένης Λαέρτιος: Βίοι και γνώμαι των εν φιλοσοφία ευδοκιμησάντων, ed. H.S. Long (Oxford, 1964), Sec. V.1, http://www.mikrosapoplous.gr/dl/dl05.html#aristotelis.

32 William of Ockham, *Ockham: Philosophical Writings*, trans. Philotheus Boehner (Indianapolis: Hackett, 1990), p. 2 and p. 11.

As this passage hints, the interpretation of Aristotle was extremely controversial in Ockham's day, as it still is today. What the last paragraph says, in a convoluted medieval way, is that kinds of things are perceptions that we formulate into words, so that universals are nothing but our common names for individual things.

Ockham may have been using Aristotle's authority to validate his own philosophical predispositions. (Ockham needed all the support he could get: he was excommunicated by the Pope[33] and his nominalist views were ultimately condemned by the Catholic Church as heretical.[34]) Nonetheless, the bottom line is that, throughout his extensive commentary on Aristotle, Ockham makes an excellent point: the immanent realism traditionally ascribed to Aristotle simply does not make sense. If Aristotle was as smart as some of the better passages of the "Complete Works" suggest, then he must have been a nominalist.[35]

So, I am of the opinion that the "Complete Works of Aristotle" is actually the "Complete Works of the Fourth-Century Lyceum." Once Theophrastus made the decision to leave the Lyceum library to Nelius instead of Strato, its fate was sealed: the lecture notes of the Lyceum instructors—predominantly Theophrastus himself—embarked on a journey that would lead to their new identity as the "Complete Works of Aristotle."

---

33 See C.K. Brampton, 'Personalities at the Process against Ockham at Avignon, 1324–26', *Franciscan Studies*, 26 (1966), pp. 4–25 and D. Burr, 'Ockham, Scotus, and the Censure at Avignon', *Church History*, 38 (1968), pp. 144–59.

34 See A. Zimmermann, *Antiqui und moderni Traditionsbewußtsein und Fortschrittsbewußtsein im späten Mittelalter Miscellanea mediaevalia: Traditionsbewusstsein U. Fortschrittsbewusstsein Im Späten Mittelalter* (Walter de Gruyter, 1974), p. 446.

35 Charlotte Witt has made a convincing case for a nominalist interpretation of Aristotle's *Metaphysics* (or, rather, of the *Metaphysics* that have been attributed to Aristotle). Her analysis requires focusing on a particular section of the *Metaphysics* that is probably authentic Aristotle. See C. Witt, *Substance and Essence in Aristotle* (Ithaca: Cornell University Press, 1989).

The question remains, however, why weren't Aristotle's dialogues—the only works he actually intended for publication—in that library? It is absurd to suppose that the worms in the Scepsis tunnel ate the dialogues and left the lecture notes merely to molder. Clearly, someone removed them. But who? And why?

In my view, the controversy over the succession of leadership at the Lyceum gives us our best clue. Strato was an outspoken atheist. Nelius was a mousy scholar. Theophrastus wanted the Lyceum to pass to Nelius even though the other Lyceum members favored Strato. This suggests to me that Theophrastus was trying to downplay the atheistic orientation of the Lyceum. He had good reason: Socrates had been executed on a charge of impiety. Aristotle had been chased out of Athens on the same grounds. If Theophrastus allowed the Lyceum to become a bastion of atheism, it would garner public disdain, thereby endangering the scientific studies Theophrastus cared most about and desperately wanted to continue. Theophrastus himself, therefore, removed and perhaps even destroyed Aristotle's dialogues. Aristotle's best friend was, in a way, his worst enemy.

What do we know of the content of the lost dialogues? The answer, alas, is: almost nothing. In the third century CE, a Greek biographer named Diogenes Laertius wrote a work called *The Lives and Opinions of Eminent Philosophers*.[36] It includes an extensive section on Aristotle that is mostly consistent with Dionysius's short biography, which we examined earlier. Writing some six-hundred years after Aristotle's death, Diogenes inserts a good bit of gossip and rumor that scholars

---

36 D. Laertius, *The Lives and Opinions of the Eminent Philosophers*, Sec. V.1, trans. C.D. Yonge, http://classicpersuasion.org/pw/diogenes/index.htm.

regard as unreliable.[37] Most important for our purposes, however, is that he provides a long list of Aristotle's works. This list includes the Lyceum lecture notes, enumerated as separate books. It also includes poetry, letters, and nineteen dialogues. Scholars have since found evidence of two additional dialogues omitted by Diogenes, bringing us to a total of twenty-one.

Chroust invested considerable energy into researching instances in which other ancient authors make reference to Aristotle's lost dialogues. These references, which may come in the form of a paraphrase or a quotation, are known as "fragments." Chroust writes,

> Barring a few isolated instances, the present status of the many prob-lems connected with the lost works of Aristotle does not permit us to establish with any degree of certainty which particular texts are genuine fragments or excerpts, and which are merely doxographical accounts of frequently doubtful value. Neither does it really enable us to determine with any degree of certainty which texts may be safely credited to Aristotle or, perhaps, to a particular composi-tion or title. All of this compounds the difficulties inherent in any attempt to reconstruct these lost works of Aristotle or present an adequate account of their philosophic content.[38]

Despite these considerable difficulties, Chroust shows that Aristotle's dialogues can be divided into two groups.

---

37 For example, Diogenes mentions a report according to which Aristotle went to Turkey because he was having a homosexual affair with Hermias. Diogenes himself doubts this story. Modern scholars believe it was invented by the enemies of Hermias to discredit him. We know Plato was gay and it is likely Theophrastus was as well, but there is no reason to think Aristotle was.

38 A.-H Chroust, *Aristotle: New Light*, Vol. II, p. xv.

The first group, known as the "major" dialogues, comprises those dialogues for which there are enough fragments that something of substance can be said about them. The dialogue we know the most about is the *Protrepticus*, which scholars have actually been able to reconstruct to a large extent.[39] Based on the clues in these fragments, scholars date the major dialogues to the years between 360 and 348, when Aristotle was a graduate student and/or instructor at Plato's Academy. In rough chronological order, the titles of the major dialogues are:

Gryllus, On the Ideas, On the Good, On Justice, Eudemus, Protrepticus, Politicus, On Philosophy.

The major dialogues reflect a preoccupation with Plato, which makes sense since they are Aristotle's earliest publications, written while Plato was still alive. Some of the fragments suggest endorsement of Platonic views while others suggest criticism of Plato. The great German Aristotle scholar, Werner Jaeger, who studied these fragments, was the first to propose the thesis that Aristotle started his career as a Platonist at the Academy and slowly evolved away from Plato, toward the views we know as "Aristotlelianism" today.[40]

The second group, known as the "minor" dialogues, comprises those dialogues for which there are so few fragments that nothing of substance can be said about them. Their titles are:

On Prayer, On Education, On Pleasure, On Wealth, On Noble Birth, On Kingship, On Poets, Sophist, Menexenus, Alexander, Nerinthus, Eroticus, Symposium.

---

39 See J. Allemang, "Hiding in plain sight," *Globe and Mail* (June 5, 2005), http:// dissoiblogoi.blogspot.com/2005/06/popular-aristotle.html.

40 W. Jaeger, *Aristoteles; Grundlegung einer Geschichte seiner Entwicklung* (Berlin, 1923).

I featured the last three dialogues in *Black Market Truth*. The *Eroticus* and the *Symposium* are complete black boxes to us: we have no information about them whatsoever. We have just one meager fragment concerning the *Nerinthus,* according to which the main character for which it was named was a farmer who came across one of Plato's works and was so impressed with it that he gave up farming in favor of philosophy.[41] In the novel, I imagined that the character Nerinthus used his Platonic education to become a high priest in the cult of Dionysus. Of course, I completely invented the content of the *Eroticus*, the *Symposium,* and the *Nerinthus.*

Most scholars assume that the dialogues in the second group are just like the dialogues in the first group: early Platonic works written by Aristotle while a student at the Academy. Once Plato died, the story goes, Aristotle began the original research that resulted in the lecture notes today known as the "Complete Works of Aristotle."

We have already seen, however, that the "Complete Works of Aristotle" cannot safely be ascribed to Aristotle. Moreover, it is striking that other ancient authors regularly refer to the dialogues in the first but not the second group. One hypothesis is that the dialogues in the first group are the best of the lot while the dialogues in the second group were so unremarkable that no one bothered to quote or paraphrase them. This is, in fact, the dominant hypothesis, reflected in the labels "major" and "minor," which were invented by modern scholars. But it is also possible that the dialogues in the second so-called "minor" group were written much later and that they contained unpopular—even radical—ideas that were deliberately suppressed.

---

41 The same fragment discusses a woman named Axiothea who disguised herself as a man in order to attend Plato's lectures. The fragment is reprinted in A.-H Chroust, *Aristotle: New Light*, Vol. II, pp. 26–27.

In *Black Market Truth*, I imagine that, after his political adventures with Hermias and Alexander, Aristotle returned to Athens to write a new, mature set of dialogues propounding nominalism. I suspect that, as Aristotle transitioned away from Platonism, he toyed with immanent realism. This level of departure satisfied Theophrastus and perhaps most of the Lyceum members. But Aristotle did not stop there. Realizing that immanent realism is an unstable compromise, he pressed on to nominalism, which is, in the end, just an extreme form of empiricism.

Because Aristotle was teaching at the Lyceum, some of his ideas made it into the lecture notes that became the "Complete Works," but the dominant voice of the lecture notes would be that of Theophrastus, who ran the school for twenty years after Aristotle's death. If my conjecture is correct, then the metaphysical view we today call "Aristotelianism," namely, immanent realism, is actually Theophrastianism.

III. The Cult of Dionysus

So far, we have seen nothing in Aristotle's life or work connecting him to the cult of Dionysus. Why then have I made the cult of Dionysus the ultimate nemesis of the novel?

To see why, we must return to the charge of impiety that was leveled against Aristotle the year before he died, prompting him to exile himself from Athens. Who brought this charge against Aristotle? The answer to this question is highly significant, in my view, and has been almost entirely neglected in Aristotelian scholarship: Eurymedon, the "hierophant" or chief priest of the Eleusian Mysteries, brought the charge of impiety against Aristotle.[42]

---

42 D. Laertius, The *Lives and Opinions of the Eminent Philosophers*, Sec. V.1, trans. C.D. Yonge, http://classicpersuasion.org/pw/diogenes/index.htm.

Ancient Greeks celebrated the Eleusian Mysteries annually in honor of Demeter, the goddess of the harvest. These Mysteries were the most sacred and secret of all the ritual celebrations in ancient Greece, culminating in an extraordinary nine-day event in the city of Eleusis, some twenty-two kilometers west of Athens.[43]

By the fourth century BCE, the Eleusian Mysteries became a function of the cult of Dionysus. Friedrich von Schelling shows that Dionysus emerged as the masculine counterpart of Demeter. He goes so far as to assert that the two came to be considered aspects of a single deity.[44] Ludwig Deubner establishes that episodes from the life of Dionysus are featured in the ritual representations at Eleusis.[45] Referring to the Eleusian mysteries, Jane Ellen Harrison concludes that "all or nearly all their spiritual significance was due to elements borrowed from the cult of Dionysus."[46] Each of these sources, while identifying the Eleusian mysteries with the cult of Dionysus, also attests to the skyrocketing popularity of this religion in the fourth century. Its hierophant was an extremely powerful figure in Aristotle's day.

As mentioned earlier, many scholars, like Chroust, see anti-Macedonian sentiment as the reason for Aristotle's exile. Kevin Clinton, however, writes that

it is not impossible that Eurymedon, the hierophant, was using this anti-Macedonian feeling against Aristotle for other, more

---

43 For a detailed description of what we know about this celebration, see: T. Taylor, *Eleusinian and Bacchic Mysteries* (Lighting Source Publishers, 1997).

44 F.W.J. von Schelling, *Einleitung in die Philosophie der Offenbarung, in Sämtliche Werke*, Vol. 13 (Stuttgart: J.G. Cotta'scher Verlag, 1856–61), p. 490.

45 L. Deubner, *Attische Feste* (Berlin: H. Keller, 1932), p. 70.

46 J.E. Harrison, *Prolegomena to the Study of Greek Religion* (New York: Meridian Books, 1966), p. 539.

personal reasons, having found in the philosopher an attitude toward the Mysteries not as unquestionably reverent as his own. The next hierophant is said to have certainly felt this way toward the philosopher.[47]

Surely the phrase "not as unquestionably reverent" is an understatement. One does not ordinarily file a criminal charge against someone—especially someone as high-profile as Aristotle—for a little lack of reverence. After all, we know Theophrastus was critical of cult practices; yet, he was never persecuted. Why were Eurymedon and his successor so angry at Aristotle?

I think Aristotle must have spoken out against them. In light of Eurymedon's determination to shut Aristotle up, it is not much of a leap to suppose that some of Aristotle's later dialogues constitute a sustained attack on the cult of Dionysus.

As I researched the cult of Dionysus, I learned why a mind as great as Aristotle's might have been concerned about it—concerned enough to set aside his scientific studies in order to speak out. During this period, local cult practices were merging together under the dominant paradigms in a phenomenon known as "syncretism." As they merged, they created a unified power base. The Greek god Dionysus merged with the Greek goddess Demeter, who in turn merged with the Egyptian god Osiris, and so on—all of them representing the paradigm of a deity who dies and comes back to life to save humanity.

The paradigm of a deity who dies and comes back to life to save humanity became dominant because it is the ultimate human fantasy. The cult of Dionysus was especially successful in promoting this fan-

---

47 K. Clinton, "The Sacred Officials of the Eleusinian Mysteries," *Transactions of the American Philosophical Society,* Vol. 64, No. 3 (1974), p. 21.

tasy because it pretended to empower women and slaves, who held important positions within its illusory world.[48] This strategy is the secret to all successful religions: give hope to the oppressed masses. Christianity learned this secret and exploited it well.

In fact, that's not all Christianity learned from the cult. As Timothy Freke and Peter Gande point out, there is an extraordinary resemblance between the two:

> The more we studied the various versions of the myth of Osiris-Dionysus, the more it became obvious that the story of Jesus had all the characteristics of this perennial tale. Event by event, we found we were able to construct Jesus' supposed biography from mythic motifs previously related to Osiris-Dionysus:
>
> - Osiris-Dionysus is God made flesh, the savior and "Son of God."
> - His father is God and his mother is a mortal virgin.
> - He is born in a cave or humble cowshed on December 25 before three shepherds.
> - He offers his followers the chance to be born again through the rites of baptism.
> - He miraculously turns water into wine at a marriage ceremony.
> - He rides triumphantly into town on a donkey while people wave palm leaves to honor him.
> - He dies at Eastertime as a sacrifice for the sins of the world.

---

48 See R.S. Kraemer, "Ecstasy and Possession: The Attraction of Women to the Cult of Dionysus," *The Harvard Theological Review*, Vol. 72, No. 1/2 (1979), pp. 55–80.

- After his death he descends to hell, then on the third day he rises from the dead and ascends to heaven in glory.
- His followers await his return as the judge during the Last Days.
- His death and resurrection are celebrated by a ritual meal of bread and wine, which symbolize his body and blood.

These are just some of the motifs shared between the tales of Osiris-Dionysus and the biography of Jesus. Why are these remarkable similarities not common knowledge?[49]

Freke and Gande pose an excellent question. I'd like to push it one step further: What would happen if these similarities *were* common knowledge? This is the question Dana asks herself in *Black Market Truth*. Would it make a difference to believers? Should it? At any rate, the fact that these similarities are not common knowledge suggests that there has been a concerted effort to hide them. This is the effort that I personify in the character of Guiseppe Torelli.

What of Saint Paul's role in the story? It is true that Saint Paul's sarcophagus was recently discovered under the altar of Saint Paul's Basilica.[50] It is also true that the Pope has so far declined to open this tomb. Though there is no reason to think it contains Aristotle's lost dialogues, as is posited in the novel, it is not a stretch to imagine that Paul could have been deeply influenced by such works.

Born around 10 CE, Paul grew up in Tarsus, a Greek-speaking town in Turkey. He was a Roman citizen as well as a Jew. These four

---

49 T. Freke and P. Gandy, *The Jesus Mysteries* (Three Rivers Press, 2001), p. 5.

50 See M.C. Valsecchi, "St. Paul's Tomb Unearthed in Rome," *National Geographic News*, December 11, 2006, http://news.nationalgeographic.com/news/2006/12/061211-saint-paul.html.

qualities: Tarsan, Greek, Roman, Jew, put him in a perfect position to mastermind a religious revolution.

As a native of Tarsus, Paul was exposed at an early age to the cult of Dionysus, which was flourishing throughout the Hellenic world. In the late nineteenth century a school of biblical interpretation known as the "history of religions" approach showed how central elements of Paul's vocabulary and concepts come from cult practice.[51]

As a Greek-speaker, Paul could have read whatever Aristotle texts were available. Paul was educated at the liberal school of Gamaliel, where students studied both Jewish Law and Greek literature.[52] In the novel, I suggest that the crucial concept of akrasia that Paul develops in his letter to the Romans comes from a poem in Aristotle's *Symposium*, which itself reflects a central doctrine of Aristotle's *Nicomachean Ethics*.[53]

As a Roman citizen, Paul would have had access to the Palatine Library in Rome. Established by Augustus in 28 BCE, the Palatine Library is regarded as the first public library. We know it contained the Lyceum library that Sulla stole from Apellicon of Teos. It also could have contained some copies of Aristotle's lost dialogues that had not yet been destroyed. On the other hand, Paul could have come across those in Turkey as well.[54]

---

51 J.B. Polhill, *Paul and his Letters* (B&H Publishing Group, 1999), p. 12.

52 See D.A. Hayes, *Paul and His Epistles* (New York: Methodist Book Concern, 1915), p. 24.

53 Of all the works in the "Complete Works," the *Nicomachean Ethics* is liable to contain the most authentic Aristotle material since the work is named after his son, who may have edited it. While Plato rejects akrasia as an illogical moral concept, Aristotle makes it the centerpiece of his theory. See *Nicomachean Ethics*, 7.1–10, http://www.constitution.org/ari/ethic_07.htm.

54 For an overview of the literary resources available at the time, see: F.G. Kenyon, *Books and Readers in Ancient Greece and Rome* (Oxford: Oxford at the Clarendon Press, 1951).

As a Jew, Paul was already a member of the oldest, most entrenched religion in the Hellenic world. Anyone who had noticed the exponential growth of the cult of Dionysus could see what Judaism needed to break out of its ethnic ghetto. Christianity is an amalgam of Judaism and the cult of Dionysus. This, at any rate, is the suggestion I make in my reconstruction of Aristotle's *Symposium*.

It is true that the cult of Dionysus, symbolized by the bull and the lamb, held wild orgies, went on rampages in the woods, and made human sacrifices.[55] It is also true that Prince Alexander's mother Olympias, rumored to be on intimate terms with snakes, was a devotee of the cult.[56] In the novel, I imagined that Aristotle's father Nicomachus became involved in the cult simply because there seems to have been a significant rift between Aristotle and his father. We infer this based on Aristotle's last will and testament, in which Aristotle makes tender provisions for all of his friends and relatives except his father.[57] Sometimes silence speaks louder than words.

In conclusion, I hope to have shown how Aristotle's history invites the flights of imagination explored in *Black Market Truth*. I'm not at all concerned that I have gone too far out on a limb. In fact, my only worry is that I haven't gone far enough. What historians tend to forget in their painstaking reconstruction of the past is that the truth is stranger than fiction.

---

55 For a classic introduction to the cult of Dionysus, see: W.F. Otto, *Dionysus, Myth and Cult* (Indiana University Press, 1965).

56 See R.L. Fox, *Alexander the Great* (Penguin, 1994). Oliver Stone hired Fox as a historical consultant for the movie Alexander (2004), in which Angelina Jolie played Olympias.

57 For a translation of one of the surviving versions of Aristotle's will, see Aristotle, *The Complete Works*, Vol. II, p. 2465.

Glossary

The third year of the 103rd Olympiad. 366 BCE.
The first year of the 108th Olympiad. 348 BCE.
The first year of the 111th Olympiad. 336 BCE.
The third year of the 114th Olympiad. 322 BCE.

Academy, The (385 BCE–529 CE). Plato's school of philosophy, founded in 385 BCE at Akademia, a sanctuary north of Athens, Greece. When Plato died in 348 BCE, he was succeeded, first by his nephew, Speusippus, and then, upon Speusippus' death, by Xenocrates. The school persisted until the Roman emperor Justinian closed it 529 CE. The Academy is considered the first institution of higher learning, providing the root of the English word "academic."

akrasia. Derived from the ancient Greek word ἀκρασία, meaning "lacking command." Akrasia is the state of acting against one's better judgment. In the *Protagoras*, Plato argues against the existence of akrasia on the grounds that it is impossible to knowingly choose evil. In the *Nicomachean Ethics*, however, Aristotle argues that akrasia is an empirically observable problem for human beings.

Alexander the Great (356–323 BCE). Macedonian king, considered one of the most successful military commanders in history. By the time of his death at age thirty-three, he conquered most of the world known to the ancient Greeks. Tutored in his youth by Aristotle at Mieza, he is said to have slept with Aristotle's copy of Homer's *Iliad* under his pillow.

Amyntas, III (King of Macedonia from 393–369 BCE). Father of King Philip II and grandfather of Alexander the Great. Aristotle's father, Nicomachus, was his personal physician.

Andromeda. A constellation of stars named for the princess Andromeda, a character in Greek mythology. Queen Cassiopeia bragged about her daughter Andromeda's beauty. She thereby unleashed Poseidon's fury, which could only be appeased by sacrificing Andromeda to the sea monster, Cetus. Chained to a rock by the sea, Andromeda was rescued in the nick of time by Perseus.

Antipater (397–319 BCE). Macedonian general who served under both Phillip II and Alexander the Great. After Alexander's death, he became supreme regent of the entire Macedonian Empire. He was also a friend of Aristotle, who named him executor of his will.

Arimnestes (348 BCE). Aristotle's older sister. Married to Proxenus of Atarneus, who raised Aristotle in Stageira after the parents of Aristotle and Arimnestes died.

Arimnestos (4th century BCE). Aristotle's brother, who died childless, according to Aristotle's will.

Aristotle (384–322 BCE). Ancient Greek philosopher. Student of Plato and tutor of Alexander the Great. Founder of the Lyceum. Author of twenty-one lost dialogues.

Aristoxenus, of Tarentum (4th century BCE). Ancient Greek philosopher. Wrote treatises on music and rhythm. Accompanied Aristotle on his diplomatic mission to the court of King Hermias of Atarneus. Reported to have been upset when Theophrastus took over the Lyceum on Aristotle's death.

Atarneus. Ancient city on the mainland of modern-day Turkey, across from the island of Lesbos. Flourished under King Hermias until he was assassinated by the Persians. Aristotle's adoptive father, Proxenus, was also from Atarneus.

Athens, ancient. Powerful, democratic city-state and cultural center. Plato's Academy and Aristotle's Lyceum were located there.

avatar. Computer user's graphic identity. A pictorial representation for interacting in a virtual world, such as Second Life.

Cardinal. Member of a college of senior officials of the Catholic Church.

Catholicism (Roman). The original form of institutionalized Christianity, which remained after the Protestant Reformation. Unlike Protestants, Catholics continue to follow the Pope and believe that the bread and wine of the Eucharist become the body and blood of Jesus Christ.

Chalcis. Chief town of the island of Euboea in Greece, approximately twenty-five miles from Athens. Aristotle's mother, Phaestis, came from Chalcis and her family owned the estate there where Aristotle died.

Christianity. The largest religion in the world. Centered on the life and teachings of Jesus of Nazareth as presented in the New Testament. Christians believe Jesus is the Son of God who suffered, died, and was resurrected in order to save humanity from sin. They also maintain that Jesus will return to judge the living and the dead, granting everlasting life to his followers.

Cloisters, The. Branch of the Metropolitan Museum of Art dedicated to the European Middle Ages. Located in New York City at Fort Tryon Park, four acres of land overlooking the Hudson River.

Cubit. Measure used by various ancient peoples. One cubit equals approximately 45 centimeters or 18 inches.

Dionysus. Ancient Greek god of wine. Known as the "Liberator," for freeing people from their normal limits through the madness and ecstasy of drunkenness. In Greek mythology, Dionysus is the son of Zeus, the king of the gods, and Semele, a mortal woman.

Eroticus. One of Aristotle's dialogues according to the third-century biographer, Diogenes Laertius. All but the title is lost.

Eucharist. Christian sacrament commemorating the Last Supper when Jesus gave his disciples bread saying, "This is my body," and wine saying, "This is my blood."

Eudemus, of Rhodes (ca. 370–300 BCE). One of Aristotle's friends and most important students. Accompanied Aristotle on his diplomatic mission to the court of King Hermias of Atarneus. On Aristotle's death, Eudemus returned to Rhodes, where he founded his own school, continued his own philosophical research, and edited copies of Aristotle's work.

Eurymedon (4th century BCE). Hierophant of the cult of Dionysus who persecuted Aristotle.

First Corinthians. A letter from Saint Paul to the Christians of Corinth, Greece that became a book of the New Testament. It contains a famous love poem often used at weddings.

four elements. Earth, air, fire, and water. Assumed by many ancient Greek thinkers, including Aristotle, to be the primal ingredients of all natural substances. Aristotle also believed the four elements to have natural motions.

Hermias, of Atarneus (ca. 342 BCE). Former slave who studied with Aristotle at Plato's Academy and went on to become King of Atarneus and the vicinity. In 348 BCE, Aristotle led a diplomatic mission, including Theophrastus, Eudemus, Aristoxenus, and Xenocrates, to his court to help him reach a peace agreement with King Philip II of Macedon. When the Persians discovered the alliance between

Hermias and Philip, however, they crucified Hermias, leaving Aristotle to marry his adopted daughter, Pythias.

Hero (4th century BCE). Daughter of Aristotle's sister Arimnestes and mother of Callisthenes, who studied with Aristotle at Plato's Academy and became a military reporter for Alexander the Great. He was accused of treachery in 328 BCE and executed.

Herpyllis (4th century BCE). Aristotle's second wife and the mother of his son, Nicomachus.

hierophant. Chief priest of the pagan Mysteries.

Homer (9th century BCE). Greek poet and author of two of the most famous epics ever written: *The Iliad* and *The Odyssey*.

immanent realism. Doctrine traditionally attributed to Aristotle based on the Lyceum Lecture Notes according to which all members of a kind share a common essence.

Ibadi. Conservative branch of Islam dominant in Oman.

Interpol. The International Criminal Police Organization, whose purpose is to facilitate international police cooperation.

Islam. The second-largest religion in the world. Originated with the teachings of the prophet Muhammad, as revealed in the Qur'an. Recognizes Moses and Jesus as prophets as well, but holds that Judaism and Christianity have distorted their message. An adherent of Islam is known as a "Muslim," meaning "one who submits to God."

jihad. A Muslim duty, generally understood in the West to mean war against those who are not Muslim.

Judaism. One of the oldest religions in the world. Based on the Hebrew Bible, or Old Testament, it has strongly influenced both Christianity and Islam. Its central belief is that there exists a single, omniscient, omnipotent, benevolent, transcendent God, who created the world and governs human affairs through laws and commandments revealed to the prophet Moses.

kafir. Arabic word referring to any non-Muslim or to a Muslim who denies the truth. Usually translated as "infidel" or "unbeliever."

Lesbos. Island across from the ancient city of Atarneus in modern-day Turkey.

Lyceum. School for philosophy founded by Aristotle and Theophrastus in 335 BCE in Lykeios, a sanctuary just outside the walls of Athens. Aristotle was succeeded by Theophrastus, who was in turn succeeded by Strato of Lampsacas. The Lyceum was sacked in 86 BCE by the Roman general Lucius Cornelius Sulla, who stole all of its books for the Palatine Library in Rome. The Lyceum was rebuilt and used for many years thereafter; the date of its ultimate demise is not known.

Lyceum Lecture Notes. Notes from lectures given at the Lyceum. Edited by Theophrastus, Eudemus of Rhodes, and Andronicus of Rhodes. Today known as "The Complete Works of Aristotle."

lynx. Medium-sized wild cat. The lynx is a cunning, solitary hunter, with large eyes and a keen sense of hearing that enables it to hunt at night. In Greek mythology, the lynx is known as "the keeper of the secrets of the forest" and is associated with Dionysus.

Macedonia. Ancient kingdom in the northern-most part of ancient Greece, bordered by Epirus to the west and Thrace to the east. Under Alexander the Great, Macedonia became the home base of the most powerful empire in the known world.

Maenad. Term from ancient Greek meaning "the raving ones," used to refer to the female worshippers of Dionysus, who were known for engaging in wild orgies involving intoxication, dancing, sexual activity, and violence.

Marcus Aurelius (121–180 CE). Roman Emperor and Stoic philosopher. Author of the *Meditations*.

Mithras. Persian god of the sun. Worshiped in the Mithraic Mysteries, whose stories, symbols, and rituals merged with the Dionysian Mysteries.

Muscat. Capital city of the Muslim sultanate of Oman.

Nerinthus. One of Aristotle's dialogues according to the third-century biographer, Diogenes Laertius. Reputed to have been named after a farmer-turned-philosopher. All but the title is lost.

New Testament. The second half of the Christian Bible. Written in Greek by various authors, but predominantly Saint Paul, between 45 and 140 CE. Its twenty-seven books were gradually collected into a single volume over a period of several centuries.

Nicomachus (ca. 374 BCE). Aristotle's father, physician to King Amyntas of Macedon. Aristotle remembers all of his family members in his will except for his father, suggesting a significant rift between the two. Aristotle does, however, refer in his will to a male descendent named Nicomachus, who could be his son or his grandson.

Nicanor of Stageira (4th century BCE). Son of Arimnestes, the sister of Aristotle.

Nikanor (318 BCE). General of Antipater. Aristotle's chief heir as first husband of his daughter Pythias.

nominalism. Doctrine discussed in the Lyceum Lecture Notes according to which everything that exists is an absolute individual. There are no common essences, as held by immanent realism, or abstract forms, as held by transcendent realism.

Odysseus. Mythic hero of Homer's epic poem, *The Odyssey.*

Olympiad. An interval of four years between celebrations of the Olympic Games, by which the ancient Greeks reckoned dates.

Olympias (376–316 BCE). Wife of Philip II of Macedon and mother of Alexander the Great. Known to have been involved in the cult of Dionysus.

paganism. Modern term for Ancient Greek religion.

Palatine Library. Considered the first public library. Established in Rome by the Emperor Augustus in 28 BCE. Destroyed by fire in 191 CE.

paleography. The study of ancient writing.

Penelope. Wife of Odysseus in Homer's epic poem, *The Odyssey.*

Philip, II King of Macedon (382–336 BCE). Son of King Amyntas and father of Alexander the Great. Destroyed Stageira when it tried to resist annexation to the Macedonian Empire. Negotiated with King Hermias of Atarneus to use his territory as a bridge to conquer the Persians. Assassinated by a young man who may have been hired by his wife, Olympias.

Plato (428–348 BCE). Ancient Greek philosopher. Follower of Socrates and teacher of Aristotle. Founder of The Academy. Author of thirty-five dialogues, all of which survive.

Provenance. Documentation of history of ownership. Required for legal sale of artifacts in order to prevent tomb raiding.

Proxenus, of Atarneus (ca. 348 BCE). Husband of Aristotle's older sister, Arimnestes. Adoptive father of Aristotle.

Pythagoras (ca. 580–500 BCE). Greek mathematician and founder of the religious movement called "Pythagoreanism," which emphasized the role of numbers in understanding the universe.

Pythias (ca. 362–336? BCE). Adopted daughter of King Hermias of Atarneus. First wife of Aristotle. Pythias bore Aristotle a daughter, whom Aristotle named Pythias in her honor, perhaps because she died in childbirth.

GLOSSARY

Romans, Letter to the. Regarded by many as the most important book of the New Testament. Written by Saint Paul.

Second Life. A virtual world on the Internet. Launched in 2003 by Philip Rosedale, founder of Linden Lab. Members create avatars through which they can meet people, buy property and build things. The Second Life world is a group of islands where avatars can walk, run, fly, or teleport from one location to another.

Saint Paul (1–67 CE). Disciple of Jesus. Wrote fourteen of the earliest books of the New Testament. Born in Tarsus, he was both a Jew and a Roman citizen, educated in Greek literature.

Santayana, George (1863–1952). Naturalist philosopher, poet, and novelist, best known for his many aphorisms.

Socrates (469–399 BCE). Considered the founder of Western philosophy. Known mostly through Plato's dialogues. Executed in Athens for impiety and corrupting the youth.

Speusippus (407–339 BCE). Plato's nephew and successor as head of the Academy. While no great philosopher himself, Speusippus abided by the views of Plato, according to the third-century biographer, Diogenes Laertius. After eight years as head of the Academy, he died of a stroke, leaving Xenocrates as his successor.

Stageira. Town in Macedonia where Aristotle was raised from age ten by his older sister Arimnestes and her husband, Proxenus of Atarneus.

Symposium. One of Aristotle's dialogues. All but the title is lost.

Theophrastus, of Eressos in Lesbos (371–287 BCE). The lifelong friend and successor of Aristotle at the Lyceum. He wrote many scientific works, some of them surviving, including the first scientific study of perfume.

Thrace. Ancient kingdom that included present-day, north-eastern Greece and the vicinity. Conquered and ruled by King Philip II of Macedon and his successors.

transcendent realism. Doctrine espoused by Plato, according to which every kind of object has its own Form, a pattern that exists in an abstract realm, separate from the objects. It is because this Form is reflected in these objects that they are members of that kind. All Forms ultimately unite in a single abstract reality called the "Form of the Good" that is reflected to some extent in every object in this world.

Vatican, The. Sovereign city-state whose territory consists of a walled enclave within the city of Rome. It is the smallest independent state in the world, consisting of only approximately 110 acres and 800 inhabitants. Vatican City is a non-hereditary, elected monarchy ruled by the Pope, who is the highest ranking clergymen of the Catholic Church.

Xenocrates, of Chalcedon (396–314 BCE). Studied with Aristotle at Plato's Academy. Accompanied Aristotle's diplomatic mission to the court of King Hermias of Atarneus. Succeeded Speusippus as head of Plato's Academy in 338 BCE.

Future Releases by ParmenidesFiction™

◆◆◆

THE ARISTOTLE QUEST
A Dana McCarter Trilogy by Sharon Kaye

Book II: The Alexander Hoard (2009)
Book III: The Savior Experiment (2010)

Also Available

◆◆◆

Pythagorean Crimes by Tefcros Michaelides